Sexton Blake

CARIBBEAN CRISIS
&
VOODOO ISLAND

Sexton Blake

CARIBBEAN CRISIS

&

VOODOO ISLAND

Michael Moorcock
and Mark Hodder

REBELLION

This edition first published 2023 by Rebellion Publishing Ltd,
Riverside House, Osney Mead,
Oxford, OX2 0ES, UK

Caribbean Crisis revised and updated from an edition published by
Desmond Reid in THE SEXTON BLAKE LIBRARY, June 1962

www.rebellionpublishing.com

ISBN: 978-1-83786-034-0

10 9 8 7 6 5 4 3 2 1

A CIP catalogue record for this book is available from the
British Library.

Designed & typeset by Rebellion Publishing

MIX
Paper | Supporting
responsible forestry
FSC® C104608

Printed in Denmark

WORKING IN THE FOLK HERO SECTOR

IN 1958, AFTER editing TARZAN ADVENTURES for a couple of years, I joined the staff of THE SEXTON BLAKE LIBRARY as Assistant Editor under Bill Howard Baker. Bill had developed the so-called 'New Order' series, which 'modernised' Sexton Blake.

I was a keen Blake reader, especially fond of the 1920s and 30s 'super-villain' stories by Skene, Teed and Brooks, but the Blake fans had been very negative about the New Order. I'd felt bound to defend it in my fanzine, BOOK COLLECTORS NEWS.

Thrown out of the Old Boys Book Club more or less for being cheeky, I had a call from Bill Baker. He had read my piece. He offered me a job when one came up at Amalgamated Press. AP put out all my favourite story papers, most of which disappeared around the time I was born.

A precocious reader, I had collected story papers since I was young, being dissatisfied by comics, except for EAGLE. From my pocket money I sent a postal order every week to a dealer, who sent me back the latest (for me) instalments of UNION JACK, MODERN BOY, MAGNET, GEM, THE SEXTON BLAKE LIBRARY and BOYS FRIEND LIBRARY where I followed the adventures of Billy Bunter, D'Arcy, Tom Merry, Nelson Lee, Captain Justice, Sexton Blake, Biggles and Nelson Lee in the order in which they had first appeared. I also had THE CHAMPION weekly delivered, the very last of the all-text story papers done by AP, which I took out of loyalty to a dying breed.

At New Fleetway House, Farringdon Road, I was expected to work on other publications in the department overseen by Ted Holmes and Len Matthews. They had been AP editors for years, producing the likes of THRILLER and DETECTIVE WEEKLY (not to forget KNOCKOUT, LION and TIGER!), and who, after the war, had started the 'Picture Libraries', pocket-sized comics featuring classic adventure stories like Captain Blood or new tales of Robin Hood, the Three Musketeers and Dick Turpin. Companions to these were COWBOY PICTURE LIBRARY featuring stories of Kit Carson, Buffalo Bill, Billy the Kid and Buck Jones. WAR PICTURE LIBRARY featured the famous Battler Britton and Roy of the Rovers was scoring everywhere. I wrote Karl the Viking for Don Lawrence and put his first colour work into an annual. I co-created Dick Daring, RFC for THRILLER PICTURE LIBRARY and dozens of serials for LION and TIGER, and I wrote the cover blurbs for Sexton Blake!

At the age of twenty-one, I realised the absurd truth. My enthusiasms had led me from Tarzan to Sexton Blake, Buffalo Bill, Dick Turpin and Robin Hood. Like it or not, I was decidedly in the folk-hero business!

We were not generally allowed to write for our own papers but were expected to supplement basic Union rates by writing for others. Although editing two issues of SBL a month, and running a letter column and other features, such as the traditional short articles, which Bill let me restore, I still had time to work on the hardback Christmas Annuals, then a feature of English comics, generally carrying stories of the regular weekly and monthly characters, like Karl the Viking, Battler Britain or Buck Jones.

I also edited and contributed to the LION and TIGER annuals, ROBIN HOOD ANNUAL, KIT CARSON ANNUAL and one or two others, mostly because, in spite of my youth, I was the only one there, other than Holmes or Matthews, who could handle short feature writing, typesetting and layouts. Most of my colleagues had only worked on comics.

I got to write about a wide variety of heroes and enthusiasms. In editing Sexton Blake, I learned basic rules of writing. I also formed a lifelong friendship with Jack Trevor Story, author of *The Trouble with Harry* and *Live Now Pay Later*, who wrote the funniest Blakes, and whose literary executor I became. The Prix du Goncourt/ Jack Trevor Story Memorial Cup is awarded by a panel of judges who generally meet at the Cafe Goncourt in Paris to decide the prize for funniest writer in English.

Bill Baker was exempt from the house rules. His best stories invigorated Blake with their snappy style and pacing. He wrote many Blakes under his own name and as Peter Saxon, Arthur Kent, W. A. Ballinger, and even Desmond Reid on occasions. He turned out some excellent work, but he was a drinker and, like his predecessors, frequently delivered hastily written stories.

Over the years Desmond Reid became the house-name for generally substandard Blakes. Sometimes it was used as part of a scam by Bill in which he paid, say, fifty guineas to an author, telling him his work was not up to scratch, then made his typist redo the manuscript with a few revisions and paid himself the remaining amount of a hundred guineas (that's how we were still being paid in the 60s). It seemed to me an iffy scheme... but I was discovering that some of the staff were worse than the villains in their stories with their various dodgy practices for stealing hefty sums of money from the firm.

As an NUJ (National Union of Journalists) member I was becoming somewhat radical in my desire to confront the bosses in various ways. We were preaching decency and generosity but practicing corruption! Behind the scenes there were frequent references to mergers as Odhams and Hulton became one. Suddenly writers were to be paid on publication—often years after their stories were written! With my freelance feature work and sales of stories and series to NEW WORLDS and SCIENCE FANTASY I could survive, but not the young married people with children who were supposed to supplement Union minimum pay with freelance work.

I was co-opted to the Union committee. Bill, still a member of Mosley's fascists, became convinced that I was a communist because one hot day I had worn sandals to work! Strangely, this secured my job because Len Matthews was certain that the Red Army would soon be marching up Farringdon Street... and, of course, I would then don a pair of rimless glasses, put on a leather jacket, stick a machine pistol in my belt, and start sending old enemies to the Gulags. Best to stay on my good side!

As a Kropotkinist and anti-communist, I found this especially amusing. Krushchev was looking after me, in his own strange way!

In 1959, after I had been working at what was still AP for some time, my friend Jim Cawthorn, the writer and illustrator, said he had an idea for a Sexton Blake mystery, a kind of locked room story in a bathysphere. I asked Bill if I could do a Blake using Jim's idea and he said "sure!"

Cuba was hot news. I was very pro-Castro, as were many in England and the USA, and supported him against the Batista regime. Part of the Blake tale discussed Caribbean politics. Bill and I had rather different views in that regard and he grumbled about my young Castro figure, but said nothing to discourage my writing. When I submitted the story, though, and to my surprise, he claimed it was substandard and he would have to get it rewritten. "We don't want a political treatise, sport. It's all over the place politically." He didn't blink.

I genuinely felt dismay and admiration. Bill was pulling the same scam on me he had pulled on others! Mind you, and to be fair, he gave it more of an overhaul than was usual before pocketing 'his share' of the fee.

Caribbean Crisis was eventually published in June 1962 in THE SEXTON BLAKE LIBRARY (fourth series) issue 501. My progressive politics were gone in favour of Bill's right-wing version. I was a bit upset but deeply relieved to see it under the Desmond Reid pseudonym.

Over the years I have been frequently asked why I didn't publish my own version. Quite simply, I had lost the original carbon. I made some attempt to rewrite it but wasn't much interested until my friend and fellow Blake enthusiast Mark Hodder suggested we "restore, revise and expand" the book by following the basic mystery of the original while amending the politics and adding new plot and descriptive elements based on his own experiences in Cuba.

This quickly led to the idea of a prequel. I'd longed to write a story set in my preferred 1930s Blake milieu, with Teed's creations Doctor Huxton Rymer, the master criminal and brilliant scientist gone bad, and Voodoo Queen Marie Galante, with whom I sympathised.

Mark and I set about plotting and writing and found that we collaborated well. I hope when you read the results you feel the same.

Should you enjoy these, we have a few other stories planned, including some about Zenith the Albino, the inspiration for my hero, Elric, some sixty years ago.

I think Mark is a great collaborator. I'm looking forward to working with him more on our favourite detective and those who inspired him. We shall introduce you to new characters and go deeper into the complicated lives of his adversaries. And, I hope, entertain you, as the eternal detective has entertained us over so many years.

We might also have a few non-Blake tall tales for the future. There are millions of stories in the multiverse demanding to be told! So why not start with the exotically rich adventures of the world's greatest detective series? Ladies, gentlemen, sentient beings everywhere, we give you our favourite sleuth, the subject of the longest running series in everyone's version of history—Mr Sexton Blake, the Consulting Detective, the qualified GP, the brilliant criminologist and the perfect companion for some fast-moving fun!

— **Michael Moorcock, Lost Pines, Texas. March 2023**

CARIBBEAN CRISIS

**Michael Moorcock
and Mark Hodder**

Restored, revised and expanded

1
into the deep

BENEATH A SKY of limpid sapphire blue, the research ship *Gorgon* rolled gently on the scintillating waters of the Caribbean Sea.

Vivid turquoise, those waters, but only to a depth of two hundred feet, where, under the vessel's keel, the sunlight faltered and gave way to an intense green twilight. Another thousand feet down, and even the faintest glimmerings were swallowed into the most intense of blacks.

What mysteries might hide in such profound darkness?

Yet a thousand feet was as nothing! For the *Gorgon* was floating over the Tanangas Trench—one of the deepest marine valleys on Earth—the ocean bedrock six miles distant!

From the squat ship, derricks stretched outward over the starboard bow, causing a slight list, and from them was suspended the most unearthly object ever seen east of Cape Canaveral.

It was a sphere of crystal-steel, blazing with the fire

of reflected sunlight, hanging barely ten feet from the surface of the calm sea.

Two men in rubber wetsuits perched upon it like grotesque frogs, balancing themselves—waiting.

On the deck of the ship, tough, sweating, brown-skinned men strained to manoeuvre the derricks. One of them was shouting, his rasping voice pitched high:

"*Oyez!* Steady on, number three! Ease her out slowly!"

The two men crouching atop the sphere looked at each other. The younger had curly blond hair and a tanned face which, at that particular moment, had blanched beneath the colour. He was clearly nervous. He said throatily, "Do we really have to do this, Paz?"

Paz, with long, lank black hair, a sharp face, and—in contrast to his companion—a disquietingly serene manner, replied softly, "If you don't have the courage—" He finished the sentence with an expressive shrug.

The other hesitated and glanced around at the ship and the sea. He fixed his eyes on a medium-sized pleasure cruiser drifting nearby, read its name—*Calypso*—and uttered a brief, quavering laugh.

"It's ridiculous, I know, but—" he paused before continuing, "but no one knows what's down there."

Paz grinned without humour, his eyes hardening. "The American professor brags that this capsule is the most advanced ever built. You'll not find any safer. And what an adventure, Señor Linwood, eh?"

Linwood muttered, "Yes, I know, I know. It's—it's just a feeling I've got, like a premonition or something."

Paz swore impatiently, his Spanish too low and rapid for Linwood to comprehend. "Get in, man! Show me what you're made of."

Linwood, with an apologetic grunt that sounded more

like a whimper, eased himself down through the open hatch and dropped into the bathysphere. His voice came hollow and echoing from inside:

"All right, I'm in position." He cleared his throat. "There's more room than you'd think."

Paz's eyes narrowed. With his companion out of sight, his whole manner suddenly altered. He now resembled a bird of prey, poised there, with his beak of a nose, and his hair ruffled around his shoulders by the gentle breeze. There was a carnivorous air about him.

He squinted up at the sun—down at the coruscating water.

"Time to say goodbye," he whispered to himself.

He unzipped his wetsuit a little, reached in, and withdrew two small plastic-wrapped packages. After examining both for a moment, he transferred them to a different pocket, zipped up, blew out a fierce, impatient breath, then turned to the crew and bellowed, "Let's get on with it! Swing her out!"

The crew scurried to obey his orders.

Electric winches began to hiss and hum.

He took a final look around, then clambered down into the sphere, clanging the heavy hatch shut behind him.

In the *Gorgon*'s control cabin, the first mate leaned over the radiophone. Soon Paz's voice came crackling out of the receiver.

"All right, Vasquez. Take us down."

Pablo Vasquez mouthed a silent expletive and made a disrespectful gesture at the apparatus. He did not like Paz at all. He did not like taking orders from him. And he did not like what Paz was doing. It was against the strict instructions of the project chief—Professor Hoddard Curtis.

Curtis had forbidden anyone to use the bathysphere while he was away, endeavouring to secure financial backing from the Marine Institute in Florida.

He had not reckoned, however, on a third visit by Paz, a government inspector from the nearby island of Maliba, in the fishing grounds of which the *Gorgon* was anchored.

Paz—and this time accompanied by a colleague!

They had the power to refuse, with a snap of the fingers, any scientific research in these waters. Vasquez dare not deny them anything, especially in his employer's absence. He preferred not to be blamed for any sudden reversal of cooperation from the Maliban authorities.

So, when Paz demanded that the bathysphere be tested, with him and his companion inside, what else could Vasquez do but agree?

"You understand," Paz had said, "that we have to be certain that you really are here only for research, and not for—"

"For what, señor?" Vasquez had asked.

"There are many rumours of sunken treasure. Old pirate ships, yes? If your professor has found gold down there, it belongs to Maliba, not to him."

"We have not found gold," Vasquez reassured. "Nor are we looking for it."

"Linwood and I will go down. If the light from the bathysphere glitters on nothing but fish, I shall be satisfied, and your professor will be permitted to continue his project without further interruption."

Now, Vasquez reached across the bank of meters to the electric winch regulator and switched on the down-drive.

"I am starting the winch, señor," he said, with ill-suppressed disdain in his voice. "Slowly for the first fifty feet."

He watched from the cabin window, as with delicate and precise grace, the big sphere began to sway downwards.

It touched the surface just as a swell lifted the ship.

As if the ocean is pushing you away—doesn't want you in it, Vasquez thought, but an instant later the bathysphere broke through the translucent blue and began its descent into the deep. The water eddied around the cables that held it; fine, woven cords of steel, which appeared far too slender to support such a mass.

Vasquez turned his dark eyes to the pressure gauges.

An indicator needle crept slowly round a large dial marked in tens of feet, then in hundreds, then in thousands.

Ten feet... twenty... fifty...

Again, Paz's voice came harshly over the line:

"Stop!"

Vasquez halted the sphere's descent.

"Is there a problem, señor?"

"No. I just want to enjoy the view for a few moments while we still have the light. I'm breaking contact for a short while. I'll call you again in a minute."

"Understood," the mate acknowledged. He flicked the switch to receive and let it stay there.

Nearly five minutes passed, and he was beginning to feel uneasy, but then Paz came through:

"All right. Proceed. Lower us down."

"Sí, señor," Vasquez responded, and set the machinery in motion.

Again, the pressure needle crept across the face of the dial.

Seventy... ninety... one hundred... two hundred...

It passed five hundred. He felt a tightening in the stomach as the gauges told of the fantastic pressures now coming to bear on the sphere. Two hundred pounds to the square inch!

The needle touched the six hundred mark and passed it.

Seven hundred…

Then the radiophone sputtered back into life:

"*It's very dark now. We're using the lamps—*" came Paz's voice. "*Can't see much. The water, it is viscous like oil. It's quite strange. I've never seen anything to compare with it—*"

Suddenly, Paz's matter-of-fact tone was cut off by a gasp.

"*Wait! There's something coming out of the— What— Dios mío! What is it?*"

His voice was suddenly shrill with excitement and horror. "*It's coming closer! It can't—it's not possible! Pull us up! Pull the sphere up! Quickly, man! Quickly!*"

Vasquez flicked the radio switch.

"Señor? What is it? What are you seeing?"

But Paz didn't answer. "*Pull us up!*" he shrilled frantically. "*Come on! Come on! It's going to— No! No!*"

Already the mate had slammed the machinery into reverse. But there was no way to make it go any faster.

"Tell me what's happening!" he cried out. "Señor Paz! Señor Paz!"

No reply.

For ten long seconds, nothing but silence, then—

The ship rocked violently and water spouted up beside it. A burst of muffled thunder reverberated from the deep.

Vasquez staggered. His elbow crunched into the glass

of one of the gauges, shattering it. He cursed and fell back, brushing fragments off his arm, smearing blood over the skin.

He grabbed the radiophone and hung onto it.

"Señor Paz? Señor Linwood? Are you there? Respond please!"

But the line was dead. There wasn't even a hiss of static. The link was broken.

He threw himself across the cabin, wrenched open the door, and tore up the companionway.

The crew were all regaining their feet. Vasquez hurried to the nearest of them and clutched his arm.

"What the hell happened? What hit us?"

The crewman shook his head, bemused, his eyes wide.

Vasquez ran to the ship's rail.

Abstractly, he noted that the cruiser, the *Calypso*—which had been loitering nearby for the past couple of hours—had gunned its engines and was speeding away.

But he had eyes only for the derricks.

Where there should have been taut, straining cables, there was only a bunched mass of steel wires—wires which, severed, had whipped up from the sea, relieved of their burden, to wrap round the pulleys in an inextricable tangle.

"Madre de dios!" Vasquez cried out. "May the saints preserve them!"

He stared down into the imperturbable ocean—now lying tranquil again over the unfathomable trench—and knew that it was impossible to save the two men who had vanished into it.

Without the cables to hold it, there was nothing between the bathysphere and the bedrock—nothing except water—*six miles of it!*

The two men were doomed, irrevocably trapped in a twelve-ton coffin of steel... sinking... sinking... sinking...

"They are finished."

Vasquez made the sign of the cross over his chest.

The eighth son of a Puerto Rican fisherman, he knew the sea. Even its shallows could be lethal. But *this!*

And all the wild tales of sea monsters he had heard in his youth flooded into his mind.

A cold fear seized him.

What had bitten through those cables?

2

dive for answers

Professor Hoddard Curtis, young and good-looking, blond of hair, broad of shoulder, and bitterly angry, gritted his teeth with suppressed fury as he was encased in inch-thick armour plating, on the deck of his research vessel, *Gorgon*.

Only two hours ago, he had returned to the ship with good news. The Florida Marine Institute had guaranteed further funding. He'd come aboard with a light heart, feeling buoyant and confident. His project could continue. Years of work had gone into the construction of his bathysphere, and soon, he would realise his dream: he would dive deeper than anyone had ever gone. He would see what had never been seen.

Then Vasquez had stepped forward to stammer out his report—

And the dream shattered.

The bathysphere was gone and could never be retrieved.

Curtis's world had collapsed around him.

Initially, the young professor could not believe it. It was

incomprehensible. Even the sight of the severed cables failed to register. Then shock set in, soon to be followed by a blind, unreasoning hatred for the men who had come aboard, disregarded his orders, and perished.

For nearly an hour, he was unable to speak.

Then, like a drowning man clutching at a straw, he ordered out the sonar equipment, to search the depths for some clue to the bathysphere's final fate.

It was a forlorn hope—but one that suddenly, incredibly, after half an hour of hopeless casting about, bore fruit.

The underwater radar had pinged—and Curtis's eyes had opened wide—for the bathysphere was not six miles down. Not even a mile. It was only eleven hundred feet below the surface.

Eleven hundred feet!

Such a depth seemed the merest trifle.

Then he remembered that the strongest deep-sea diving suits in the world had never been tested below a depth of nine hundred feet. Curtis had a pair of them on board. He had no means of knowing whether they would stand up to an extra two hundred pounds of pressure.

But he was going to find out.

Was his life's work worth his life? Yes! If five long years of unremitting toil were to mean anything, he had to risk the descent. He had to see the bathysphere, to find out what had gone wrong.

Now, as Vasquez and one of the crewmen helped him into the suit, Curtis thought about Paz's words, as reported by the first mate.

"There's something coming out of the— What— Dios mío! What is it?"

He had studied marine life for years. He knew there were gigantic creatures occupying the darkest fathoms—

oarfish, squid, jellyfish, spider crabs, and more, all of awe-inspiring dimensions—but a creature capable of severing steel cables?

And he recalled how, over the fortnight that the *Gorgon* had been here, there had been two occasions when the sonar had pinged unexpectedly, its signal bouncing off something huge moving deep below—some mysterious *leviathan*.

A surge of claustrophobia overwhelmed him as the bulky steel helmet slid down over his head and locked with a clunk into the collar of the suit's big cylindrical torso.

His mouth went dry. He blinked rapidly, gripped by sudden terror.

But it had to be done. He could not abandon the sphere.

With a wrench, he forced his attention back to the job at hand. He ran through the routine check to ensure that all the parts of the suit were functioning as they should.

He thumbed switches to test the remote control "hands"—lobster-like pincers; metal claws resembling those used in nuclear laboratories to handle radioactive isotopes—then he flexed the hinged arms.

Next, he satisfied himself that the built-in air supply was functioning faultlessly.

Finally, the radiophone.

"Receiving?" he transmitted.

"*Yes, señor*," came the response from Vasquez, who had gone to the control cabin.

"Let's get on with it, then."

A crewman came forward holding a weighty hook—attached to a cable suspended from one of the derricks—and moved behind Curtis, out of his range of vision.

There was a heavy clack as the man affixed the hook to a metal loop just below the back of the diving suit's collar.

He stepped back into view and gave a thumbs up.

Curtis nodded.

He was ready to be lowered into the ocean.

HE DESCENDED AT six feet per second; a body within a body, a skull within skull.

His anger continued to simmer, but fear was fast supplanting it. "What the hell am I doing?" he wondered. "This is crazy. I have lost my mind!" But his desire for answers was more powerful than those surging emotions. His dedication. His obsessive desire to lead the world in deep sea exploration.

Sunlight played on the blue-green surface above, but the gloom quickly increased, and he was soon enveloped by the deep Caribbean, sinking into a world of silence; a world of swirling and scintillating plankton, half-glimpsed movements, and below him, impenetrable darkness.

He spoke into the microphone, his words sounding unnaturally loud in the confines of the helmet.

"How far down?"

"*Six hundred feet, professor,*" came the voice of Vasquez. "*Still descending. Cómo estás?*"

"I'm all right. Give me regular readings."

Curtis was no stranger to deep diving, but he'd never made a foray into the depths without considering what they could do to him. Carelessness was fatal. A suit, if not exhaustively checked, could carry a fault. Any breach in it, and the water pressure would slam in, turning a six-foot man into a tight package of condensed flesh and bone.

So much easier to bury, Curtis thought with morbid humour. *If all men died so neatly, the undertakers would go out of business.*

The radiophone crackled.

"*Seven hundred feet.*"

"Okay. Keep going."

Curtis clicked the switch that activated his headlamp. Its illumination cut a tunnel through the dense twilight, turning swirling motes into star-like sparks, briefly flaring off small, silvery shapes that instantly darted out of its path.

Down... down... down...

"*Eight hundred feet.*"

At this depth, a sinking wooden ship would be crushed to splinters in moments, like a toy beneath a sledgehammer. Even metal could buckle into shapes beyond all recognition.

The suit distributes the pressure evenly, Curtis told himself. *Geometric strength. It has no weak points.*

But perspiration beaded his forehead and dribbled into his eyes, and his heart hammered wildly.

"*Nine hundred feet.*"

"Acknowledged."

Again, Curtis silently raged at Señor Paz and the Maliban government. Three times the man had come to the *Gorgon*, prying, asking endless questions, getting in the way. And the third time, with his colleague, taking the bathysphere on what amounted to a joyride. Damn them both!

He jerked his head to drive the thoughts away.

Now, he could sense the intense pressure clamped around him, could hear his breath rasping inside the helmet, smell the sweat on his skin. His ears strained for the slightest creak of metal, the faintest groan of steel, the one little warning that would come an instant before he was crushed into oblivion.

A cliff of black rock, glistening with slime, rose within arm's reach as he dropped into the marine valley.

"*One thousand feet.*"

Curtis took a deep breath.

"Okay, Vasquez," he said. "Bring me to a stop. I'm right beside the rock face. I should see the sphere on a ledge below me any moment now."

His descent ceased. He hung in the water, swaying slightly as slow-moving but powerful tides heaved against him.

He extended his left arm, used a switch to open its claw, then another to clamp it like a vice onto a jutting rock. Thus steadied, he manoeuvred with difficulty so that his lamp shone downward.

He strained, directing the illumination.

Suddenly, his light reflected from a silver orb.

"Got it!" he cried out. "It's on a narrow ledge. Hold on a moment, I'm just—" he grunted with effort as he adjusted his position.

"*Professor, what's happening?*" Vasquez demanded, his tone anxious.

"It's all right, I'm getting a clearer view. The sphere is jammed against an outcrop. There's about three feet between it and the edge of the shelf. No danger of it falling. I think we can recover it without too much difficulty. Wait—"

He disengaged his grip.

"Right. Lower me, nice and slow."

He began to sink.

It took about three minutes, then his feet hit the ledge and the cable drooped around him.

"Stop," he ordered. "I'm there."

He moved towards the sphere. Clouds of sand and organic matter billowed around his feet. An eel-like creature shot through his light beam, passing his faceplate like a blazing arrow.

After what seemed an age, he was able to touch the sphere. He worked his way around it slowly, reassuring himself that it was secure and not about to roll off the edge to fall fathoms down.

At length, his faceplate was opposite the bathysphere's porthole.

He pressed his face forward, directing his headlamp into the dim interior.

ON THE RESEARCH ship, Vasquez was watching the dials and praying. His heart was pounding, and he was trembling—already terrified of the monster that, he was certain, was about to eat his employer.

Curtis's voice crackled over the radiophone.

"*I'm beside it now. I'm looking in. The equipment has taken some hard knocks, but the sphere itself is intact aside from a smallish, ragged split near the top, where the cables ripped off.*" His tone lowered. "*I can see a body—not a nice sight, it's been badly crushed by the pressure...*"

There came a moment of silence, then—

"*That's strange...*" Curtis sounded puzzled.

There was another pause, longer this time.

"Professor?" Vasquez prompted.

"*Wait, I'm just looking for... but... it's not possible!*"

"Professor?" Vasquez said again.

"*There's only one body, Vasquez. The other one has*

gone—disappeared. How? No one could get out alive at half this depth—"

His voice broke off.

Vasquez stared in bemusement at the radio apparatus.

When Curtis finally spoke again, his voice was pitched high with a new note—a note of near hysteria.

"God Almighty! I don't believe it!"

Vasquez, overcome with superstitious dread, banged the transmit switch and yelled, "What is it? What have you seen? Tell me!"

"The body! The man's been murdered! He's been stabbed in the back! I must be going mad, but I can see it! I can see the knife! He's been stabbed in the back!"

Vasquez made no reply to that. He ceased to feel the oppressive heat of the Caribbean afternoon. Cold sweat broke out all over his body as the uncanny implications of the professor's words registered in his mind.

One dead body was floating in the sphere—murdered. And the other man had vanished.

But how?

3

sweet persuasion

SEXTON BLAKE, SITTING at his desk in his office in Berkeley Square, stirred his mid-morning coffee, his expression abstracted and thoughtful.

He was reading the latest edition of the *Daily Post*, and his eyes focused on a front-page article:

TERRORISM INCREASES IN MALIBA

PRESIDENT NONALES TO SEEK US AID

The People's Liberation Army of Juan Callas last night struck a new blow at the Government of the trouble-torn Caribbean island of Maliba when it pulled off a well-planned raid on an Army garrison, only a few miles outside the principal city, Carabanos. CHARLES FLEMING reports:

The island's Police Chief, Captain Carlos Tarratona, said tonight: "This is the fifth successful raid by subversive forces so far this year. In view of these increasing outrages, the President, Doctor Nonales, is to consult American representatives with a view to seeking US aid to defend our national sovereignty."

Tarratona claimed that this latest attack, like others preceding it, was communist-inspired, and accuses the Soviet Union of interfering in Maliba's domestic affairs.

After the attack, the city waits in an uneasy silence and the streets are deserted except for the rumbling of army tanks as security forces patrol the capital.

At the bottom of the column, it advised:

"See pictures on page 3. More about Maliba in AROUND AND ABOUT, page 6."

Blake frowned, compressed his lips, and turned to page six.

AROUND AND ABOUT was the gossip column written and compiled by his old friend Arthur "Splash"

Kirby, one of the *Post's* top journalists. It struck Blake as an odd location for further news on Maliba.

The column ran along the usual lines. He swiftly scanned through reports of celebrity dalliances and breezy observations on London life before coming to the sub-heading:

MALIBAN MYSTERY

From the Caribbean trouble-spot of Maliba comes this report on the latest events in the life of the famous American "boy professor" and marine biologist Hoddard Curtis. Curtis is the man who has perfected a new kind of bathysphere, a significant advance in the field of deep-sea exploration.

It has just become known that three days ago, while the professor was away on a trip to Florida, two fisheries inspectors from the Maliban government exceeded their authority by taking his bathysphere out for a spin in the deep.

Just how wrong they were to do so is shown by the fact that they went down but failed to come back up.

Upon his return from America,

Curtis risked his life in an untested deep-sea diving suit and located his invention more than a thousand feet down.

Then came shock number two, for when he shone his under-sea torch through the porthole of the bathysphere, he found that one of its two occupants had disappeared—leaving the other with a knife in his back!

Experts agree that no one could escape alive from the bathysphere at even half that depth.

How one man came to be stabbed and the other spirited away, presents a mystery that would challenge even the famous Baker Street sleuth, Sexton Blake.

Maliban authorities have so far refused to comment.

Blake allowed himself a brief smile at the reference to himself, but as he came to the end of the article, his smile became a puzzled frown.

For a moment, his fingers drummed thoughtfully on his desk. Then he picked up the telephone.

His office telephonist and receptionist, Marion Lang, came on the line.

"Yes, Mr. Blake?"

"Marion, get me Splash Kirby's office at the *Post*, would you?"

"Right away, Mr. Blake."

He replaced the receiver on its cradle and glanced up as his secretary came in.

Paula Dane was tall, sophisticated, and stunning. Her blue summer dress, covered by a light, pale yellow cardigan, swayed from her hips as she walked. Her honey-blonde hair glowed softly in the morning sunlight that streamed through the window, and the scent of fresh lavender wafted in with her as she entered the office.

With a twinkle in her eyes, she declared, "Dictate, oh master, and verily I shall transcribe!"

Before Blake could offer a suitably dry retort, the telephone rang. He gestured for Paula to take the chair beside his desk, then scooped up the receiver.

"Hello?"

"Kirby here," came the bright and cheery voice of the columnist. "I accept."

"Accept?" said Blake. "Accept what?"

"Dinner at your place, tonight. Mrs. Bardell's finest fare! I predict lamb with mint sauce, peas and new potatoes. A bottle of Bordeaux. The delectable Paula attending. Brandy and cigars afterwards. Shall we say seven?"

"Mrs. Bardell is visiting her great-niece in Devon."

"What's so great about her?"

"Her age, primarily. You know the Bardell genes. Listen, Splash, I've just been reading your item on Maliba—"

"Ah! The bathysphere mystery? I thought that would hook you. Have you solved it yet?"

"No, I haven't."

"Too busy loafing around, I suppose? You've not been the same since you hired staff."

Blake smiled. "I'd like some more information."

"Shoot," Kirby invited.

"Why did you write it?"

There was a pause. "Pardon me? What's the matter? Don't you like it?"

"On the contrary," Blake replied. "I'm fascinated by it. But by the same token, millions of other readers will be, too. I mean, why you in particular and not the news boys? This is front page material, surely?"

Kirby paused again. "You're right, of course—but the problem is the story's reliability. Our man in Maliba is having trouble getting his stuff through. The police hamper him at every stage. There's a lot of unofficial censorship going on, and we haven't been able to get anything verified. We don't even know the names of the victims... and how could the article gain a headline without those? It's damned frustrating, Blake!"

"Censorship?" Blake asked. "On a story like this? Why?"

"That's the million-dollar question. It's hard to see how the bathysphere case can have a political angle, but presumably it does. As soon as we get it corroborated, we'll make a bigger story of it, but in the meantime His Royal Highness the Editor is playing it safe, which is why he gave it to me to handle as a piece of harmless gossip."

"You know nothing more about it?"

"Not a thing, old chap. I had to pad it out as it was. As soon as I have any more facts —the names!—I'll let you know. Okay?"

"Okay. Thank you."

"When's she back?"

"When's who—oh— You're aware that London has restaurants?"

"It's not the same."

"Because they cost you money? Splash, go make yourself a cheese and pickle sandwich."

Blake hung up. He turned to his secretary. "He's incorrigible."

"Either that," she said, having got the gist of it, "or he has malnutrition."

Blake glanced at the notebook poised above her knee. "Dictation?" he asked. "What dictation?"

"A couple of letters—one to the solicitors and one to Sleepwell Life and Property about last month's fake-suicide investigation."

"Humph! Can't they wait until this afternoon?"

"They can—or, if you're busy, I could deal with them myself." Paula gave a sight shrug. "But you don't have any appointments until Sir Gordon Sellingham at eleven, so—?"

Blake glanced at the clock on the wall. "I think we have a file on Maliba in the Index. I'd rather have a look at that before he gets here."

"Maliba? In the Caribbean?"

"Yes."

Paula rose with a quick, "Half a mo" and went to get the file.

She returned with a thin folder, which she placed on the desk.

"Why the interest?" she asked.

Blake put a finger on the file and pulled it over. He opened it and said, "Sir Gordon owns its largest sugar refinery."

"Ah, I see. Well, if he has a case for you, and it involves a trip to the sun-kissed Caribbean, I hereby offer my services."

He raised an eyebrow at her. "I bet you do."

"It's been a while since I had a nice tan."

"Sorry, Paula, nothing doing. I want you to join Tinker

35

in Sheffield. That poisoning he's been looking into has turned into a case of industrial espionage. Your skills at infiltration are required. Take the morning train."

Paula groaned. "Sheffield? It's been pouring with rain there for three weeks solid!"

Blake pulled several newspaper articles from the folder and spread them out in front of him, examining the headlines.

In a distracted tone, he murmured, "I won't begrudge Wellington boots on your expense account. Show Sir Gordon in as soon as he arrives, will you? In the meantime, you can deal with those letters while I go through these cuttings."

"All right," said Paula. "But be warned, those Wellingtons will be diamond-studded!"

She whisked elegantly from the office.

FORTY MINUTES LATER there was a discreet tap on the door and Paula ushered in a tall, slightly stooped man. He was wearing old-fashioned pince-nez and was bald, with a very shiny scalp gleaming through the long strands of greying brown hair that he'd meticulously combed over from a parting on the left.

His face was unnaturally pink. The high colour, Blake observed, was gathered particularly on his cheeks, and spanned the bridge of his nose, forming a butterfly shape.

Lupus, the detective thought, immediately recognising the symptom.

His visitor was holding a briefcase in one hand and an expensive-looking hat in the other. He was attired in a sombre, charcoal grey suit.

"Sir Gordon Sellingham, Mr. Blake," Paula Dane said formally.

Blake rose and shook hands with the man over the desk. "Thank you, Paula. Take a seat, Sir Gordon."

As Paula withdrew, clicking the door shut behind her, Sir Gordon lowered himself into one of Blake's comfortable chairs, uttering an ill-suppressed moan as he did so.

"Horribly stiff in the joints today," he declared. His voice was surprisingly deep and throaty. He placed his hat on the floor and his briefcase across his knees.

Blake opened his monogramed silver cigarette box and offered it to the millionaire.

Sir Gordon waved it away. "Thank you, but my doctor advises me not to. As a matter of fact, he advises me not to indulge in anything at all that might be remotely worth indulging in. I absolutely despise the fellow."

Blake allowed himself a faint smile. "I deal in investigations, Sir Gordon, not in assassinations."

"Ha! I could make it worth your while!" Sir Gordon clicked open the clasps on his case but didn't lift the lid. "But we'll leave my irritating medico for another occasion. Today, I have something rather more urgent for you."

Blake put his cigarette box aside. "You'll appreciate that I don't accept every proposition that's brought to me."

"You'll accept this one, I'm certain of it. I've had you looked into, I've studied your reputation, and I can promise you this has all the ingredients necessary to interest you."

Blake nodded. "Very well. Tell me all about it."

"I intend to send you on a highly confidential mission, Mr. Blake. It concerns large sums of money, the life of a man, and a new trouble spot in the Cold War."

"Maliba?" suggested Blake.

Sir Gordon leaned back in his seat. "By the Lord Harry! How on earth did you know?" He peered down at himself, at his cufflinks, his suit buttons, his shoes. "I see nothing on me. What possible clue have you spotted?"

"No clue," answered Blake. "I read the newspaper."

His prospective client looked deflated and murmured, "Ah, of course. Yes, there have been reports."

"Quite so," said Blake. "And I'll confess to some interest in them. Perhaps you'd like to fill in the details?"

Sir Gordon finally opened his briefcase and took out a sheaf of papers. He passed them over. "I'll leave these with you to look over when you've the time."

Blake took them, flicked through the pages, and with a twinge of amusement saw that most were the same cuttings he had in his own file.

"But all you need to know for now," continued Sir Gordon, "is that the affair hinges on the current political set-up in the Caribbean. You know, I suppose, that I own a great deal of the Maliban sugar industry?"

"Yes, I'm aware of the fact."

"And you know that Doctor Nonales is the President of Maliba?"

Blake nodded.

"Well, let me tell you, his administration is totally corrupt. And the police operate more like the Mafia. Crooked as corkscrews, the lot of 'em."

"Then you favour Juan Callas and his so-called People's Liberation Army?" Blake asked.

Sir Gordon raised a hand. "Ah! You'd think so, wouldn't you? But that is just where you're wrong, Mr. Blake. The fact of the matter is that, if the rebels overthrow Nonales and make a democracy of the island, its industry will be utterly paralysed. Everything will grind to a complete standstill."

Blake frowned and angled his head enquiringly. "Why so?"

"Because democratic governments impose rules and regulations. Maliba prospers without 'em! It always has done. You can't take away an ages-long tradition without bringing the machinery to a halt—any more than you can take away the ball-bearings of a centrifuge in a sugar refinery."

"Then you favour corruption?"

"Great heavens, no! But any opinion I might hold is by the by. The fact that you and I live in a country where corrupt practices are discouraged doesn't invalidate their effectiveness. And, really, it's only a matter of perspective. A custom deemed corrupt from one angle is perfectly acceptable—and positively encouraged—from another. Ask any of them—corruption is the only way that anything gets done. Their industry thrives on it."

Blake sighed. "Go on."

"I'm not a man to mince words, Mr. Blake. The *status quo* is favourable to me. I don't want there to be change. If Juan Callas overthrows Nonales, there'll be another Cuba in the Caribbean."

"I take it you're referring to the rumours of Soviet meddling?"

Sir Gordon nodded. "The island's police chief claims that the rebel army is swarming with communists. If it's true, my refinery is as good as gone."

Blake put his elbows on his desk and steepled his fingers. "As far as I've been able to ascertain from the reports I've so far read, there's no solid evidence to support his assertion. In fact, there's speculation that

President Nonales is having him make that claim simply to encourage American funding."

"Maybe so," Sir Gordon admitted grudgingly. "But I can't afford to take any chances, and with the news censored at its source, I'll never know anything for sure unless I can get someone reliable out there to assess the situation. If it's as bad as it's painted, I may need to cut my losses and sell the business."

"But you already have people out there, running the refinery. Can't they enlighten you?"

"I don't trust them to be impartial, Blake. I employ them to navigate the corruption but, inevitably, that makes them vulnerable to it. Given an appropriate 'backhander,' they might tell me anything."

Blake was silent for a moment. Sir Gordon's "mission," such as it was, amounted to very little: merely a nebulous request for him to go to Maliba and have a nose around.

He lowered his hands and tapped a finger on the sheaf of papers. "You mentioned that a man's life is in danger. What about that?"

Sir Gordon pursed his lips, and the patch that marred his face turned a shade redder.

"It's my son, Peter. I fear he'll be the ruin of me if I don't rein him in. I should never have allowed him to attend Oxford. He's been living in cloud-cuckoo-land ever since he graduated. The place is a hotbed of socialism."

Blake's brow puckered. "I don't quite understand."

"When I told you that I needed someone reliable in Maliba, it's because I've learned a hard lesson. I sent him—a naïve fool with a headful of pie-in-the-sky ideas and a bucketful of money. The last I heard from him, he'd got it into his thick head to start purchasing weapons for the rebels."

"Is he a communist?" Blake asked, his eyebrows going up.

"Hah! He doesn't know what he is," snapped Sir Gordon. "But certainly, the communist movement has had reason to be grateful for his chequebook before now. This is just one hobbyhorse in a long line of senseless frivolities. A year ago, he financed a campaign for banning H-bombs. Before that, he got in with a rabid crowd of ne'er-do-wells that ran around denouncing all my friends as fascists. Before that—"

Sir Gordon's voice, which had got louder and begun to sound hoarse, cut off.

He coughed, drew a breath, and continued more softly:

"I thought that by trusting him with an important mission, I'd put him on the straight and narrow. More fool me! Perhaps the rebels can't be stopped, Mr. Blake, but I will not stand idle while my own flesh and blood helps them to ruin my business."

"Can't you simply cut off his allowance?"

"I did that years ago, but he still has the half million he inherited from his late mother, God rest her soul."

"But why do you think Peter's life is in danger? Is it just because he's playing with political dynamite?"

"No, it's gone beyond that," Sir Gordon responded sourly. "He's missing. No one's seen or heard from him for days. My manager out there—Tucker—has had her people keeping a close watch on him, but she tells me he's disappeared without a trace. I can't make too much noise about it or the rebels will raise a hullaballoo— '*Capitalist Interferes in Maliban Domestic Affairs!*'— you know the sort of headline. It would be on every front page."

Blake said, "So, you want me to—?"

"Go there, locate him, and bring him back," Sir Gordon said, then added firmly, "By force if need be."

Blake smiled thinly. "I told you in jest, Sir Gordon, that I'm an investigator not an assassin—but, in all seriousness, neither am I a strong-arm man. Your son is presumably over twenty-one. I can hardly kidnap him and drag him—"

"You'll be saving his life!" Sir Gordon interrupted. "If he isn't already dead, that is. Can't you see how he's caught between two fires? Either Nonales will rumble what he's up to and throw him into a prison cell—or the rebels will bump him off as soon as he's served their purpose. They'll hardly want to be associated with the son of a capitalist when the time comes for handing out medals."

"Yes, I see what you mean."

"Will you take the case, then?"

"I'll need to give it some thought. Can I phone you back later and let you know?"

"You can. Here, have these—"

Sir Gordon drew two envelopes from his case and placed them on Blake's desk.

"Two letters, which you'll require should you accept. One, written in Spanish, establishes the fact that you are working on my behalf. It will smooth the way if you encounter any bureaucratic difficulties. The other, in English, introduces you to Miss Tucker, at the refinery. Oh, and you'll need this—" He extracted a wallet from his jacket pocket and took a passport-sized photograph from it, which he handed over. "This is Peter."

Blake looked at it and murmured, "A handsome lad."

"He has his mother's good looks," Sir Gordon responded. "But the family goldfish's brains."

He rose to his feet, wincing and putting a hand to his hip, which obviously pained him.

"I should warn you in advance," he said, "that my manager, Amelia Tucker, is a tough old bird. Rather hard and unpleasant in manner, but excellent at her job. She came to me a year and a half or so ago—October of 'fifty-nine, it was—and I thoroughly disliked her the moment I set eyes on her, but she had a fistful of glowing references, and my previous manager, Cranston, had just been killed, so I took a chance, and I've not regretted it. Don't let her prickles bother you."

"Killed?" Blake asked, his curiosity piqued, as it always was, by that particular choice of word.

"A hit and run. Everyone drives like a maniac in the tropics. They go fast to beat the heat. And they're full of rum, of course."

He shook hands with the detective and moved to the door.

"I'm confident you'll make the correct decision, Blake."

He stopped, turned, and smiled.

"And when you get back, we'll have a talk about my dastardly doctor, eh? Good day!"

He marched from the office.

Blake sat back in his chair, took a cigarette from the box, and lit it. He smoked and contemplated.

Young Peter Sellingham's life was certainly in danger if he was meddling in subversive activities, there was no denying that.

A trip to Maliba promised to be interesting.

And, of course, there was that stranger item—the mystery of the bathysphere.

He started to sift again through the newspaper cuttings.

4

"the man"

IT WAS A few minutes before noon when Sexton Blake closed the Maliba file, to which the material brought by Sir Gordon Sellingham had now been added.

Leaning back behind his desk, he massaged a crick out of his neck and considered what he'd read.

Maliba was remarkable for being the easternmost of the Spanish-speaking Caribbean islands. Unfortunately, news reports concerning its recent history were far from helpful. Drawn from sources all over the world, they were either confusing or downright contradictory.

According to left-wing papers, the government of Doctor Nonales was a bastion of fascism while the rebels were merely staunch democrats. According to right-wing papers, Nonales was a benevolent paternalist while the rebels were rabid Reds.

The truth probably lay somewhere between the two— in which case the affair was a purely domestic one which did not warrant interference by outsiders.

On the other hand, if the claims made by Police Chief

Tarratona—the president's mouthpiece and muscle—
were true, and the communists were really backing
the rebels, then an investigation was both justified and
necessary.

Blake had to be certain. And there was only one man
who could tell him what he wanted to know.

He rose from his chair, picked up his hat and coat, and
went out into the outer office.

Paula Dane and Marion Lang looked up with curiosity.

"I'm going out," Blake said simply. "Expect me when
you see me."

Paula Dane nodded but did not say anything. Blake's
words were a formula she knew from experience—they
meant he was going to seek the counsel of a certain
individual who was wizened and old and infinitely wise;
one who ostensibly managed a small export/import firm
in Belgrave Square, but whose exports and imports were
of a highly specialised nature.

His proper title, never spoken and seldom written, was
"Director of the Inter-Service Co-Ordination of Strategic
Intelligence and National Security."

Most people who knew of him, which was very few
indeed, referred to him simply as "the man."

And of those few, even fewer were aware that such power,
knowledge, and foresight as was his was comparable only,
perhaps, to that of the ancient Oracle of Delphi.

His name was Eustace Craille.

BLAKE FOUND HIM sitting behind his desk in front of a
map of the world, his attention riveted on a column in
Pravda, which he was reading by the light of a powerful
lamp.

His right hand was resting on the desk, gripping a stubby cigarette holder from which a thin pencil-line of aromatic smoke was climbing steadily towards a ceiling obscured by fumes.

Craille habitually kept his curtains drawn. It was good for security. But it was also bad for health, and the smoke of the old man's Egyptian cigarettes produced a spasm of coughing from Blake as he was shown in by a full-lipped, softly contoured brunette, who spoke with a husky voice.

"Mr. Blake, sir."

Surprisingly, the girl was the same the detective had seen on his previous visit.

"Do I take it that you've found your soulmate, at last?" he asked after she had exited, closing the door behind her. It was rare for Craille to keep any of his beautiful women for very long.

"She's due to go at the end of the week," the old man rasped in his dry voice. A gleam crept into his hooded, hawk-like eyes. "Still wondering where I get them from, are you?"

Blake smiled. "I know it's not from a secretarial agency. I'm more intrigued by what your neighbours must think."

"They think exactly what I want them to think," said Craille. "The price I pay for security is the loss of my respectability. I am, apparently, a lecherous old goat with considerably more money than morals. Who cares? It helps to explain the secrecy."

"And the girls? Do the neighbours dismiss them as cheap tarts? How do they feel about that? Good god, Craille, why would any of them want to work for you?"

"Because they gain valuable knowledge, intensive

training, and afterwards they are promoted into fieldwork."

Blake arched an eyebrow. "Are you telling me they are agents?"

Craille threw the copy of *Pravda* into his huge waste-paper basket.

"Now why," he said, "would I tell you a thing like that?"

He gestured towards a seat. Blake sat in it.

Craille drew on his cigarette and, expelling a billowing cloud, said, "All right—why are you here?"

"Because I've just had a visit from Sir Gordon Sellingham, the millionaire."

"Ah. And he asked you to go to Maliba to find his son."

Blake became very still. He narrowed his eyes and said in a low, icy tone, "If you've planted a listening device in my office—"

Craille interrupted with a dismissive flick of his hand. "You've accepted the job?"

The detective allowed a moment of silence to pass before he responded.

"No, not yet. I haven't decided. I need to know more about whatever Peter Sellingham has got himself mixed up in. The political situation."

Craille gazed at him steadily. "What do you want from me?"

"Hard facts rather than newspaper rumours and sensationalism."

Craille grunted. There was a frown on his brittle-skinned face. "Yes, that's what I want, too. I've been thinking of sending someone over there—"

"Then you can't help me?" Blake asked.

Craille rotated his cigarette holder between skeletal

fingers and drew another lungful of the strong, perfumed smoke.

"I can tell you what I know from Her Majesty's Government—from Henderson, our Vice-Consul on the island. Juan Callas is no communist. He's out to overthrow the Nonales government for one good reason and one alone: it needs overthrowing. That said, there's no shortage of communists in that part of the world right now—you know what's happening in Cuba."

"Has the rebel army been infiltrated?" asked Blake.

"If you believe Doctor Nonales, yes; and, according to his police chief, the city of Carabanos is swarming with communists, all eager to join Callas up in the hills where his so-called freedom fighters are encamped. But truth be told, there's no credible evidence to support the assertion. Our assessment is that there's currently just one full-blown Soviet agent with feet on Maliban soil. We know that because he was spotted by the CIA running guns from Brazil to the island."

Craille peered through the room's miasma.

"Blake, the Soviets have got their claws into Cuba in the west of the Caribbean. If they gain a hold in Maliba, in the east, then all the islands in between are liable to fall like dominoes. We can't allow that to happen."

He drew on his cigarette, blew out the smoke, leaned back in his chair, and continued, "So—a private detective searching for a lost youth. Nothing untoward about that. It's a good cover, don't you think?"

"Under which to go in and apprehend the Soviet agent, do you mean?"

"Yes."

"No," said Blake. "It's lousy. But it will have to do."

"You'll accept the assignment?"

Blake made his customary pause for last-minute thoughts, but he hardly needed to consider it any further.

"I accept the assignment. Tell me about him."

Craille took a file from a drawer and slid it across the desk.

Blake opened it. At the top of the first page there was glued a small, grainy photograph of a man with short black hair, his features bony but indistinct and half-concealed by shadow.

The photo was stamped: "May 1960." It had been taken eleven months ago.

Underneath:

ORTIZ, SEBASTIÁN

Argentinian, born in Córdoba, October or November 1924. He participated in the coup d'état of 1943 (aged 19), but after he executed five men and one woman without being ordered to do so, he was himself placed under arrest. Two days before his trial, Ortiz murdered a guard and escaped with the assistance of an as yet unidentified woman. Members of the Communist Party helped him to flee the country. He made his way to Moscow, where he was recruited by the NKVD and trained as an espionage agent. He is skilled in the use of multiple weapons, in unarmed combat (particularly kickboxing), and in the concoction and application of poisons. He speaks fluent Spanish, English, French, and Russian.

See pp 12-31 of File "B" for espionage, and pp 43-65 for his confirmed assassinations of Gretchen Meyer (H55327), Emil Hácha (K87366), and Andrew Arthur Franklyn (R44438).

ORG.: employed (1947-1950) by GOSUDARSTVENNOYE POLITICHESKOYE UPRAVLENIYE (G.P.U., State Political Department), and (1950-1957) MINISTERSTVO GOSUDARSTVENNOI BEZOPASNOSTI (M.G.B., Soviet Ministry of State Security). Current position unknown.

SPECIAL OBSERVATIONS: This man is a senior-ranked master spy in the Soviet network. His abnormal degree of personal power, and the freedom of action which the Soviet authorities have consistently allowed him,

```
indicate that he is one of their
most trusted operatives.
```

```
(Compare photograph above with
man in group-shot, P. 43, taken
at time of 40th Party Conference
in Moscow, 1957).
```

APPROACH WITH EXTREME CAUTION.

On the next page, there was a detailed physical and psychological description of the man. On page three, an analysis of Ortiz's special skills. The remaining seventy pages were devoted to the missions he was known to have undertaken, plus others in which his involvement was suspected but not confirmed.

As Blake skimmed through them, he whistled softly.

"Yes, an impressive record," Craille observed, in his creaking voice.

"I would have chosen the word *appalling*," countered Blake. "If he is on Maliba, then there can be little doubt that the Soviets intend to take the island—but I must say, you appear to lack any convincing evidence of his presence. The gunrunning from Brazil?"

"Two CIA agents identified him," Craille said. "They have no doubt about it, despite that he was using a false identity. He was overseeing the loading of weapons— mostly German, World War Two era—onto a ship bound for Maliba. He went aboard and did not disembark— possibly because he realised he'd been identified. The ship sailed."

Blake stood. "Anything else?"

"Yes. He was using the name Paz."

"Paz?" Blake echoed.

"Paz," repeated Craille. "Benjamin Paz."

5

change of climate

EIGHTEEN HOURS LATER, armed with the two letters written by Sir Gordon Sellingham and a wallet full of American dollars, Sexton Blake fastened his safety belt as the Comet IV airliner prepared to land at Maliba's only airport.

The flight through the long night had been uneventful, but there was a great deal to think about.

Before leaving London, there had been barely sufficient time to telephone Edward "Tinker" Carter to get an update—and issue advice—concerning the Sheffield case, and to alert him to Paula's imminent arrival.

Blake had then raced to catch his plane. Everything depended on him reaching Maliba as soon as possible, before any further developments might render his scanty information invalid.

Now, as the aircraft descended, and, in a sea of sapphire blue, the island of sugarcane, palm trees, and coral-white beaches loomed ahead, the detective was conscious that there was much to do and that a lot depended on it.

The tropical scenery looked tranquil, dreamlike,

shimmering beneath the early morning heat haze like a mirage. He wondered whether events over the next few hours might shatter that illusion of peace.

The airliner's wheels bumped once, gently, on the airport's single runway, then it settled, slowed, and taxied to a halt beside the stark white block that served as a terminal.

THE PASSENGERS DISEMBARKED at eight-thirty in the morning into the humid embrace of a Caribbean spring. It was an unseasonably hot April. Despite the early hour, the heat already came at them from every direction, reflecting from every surface, soaking immediately into every pore as they stepped from the air-conditioned coolness of the aeroplane and crossed to the customs hall.

The inside of the building was modern and clean. They were received by expressionless, hard-eyed officials, who scrutinised their passports with excessive suspicion, and allowed them to pass with apparent reluctance.

Armed police watched over the proceedings.

When asked the reason for his visit, Blake produced the first of his letters from Sir Gordon.

He was permitted through.

With considerable relief, he emerged from the terminal, but was then immediately reminded that all was not well in the Republic of Maliba. Soldiers, in drab, olive uniforms, stood sentry duty at sandbag and barbed-wire machine gun emplacements all around the perimeter of the parking area.

The airport, it appeared, was a forbidden zone to Maliba's citizens—and a strategic key point to anyone planning insurrection.

He crossed to where a smooth, gleaming American-built airline bus was waiting to whisk the latest arrivals from the airport to Carabanos.

He climbed in, gave his destination and fare, then settled in a seat behind the driver.

Soon, everyone else was aboard, and the vehicle set off.

A warm breeze fanned the detective's face as he took in his first ground-level view of the island.

To the west, a dormant volcano dominated, its slopes heavily forested. Two low mountains rose beside it, with roads zigzagging through their trees, connecting the bauxite mines, which in the past three years had brought unaccustomed wealth to Maliba.

The land sloped down and northward from these heights, then curved eastward, hilly, and narrowing to a point, forming—in its entirety—an irregular comma shape. The airport was almost exactly in the centre of it, with Carabanos eight miles distant on the northern coast. There were two large towns: Santa Maria at the foot of the volcano, and Ángel Dorado in the south-east.

Dazzling blues, turquoises, and vivid, juicy greens predominated, the sky, the sea, and the lush, dense flora. Everything else was bleached by the sun to the palest of browns and greys. The Maliban colours—blue and orange—were painted here and there, bright where fresh but mostly washed out.

It dawned on Blake, as the bus rumbled and rattled on, that these two colours were employed everywhere for decorative purposes rather than in nationalistic fervour. He was struck by the absence of flags. In fact, he didn't see a single one. This was, in his experience, a very unusual circumstance in any country on the brink of revolution.

The road linking the airport and city was well-maintained. President Nonales had obviously recognised its value. Advertising hoardings crowded along its length, all promoting American and European luxury products, "tax-free!"—the finest Havana cigars—the best Caribbean rum—the most modern hotels—the top casinos—

Come, foreigners! Blake thought. *And bring your money!*

As the vehicle drew closer to the city, the hoardings gave way to market stalls and to vendors selling sugarcane milk and coconut water. The air blowing through the bus suddenly brought with it the spicy odours of street food.

He caught a glimpse of a white beach and extremely tall palms. Then, board houses and little shops—many slumping and ramshackle, some little more than hovels—obscured the view. Soon came larger buildings, each coated with flaked and blistered whitewash and adorned with faded canopies and rickety window shutters.

Restaurants, bars, and stores of all descriptions began to appear. Aside from the bars, nothing was open, it being Sunday. For the same reason, the people were wearing their best. Shoes were shiny, shirts ironed, and the dresses smart and surprisingly fashionable.

Carabanos hugged the harbour for its livelihood. It was a small and tightly packed city, seething with humanity; noisy, resplendent and vibrant but, on closer inspection, decayed and crumbling.

To where, or perhaps who, the detective wondered, *goes the reputed wealth from the bauxite?*

The bus slowed and stopped outside a large hotel. It was an old colonial edifice, the ghost of a history best forgotten, and was adorned with a sign stating HOTEL

PALMA, which was justified by the two palm trees shading the entrance.

The driver leaned from his seat, looked back at Blake, and called, "Aquí, señor!"

Blake tipped him and disembarked—the only passenger to do so, the rest destined, he supposed, for cheaper accommodation.

Carrying his light suitcase, he entered the hotel through its frosted glass doors.

The lobby resembled a small, late Edwardian ballroom. Red plush, rather worn, was everywhere, framed by ornately carved woodwork, all painted gold. Big mirrors adorned the walls. It was dimly lit, and a roof-fan, turning lazily overhead, kept it refreshingly cool.

A radio was on, tuned to a news channel and turned up loud.

Blake stopped dead and his mouth fell open.

The announcer was speaking fast, almost hysterically, his Spanish flowing one word into the other with such desperate rapidity that the detective, fluent as he was, found it almost impossible to follow.

"...the anti-Castro invasion... crushed completely in less than seventy-two hours but with heavy casualties suffered by both the government forces and the rebel army, which... flee the island but were stopped by aircraft which bombed their craft to cut off their... while other battalions were trapped in a swamp and forced to surrender. The rebel position in Playa Girón was overrun by half-past five and the... pressed the invaders without respite... discovering that, unquestionably, the armaments were of American origin... can be no doubt that the imperialist government of the United States has... and the iniquitous plot will... who this morning* *condemned Kennedy and called upon First Secretary Khrushchev to immediately place a…"*

A wizened porter, standing beside the radio, noticed Blake and quickly clicked it off, hurried over, and greeted him.

He was a small man, mixed Latino and Carib, dressed smartly in a white uniform, and with a peaked cap pressed firmly down on his head.

"Señor?"

"What has happened?" the detective asked. "The news?"

The man tapped his ear. "Pardon, señor, a little deaf. You said?"

Blake repeated himself, louder.

"Ah! The news, señor! But you have not heard?"

"I've been on an aeroplane."

"Ah! You are American?"

"British."

"Gracias a dios! It is Cuba, señor. An army of exiles, they landed yesterday at Playa Girón on the southern coast—a counter-revolution to overthrow Fidel Castro. Much fighting! But they were defeated, and now Castro, he says the attack was financed by the Americans, by President Kennedy and the CIA. He has the evidence! Madre mía! It is a disaster, no?"

Blake ran his fingers back over his hair and blew out a breath. "Phew! Yes, that's going to complicate matters."

"Si, señor, for the world, I think. But do not worry. We are a long way from Cuba here, and we do not have the politics. No one will bother with Maliba."

Blake murmured, "Well, that's good to hear."

The porter put a finger to his ear again.

"Señor?"

"I said: I have a room booked. Mr. Sexton Blake."

He was deliberately using his own name. He had travelled so extensively for so many years that recognition could never be discounted. It was better to hide nothing than to attempt a deception, get caught out, and thus stimulate curiosity.

The porter took his suitcase, called out "Maria!" and led him to the reception desk.

A pretty girl stepped in through a doorway, leaving the ribbons of a plastic curtain swaying behind her. She was wearing a pale blue and orange Sunday frock that left her chocolate-brown arms and shoulders bare, a scarf of the same colours holding back her braided hair. She greeted him with a bright smile and placed her hands, with a clatter of bangles, on the desk either side of a reservation book.

"Señor Seaton Begg," the porter said.

"Sexton Blake," the detective corrected.

"Sí," the porter agreed. "He is British, Maria."

Maria's smile widened. "Will you sign the book, Señor Blake? I hope you enjoy your stay on Maliba. We are a welcoming people."

Blake signed. "Yes, I saw the gun emplacements."

The girl's smile faltered.

He made reparation with a smile of his own. "Forgive me, that was rude. I have just received a shock—the news from Cuba—and after seeing the soldiers around your airport—"

"Uff! They are nothing to be concerned about," she said. "Just an exercise, I have heard."

She reached out and switched the radio back on, twisted its dial, and tuned it to a music station. An insistent and happy-sounding rhythm pumped out, filling the lobby.

She raised her voice. "This—not the soldiers—this is our Maliba! You like Jimmy Cliff, Señor Blake?"

"That's the artiste? Yes, the music feels—um—appropriate."

"On the island, we say: 'Cuando hay problemas, solo baila!' You understand?"

Blake's smile widened. "When there are problems, just dance. It's a nice philosophy."

"It is the way we live, señor."

She took a key from hooks beneath a shelf and gave it to the porter. "Room twenty-six."

Blake thanked her and followed the porter toward the lift.

OVER BREAKFAST IN the hotel restaurant, the detective read the local newspapers, all crammed with the hullabaloo from Cuba.

America, if the reports were to be believed, had made a gigantic error of judgement. It had, in effect, strengthened Fidel Castro's position and handed an open invitation to the Soviet Union.

The communists were at America's doorstep.

One end of the Caribbean secured.

At the other end—Maliba.

What this meant for Blake's mission, it was too soon to know. He suspected, however, that the Soviets would become more brazen; that they would now act more quickly, and would find it a lot easier to justify their occupation of the little island.

Where before he had given himself a week to complete his mission, he now gave two days at most.

The newspapers taught him something else: Maliba's censorship was not confined to foreign correspondents.

There was no suggestion that the developments in

Cuba could impact Maliba. There was no mention of any political disturbance "at home." Instead, the idea that "it could not happen here" was forcefully promoted, and page after page was devoted to feature articles in which the latest "security force exercises" were outlined and explained in the most positive terms. No communist, it was stated, could ever set foot on the island without being immediately captured and incarcerated.

The People's Liberation Army was mentioned nowhere. Doctor Nonales had evidently decided on a policy of "no publicity, no public interest."

Blake folded up the papers and finished his breakfast. He decided that his first move should be to trace Peter Sellingham's movements, and to begin by visiting the hotel from which the young man had last written to his father.

A few minutes later, dressed in a light, tropical suit, he left the hotel and set out on foot toward the centre of the city.

THE DAY WAS heating up, the air thick with moisture and filled with noise.

Music was ubiquitous. Radios played, it seemed, from every window and every doorway. Men, with leathery skin and a myriad of wrinkles, sat on steps and strummed guitars. Women were singing. Drums throbbed incessantly.

Every bar and café in the narrow, twisting thoroughfares—even the smallest of them—provided a venue for musicians.

Added to this, roadside hawkers declared their wares in singsong tones, while what passed for normal conversation—and everybody was talking—sounded, to Blake, more like yelling.

The sheer intensity of the hustle and bustle was incredible.

And evidently, with the shops closed, Sunday was the best day for independent vendors.

Donkey-carts, horse-carts and hand-carts were everywhere, piled high with fruits, vegetables, brightly coloured sweetmeats, black cheroots, and cheap cigarillos.

Here and there, men and women sauntered along with their arms outstretched and draped with clothes, with sandals strung around their necks, and a tower of hats rising from their heads. A person could purchase from any single one of them a complete outfit.

Others were adorned from head to foot with a multitude of rings, bangles, necklaces, headscarves, and leather belts.

Even at this early hour, there were oil stoves on every corner. Vendors fried churros, which they liberally sprinkled with sugar and cinnamon, or plantains, served with hot butter sauce, or ferociously spiced chicken wings, or goat curry, and a plethora of other traditional foods, everything available for just a few cents.

The aromatic, bitter-sweet smell of coffee penetrated everywhere, disguising the less wholesome odours— the stench of rancid oil, pungent garlic, badly plumbed lavatories, and, above all, of perspiring humanity.

Carabanos seethed, a great melting pot—Creoles, Spaniards, Carib-Indians, Afro-Caribbeans, Europeans, Americans, and even Chinese—every shade of skin from the whitest to the blackest, and in profusion.

There was no apartheid—no racial divides. It was impossible to discriminate at all.

And, to Sexton Blake, all of this was wonderful.

More than anything, it was the vitality that impressed him, the sense that the islanders fully engaged with life and lived it to the full. Their zest was palpable. It got under his skin. For all the squalor—because plainly there was squalor—and for all the poverty—because that, too, was in evidence—he found himself filled with admiration for these people, and rather envious of their outlook. *Just dance!*

It was midmorning by the time he turned a corner and saw his first port of call.

The grandiosely named HOTEL MALIBA was in, by the looks of it, the city's most dilapidated district. Its buildings were in a severe state of disrepair, many windowless, some collapsed, the streets piled with rubbish.

It looked just the place for a young and wealthy idealist like Peter Sellingham.

The reek of yesterday's fried fish greeted the detective as he pushed open the hotel's wooden front door and entered.

There was no reception desk, just a bell on the wall.

Blake rang it and waited.

No one came.

He tried again.

A further minute passed before a man shuffled in. He was dressed cleanly enough but, beneath his thick drooping moustache, he was unshaven, his chin made blue by stubble.

"Buenos días, señor," he said, revealing crooked, tobacco-yellowed teeth.

Blake greeted him. "I understand that a Peter Sellingham resides here?"

"The young Englishman?" the man queried. "Sí, señor,

he did, but not for three or four—maybe five—days. He departed and has not returned."

Blake feigned anxiety. "He's gone? But I was supposed to meet him here this morning. He must have forgotten. Do you know where I might find him?"

The other shrugged.

Blake drew a ten dollar note from his pocket and considered it in an abstracted fashion. He sighed and shook his head. "Such an absent-minded young man. I suppose he neglected to leave a gratuity, too."

The man coughed and nodded. "That is true, señor. Perhaps you will find him at the Ostra."

"Ostra?"

The word meant *oyster*.

"A cantina," the man said. "A drinking bar two streets from here." He gestured. "On the right as you go out of the door. You cannot miss it."

"You have been very helpful." Blake looked at the note in his hand as if seeing it for the first time. "Oh! By the way, I'm sure my friend would want you to have this."

He passed over the money and departed.

Back in the glaring sunlight, he glanced at his watch.

He doubted that Sellingham would be at the bar so early in the day. The Ostra could wait.

Now to fulfil the obligation of every foreign visitor and make himself known to the authorities. It would be a mistake to avoid doing so, and he would at least find out to what extent the police might assist or obstruct him in his search for the missing man. The letter from Sir Gordon was in his pocket. It would prove his *bona fides*.

There was, however, an outstanding question. How did the police regard the foreign millionaire who dominated the island's sugar production?

6

end of a master spy

THE HEADQUARTERS OF the Maliba State Police were, as Blake had instinctively anticipated, in one of the most imposing buildings on the island. It stood in the capital's main plaza, directly opposite the Presidential Palace, a massive, multi-storey edifice of immaculate white concrete, elaborately adorned with rococo guttering and ornate facing.

Like the airport, it was a strategic key-point, protected by a high barbed-wire fence and sand-bag machine-gun emplacements.

He entered the narrow gate, with armed guards watching his every move, and crossed to the main steps of the building. Inside, more guards took up the scrutiny, but made no move to hinder him as he approached the front desk.

A sergeant, in a bottle-green uniform with abundant gold braid—and more medals than had ever been won on any Western battlefield— greeted Blake with a broad, genuine smile. He eyed the detective's suit with obvious envy.

"American?"

"English."

"How can I help you, señor?"

"I wish to see the Chief of Police," Blake said crisply. He took Sir Gordon's letter from his pocket and handed it over. The sergeant read it through and looked impressed.

"Please, if you will wait one moment." The man gave a nod of reassurance and disappeared through a door. A few moments later, he returned—still smiling.

"Captain Tarratona will be very pleased to see you, señor."

Blake murmured a thank you and allowed himself to be ushered through the door, along a corridor, and up a flight of stairs.

The sergeant stopped before a highly polished double-door and knocked.

A languid voice called, "Come!"

At the sergeant's behest, Blake entered alone.

The door clicked behind him.

The room was large and high-ceilinged, with two tall narrow windows, a small chandelier, and an extravagantly carved cornice running along the top of the pale-yellow walls.

A magnificent desk, which any Victorian industrialist would have been proud of, was positioned in the middle of the chamber. Against the wall to the left of it stood a Queen Anne sofa, with two chairs of the same style facing across a low coffee table.

Gleaming metal filing cabinets lined the wall to the right of the desk.

Though he was careful not to show it, Blake felt amused by the room's opulence, recalling his old Scotland Yard friends—Coutts, Harker, Venner and the rest—in their gloomy little offices.

"Bienvenido!" said a large man, heaving his bulk up from behind the desk. "Welcome, Señor Blake."

He was in his mid-to-late forties, coarse-featured, swarthy, and with a streak of startling white running through the left side of his thick, greased black hair.

His uniform was the same bottle-green as the sergeant's, but with even more medals.

He shook Blake's hand—his own was like a slab of meat—then drew up a chair for him.

"I am Captain Carlos Tarratona, señor. It is good to have you here. How do you like beautiful Maliba, the emerald of the Caribbean?"

"If that's what you call it," Blake responded, as he sat down, "I can see why. It's very green—and I like it very much."

"That is good to hear." Tarratona settled back at his desk. "A drink, perhaps?"

"No, nothing, thank you. The sergeant showed you the letter from Sir Gordon Sellingham?"

"He did." The police chief scratched his baggy chin thoughtfully. "Sir Gordon is an important man. He has brought much prosperity to the island."

And how much of it, Blake thought, recalling what his client had said about corruption, *has gone into your pocket, my friend?*

"If you are here at his behest," the police chief continued, "then I am only too happy to assist you. Although—" he went on, with a quizzical frown, "—Sir Gordon has omitted to write exactly who you are or what business you are pursuing on Maliba."

"I work for marine insurance," Blake replied blandly. "I'm a private investigator."

"Ah, yes." The captain smiled. "I thought your name

was somehow familiar. Sexton Blake. It is an unusual one, no? Maybe I have seen it in the newspapers?"

"It's not impossible that I have been mentioned in print, I suppose."

"Well, how can I be of service to you?"

He proffered a box of cigars.

"Perhaps you could help me to get my bearings," Blake said casually. He took a cigar. "Thank you."

"Bearings?"

Tarratona struck a match and offered its flame.

Blake got his cigar going, drew on it, and raised his eyebrows. "Excellent!" he murmured. "Cuban?"

"Sí, señor."

The police chief lit his own, took a puff, and waited.

"I heard," Blake continued, "that there was some sort of political trouble brewing, and to judge by the security around this building and the airport, there is. Usually, in such circumstances, the authorities impose emergency laws and regulations. I don't want to inadvertently infringe on any, so I thought it best to seek your counsel."

"What charming courtesy!" Tarratona grinned. "But really, there is no cause for anxiety."

"No?"

Tarratona made an extravagantly dismissive gesture. "Pah! A few hot-headed students—what do you call them? Beatniks?—nothing more. They are the same the world over. There is no trouble in Maliba."

Blake leaned back in his chair. "The press—I mean the English press—made it seem quite alarming."

"Of course! To boost circulation! In your country, newspapers are a business not a service, Mr. Blake, and when has the truth ever been compatible with commerce?"

Blake nodded thoughtfully. "Well then, I feel much encouraged. If I can proceed without tripping over toes..." He let the sentence tail off.

Tarratona eyed him for a moment, then took the bait.

"Proceed with what, Señor Blake?"

"Oh, it's pretty straightforward. Sir Gordon has lost track of his son. You know how negligent young men can be, especially when they have more money than sense. I'm here to track him down and send him home."

"Ah," Tarratona said.

"Apparently, he was staying at the Hotel Maliba, but I just learned that he left there some days ago. I don't suppose you have any idea where I might find him? His name is Peter. Peter Sellingham."

Tarratona threw out his hands in an exaggerated shrug.

"Foreigners are free to come and go as they please. We do not monitor their movements. He could be anywhere."

Blake examined his cigar appreciatively, gave a decisive nod, and got to his feet.

"You've been most gracious, captain. Your time is valuable. I shan't impose on it any longer."

"It's been a pleasure." The police chief rose, smiling, to shake hands. "I'm sorry that I can't be of any better assistance. But, please, call any time."

"I will," Blake promised.

It was only as he was reaching for the doorknob that Tarratona said casually, "A moment, please."

Blake turned. "Captain?"

"I'm a little confused. You said you worked for marine insurance. If that is the case, why have you been employed to search for—?"

Blake made a dismissive gesture. "Oh, nothing, a different matter—a side issue. The insurance case involves a witness to arson. He's required for a lawsuit due in Brazil. There is a chance he's in Maliba."

"Another man you are looking for?"

"Yes."

"You should have said. What is his name?"

"Benjamin Paz."

The police chief frowned. "Paz?"

"You know of him?" Blake's surprise was genuine.

"Madre mía! Yes, I know of him!"

Blake paced back to the desk, keeping his excitement tightly constrained. If Tarratona was aware of Paz's true identity, it was crucial that Blake gave no indication that he also knew the truth.

"This is more than I expected, captain. It didn't occur to me that you might be familiar with him. Sellingham, yes—he is the son of an important man—but this Paz fellow—"

Tarratona's eyes widened. "Señor, I know of him because he masqueraded as a government inspector and went aboard an American research vessel out over the— you have heard of the Tanangas Trench?"

"Yes."

Tarratona rubbed his chin.

"*Gorgon* is the name of the ship. This Paz, he boarded it with another man, named Linwood. Together, they went down in a bathysphere. We do not know why they did it. And—well—it failed to return. The following day, it was located. Paz's body was inside, stabbed in the back—murdered! And Linwood was missing!"

7

deep sea mystery

BLAKE'S MIND WAS reeling as he left Police Headquarters.

Kirby's bathysphere story! The victim was Benjamin Paz—who was really Sebastián Ortiz, Soviet master-spy!

It seemed incredible that a man on Eustace Craille's "most wanted" list—a man with supreme combat skills—could have perished in such a bizarre fashion. If true, it represented an ironic twist of fate—and a tremendous stroke of fortune.

Yet, Blake felt uneasy.

Who was the other man—Linwood?

Why had he and Ortiz gone to the research vessel and taken its bathysphere fathoms down?

He had to find out. Sellingham could wait.

He hailed a taxi and was driven from the city's main plaza, heading for the waterfront to find a boat that would take him to the ship in question—the *Gorgon*.

* * *

THE HARBOUR OF Carabanos was a Spanish construction, built with granite two hundred years ago. Slave labour did the work. Spanish soldiers garrisoned it.

It was to this harbour that Sir Henry Morgan had sailed with three small English frigates. The Conqueror of Panama had taken Carabanos with ease, and the port had then become the haunt of every freebooter on the Spanish Main. The harbour district was rich with legends concerning Blackbeard, Kidd, and Morgan himself.

But now a new piracy had taken over the port—in the form of the fees charged by boatmen who hired out vessels to tourists.

Blake—thankful that it would go on Craille's expense account—paid for a motorboat and inquired as to the position of the *Gorgon*.

Minutes later, he was steering the craft out to sea at a steady twelve knots.

The deep waters glittered like a carpet of jewels, and as the island fell behind him, the humidity lessened a little, giving him a measure of relief. He filled his lungs with the fresh, salt-tanged air.

Carabanos, seen from a distance, lost its squalor and shabbiness and took on a romantic aspect, glamorous and alluring, the sun flaring from its white walls, the greenery humped around its borders, the slender palms towering high above.

It sent Blake's thoughts careening into the past, back to his encounters with Marie Galante, the Voodoo Queen of the Caribbean, and Doctor Huxton Rymer, a master crook who frequently succumbed to the lure of the tropics.

Rymer would have liked Maliba.

The bauxite mines, Blake thought. *Rymer would have*

latched onto those and leeched a fortune from them, at the island's expense!

It was not often that Sexton Blake reminisced, but the steady rhythmic throb of his boat's motor and the gentle rise and fall of the water lulled him into a reverie. For the better part of forty minutes, he permitted himself the indulgence.

Then Professor Hoddard Curtis's deep-sea laboratory—the *Gorgon*—came into view, and all the memories fled. Blake snapped back into the present, reminding himself that Maliba was threatened not by a master crook, but by a master spy—who was, if all accounts could be believed, now dead.

The vessel was lying low in the water. Every time a long, lazy swell lifted his motorboat, the detective caught a glimpse of its deck, and saw that it was littered with air tanks, diving gear, coiled rope, chains, and unidentifiable equipment. Men were pottering about here and there in a desultory sort of way, but one in particular caught Blake's attention—a man in a white shirt and tan trousers, carrying a clipboard and moving towards the stern.

As Blake drew closer, he saw that this individual was tall and quite young, with an athletic build, and curly blond hair bleached almost colourless by the sun.

Cupping his hands around his mouth, he called, "Ahoy there! Can I come aboard?"

The man stopped and stared at him for a moment before shouting back, "No reporters allowed!"

Blake drew alongside.

"My name's Blake. I'm not a reporter. I want to see Professor Curtis."

"Not a reporter?"

"Definitely not."

"All right. I'm Curtis. Come aboard."

Blake steered to where another motorboat was already moored to a steel ladder hung against the ship's hull. He roped his craft to the other, stepped across it, then ascended to the deck of the *Gorgon*, where he was greeted by the professor.

He shook the young man's hand. "Sexton Blake."

"Pleased to meet you. What can I do for you, Mr. Blake?" Though his manner was polite, Curtis didn't smile. His mouth was set hard, and he was obviously under considerable strain.

Blake said, "I'm investigating the men who stole your bathysphere. In particular, the one named Benjamin Paz."

"You're police?"

"No. I'm from marine insurance."

"I haven't put in a claim yet. How could you possibly—?"

Blake raised a hand to interrupt. "Forgive me. You misunderstand. I do not represent your insurer. I'm seeking the witness to an affair that occurred some months ago. I believe that Señor Paz is—or was—the man in question."

Curtis furrowed his brow. "First the CIA and now you. I'll tell you the same as I told them. If you want to see Paz, you'll have to dive more than a thousand feet down. He's in my bathysphere. The bathysphere I spent years developing, in which I invested my every last cent, and which he—damn him!—decided to take for a joyride. He's down there now, Mr. Blake—with a knife in his back."

"I understand your frustration—"

"*Anger!*" Curtis corrected.

"Yes, quite so. If you could just tell me what happened, then I'll get out of your way."

Curtis turned his head and yelled, "Vasquez!" then looked back at Blake. "I wasn't here. My first mate will tell you."

Blake nodded and looked curiously at the man who answered the young scientist's summons. Vasquez was a big, bluff fellow—a seaman to his core. Curtis told him what to do, and he did it, describing the loss of the sphere with no deviation, in straightforward terms, answering Blake's occasional questions with neither hesitation nor uncertainty.

When he finished, the detective said, "Thank you, Señor Vasquez. Just one last thing. The man named Linwood. You say he was the younger of the two and appeared to be subordinate to Paz?"

"Sí, señor."

"Is there anything else you can tell me about him?"

"No, señor." Vasquez began to say something else but stopped himself.

Blake looked steadily at him.

The man cleared his throat then stammered, "Only—only that—that he seemed a little nervous."

"About going down in the sphere?"

"Yes, but also, just generally. He was—preoccupied."

"With what, do you think?"

"I don't know."

When Blake gave an acknowledging nod, Curtis said, "Thank you, Vasquez. You can get about your duties."

Vasquez nodded and departed.

Blake looked over the rail, down at the calm sea. "You said more than a thousand feet, professor?"

"A hundred and eighty-five fathoms, to be precise."

"Beyond salvage?"

"No," Curtis answered. "As soon as the equipment arrives from the States—tomorrow morning, all being well—I'll go down there. There's a split in the sphere where the cables attach. I'm waiting for a device like an expandable grappling hook. I'll insert it through the hole, open it, and it'll give sufficient hold to haul the whole thing up."

Blake's nostrils flared slightly. "Hole? What made it?"

"A small explosive, by the looks of it, but if you ask Vasquez, he'll tell you it was a sea monster."

"Explosive? Can you account for that?"

"Not at all. I'm almost inclined to believe the other explanation."

"But that's just superstition, surely?"

"Vasquez was in radio contact with Paz. The man saw something. He was screaming with horror." Curtis shrugged. "I can't discount some as yet undiscovered form of deep-sea life. We've had anomalous sonar readings hinting at something big moving about down there. We don't know what lives at the bottom of the Tanangas Trench, Mr. Blake. I've spent years of my life and thousands of dollars endeavouring to find out."

Blake looked out at the sea again.

"The hole in the bathysphere, could a man have squeezed through it?"

"No. As I said, it's just a split—a rupture in the shell. If you mean to suggest that one man stabbed the other, then swam out through the opening, it's absolutely impossible."

"Maybe sucked out after being crushed by the water pressure?"

"No. The corpse left behind was malformed, but not so compressed as that."

"Malformed? Then, how did you know it was Paz?"

"Paz had shoulder-length black hair. So did the corpse. Linwood was as blond as I am."

Blake shook his head in bemusement. "So, it looks like Linwood murdered him. But then what? How did he get out of the bathysphere?"

"I've no idea," the professor said. "It's simply inconceivable."

Just then, two men came up on deck and walked towards the detective and marine biologist. They were both wearing fedora hats and highly polished tan shoes, light-weight grey suits, and pastel-coloured ties—attire suitable for New York, perhaps, but certainly not for the tropics.

Curtis murmured. "Here are the CIA men."

"They're still here?" Blake exclaimed. "I didn't realise."

One of them appeared to be carved out of rock. There wasn't an ounce of surplus fat on him. He was big and angular and solid. His skin was swarthy. An émigré from south of the US border, Blake thought—Mexican.

The other was taller but very much thinner, with wolf-like pale grey eyes.

As they approached, the bulky one looked at Curtis and jerked a thumb at Blake. "Who's this?"

"Insurance man. Have you finished bothering my crew? Can they get back to work?"

"Yes, professor," said the Mexican. "We'll talk to this guy, now, though."

Curtis nodded, mumbled, "All yours," and moved off, giving his attention to his clipboard.

"Mister—?" said the Mexican.

"My name's Blake," the detective responded.

"Navarro. Agent Navarro. This is my colleague, Agent Kellaher. Central Intelligence Agency. And you—insurance, you say?"

"Yes. I'm tracing a man—a witness."

"What name?"

"Benjamin Paz," Blake said evenly.

The two men looked at each other. Then they both looked at Blake.

The Mexican said:

"Come into the cabin."

THE CABIN WAS packed with diving gear, winch meters, air regulators, radio, radar and sonar consoles, and miscellaneous electronic equipment.

Blake, looking around at it all, realised what the loss of the bathysphere really meant to Curtis. Without it, most of this paraphernalia was useless.

He leaned casually against a small table. "Very well, gentlemen, what do you want to know?"

"Who're you really working for?" Navarro snapped.

Blake studied the man's coal-black eyes, then said slowly, "Can you show me some official identification?"

The Mexican snarled, "We'll ask the questions. This is an American ship."

"Maybe so," Blake responded, "but it's moored in Maliban territorial waters—and outside of US jurisdiction. You can ask whatever you like, but that doesn't mean I have to answer."

Navarro's face turned ugly, but Kellaher intervened, gently smacking the back of his hand against his colleague's arm. "Hey, c'mon now, Miguel, you know he ain't under any obligation." He addressed Blake. "All we're askin' is for a little friendly co-operation. It might be that commie agents murdered Benjamin Paz."

"For what reason?" Blake cut in.

"He was a Maliban government inspector. Rumour has it that the island is seeking US backing. And as my partner said, this is a US ship."

"Ah. You suspect that everyone, including Curtis, is a little more than they claim to be?"

"Uh huh," Kellaher confirmed. "And as for you—"

He took a packet from his pocket, put it to his mouth, pulled out a cigarette with his teeth, then offered the pack to Blake. The detective declined with a slight shake of the head.

Kellaher raised a brass lighter and flipped it open. It made a loud and distinctive *click-clackety-click*. He lit up, and continued, "As for you—either you are or you ain't, and if you ain't, how 'bout we exchange information—as friendly allies, you get me?"

In the past, Blake had from time to time worked with American agents—but Craille didn't approve of arbitrary deals of the sort Kellaher was proposing—and, besides, the detective was too old a hand to take anything for granted. He was not yet convinced that these two men were really from the CIA.

He said, "I'm not here to get tangled up in politics. I'm simply a marine insurance investigator who's been commissioned to locate Paz and subpoena him, nothing more."

Kellaher turned to Navarro with a shrug. "If he's just a gumshoe—"

The Mexican sneered. "*If* is the word."

Kellaher stepped back to the cabin door, opened it,

and said, "Enough. We're getting nowhere. You can go, Blake. But be aware—we'll be keeping tabs on you."

Blake fixed Kellaher with an unwavering gaze for a moment, then, ignoring Navarro, he departed.

On deck, he found Curtis leaning over the ship's rail. The professor, without turning his gaze from the sea, asked, "The third degree?"

"No," Blake responded. "More a case of clutching at straws."

He looked down at the water.

"What time tomorrow do you expect to have the bathysphere up?"

Curtis glanced at the derricks. "Midday, I should think."

"In that case—just so I can confirm the dead man's identity to my satisfaction—would you mind if I was here?"

The professor shrugged. "No, that's fine, so long as you stay out of the way."

The detective was deep in thought as he climbed down the ladder, across what he now realised was the CIA men's boat, into his own, and began his return journey to the harbour.

If Vasquez's account of the bathysphere incident were true—and Blake had no reason to doubt it—then a line could be drawn through the file of Sebastián Ortiz.

Eustace Craille would be happy, insofar as that emotion could ever be ascribed to him.

Meanwhile, there were other matters to pursue: Peter Sellingham; and now, in addition, Blake had to find out who this man Linwood was, and why he had murdered Ortiz.

Something else occurred to him. Kirby had complained

that the Maliban government had imposed censorship on the bathysphere incident. Why were they doing so? Could it be that they were aware of Paz's true identity?

And if that was the case, why had Captain Tarratona been so quick to put Blake on the man's trail?

8

harsh words exchanged

As SOON AS he was ashore, Sexton Blake selected a small, clean-looking eatery and enjoyed a late lunch of fried blackfish, which he washed down with a cool beer. He did not linger over the food, as delicious as it was, but the short break gave him time to gather his thoughts.

Now, more than ever, he had to locate Sellingham. Craille wanted insight into the island's politics. If Blake could contact the rebel forces of Juan Callas—perhaps in the guise of a supportive foreigner—he might be able to gauge the true measure of communist influence. Young Sellingham was his only link.

The siesta was imminent. The streets were already emptying, becoming uncannily quiet.

In the last few minutes before that long, all-embracing pause, Blake managed to locate a car-hire firm—open on Sundays for tourists—and rented an Oldsmobile convertible for another exorbitant fee.

He took the main road through the city towards the airport and Sir Gordon Sellingham's sugar refinery, situated a mile and a half inland. Blake knew that, being British-owned and fuelled by international commerce, the place functioned around the clock, observing neither a religious nor local custom-imposed hiatus.

There was a refreshing breeze in the open car, but the drive was not a long one, and just ten minutes after leaving the city centre, Blake steered through the gates of the large industrial plant. A moment later, he brought the convertible to a halt outside the main building.

It was a tall, modern, steel and concrete structure of the functional American pattern, and was sign-boarded: ADMINISTRATION BLOCK.

Inside, he was greeted warmly by a girl of African descent, her hair in cornrows and decorated with coloured beads, and her eyes magnified by a large pair of plastic-rimmed spectacles.

"Good afternoon! Can I help you, sir?"

Blake produced the second of the letters Sir Gordon had given him. "Where can I find—" he glanced at the envelope, "—Miss Amelia Tucker, the manageress?"

The girl pointed to a grey-carpeted stairway. "First floor, sir—you can't miss it—her name's on the door."

Blake saw uncertainty in the girl's expression. He reassured her. "My name is Blake. I believe Miss Tucker is expecting me?"

"Oh! Yes! Sir Gordon got word to us that you were due today. Go right on up."

Blake took the stairs two at a time to the broad first-floor landing. A door to his right bore the words: A. R. TUCKER—MANAGERESS. He was about to tap on it when the noise of an altercation reached him from the other side.

A man was yelling. He was furious about something and making no bones about it.

"You lousy crook! I'm glad I'm getting out!"

"You have no choice, Worple." This was a deep-toned, female voice which cut through the strident torrent. "You have no choice at all. Collect your money downstairs and leave. Go home, there's nothing more to be said."

"Oh, isn't there, you old hag? Nobody calls me a liar and gets away with it. I've got plenty to say—and I'm going to say it, Miss blasted Tucker!"

"The company has heard quite enough from you, Worple. If you think you can spread scandalous lies about me—and about the son of our managing director—without consequences, you must be insane."

"It's true!" shouted the man called Worple. "All true!"

Blake had been about to step away from the door and wait on another part of the landing until the quarrel was over. Now, though, he was all attention.

"I don't know what you mean to achieve by this," came the voice of Miss Tucker, "but whatever it is, you'll not succeed."

"You can't cover it up," snarled Worple. "I saw you with my own eyes. You were with Peter Sellingham that night. And you're not the only one he's got his claws into. He hangs out with every tart on the island, and in the filthiest parts of the city."

"What you're suggesting is disgusting—I'm old enough to be his mother."

"Exactly!"

This appeared to be Worple's parting shot. The door banged open and a small man, portly and with a face redder than a pillar-box, his expression one of righteous indignation, almost collided with Blake. He pushed past the detective and stamped off down the corridor, leaving a faint scent of whisky in the air.

Miss Amelia Tucker saw Blake standing there.

"Can I help you?" she said, her tone hard.

He saw a sudden glint of fear in her eyes, due, he supposed, to her realisation that he had overheard the raised voices.

She was a tall, grey-haired woman, rangy in limb, slim-hipped, and wide at the shoulder. In youth, she may have been athletic and beautiful, but the years had etched a profusion of deep lines and sun damage into her face. While the underlying bone structure was well-proportioned, the skin clung too closely to it, making the cheekbones like blades over dark hollows, the eye sockets shadowy craters, and the jaw too heavy and angular. She appeared almost mummified, an unpleasant effect that suggested inhumane cold-bloodedness.

She was wearing a plain white shirt, knee-length skirt, and flat shoes.

Her office was unremarkable, with a high window, metal filing cabinets, document folders piled onto shelves, a safe in one of the walls, and a door, half open, through which he could see a bathroom.

"My name is Sexton Blake," the investigator said, stepping inside. "I'm here on behalf of Sir Gordon Sellingham."

"Ah yes, Mr. Blake, I've been expecting you." Her tone altered, and her thin lips stretched tightly over large teeth, more a grimace than a smile. She walked over to her desk and lowered herself into her chair. "I am Amelia Tucker. I apologise—you arrived an inopportune moment. One of my employees was demanding rather a lot more than we can afford to give him. Ridiculous, really. He already receives a very generous salary, but—well, the tropical heat, tempers flare, and—" She shrugged.

Blake responded with a dismissive gesture, though he mentally filed every word of the argument for later consideration. He gave her the letter from Sir Gordon, which she read carefully.

While she was thus preoccupied, he scrutinised her closely. The attempted smile had revealed a sizeable gap between her top front incisors, and the moment he saw it, Blake formed the conviction that he had encountered her somewhere before, a long time ago.

His memory was a remarkable one but, on this occasion, it let him down, and he pushed the puzzling sense of familiarity aside as she looked up and said, "How can I help you?"

"Would you tell me what you know of Peter Sellingham's movements?"

Miss Tucker sighed. "Precious little, I'm afraid. I know he's on the island, of course. Sir Gordon asked us to keep an eye on him and see that he didn't get into trouble. But—" she held out a hand, palm up, "—you know what young men are like these days, Mr. Blake. Peter is all fire and no heat, a pseudo-revolutionary attracted to Maliba by the political situation and, I daresay, in it far over his head—"

"In what, exactly?" Blake asked.

"Who knows? The last news I had of him was when his bank manager in Carabanos telephoned to ask if I knew where he was. Apparently, Sellingham had been drawing large amounts from his account, and the bank was concerned that he'd been spotted consorting with rather—er—unsavoury types."

"And you told the manager—?"

"The same as I'm telling you," Miss Tucker replied. "That Sellingham called here on the day he arrived in Maliba, and I've not encountered him since."

"I see," Blake murmured, recalling her previous visitor's words: *'I saw you with my own eyes. You were with Peter Sellingham that night.'*

"I'm sorry I can't be of any better help to you, Mr. Blake."

She met his gaze calmly. Again, he felt that strange, vague feeling of familiarity.

"I wonder," he said. "Have we met before?"

"I'm sure we haven't," she replied.

"Well," he said, "I won't waste any more of your time. Good day, Miss Tucker."

She reached out and shook his hand, her fingers long and big-knuckled, the nails bitten to the quick.

"Good day, Mr. Blake."

He left the room, closing the door behind him, crossed the landing, went down a few of the stairs, then stopped, waited for a minute, and crept back up. He put his ear to the door.

It was the oldest trick in the book.

And it paid off.

She was on the phone.

"No, I'm telling you, it's him—Sexton Blake!—and he's asking questions. We need to move everything forward and get out of this now, while the going is still good. The bank first thing in the morning, all right? You know what to do. What? No! Don't be a bloody fool! Do as I say, and just before the fighting starts, we'll make for the—"

Hearing someone coming up the stairs, the detective stepped back, turned, and descended.

In the lobby, he paused in front of the company noticeboard.

Amelia Tucker had been hiding something. There was no doubt about it—and he wanted to know what it was.

A moment later, he saw what he was looking for—a list of the home addresses and telephone numbers of the company's executive staff.

Halfway down the list was the name: Worple, Albert—Hotel Europa, 57 Avenida Santa Maria, Carabanos.

With a grunt of satisfaction, Blake departed. He got into the Oldsmobile, reversed and drove out onto the main road—back towards Carabanos—and the Avenida Santa Maria.

9

man with a grudge

BLAKE REACHED THE centre of Carabanos and drove past the Presidential Palace and Police Headquarters. A glance in his rearview mirror revealed that a sleek, black limousine of the type used by the Maliba State Police had accelerated out of the headquarters and was now stuck doggedly on his tail.

The Avenida Santa Maria came up on his left. He did not turn into it but drove on past, coming to a stop three blocks farther on, outside the International Press Club.

He got out of the car and crossed the pavement to a tobacco kiosk. Casually, he turned to glance at his car and from the corner of his eye saw the vehicle bearing the State Police insignia glide to a halt at the kerb.

Blake did not hurry. He bought a packet of cigarettes and was strolling back towards his Oldsmobile when a peaked cap was poked out of the police car window and the sleepy voice of Captain Tarratona called out:

"Ah, Señor Blake!"

"Good afternoon, captain."

"Good afternoon. Just a word, señor—a friendly word of advice, if you will." He smiled. His voice was a soft purr. "I think it best that you stop your prying. You should probably leave Maliba as soon as possible."

Blake's expression hardened. "I am investigating, captain, not prying. It is what I was sent here to do."

"I mean no offence, señor—but an important person, a powerful person, has suggested that you are becoming a little too curious about—ah—internal affairs."

He flashed his teeth, saluted extravagantly, and muttered a word to his driver.

The car swept away, leaving Blake standing perplexed.

For whom was Tarratona speaking? he wondered. The president? Or was that mention of a powerful person simply a reference to Tarratona himself?

"Damn," he muttered. The sudden alteration in the police chief's manner complicated matters. Blake knew now that he was being watched and, at best, was currently regarded as a meddler. At worst, maybe as a spy.

Proceed with caution!

Crossing to his car, he got in, and drove as far as the next intersection before turning off to double-back on his tracks.

A few moments later, he was once more approaching the beginning of Avenida Santa Maria. There was no longer any sign of the police car.

Blake steered into the avenue and slowed, cruising along the pavement, searching for number 57.

Street name notwithstanding, he was now on the outskirts of the Jewish quarter, one of the more exclusive and well-maintained areas of Carabanos, where many of the European and American employees of the foreign-owned industries lived.

Soon the detective spotted the number he was looking for. The Hotel Europa was a small, neat building nestling back from the road, reached by a narrow semicircle of pebbled drive.

Blake turned in through the gates and parked his car beneath the shade of some tall palms. He got out and walked across to the hotel entrance.

It was clean and smart—a reminder that Europeans in Maliba drew substantial salaries.

Except Worple, who is no longer drawing his, Blake thought wryly as he walked up the three steps and pushed open the carved wooden doors.

He entered a small, well-cooled vestibule.

A distinguished-looking, white-haired European was standing behind a small reception desk. Blake guessed that he was ex-Indian Army. He had a white handlebar moustache, a florid face, and a ramrod straight back.

"Good day. How may I assist you, sir?"

Blake smiled at the precision of the voice and the old-fashioned civility.

"Do you have a Mr. Worple resident here?"

"Yes, sir, we do."

"Perhaps you could tell him I'd like to see him for a few minutes. My name is Blake."

"Certainly. Just one moment, please, Mr. Blake."

The man moved to the telephone switchboard, picked up the receiver and dialled a single number.

For long seconds there was no reply, but at last the buzzing stopped and a torrent of sound poured forth from the receiver, causing the desk clerk to hold it away from his ear.

From where Blake was standing, it sounded like slurred, incoherent abuse from a very inebriated man.

The clerk raised his voice over the incomprehensible din.

"Mr. Worple... Mr. Worple! If you—if you could—sir!—please! There's a gentleman here to see you. A Mr. Blake."

The abuse faltered, then abruptly stopped.

Blake heard the response, made tinny by the phone:

"You tell 'im, I'll be... be right there."

The line went dead.

The clerk put down the receiver and turned to Blake.

"He's on his way down, sir."

Blake thanked him and waited.

After a minute had passed, the clerk cleared his throat and said, "A bad business over in Cuba, sir."

"Indeed," Blake agreed. "But it's a thousand miles away. Do you think it might affect Maliba?"

"Pardon me for being blunt, sir, but if Kennedy and Khrushchev start tossing nuclear missiles about, I fear it will affect everyone."

Blake nodded. "True, but I would hope that if matters deteriorate to the point where—"

He broke off as a loud thump sounded from the top of the stairs.

Albert Worple came stumbling down. He staggered toward the detective, waving a bottle of Old Kentucky Bourbon. It was three-quarters empty.

"Sorry to 'ave kept you waitin', Blake." He smiled crookedly and swayed. "I 'ad a bit of a shruggle—struggle—to put my shoes on."

Blake had met some hard drinkers in his time, but he was amazed at how inebriated Worple had become in the short period since leaving the refinery.

"That's all right, Mr. Worple. I'd like a word with you, if I may."

Worple spread his arms out wide, the whiskey slopping in its bottle. "O' course, Mr. Blake. Sent by his lordship, were you? Come to sort out that ol' hag Tucker?"

He tottered to one side. Blake reached out an arm to steady him.

"Sort her out, Mr. Worple?"

"Give 'er the bloomin' sack—and make me the manager!"

"Let's go in here, shall we?" Blake gave the clerk a nod, then took Worple's bottle from him and guided him through a door marked LOUNGE.

The chamber was furnished in an English style, reminiscent of a south coast boarding house, and entirely out of keeping with the tropical climate.

Blake helped Worple to settle on a lumpy, overstuffed settee, and surreptitiously put the bottle on the floor beside it, out of sight.

He said, "So you think Sir Gordon sent me here to replace her with you? Why would he want me to do that?"

"'Cos of her leadin' his precious son astray, that's why!"

"How is she doing that? And where is Peter Sellingham?"

The urgency of his tone had little effect on the drunkard, who said with an exaggerated wink, "Could be anywhere. I guess his girl will know."

"His girl?"

"Fransh—Franshesh—Francesca. Cor! You should see her! Lovely, she is. More than he deserves."

He leaned his head on the back of the sofa and closed his eyes.

Blake said, "Hey!" and gave him a shake. "Where will I find her?"

"Huh?"

"Where will I find Francesca?"

Without opening his eyes, Worple slurred, "Um... in the same filthy dive he was in with the old hag Tucker. The bar where the so-called revolutionaries meet to plot and plan and make themselves feel important."

"And you saw Miss Tucker there with him? Are you sure about that?"

The drunk man blinked, focused, and curled his lip aggressively. "You callin' me a liar, mister?"

"I'm asking you to explain."

Worple licked his lips. "Where's my bottle?"

"I don't know," Blake lied. "But I'll get you another one if you answer me truthfully."

Worple sighed, and with a big effort pushed himself upright.

"Tell you what, you can buy it for me there, at the bar. Maybe Fransh—Franshesh— Maybe she'll be there. I'll take you."

"All right," Blake said. "Let's go."

TEN MINUTES LATER, as Blake drove back across the centre of Carabanos with Worple semi-conscious in the seat beside him, he became aware, for the second time that afternoon, that he was being followed.

Another police car was tailing him, though keeping well to the rear.

Blake quickly swerved into a side street, accelerated, veered into another, then rounded a third corner to see just how badly the Maliba police wanted him under surveillance.

At first, they stayed doggedly on the tail of his

Oldsmobile, but when it became clear that Blake was aware of their presence, they dropped back and allowed him to shake them off.

Blake steered back onto the main streets.

What were they trying to do? Were they really anxious to keep an eye on him, or were they just attempting to intimidate him?

Captain Tarratona's warning had been firm enough: "Stop your prying."

Again, Blake asked himself, why the shift in attitude? The man had greeted Blake cordially enough that morning—even defied state censorship by identifying Paz as the bathysphere murder victim—but now, just a few hours later, he was telling him to leave the island.

What had happened in that time?

One thing was sure. Someone had exerted their influence. Someone was attempting to stop Blake's investigations. Had he stumbled on something that imperilled them?

The question of identity was intriguing—because it was probable, Blake thought, that it was someone he'd already spoken to. And the list of possibilities was very short. Barring Worple—who was slumped beside him—and the people who merely worked at hotels and reception desks, Blake had spoken to only five people: Tarratona, who had delivered the message; the marine biologist, Hoddard Curtis; Navarro and Kellaher, ostensibly of the CIA; and Miss Amelia Tucker.

One of those wanted him out of the way.

Blake had a shrewd idea which of them it was.

10
Francesca

THE BLUES, TURQUOISES, and greens of Maliba intensified as the afternoon wore on. The temperature was as high as it was going to get, the air warm and clammy, with no hint of a breeze.

Worple's directions were slurred and confused, but—more despite them than because of them—Blake eventually succeeded in guiding the Oldsmobile to the intended destination.

Driving was easy. The streets were empty, the siesta casting its blanket of silence.

The bar, when they found it, was the one mentioned by the hotel keeper at Peter Sellingham's sleazy guesthouse. The Ostra. It was a fifth-rate barrel house.

Blake helped Worple out of the Oldsmobile, made sure to lock the vehicle's doors, and with one arm supporting his unsteady companion, entered the bar.

It was dark inside after the brightness of the streets. The sunlight scarcely penetrated the narrow slits of the single shuttered window. The only real light came from behind the bar, where an illuminated display of cheap wines and doubtful-looking rum glowed garishly in a dozen different colours.

The air was thick with tobacco smoke. Tables stood in booths along the right-hand side of the room, opposite the long bar. A few couples snuggled furtively together in the murkiest of these booths, while in others, men played cards, threw dice, talked in low voices, swore, spat, smoked, and drank. They were all, from what Blake could see of them, an uncouth lot—the dregs of Maliban society.

Narrowed, furtive eyes darted looks of suspicion and hostility as the two men entered, and were then averted.

In the darkest booth of all, a figure was indistinctly outlined. Someone was sitting there alone, in silence.

Worple broke away from Blake and lurched towards the bar. He clambered clumsily onto one of the stools. Blake sat beside him and said to the ebony-skinned barman, whose "Sunday best" consisted of bright orange shorts and a navy-blue vest, "A bottle of Old Kentucky for my friend, and for me, a cola."

"Sí, señor."

The barman reached for a bottle and set it on the counter with a thump. He poured a glass of cola for Blake. The detective handed him a banknote and murmured, "Keep the change."

The man gave Worple a glass and poured the first measure of Bourbon for him. Worple eyed it morbidly, picked it up, and sank it in one gulp.

"That damned hag," he said loudly, picking up the conversation where he and Blake had left off. "It should've been me made manager after Cranston copped it, not her." He swayed on his stool, belched, and snarled, "Specially as it was her who killed him."

"Keep your voice down," Blake cautioned. "What are you talking about? He died in a hit-and-run incident, didn't he?"

"Yup. An' who do you think paid the driver?"

"That's quite an accusation, Worple!" Blake exclaimed. "Got any evidence?"

"Nope." He picked up the bottle and, rather than refilling his glass, drank straight from it.

"The police didn't find anything suspicious?"

"The police didn't investigate."

"Why on earth not?"

"Hell, Blake, I wouldn't be surprised if it was a police car that ran him down! She's got Tarratona in her pocket. It was her who financed his rise to the top. You know he's not even a native islander?"

This was news.

"Where's he from?" the detective asked.

"Dunno. He arrived about a year and a half ago, just before she did. Started shooting his mouth off about how the police should be better organised. No one was interested. Then—"

He swigged bourbon and, for a moment, his eyes glazed over, the lids drooped, and his head slowly fell forward.

"Worple!"

"Huh?"

Worple grunted, straightened, and sighed. Then he appeared to get his second wind.

"Huh?" he repeated.

"Tarratona!"

"Yes, Tarratona. So, the old hag arrived, and suddenly, he was handing out cash like there was no tomorrow. His police force—his *Gestapo*—they are all bought men.

Then he purchased uniforms for them. Then weapons. Where do you think he got all that money, eh?"

He started to raise the bottle again, but Blake caught his wrist and held it.

"Are you suggesting that Amelia Tucker, the manager of Sir Gordon Sellingham's sugar refinery, owns the police?"

"Owns them? She and Tarratona bleedin' well *invented* them!"

Worple sighed, and murmured, as if to himself:

"The way this island has changed, so fast—going to the dogs, it is—it's all down to those two."

Blake released his grip and sat back, stunned.

The police were widely regarded as being the Maliba president's "muscle." If they in fact belonged not to him, but to Tucker, did Doctor Nonales have any strength at all? The entire notion that he was a brutal, dictatorial fascist—as reported in the English language newspapers—was cast into doubt. Maliba's political complexion was something else entirely.

Which raised the question: who, exactly, were the People's Liberation Army fighting?

Now, even more, he needed Peter Sellingham to take him to Juan Callas, the leader of the rebels.

"Worple," he said, "don't drink yourself insensible. I need you alert enough to point out Francesca as soon as she comes in."

"She's already here," Worple slurred. He jerked a thumb toward the person in the shadowy booth.

Blake squinted through the haze of tobacco smoke and realised, for the first time, that it was a woman.

"You didn't think to tell me?" he muttered, then left Worple and crossed the room.

He reached the booth and sat down without waiting for an invitation. He could see the girl better now, and she was certainly worth seeing. *A real Sophia Loren*, he thought, and as out of place in the grubby bar as a diamond in a coal-pile. Her hair was long, black, and curled down around her shoulders. Her eyes were also dark, big, and at that moment wide with irate surprise at his intrusion.

She hissed like a cat. "Qué quieres?"

"What I want," Blake said firmly, in Spanish, "is to speak with you about Peter Sellingham. You know him, yes?"

"No."

She snapped out the denial with an air of certainty, and flicked her hand, waving him away. As far as she was concerned, the conversation was over.

Blake was not so easily discouraged. "Tell me the truth!"

"Señor! I have no reason to lie. I know of no Peter— whatever-you-called-him. Go away! You are annoying me."

Her eyes flared in anger—but now there was a hint of fear in them, too.

"I need to find him. His life may depend on it," Blake insisted.

"I have told you," the girl said in a fierce tone, "I have never heard of him."

Suddenly, she was on her feet. Before he could stop her, she was making for the street door.

Blake ran across to Worple and grabbed his shoulder. "That girl! Look at her! Are you sure she's the one?"

Worple turned on his stool and squinted at the girl as she crossed the threshold and departed.

"I'd know those legs anywhere," he said with a drunken

leer. "That's her, all right. What a girl like that sees in a dolt like Sellingham—"

Blake hurried away from him. As he reached the door, Worple shouted after him, "His money, of course!"

The detective was about to step outside when a hand smacked down on his shoulder and fingers dug in. He was yanked backwards, spun around, and slammed hard against the wall.

"Pardon, señor—"

The voice was ugly and it matched the face. Blake looked up into black slanting eyes, set above heavily pockmarked cheekbones, in the mahogany-skinned face of the tallest Carib-Indian he'd ever seen.

"What?" Blake demanded.

"Señor," the man said softly, ominously, "you are a visitor to our island. I think you do not understand all of our customs. There are many beautiful women in Maliba, eh? You have seen them? Many! Take your pick—but not Francesca. Francesca, she belongs to someone special."

Two big men, who had been playing cards, rose and moved to support the Carib-Indian. Others sat and stared, tense and poised.

Blake had no time for this.

"My apologies," he said. "I understand. I'll stay away."

"Ah, you tell me that now, señor," the Carib said, "but in the morning, perhaps you will have forgotten. A little reminder may be necessary, no? Something for you to see when you look into the bathroom mirror."

His left hand was still clamped around Blake's right shoulder. The other hand, fisted, went back, then shot forward.

The punch, intended to flatten Blake's nose, never landed.

The detective let his knees buckle, dropped beneath the blow, then came surging up, the whole of his bodyweight behind the heel of his hand. It impacted the point of the Carib's jaw with a loud clack, and the man went backward like a felled tree, out cold before he hit the floor.

His two cohorts bellowed and charged.

Blake jumped forward and sidestepped, his arm hooking around the lead man's neck, heaving, adding to his opponent's momentum, and causing the man to power helplessly headfirst into the wall, leaving a big dent—and an untidy heap beneath it.

Simultaneous with the wince-inducing *thud!* of skull against plaster came an agonised *oof!* as the detective's foot swung into a tender region of the other man's anatomy, leaving him, seconds later, lying on his side, screwed into a tight, whimpering ball.

Chairs scraped back. Men stood up.

Blake's hand went into his jacket and out again.

"Don't!" he barked, his pistol levelled.

Slowly, they all regained their seats.

He paced over to Worple—"Come on!"—and dragged him out of the cantina.

OUTSIDE, WHILE SLIPPING his weapon back into its holster, Blake caught a glimpse of Francesca as she darted into an alleyway.

He propelled the near-insensible Worple to the Oldsmobile and bundled him into the back seat. "Stay here. I'll be back in a few minutes."

Worple slopped his bottle in careless acknowledgement.

Then Blake was away, striding swiftly towards the

alley, shouldering past people freshly emerged from their siesta.

Carabanos was coming alive again.

Once in the alley, he was running.

He caught up with the sound of fast-clicking heels, rounded a bend, and, in a narrow passageway, spotted the girl only a few yards ahead of him.

As he bore down on her, she spun to face him, a look of angry defiance on her face.

"You again! Why do you follow me?" she demanded. "Must I call for help?"

Blake raised his hands placatingly. "Señorita, please believe me, the situation is urgent. Peter Sellingham is in danger. I only want to help him."

"That name again! How many times must I tell you, I do not know him!"

He took from his pocket the photograph that Lord Gordon had given him and held it out to her. "Are you certain?"

The girl looked at the picture and immediately her eyes widened with recognition.

"Where did you get this?" she demanded, suddenly less certain of herself.

"It doesn't matter. You recognise him, that is enough. Where is he?"

"I don't know. Let me go—" She turned to hurry away, but Blake intercepted her, blocking her path.

"If you don't help me, his blood will be on your hands."

She looked up into his eyes. "Blood? What are you talking about?"

Blake spoke quietly and rapidly. "Sellingham has been financing the People's Liberation Army. He's a naïve idiot. He thinks it's all an exciting game. I was sent here from England by his father to find him and take him home before the government orders his arrest and has him executed."

A look of scorn spread across the girl's face. "Government? What government? There is no government."

Blake frowned. What Worple had said about the police was still uppermost in his mind. He tested a theory—

"But President Nonales?"

—and had it confirmed:

"Hah! He is nothing. He has no power. We people of Maliba don't require leadership. We tolerate his pomposity only because he is useful to us as a point of contact for the governments of other countries."

"So, he *does* represent you?"

"No. He is little more than a telephone receptionist."

Blake slipped the photograph of Sellingham back into his pocket.

"I don't understand," he said. "If there's no government, who makes policy, who establishes the law?"

Francesca laughed. "No one! We have no need of such things. We are not children."

Blake felt bemused. "So—what? Are you telling me that Maliba exists in a state of anarchy?"

"Call it whatever you want, señor—it is what it is."

Blake thought, *My God! If Worple is correct!* and asked: "If you have no laws, why the police?"

Francesca looked nervously at one end of the passageway, then the other. She caught her lip between her teeth, frowned, then came to a decision. The photograph had got through to her.

"We had better talk in my car," she said. "It will be safer."

She set off and Blake fell into step beside her. The passage gave onto an open square containing a fountain and some maple trees. A long, white, American convertible occupied one corner, its roof up. They walked across to it.

Blake thought, *From that seedy bar to this!*

She tapped on the side window. The door opened, and a man got out. He opened the rear door and held it while Blake and the girl got inside.

"Tomás, wait outside, please," she said to him.

The man nodded, closed the door, moved to the front of the car, and sat on its hood. He took out a cigar and started to smoke.

Francesca looked steadily at Blake. "Who are you, señor?"

"My name is Sexton Blake. I'm a private investigator. Sir Gordon Sellingham, who owns the main sugar refinery on this island, commissioned me to find his son, Peter."

She held his eyes a moment, then gave a slight nod of satisfaction.

"I believe you."

After another pause, she echoed the question he had asked. "Why the police?" then fell silent again, becoming lost in thought.

He prompted her. "I've been told there were none until recently."

"Not like we have now," she confirmed. "Before, we only needed the Consejeros."

Blake raised a questioning eyebrow. The word meant "Counsellors," but the way she said it—her tone and expression communicating a mix of affection and respect—implied a deeper significance.

"They were—" She stopped, picking her words carefully. "They were what you might call a loose affiliation of advisors, mentors, guides, counsellors, mediators, tutors, and referees. They interceded where required and were highly valued for their wisdom, compassion, and restraint."

"How were they organised?" Blake asked.

She shrugged. "They weren't. They were simply those of us who undertook to resolve disputes, maintain standards of safety, and to set a forfeit where there was wrongdoing. It was all loosely arranged. Only a few people chose such a role on a full-time basis. There were no ranks or uniforms, no headquarters."

"And then Carlos Tarratona arrived."

She nodded, and he saw a dangerous glint appear in her eyes.

"That cabrón!" she hissed. "He came spreading the idea that foreigners were taking advantage, that we had no defence against their—as he put it—*rapaciousness*. We believed him."

"Why?" Blake asked.

She shrugged. "I think, señor, that we made a misjudgement some years ago, when the money from the mines—you know that we mine bauxite here?"

He nodded.

"When that money started to come to the island, we thought to create a tourist industry. We improved the airport and the road that runs from it to the city and through to the harbour. We built new hotels, better access to our beaches—many things. People came. They brought money. They also brought ideas and attitudes that—" She paused, then went on, "—that are not *simpatico*. You understand?"

"I do," he said, recalling the cost of hiring the motorboat and the car. "And I can see, now, why Tarratona's ideas caught hold."

"Yes, we made a bad mistake. To counter minor corruption, we allowed him to develop the police into what they are today, and have ended up with much more serious corruption! It came quickly—the uniforms, the weapons, even the military fatigues. You saw them outside the airport?"

"I thought that was the Maliban army!" Blake exclaimed.

"There's no such thing. It's all the police! And now they accuse innocent people of being communists and throw them into cells. No family is safe. And it's all a lie! A filthy lie to keep us scared, to make us suspicious of each other."

"To what end?" Blake asked. "What purpose is served by this—"

"By this reign of terror? I do not know."

The detective was thoughtful. A couple of minutes passed, then he murmured, "So the People's Liberation Army is not fighting the president. It's fighting the police."

"Sí, señor."

"Back home, I read that the rebels had attacked an army base and that tanks were patrolling the city at night."

"Have you seen any tanks?"

"No."

"Because there are none. And the army base was a police training camp."

He nodded. "I was aware of censorship, but I didn't know that news was being falsified as well."

"The press can easily be made to lie," she noted. "It doesn't take much. A few bribes, a few threats. The truth is only ever what the majority decides to believe."

Blake made a sound of agreement. He frowned and clicked his tongue. "What you've told me makes it even more important that I find Sellingham. You really don't know where he is?"

She looked puzzled. "It makes it more important?"

"Yes," Blake said. "Because through him, I might be able to meet Juan Callas."

"For what purpose?"

"To warn him."

She waited for more, but Blake shook his head. "No, señorita. As Sellingham's girlfriend, you are in more than enough danger. The information I have for Callas might get you killed."

She snorted disdainfully.

"I am not the Englishman's girlfriend. I am betrothed to another."

Blake blinked. "Then how—?"

"How do I know him? It was I who recruited him."

"You?"

"Sí, señor! I am engaged to Juan Callas, I am also a recruiting agent for the People's Liberation Army. Why else do you think I frequent that filthy cantina? It was there that I met this young man. I have met him there often—he hands money to me and I ensure that it gets to Juan—but I did not know his name was Peter Sellingham."

"That," the detective said, "casts rather a different light over the matter."

She gave a wide, exaggerated shrug. "So, you see, I am always at risk. Whatever you have to tell to Juan, you can tell to me. I will pass it on to him."

Blake came to a decision.

"Very well. Tell him this. All the communist hysteria spread by the police has a basis in truth. I have credible evidence that at least one high-ranking Soviet agent has visited Maliba. He is now dead, but there may be others. Some might have already infiltrated the People's Army."

Francesca regarded him steadily for fully ten seconds before she put a hand on his arm, tipped back her head, and laughed.

11

"the charge is murder!"

FRANCESCA SHOOK HER head. "I do not know from where your information comes, but it is old, and it does not matter anymore."

"You must believe me! Your revolution is going to—" Blake began.

"No!" she snapped. "It is not a revolution! It is *restoration!* It is *liberation!*"

Blake conceded the point. "Very well, your liberation. It will be hijacked. You will do the fighting, but the Soviets will score the victory."

The girl sighed and looked out of the window. The shadows were growing longer. A light had just flicked on beneath the fountain, making the frothing water flash and glitter.

In the distance, church bells started to ring.

"I will tell you something, señor, and *you* must believe *me*. There is no communist threat. All the communists—I mean the *real* communists, not the innocents that the police harass—they were dealt with forty-eight hours ago."

Blake jerked back. "What?"

"And we have this man you call Sellingham and his friend to thank for it."

"His friend? What friend? And what do you mean, dealt with?"

"I will explain," said Francesca. "It was not difficult to recruit men to our cause. We have nearly one and a half thousand camped in the hills. But we had no money for guns and no means of shipping them into the country. When I met the young Englishman at the Ostra, he was like a gift from heaven! He was wealthy and very enthusiastic. With his donations, we were able to purchase weapons. Only the shipping problem remained, and fortunately, he had a friend who was well-experienced in such matters."

"This other man—what is his name?"

"It is not a man," Francesca smiled. "It is a woman. Her name is Amelia Tucker."

Despite the humidity, Blake's skin suddenly went cold.

Tucker had armed the police. Now, he was learning that she had also helped to arm the forces opposed to the police!

And again, he experienced that uneasy suspicion that his and Tucker's paths had crossed at some point in the past.

"It was Miss Tucker," Francesca went on, "who warned us about the communists so that we could act in time."

"How did she become aware of them?" Blake demanded.

"By playing a double game. She has cultivated a friendship with Captain Tarratona. From him, she learned that—among the many innocents that he has tortured and incarcerated—he discovered a courier who was carrying a list of communist agents active in the Caribbean. Some men on that list, she told us, had probably joined the People's Liberation Army."

"You have foreigners among you?"

"Yes. Mainly from the other islands, but also a few Europeans, drawn to our cause." She reached up and ran her fingers through her hair, pushing back the long, dark curls. "It seemed incredible, for if it were true, then we ourselves posed a greater danger to Maliba than even Tarratona and his thuggish police."

"That is my concern," Blake agreed.

"It need not be. It is no longer a problem."

"How so?"

"Miss Tucker discovered from Tarratona that the list had been sent to the main police training camp, so that new trainees could become familiar with the men whose names were on it. General Ramon de Vega—a professional soldier from Cuba who had recently joined us—offered to organise and lead a raid on the camp. It went better than we could ever have hoped. He took possession of the list and, from it, he was able to weed the infiltrators out of our group. They had been very clever. Some had become Juan's most trusted lieutenants."

She shook her head in wonder.

"If it hadn't been for Miss Tucker, we would never have known."

Blake gave a noncommittal grunt. He put his fingers to his chin and rubbed it. Something wasn't adding up, but he couldn't get a grip on what it might be.

He returned to his original question:

"And you truly don't know where Sellingham is?"

"I know only that he is in hiding."

"Why?"

"He wanted greater involvement. Not to merely sponsor us, but to fight alongside us, too. We had been careful to keep him apart—he has never met Juan, de

Vega, or any of the others—but we thought we might lose his support if we refused him. So, we gave him a mission."

Sexton Blake had been an investigator for a very long time. He was aware of how his mind worked, and now, feeling the peculiar sensation of gears engaging at some deep unconscious level of his intellect, he knew immediately that a revelation was coming.

"What mission?" he asked.

"That list," she said, "had been intended for the chief of Soviet operations on Maliba. It identified him. He was posing as a man responsible for patrolling Maliba's fishing grounds, a position he could use to smuggle communists onto the island. Those who'd infiltrated us may have given him the names of our most important members—but he would not know your young Englishman, for, as I say, we kept him apart."

"So?" Blake asked.

"So, de Vega had us send Sellingham to this chief of Soviet operations, posing as a potential communist recruit. His mission: to assassinate the man."

The detective's voice was suddenly hoarse. "You sent Sellingham to kill a Soviet agent?"

"He wanted to do it."

In almost a whisper, Blake said, "Sellingham—you recognised his photograph but not the name. What did he call himself?"

"Jimmy," she said. "Jimmy Linwood."

"And the man he killed?"

"Benjamin Paz."

And there it was.

* * *

BLAKE SANK BACK in the car seat, uttering a low whistle of amazement.

Sebastián Ortiz, alias Benjamin Paz—Soviet master spy—had been liquidated... by an amateur!

"Linwood—Sellingham—could you find out where he's hiding?" Blake asked.

"I could try."

"Yes, please do. You can telephone me at the Hotel Palma as soon as you have news. And, Francesca, that list of communist agents—it has served its purpose for your people—but for mine, it still has value. Do you think you can get me a copy?"

The girl hesitated, then opened her handbag, took from it some folded papers, and handed them over.

The detective opened the document and ran his eyes briefly down the list. There were more than a hundred names, each followed by short descriptive notes written in the traditional style of police dossiers.

Valuable intelligence! These individuals could be investigated by Craille's people, their movements traced back, their contacts explored. It could lead to the exposure of other operatives, even of senior spy masters.

He refolded the papers and slipped them into his pocket.

"Thank you. Now I must make a telephone call. Is there a booth near here?"

"There is one not far from the Ostra," said the girl. "I'll drop you there."

She knocked on the window and her driver, discarding his cigar, entered and started the engine.

Worple, Blake thought, was still waiting in the Oldsmobile. The bottle of Old Kentucky would keep him happy for another half hour or so. More likely, he was snoring.

The white convertible swung around, exited the square, and turned into a main thoroughfare.

WHEN BLAKE GOT out of the car, he leaned in and asked a final question.

"When will your people move against the police?"

"Tomorrow," she said. "A small explosion will signal the beginning of the end for Tarratona."

She pulled the door shut, and the car moved off.

Blake entered the telephone kiosk, took out his notebook, and looked for a certain number. He dialled it, was put through to the British Consulate, gave a codeword and an identification number, waited, then heard the voice of the Vice-Consul—Henderson.

"Urgent?" Henderson said, by way of a greeting.

"Yes. I want to see you—personally."

"Where are you?"

Blake told him.

There was a pause, then Henderson said, "You're facing the telephone?"

"Yes."

"Look to your right. The second turning on the left side of the street."

"Got it."

"That's the Avenue San Cristobal. About halfway along it, you'll find the Astoria Hotel. It's a couple of minutes' walk from where you are. I'll be there in a quarter of an hour. Wait for me in the cocktail lounge."

The line went dead.

Blake hung up and pushed out of the booth. He headed along the neon-lit street.

Dusk had fallen with tropical abruptness, and the

air was suddenly thick with mosquitoes. Music blared from every building. The streets were crowded again, the atmosphere party-like. The islanders, it seemed, possessed almost nothing yet enjoyed almost everything. Again, Blake wondered: money from the bauxite mines had gone into tourism, but where was it going now? With such a resource on the island—required the world over for the manufacture of aluminium—no city, no town, no village should be in the state of disrepair in evidence all around him. Someone, somewhere was benefitting from those mineral deposits? Who? A foreign power, perhaps?

It wasn't a part of his assignment to investigate the island's economy, but it was certainly another element in the puzzling picture that Maliba presented.

Following the example set by the crowd, he gave a patrolling policeman a wide berth, and noticed how all conversation stopped within range of the uniformed man's hearing.

He slapped a mosquito from his cheek, waved away a man who presented him with a choice of cheap wristwatches, passed a sugarcane milk vendor, felt thirsty, but did not have time to stop.

Amelia Tucker, that odd, wrinkled, formidable Englishwoman, bothered him immensely.

THE ASTORIA HOTEL was a cosmopolitan place; a luxury hotel owned by an American company and built primarily for American customers. Blake noticed the air-conditioning first. A blessed relief. Then he became aware that, among the tourists in the cocktail bar, there was a liberal sprinkling of Europeans, and many of them looked like press correspondents.

It was one of the surest signs of a revolution brewing, this sudden swelling of foreign press-corps. An ominous reminder that on Maliba, a grievance was coming to a head.

Blake chose a corner table, and over a wonderfully chilled, thirst-quenching beer, he drafted a concise Intelligence appraisal of the island's political situation on a page of his notebook. By the time Henderson arrived, he was ready to make his business brief.

"I want you to pass three items to London for me," he told the Vice-Consul quietly. "Highest priority for the personal attention of the Director of SINSEC."

Henderson nodded.

"The first two may be tele-printed exactly as they stand and need no reply." Blake gave him the list of communist agents and his Intelligence report. "The third is a request for authentication on the identity of two men claiming to be agents of the CIA. Navarro and Kellaher, both currently operating in Maliba."

"Got it." Henderson nodded as he slipped the papers into his pocket. "How soon do you want the response? Before morning?"

Blake calculated rapidly. "You'll be through well before midnight. London will be able to answer my query within three or four hours. You'd better arrange to contact them again before breakfast tomorrow. I'll get in touch with you some time after."

"Right."

Henderson rose to his feet with a swift but casual glance round the room. No one had paid any attention to the two men.

He gave Blake a cursory nod and left for the hotel entrance.

Blake allowed four minutes to pass before draining his glass and making for the same exit.

ONCE IN THE street, the detective set off at a brisk pace, heading back to where he had left the Oldsmobile with its drunken occupant.

On the whole, he had got a lot done in a single day, but there were still blanks, and he felt the edginess that always possessed him whenever he was missing something that ought to have been obvious.

Now, as he made his way back towards the poorer quarter of the town, a small detail gleaned from his meeting with Eustace Craille popped into his mind unbidden.

Sebastián Ortiz, the Soviet master spy, while purchasing weapons in Brazil, had become aware that his identity was compromised.

He knew, then, that his cover-name, Benjamin Paz, was known to be false.

Therefore, by all the laws of espionage, he should have changed it.

But he had not.

Why?

Before Blake could consider the question, the wail of an approaching siren cut into his thoughts.

Barely a moment later, the crowd parted, blazing headlights lit up the street, and the siren died to silence as a long sleek limousine glided up against the kerb.

The car doors opened, and uniformed men swarmed out to surround him.

"Come with us!"

They seized Blake and manhandled him into the car.

He knew when not to resist.

Chief Tarratona was on the back seat.

"I think the Americans say, third time's a charm, Señor Blake."

Blake's jaw hardened and his blue-grey eyes glittered dangerously as he looked at the police chief's mocking smile.

"What is this?" he demanded.

"This, señor, is an arrest." Tarratona nodded to the driver. "Despáchense!"

The car lurched away from the kerb, turned sharply in the middle of the road, and sped off, sirens wailing again, in the direction of the central plaza.

"With what am I charged?" Blake's voice was quiet, threatening.

"The charge, señor?" Tarratona said. "Why, it is murder, of course."

"Interesting. Who was the victim?"

Tarratona chuckled. "Ah, you are forgetful? That is a pity. But no matter, I shall remind you."

The car turned in through the main entrance of the Maliba State Police Headquarters. Tarratona leaned forward and gestured to the driver to pull up beside a car parked under a glare of temporary floodlights.

Uniformed detectives were swarming around the vehicle, taking photographs and making measurements.

The police limousine drew to a halt. Tarratona jumped out and held open the door for Blake. "Come, señor."

Blake stepped out onto the concrete yard and recognised the vehicle at the centre of all the attention. It was his own hired Oldsmobile, which he had left in the street outside the Ostra.

Tarratona paced across to it and, with a dramatic gesture, invited Blake to examine the back seat.

"You are arrested, Señor Blake, for the murder of this man!"

Blake looked inside and saw Worple.

He was spread-eagled on the back seat, with a fatuous grin on his face and a black-handled stiletto buried to the hilt in his heart.

His stiffening fingers gripped an empty bottle, as if it were the only thing worth dragging into the hereafter.

Its label announced:

OLD KENTUCKY—PUTS LIFE INTO THE PARTY.

12

a remarkable woman

SEXTON BLAKE SPENT the night in a filthy police cell. It was not the first he had ever slept in, but that did not make it any more tolerable. Worse than the confinement was that, while he did not know everything, he knew enough to be aware that time was fast running out.

At first, he had attempted to remonstrate with his captors—challenging them to prove his guilt. But his repeated demands for an explanation were greeted first with polite evasion and finally with unconcealed indifference.

The police attitude was simple: a man had been murdered, and a suspect had been pulled in. In due course, that suspect would be tried and executed.

Grimly, Blake realised that the police were no more convinced of his guilt than he was himself—and it didn't matter.

Worple's death had only been the pretext, a useful excuse for throwing him into jail, though with the added advantage, he suspected, of permanently shutting up a man who was talking too much and too loudly.

Patently, someone wanted Blake out of the way—either Tarratona himself or a person who had a lot of influence at police headquarters.

And where the latter was concerned, there was now only one candidate.

THE SOUND OF a key turning in the lock of his cell door roused Blake. He had been denied an evening meal and had managed only three hours of sleep.

He was not in a good mood.

The door swung open. Two armed escorts stood there. "Come!"

Blake rose from the stained, naked mattress that served as a bed and stepped out of the cell, eyeing the pair bleakly.

"Do you intend to put me against the wall without even the pretence of a trial?" he demanded acidly.

The police guards made no reply except to urge him forward along the corridor. "Move! Hurry!"

He was hustled out of the cell block, up two narrow flights of stairs, along one corridor and into another.

He was halted outside the office of Captain Tarratona.

The guard in front opened the door and marched Blake in.

The fleshy, freshly shaved face of the police chief looked up from a document on the desk. To Blake's surprise, he was wearing a light casual suit rather than his usual dress uniform.

"Ah, Señor Blake." A sleepy smile of welcome lit up Tarratona's face. "Please come and take a seat." He rose and brought a chair forward for the detective, dismissing the guards with a nod.

As Blake sat, he noticed two smart attaché cases beside the desk. He looked at the wall clock. It was ten forty-five.

"I hope your stay here last night was not uncomfortable."

"Cut the comedy," snapped Blake. "What is all this?"

A pained expression spread across the police chief's features. "Señor, believe me, I apologise for the way you have been treated. I apologise sincerely! But—" he shrugged massively, "you could have saved yourself all this unnecessary discomfort, if only you had been frank with me in the first place."

Blake scowled. "Oh?"

"Sí, señor!" Tarratona nodded vigorously. "Why did you not explain that the young Englishman you came here to find was consorting with rebels and subversive riffraff? Had we known, perhaps we would have understood your presence at a disreputable den of vice in the city's most notorious district. As it was, we had no reason to account for it, so clearly your behaviour aroused suspicion. We were obliged to conclude that you were a foreign agitator. A communist. The kind of person who would not hesitate to murder an innocent European like the unfortunate Mr. Worple."

"And now you've changed your mind?" Blake ventured.

"But of course, señor! The situation is explained to my satisfaction. There is no reason to detain you any longer."

Tarratona reached into a drawer and pulled out a plastic tray, upon which lay the various items taken from Blake's pockets. He slid it over the desktop and gestured for the detective to reclaim his property.

"An interesting notebook," he observed. "What language is it that you write?"

"Just a form of shorthand," Blake murmured.

"Not a code such as is used by spies?"

"No."

"Ah, that is good. Now, about this—" Tarratona took Blake's shoulder holster and pistol from another drawer and placed them on the desk. "You are at liberty to carry your weapon, my friend, but under the circumstances I have thought it best to withhold your ammunition."

Blake made no response. He stood, removed his jacket, strapped on the holster, replaced the jacket, and remained standing.

He said, "You received an explanation? From whom?"

"Why, from your friend, señor! The lady has vouched for you and is now waiting for you in her car outside. The big white one. You will find it parked by the entrance gate. Go now, and thank her!"

SEÑORITA FRANCESCA, BLAKE decided, was either tremendously brave or tremendously foolish. Talk about walking into the lion's den! She was resourceful, too—because he could not for the life of him imagine how she had secured his freedom. What could she possibly have said to Tarratona? And why had he believed it? Did he even know who she was?

It was only when he exited the station, crossed to the car, opened the rear door, and got inside, that he realised his mistake.

"Good morning, Mr. Blake," said Amelia Tucker.

She was wearing khaki cargo trousers, blue deck shoes, and a pale blue jacket over a white shirt.

Her driver put the car into gear and steered it out of the main plaza.

"They didn't treat you badly in there, I hope."

Blake gave a grim smile. "I've known worse places."

"I'll bet you have," said Tucker. "That is to say, I didn't realise until late last night that you're *the* Mr. Blake. Sheer idiocy on my part, of course. It's not as if your name is a common one. But for some reason, it simply didn't click at our first meeting, and knowing Sir Gordon, I wasn't convinced that I could trust you—not until the police framed you for that horrible murder. Poor old Worple! He was an unpleasant little fellow but—"

"Knowing Sir Gordon?" Blake queried.

The car, he noticed, was heading out of the city and in the direction of the refinery.

"Hm! A tricky situation," she said. "He is, after all, my employer. But Sir Gordon, you see, is very much in favour of the corruption that prospers on Maliba—the bribes and backhanders and so forth. His business flourishes because of it. Naturally, I would expect any detective he sent here to be the sort of man who might excel in that sort of environment."

"You mean a dishonest one?"

"Yes."

She pulled a cigar case from the pocket in the door.

"These are Cuban Partagás. Rather strong and peppery, certainly not to everyone's taste. It isn't a very ladylike habit, I fear, but I picked it up along the way and became incurably addicted. Will you?"

"Thank you."

He took a roll of tobacco.

She struck a match and offered it, then lit her own, rolled the smoke around her mouth, put her head back, and expelled a perfect ring.

At that exact moment, Blake remembered who she was and where they had previously met.

It was a momentous revelation—but he showed not a flicker of emotion, and did not allow the recognition to reach his eyes.

Tucker said, "Señorita Francesca came to me last night and made it clear that you have independent views about the liberation movement. To put it plainly, she told me that you are on our side."

She paused for a moment, as an old flatbed Army truck roared by, carrying olive-uniformed men into the city.

"She also informed me," she continued, "that you were arrested for the murder of my assistant-manager—I should say *ex*-assistant-manager—um, I mean 'ex' because I fired him, not because he has been—"

She gave a slight cough, muttered, "Oh dear," and put her cigar to her mouth. When she removed it, she resumed, through a billowing cloud:

"Francesca, the dear girl, wanted me to come and get you out right away, but my influence with the police is a delicate balance. Push too hard, and it will be lost. Had I immediately come to your rescue, my eagerness would have prompted awkward questions. Therefore, I regret to say, you were condemned to an uncomfortable night."

"I'm grateful you got me out when you did," Blake told her.

"I was cutting it fine, Mr. Blake. Did you notice the truck that just passed us?"

Blake nodded. "It was full of troops."

"Tarratona is pulling all his forces into the capital. His time is running out, and he knows it."

"When will the balloon go up?"

"During the siesta. The signal will be provided by a grenade thrown into the middle of the main plaza, where it will detonate without hurting anyone. When it is heard, the People's Liberation Army will sweep into Carabanos. General de Vega will lead the attack on police headquarters, and Juan Callas will secure the radio station. He will be on air within minutes telling the population to stay calm."

"And now?" Blake asked. "Where are you taking me?

"To the refinery. There are some documents I need to secure for Sir Gordon on the off chance that the rebellion doesn't go according to plan. Unlikely, but better to be safe than sorry. You can freshen up while we're there, then I'll drive you out beyond the city."

"Why?"

"You came to Maliba to find Peter Sellingham, didn't you? I'm going to take you to him!"

A MOMENT LATER, the car reduced speed as Sir Gordon's sugar refinery loomed up ahead. The driver steered into its compound and pulled up outside the administration block. He got out and opened the back door. Tucker and Blake disembarked.

"Leave the car here, Raul," she instructed the man. "Get the other one and wait for Brigette. Then drive her home and go home yourself. Keep your family safe until it's all over."

"Yes, ma'am," he said. "Thank you, ma'am."

"This way, Mr. Blake. There's a bathroom adjoining my office, and I think you'll find an electric razor in there."

They entered the lobby. The girl with spectacles and cornrow hair greeted them.

"Bring coffee and some sandwiches up to my office, would you, Brigette?" Tucker asked her. "Then Raul will take you home. He's waiting outside."

She turned to Blake. "You must be famished."

"I am," he responded.

They ascended the stairs.

"Where is everybody?" the detective enquired.

"I've closed the refinery for the day," she said. "Ostensibly for a safety inspection but—well, everyone knows what's going to happen. You can feel it in the air, can't you?"

At her office door, she stopped. "Make yourself comfortable. I'm going across to the cable centre. I need to wire the bank, transfer some funds. I'll join you in twenty minutes or so."

Blake nodded, went inside, and shut the door behind him.

He waited a minute, then softly opened it and looked out. No one was there. Satisfied, he closed the door again and crossed to the telephone on the desk.

He dialled through to the British Consulate and asked to speak to Henderson. Moments later, he heard:

"Blake! Is that you? I've been waiting—"

"This is an open line," he cut in. "Just answer my questions. What's the word on our two American friends?"

"Positive," came the reply. "Definitely working on your side of the industry. But about that price list you gave me—"

"Yes?"

"Your London office says negative. Repeat, negative. Trade references won't stand up. Regard it as spurious."

"Got it. Thanks, Henderson."

He hung up, went to the window, and looked out at the silent refinery.

So, the list of communist agents was spurious. It did not hold up to scrutiny.

He stood there for five minutes, deep in thought until Brigette entered with coffee and a plate of chicken sandwiches. He thanked her, waited for her to depart, then went into the bathroom, found an electric razor, shaved off his twenty-four-hour stubble, and washed his hands and face.

Returning to the office, he ate the sandwiches, drank the coffee, and prepared himself for what he knew was to come.

BLAKE WAS STANDING beside the door when Amelia Tucker entered. He was examining a large, framed monochrome photograph on the wall, a view of the island's harbour, taken in the 'thirties.

"Are you all set?" she asked, moving across to the safe.

"Yes," he murmured. "I have all I need."

She missed the peculiarity of his answer and applied herself to the combination lock. "There's a case of documents I should take with me."

"He was an extraordinary man, wasn't he?" the detective responded.

"Who?" she asked, opening the safe door. She pulled a black attaché case from inside.

"Doctor Huxton Rymer."

"I'm sorry, you've lost me. Who is that?"

She closed the door and twisted the dial to re-lock it.

"One of recent history's greatest criminals," he said. "I was thinking about him yesterday."

"Why so, Mr. Blake?"

She stepped to her desk, placing the case upon it.

"He always had the uncanny ability," Blake continued, "to discern an opportunity for some audacious criminal enterprise that few others would have seen. Admittedly, there were three or four crooks of similar talent in his day, but none quite so intelligent, and none since the nineteen thirties—bar one."

"Really?" she said quietly.

He made a noise of affirmation, watching her reflection in the glass of the framed photograph.

"That one—she was a rather remarkable young woman named Violet Damm. When I first met her, she was keeping company with Rymer. And I encountered her a few times after that, too. She developed a unique *modus operandi*."

"What was it?" Her voice was almost a whisper.

"She would always sow political turmoil to distract from her criminal schemes."

Tucker remained silent.

Blake slid out his pistol, turned, and aimed it at her.

"Hello, Violet."

She smiled, displaying the gap in her teeth.

"Hello, Sexy. Long time, no see."

13

how to make a killing

VIOLET DAMM, NO longer Amelia Tucker, laughed, opened a desk drawer, and reached into it.

"Your pistol isn't loaded," she said. "This one is."

She raised an APS machine pistol.

"Really, Sexy—" she started.

"You can cut that out!" he snapped.

"—I'm positively distraught. I've been lying my head off. You could have saved me all the trouble. How on earth did you fail to recognise me? We have *history!*"

"We do, unfortunately," he agreed, holstering his useless weapon. "But you are much altered—to look at, anyway."

"More than a quarter of a century older." She turned her head slightly and peered sideways at him. "As are you, yet you haven't changed one iota. Why not? What's your secret?"

"If I have one," he said, "it will never be told. I heard a rumour, after our last encounter—nineteen thirty-nine, I think?"

"Yes."

"—that you had found your way back to Germany. I thought perhaps you'd been killed there during the war."

It seemed to Blake that she was not going to answer, she took so long to do so, but—

"You're correct, I did return to Germany. I thought perhaps there'd be some gains to be made, but—my god, I couldn't deal with it. The maniacal fervour of the politics had become—well—many bad things can be said of me, Blake, but I am no anti-Semite."

"True," he agreed. "I've never known you to discriminate. You'll fleece anyone, whatever their race, creed or colour."

She gave a bark of laughter.

"That's right!"

She lowered the gun slightly, aiming at his heart, then raised it back to his face, as if considering where to shoot him.

After a pause—searching his eyes for any sign of fear—she went on:

"I tried Spain, but that was just as bad. The civil war was too savage even for an opportunist such as I. In the end, I joined a boatload of refugees at Vigo and made the voyage to South America. I always liked the tropics, you know that. I've been here ever since." She sighed. "But alas! I am Dutch, and Dutch skin is not suited to the sun. You can see what it has done to me."

"As a gentleman, I'll not pass comment," he said. "But I'd ask you to consider whether it is the effect of the sun without—or of the darkness within."

"Ouch!" she murmured.

She squinted down the pistol's sights.

He watched her.

Half a minute ticked by.

Then Blake said, "Obviously, your plans are coming to a head and you had me jailed before I could interfere with them. Did you murder Worple?"

"Not personally, but I'll take the credit."

"What I don't understand is why you got me out—or why it is that I'm still alive."

Her smile was not pleasant.

"Ah, Blake, I'm not one of those crooks that admires you, not one that plays the honourable game with you. Not at all. I hate you. I've hated you for years. It would be easy and immensely satisfying to kill you right here and now."

Again, she shifted aim, contemplating a shot to his stomach, to his heart, to his head.

"But there would be no profit in it, and—as you are well aware—I'm inordinately fond of easy money."

The gun settled, its barrel directed at the point between his eyes.

"And it so happens," she continued, "that there are a number of competing criminal organisations and spy networks eager to get their hands on you. It's incredible what high prices a potential for revenge can command. I intend to sell you to the highest bidder."

"Ah," he said. "My fate is sealed."

"Emphatically."

"In which case, you can brag to your heart's content. What's the game? Is it the bauxite?"

She grinned her characteristic gappy grin—so guileless-looking yet so deadly. "Clever man."

She spread her left arm in an all-embracing gesture.

"The refinery provided the perfect cover for the laundering of money. I've been able to divert considerable revenue from the mines into my accounts. I shall depart Maliba with nearly six million, all told."

The door opened.

"And here it is," she declared. "Very timely!"

Carlos Tarratona stepped in, with an attaché case in each hand.

"Ah," Blake said. "The lowly henchman."

"Shut your mouth," the corpulent police chief snapped. He crossed to the desk and put the cases beside the one already on it. He then positioned himself beside Violet Damm, an arm's length to her left.

"That was quick," she noted.

Tarratona smoothed his greasy, white-striped hair. "I telephoned the bank manager at his home at seven this morning. He went in early to get everything prepared. It was delivered to me literally two minutes after he—" he indicated Blake, "—climbed into your car."

"No trouble?"

"None," he responded. "The bank was falling over itself to cooperate. They were never going to refuse the police chief, were they? Not when the island is in danger of being overrun by communists."

He smiled, and added:

"Nearly three million each in bearer bonds."

"Thank you," said Violet Damm.

She swung her arm around and shot him through the head.

"—but I don't like half measures."

Her gun was directed back at Blake before Tarratona's corpse hit the floor.

Blood and grey matter oozed down the wall.

"He was going to betray me," she declared. "I'm certain of it."

"I think you'll find that he already has," Blake said.

"What do you mean by that?"

He smiled. "All in good time, Violet."

Crouching, not taking her eyes from the detective, she went through the dead man's pockets until she located a set of keys, which she appropriated before straightening.

She picked up one of the cases and, holding it in her left hand, moved back. "Come and get these," she said to Blake, jerking her chin toward the remaining two cases. "Move carefully. I'll kill you in an instant if you try anything. Back out of the office door, and against the wall opposite, nice and slow, your eyes on me all the time. Don't try to dive aside—you won't make it."

He did as he was told.

She moved to the doorway.

"Now down the stairs and out to the car."

He obeyed and they reached the vehicle without incident. She had him place the attaché cases on its back seat, then kept her gun on him while she got in beside them, and he occupied the driver's position.

"To the harbour," she instructed.

"I thought you were taking me to Sellingham?"

"I lied. I don't know where Sellingham is."

He started the car and drove out of the refinery compound.

After five minutes of silence, Blake said, "Will you continue the story? I'm curious."

"Story?"

"You sailed from Vigo, got to South America—what then?"

He noticed that traffic was heavy, mainly heading out of the city. Truckloads of police troops were heading in, the men unaware that they were now leaderless.

141

"I ended up in Argentina," she said. "My fortunes improved. The coup d'état of 'forty-three can be attributed to me, though it never will be, I played it so cleverly. It was during that escapade—which earned me a handful of diamonds—that I gave some assistance to a young man named Sebastián Ortiz."

Though she was sitting behind him, with her pistol pressed against his neck, Blake kept his expression neutral, knowing that she could see his face in the car's side mirror.

"After that, I settled in Cuba, and for a few years lived rather comfortably. I became quite the socialite, Blake! I was rich, and—if you'll excuse me saying so—I was beautiful; so much so, that I attracted the attention of President Batista. For two years, we were lovers, but—curse the climate!—I lost my looks—overnight, it seemed—and Batista lost interest. To his credit, he continued to provide for me, and even assigned a guard to protect me against his wife, should she choose to be vengeful. The name of that guard was Carlos Tarratona."

"All the pieces falling into place," Blake murmured.

Damm pressed her gun harder against his neck. "Take the next right. We'll circle through the outlying districts. The police are probably barricading the city centre."

Blake glanced at his wristwatch.

If Professor Hoddard Curtis was on schedule, he would be raising the bathysphere right about now.

Damm resumed her account.

"Batista fled Cuba in January of 'fifty-nine, taking with him the wealth he'd accrued through graft and payoffs—but not all of it. He'd made a mistake, you see. Over the years, he had employed me to hide the money."

Despite his dire position, Blake chuckled. "And you hid a sizeable portion of it in your own pocket."

142

"Of course."

She paused. Blake heard a match striking and, a moment later, a cloud of cigar smoke rolled past him.

"Two days before Batista's departure," she went on, "and to my great surprise, Sebastián Ortiz—whom I hadn't seen or heard from for sixteen years—knocked on my door. He declared himself a Soviet spy and warned me that Castro was about to invade. He got us out of Cuba—me and Tarratona, money and all—and took us to Martinique. There, he explained that he'd been tasked with establishing a Soviet foothold in the eastern Caribbean. He called upon my skills, and I was happy to supply them—for a fee, of course. It wasn't long, however, before I realised that, while Martinique might have suited the Soviet's purposes, it didn't suit mine at all."

"You couldn't find anything to get your avaricious claws into?" the detective suggested. He accelerated past a slow-moving bus.

"Not a single thing. Forested hills, arable land, and gorgeous beaches—what the hell am I supposed to do with those?"

"Open a hotel," he proposed. "A nice, honest business."

"All the more unsuitable," she responded. "Which is why I had a little poke around the neighbourhood."

"And found Maliba."

"With its bauxite mines."

Blake saw tall palm trees shimmering over the buildings ahead. The harbour was not far now.

"Ortiz was easily convinced, so the three of us relocated and—"

"Wait!" Blake interjected. "If memory serves, there were riots in Martinique in—"

"December, 'fifty-nine. Yes, our doing, I'm afraid. The aftermath of an abandoned project."

"Violet, have you ever spared a moment's thought for the chaos you habitually leave in your wake?"

"Why would I?"

"Conscience?"

"Great heavens! I'm a criminal, Blake!"

He shook his head despairingly.

She continued:

"Tarratona got to work here first, spreading the notion that a well-organised police force was required to combat a growing communist threat. I then identified Sir Gordon's refinery as the means through which to launder money in both directions—Soviet finance coming into the island, and my gains going out."

"The latter being kept from Ortiz, I suppose?" the detective asked.

"Yes."

"Who was it who killed the refinery manager, Cranston?"

"Tarratona—who's now beyond the reach of the law, I think you'll find."

Blake slowed the car as it drew alongside the harbour.

"Park by the marina," Damm ordered. "I'm going to pocket my pistol, but my finger will be on the trigger, and it'll be aimed at your back, so don't try anything."

"I won't," Blake said. "I'm finding it far too interesting."

He stopped the car in an appropriate spot. They got out. She instructed him to take two of the attaché cases and retrieved the third herself.

"Down to 'D' dock," she directed. "A cruiser named *Calypso*."

"Ah, the keys to which you took from Tarratona's pocket?"

"Yes."

He led the way.

After a short silence, he asked, "How did you get Cranston's job? Did you bribe Sir Gordon?"

"I didn't need to. He's old and ill. He didn't want any fuss. I showed him some fake references, and he employed me on the spot. I took up the position, started to receive Soviet funds, and with them Tarratona was able to build his commie-obsessed police force."

"And with the same money, Ortiz started shipping arms from Brazil?"

"He did."

"As 'Benjamin Paz'?"

"Yes."

"You're being very forthcoming."

"I'm proud of the whole endeavour. It might well be my best. I'm happy to discuss it. And you're no longer any threat, Blake—I'm selling you into slavery—or into the grave."

He stopped alongside a fifty-foot, white and blue boat. "Here it is."

"Into the wheelhouse," she ordered. "Charts in the drawer to the left of the wheel. Plot a course to Puerto Rico. There's fuel enough."

Blake obeyed, and five minutes later, he pulled in the mooring rope, caught the keys she tossed to him, started the motor, and steered the boat out of the harbour and onto the calm Caribbean Sea.

"So," he said, to resume the conversation, "you armed the police, and they set about brutalising the Malibans and rounding up so-called communist sympathisers?"

"In fact, anyone and everyone we felt might get in our way," she confirmed. "Including key personnel from the Bauxite mines."

She moved the pistol from her right to left hand. Blake noted this—better to strike while the weapon was in the less coordinated hand—but he was not yet ready to make a move. He wanted to hear more.

"In this way," she went on, "we made anti-communism oppressive, and President Nonales, where international politics is concerned, got the blame."

Blake made a subtle course change.

If Damm had glanced to the rear, she would have noticed that the boat's wake was now curving, the craft bearing gradually eastward when it should have been going west. However, looking back would have meant taking her eyes off Blake—and she was not stupid.

She said, "The most vocal opposition came—would you believe it?—from a simple garage mechanic, a man named Juan Callas. He was just what Ortiz and I had been waiting for. We soon discovered that his girlfriend, the delectable Francesca—she looks like Sophia Loren, doesn't she—?"

"She does."

"—she was recruiting men and women to form a resistance. I contacted her and offered to help finance it. Thus, the People's Liberation Army was born."

"Have you met Callas?"

"No. Francesca is the intermediary. I've had no personal contact with Callas or de Vega or any of the other leaders. No need for it."

Blake, standing at the wheel, said over his shoulder, "And when Peter Sellingham turned up?"

Her laughter was deep and genuine.

"The idealistic fool! He donated thousands to the cause. He gave the money to Francesca, she passed it to Callas, and he gave it to me for the purchase of weapons. I kept it for myself, obviously. The arms for the resistance come from the same source as the ones for the police—the Soviets are paying for everything. And willingly. You see their game?"

"I do. If the people are made to fear the commie-hunters more than they fear communism itself, it makes it easy for communism to slip in through the back door—that door being, in this case, the People's Liberation Army."

"Exactly as Ortiz intended all along."

Blake spotted a small ship on the horizon. He made an almost imperceptible course correction and started to very gradually ease off on the throttle, so slowly that Damm would not notice the subtle diminishing of speed.

He had almost heard enough.

"What of that list of Soviet agents?"

"Ah, you heard about that, did you? It was fake—cooked up between Tarratona and me to identify the so-called Benjamin Paz as a Soviet agent. General de Vega had him killed. You'll never guess who did the dastardly deed."

If she had noted the position of the sun, she would have realised that the cruiser was now heading in the wrong direction. She was, however, too busy blowing her trumpet.

"Who?" Blake asked, artlessly.

She chuckled, a gloating burble that sent hackles up Blake's spine.

"Sellingham!"

"Oh," Blake responded. "Really?"

"Yes," she said. "There's an American research vessel

out here somewhere. Ortiz suspected it to be a cover for the CIA. Sellingham, posing as a potential asset, accompanied him to the ship and they both went down in a bathysphere. Ortiz didn't come back."

"And the intrepid assassin?"

"Got away somehow. He's hiding. I don't know where. I don't care."

Blake used his right hand to shield his eyes. The sky was a white glare, its light reflecting from the sea in stabbing scintillations that brought tears and made his vision swim. When he turned his head to look at Violet Damm, she wavered before him, and he knew the reverse was true.

"Oh, Violet," he murmured. "You are, on so many counts, mistaken."

He jammed the throttle forward.

Abruptly, the boat accelerated, and its prow jerked up.

Violet Damm lost her balance.

Blake twisted and pounced.

14

a questionable corpse

BLAKE SNATCHED THE pistol out of Violet Damm's hand. Her reaction was instantaneous; she chopped sideways and knocked the weapon from his fingers. It went spinning over the side of the boat.

More than twenty-five years ago, during their first encounter, Damm had taken Blake completely by surprise, delivering a savage uppercut that had put his lights out, an achievement of which only a handful of male master-crooks could have ever boasted.

She was close on fifty years old now—and looked much older—but it immediately became apparent that she had lost nothing of her brute strength, speed, and endurance.

And she was utterly lacking in restraint.

He jerked his head aside, anticipating a repeat of that historic knockout blow, and instead received a knee in the groin.

His legs buckled, and as he went down, her fist cracked into the side of his face.

Reeling, Blake threw himself forward, wrapped his

arms around her midsection, and sent her thudding onto the deck, with the weight of him adding to the force of her fall.

Punches rained onto his head. He rolled aside and grunted as she swivelled and crunched her heel viciously into his ribs.

Then they were both on their feet again.

It had once been written of Sexton Blake that the heavy-weight amateur championship was his for the asking, so the struggle that ensued should have been absurdly one-sided.

It was not.

For a start, the detective was hampered by his inbuilt reluctance to hit a woman, even one as deadly as Violet Damm. But also, his opponent was perhaps the most unpredictable fighter he had ever encountered. Imbued with the rage of a maniac, she showed none of the giveaway signals that, usually, he was able to discern and act upon even in the midst of the most frenzied of brawls. With a man, he could see a punch broadcast in his opponent's eyes a split-second before it was delivered. Not so, with Damm.

She came at him like a hurricane.

Rocked on his feet, he took knuckles to his nose, to the side of his neck, and again and again to his ribs on the right side, against which that heel had crunched previously. His shins and knees were kicked. He was bitten, scratched, yanked off balance, and chopped. Twice he fell, and both times barely made it back up again.

Once, that haymaker of hers came sweeping up and caught his chin, only just off target, and his senses dimmed to a pinpoint. For the next few minutes, he was nothing but instinct, blocking, ducking, twisting out of her clutches, tripping over the attaché cases, and rebounding off the wheelhouse bulkheads, blood spattering from his nose.

They were going at it hammer and tongs in very close quarters. Every time they slammed from one side to the other, the cruiser rocked, causing it to snake from side to side as it ploughed through the water at its maximum speed of twenty knots.

Blake regained focus.

He abandoned all principles.

He stepped back and went for long shots—endeavouring to keep her nails and teeth from his face and neck, from his hands and wrists—and struck out with every ounce of his remaining strength. His left fist caught her jaw, and it was like punching granite. His right came across and she ducked under it. He leaned into a jab, and she evaded it, grabbed his arm, and jerked him forward into her knee, which came up high to once again punish the battered ribs.

As he doubled over, her fist impacted his left eye with the kick of a mule. He was sent sprawling backward, nearly out again—only some sixth sense still engaged, aware of her dropping on top of him, feeling her fingers at his neck, circling it, digging in, tightening inexorably—

—and dimly recognising that his hand had fallen against a cold metal object.

He gripped it and swung it savagely into the side of her head.

A loud clang resonated down his arm and into his shoulder.

She keeled over and was still.

Blake lay on his back, his eyes filled with the blazing white sky, the deck jumping and jolting beneath him.

He turned his head and saw that he was holding a small aqualung. Dropping it, he rolled to all fours, heaved himself up with a groan, and toppled against the helm. He pulled the throttle back, slowing the *Calypso* almost to a stop.

Through blurring eyes, he saw the science vessel not far ahead.

He staggered to the gunwale, where a length of neatly coiled rope was hanging from a cleat, took it, and collapsed beside Violet Damm.

Rolling her onto her stomach, he pulled her wrists behind her back, looped the rope tightly around them, and knotted it.

She moaned and blinked.

"Blake," she whispered.

"It's over," he said.

Kneeling, he pulled a handkerchief from his pocket and pressed it against his bleeding nose. Already, he could feel his left eye swelling to a slit.

He lurched up to the wheel, took a hold, and steered toward the *Gorgon*.

The bathysphere was up.

The CIA motorboat was roped to the ship's starboard ladder. The *Calypso* was considerably bigger than that craft, so rather than mooring against it as he had done before, he circled to the other side of the research ship.

Damm sat up just as he drew the cruiser to a halt and tied it against the *Gorgon*'s port-side ladder. She said, "Next time, I'll kill you, Blake."

The detective looked up and saw the CIA man, Kellaher, peering down.

"Give me a hand," Blake called, pocketing his stained handkerchief. "I have a prisoner."

Kellaher swung over the rail and descended.

"What in tarnation happened to you?" he asked.

"She did." Blake nodded towards Damm. He stepped over to the corner where the three attaché cases had come to rest after being knocked around the cabin. The aqualung had rolled against them. He blinked at it, and his right eyebrow rose a little. A slight smile stretched his swollen lips.

Picking up the cases, Blake passed them to Kellaher. "Take these up then come back to help me with her. I'll explain everything later. It's a long story."

This was done, and the two of them manhandled the woman up the ladder while she cursed and insulted them, then dragged her over to where Navarro, Professor Curtis, and Vasquez were standing, near the sphere.

"Agent Kellaher, Agent Navarro," Blake said, "this is Violet Damm."

Navarro looked amused. "Her knuckles are bleeding. Did she do that to your face?"

"Regrettably."

The Mexican grinned. "With a name like *Violent Dame*, you should've seen it coming."

"Violet Da—" Blake started to correct. He ran his tongue over his teeth. "Never mind."

He gestured toward the attaché cases, which Kellaher had placed on the deck. "There's nigh on six million in bearer bonds in those cases. She stole it from Maliba. Can I trust you to look after it for a while?"

"You can," Kellaher confirmed.

"And I very much expect that Miss Damm is high on the CIA's 'Persons of Interest' list. Guard her carefully. She's tricky and she's dangerous."

Blake's legs felt like they might fold beneath him.

He didn't let them.

Kellaher—a perceptive man—stepped forward, took Blake's arm, and pressed a silver pocket flask into his hand. "Take a swig of that. It'll buck you up some."

Damm commented: "Strychnine, I hope."

But it was neat bourbon, and it did the trick.

"We made enquiries with those in the know," Kellaher murmured. "Got the lowdown on you, Blake. Impressive record."

Blake grunted. "I did likewise. Glad we're on the same team."

He turned to Curtis and gestured toward the dripping sphere. "I see you've opened the hatch, professor. What did you find?"

With a look of distaste, Curtis pointed to what Blake had taken for a heap of oilcloth, but which he now saw to be a wetsuit stuffed with some indescribable substance somewhat reminiscent of lumpy, discoloured blancmange.

Blake had to fight down a surge of nausea when he realised what it was.

"The fisheries' inspector," Curtis said. "Señor Paz."

Kellaher added, "Otherwise known as Sebastián Ortiz."

"And good riddance to him," Damm put in.

"I can't disagree with her," Navarro declared.

Blake eyed the CIA men. "Was it you two who identified him in Brazil?"

"Yup," Kellaher confirmed. "Been on his tail ever since."

Blake stepped closer to the corpse. The water pressure had crushed it beyond any hope of identification.

He saw the handle of a knife caught in a fold of the

rubber, Putting his right hand over his nose, he took another step, and crouched beside the gruesome, reeking remains.

"How do you know?"

"Know what?" Navarro asked.

"That this is Paz."

"How could it not be?"

"There were two men aboard. Only one body has been recovered—and as we can all see, it is unrecognisable. Why should we assume it belongs to one and not the other?"

Curtis took a step closer. "Paz was the one heard screaming for help when the bathysphere was a thousand feet down."

Blake squinted at the sphere—difficult to look at with the dazzling sunlight reflecting from it—and asked, "Have you checked all the equipment, professor? Are you satisfied that it's all present?"

"It's all there," Curtis confirmed.

"And no one could have left the bathysphere at that depth, when the screaming began?"

"At that pressure, they wouldn't even be able to open the hatch, and if by some miracle they did—" The professor jerked his chin at the corpse, "—*that.*"

Blake shifted position, lowering a knee to the deck and resting his weight on it, wincing as his battered ribs complained.

"So again," he said, "we return to the fact that one man has vanished from the sphere. Now let us eliminate the impossible and disregard the miracle. With what does that leave us?"

They looked at him blankly.

He raised his eyebrows.

"Does it not follow inevitably that the man who left the bathysphere must have done so much earlier—at not more than, say, fifty feet?"

Curtis frowned. "I suppose, with an aqualung, it could be done—"

"Was there one aboard?"

"Yes, of course. Standard equipment."

"Is it still there?"

The professor crossed to the sphere and peered in through the hatch.

He turned, his eyes wide.

"Gone."

"Then that's what happened," Blake said flatly.

Curtis exhaled loudly in exasperation. "If you're suggesting that Linwood killed Paz then left the bathysphere when it was no more than fifty feet down, explain to me how Paz was screaming about an attacking sea monster at a thousand feet!"

Blake said patiently, "He couldn't have been. Therefore, he wasn't."

"Señor!" Vasquez objected. "I heard with my own—"

Blake stopped him with a raised hand and addressed Curtis.

"Professor, you said all the equipment was present. But you overlooked the fact that the aqualung was missing. Will you look again, please?"

Curtis, still standing by the open hatch, turned and leaned in. For a full minute, he scrutinised the interior.

The others waited, the silence broken only by Kellaher lighting a cigarette with his noisy brass lighter—*click-clackety-click*.

Then came an echoing cry of puzzlement, and Curtis clambered into the sphere. When he dropped back out and turned to face them, he was holding a small object in his hand.

"Nothing else missing," he said. "But something added. I don't know where this came from. It was taped to the radio transmitter."

He handed it to Blake, who examined it, and said, "Soviet design. A small, battery-powered tape-recorder. Rather ingenious. Sturdy and encased in rubber. Completely waterproof." He held it up for them all to see. "This little device brings with it some serious implications. It's not the sort of thing that Ortiz would be carrying around with him. He must have requested it and received it in short order. That suggests to me that there's a Soviet submarine in the region. An explanation, perhaps, professor, for those anomalous sonar readings you mentioned."

Kellaher and Navarro glanced at each other.

Blake pressed a switch on the recorder, waited a moment, then pressed another. From the little box there came a loud voice:

"—*ing closer! It can't—it's not possible! Pull us up! Pull the sphere up! Quickly, man! Quickly!*"

He clicked it off.

"Vasquez," he said, indicating the Puerto Rican, "paused the bathysphere's descent at around fifty feet. Everything he heard over the radio connection after that—including the stretches of silence—was pre-recorded on this."

"But—señor!" Navarro objected. He threw his hands up and spoke rapidly in his native tongue. "Por qué Paz ocultaría su propio asesinato?"

Why would Paz obscure his own murder?

"Because he wasn't murdered," Blake responded.

Curtis cried out, "He's right in front of you, man!"

Blake looked at Vasquez. "When they took the bathysphere down, did you happen to notice any other vessels nearby?"

"Sí," the first mate responded. "The one you came in. The *Calypso*."

"Precisely. And if you care to look, you'll find in its wheelhouse an aqualung with *Gorgon* printed on its side."

Violet Damm muttered, "Oh my god."

"What?" Kellaher snapped. "What?"

Sexton Blake wrinkled his nose in distaste, reached for the corpse, caught hold of its long black hair, and peeled it back, removing the grips that held it to the curly blond hair beneath.

"This is Linwood," he said bleakly. "Better known as Peter Sellingham."

Violet Damm said, "Let me go, Blake. Let me go, so I can find the filthy double-crosser and stab him in the heart!"

Kellaher looked from her to Blake. "You mean—?"

"Ortiz was aware that you spotted him in Brazil," Blake said. "His cover identity was blown. In addition, this woman—" he cocked a thumb at Damm, "—had falsified a list that exposed him to the People's Liberation Army. He knew it—because Carlos Tarratona told him."

"That treacherous dog!" Damm spat.

Blake gave her a shrug. "You betrayed Ortiz, Tarratona betrayed you, you betrayed him, and Ortiz has come out on top."

Kellaher looked from one to the other.

"I get it," he said, slowly. "Holy smoke! I get it. He faked his death."

Blake got to his feet, wincing.

"He did. In his guise as a fisheries' inspector, he'd already been aboard the *Gorgon*, and had seen the bathysphere. Now he made use of it. Sellingham—as Linwood—was posing as a potential communist recruit. I'll wager that Paz demanded a show of courage—Linwood must accompany him down into the depths. Sellingham had little choice but to comply. Paz had the sphere stopped at fifty feet, then stabbed his companion to death. As Paz, he wore a wig. He removed it and put it on Sellingham, securing it with grips. He then strapped on the aqualung, attached the recorder to the transmitter, pressed the play button, and opened the hatch. The bathysphere flooded. He closed the hatch, clipped a timed explosive to the base of the cables, and as the sphere continued its downward journey, he swam away."

The detective crossed to Damm, met her eyes, and continued:

"Ortiz was picked up—by Tarratona in the *Calypso*."

She snarled, "That skunk!"

"Even a crook, Violet, should never trust a crook. I daresay Tarratona would have shot you—had you not shot him first. He enjoyed his power as police chief. The Soviets, through Ortiz, probably guaranteed him the role in perpetuity, along with a sizeable share of the money you stole."

She gritted her teeth, her jaw muscles standing out like bunched wire.

Kellaher drew his pistol and checked that it was loaded.

"Ortiz is alive," he said. "Where is he?"

"He's with the rebels waiting to seize control of the island," said Blake, "and I've got to get there before it happens."

"I'm with you."

"Me, too," Navarro put in.

"No," Kellaher said. "You stay here, Miguel. Guard those attaché cases and that woman."

"But—"

"It's an order."

Kellaher was apparently the senior in rank, for Navarro nodded and stepped back, glowering but offering no further objection.

"I need a weapon," Blake said.

There were, however, only two aboard—the pistols belonging to the CIA men—and the detective was unwilling to leave Navarro unarmed. Even with her hands bound behind her back, Violet Damm was a dangerous woman.

So, he and Kellaher headed back to Maliba in the *Calypso*, there to hunt one of the Soviet Union's most dangerous agents—

—and Sexton Blake had only his fists.

15
el final violento

BLAKE AND KELLAHER reached Maliba and ran up to the Carabanos waterfront, where the CIA man had parked a bright red '46 Plymouth Special De Lux 4-Door Sedan.

"At least we won't be conspicuous," Blake quipped as he occupied the front passenger seat.

"She's a beaut," Kellaher said, starting the engine. "Cost a fortune to rent, though, and she sure guzzles the gas." He pulled into the road. "Where to?"

"You know the poorest quarter? There's a bar, the Ostra. We need to get there fast, so go through the city centre. We might have some barricades to deal with. Do whatever it takes."

"Gotcha," Kellaher said, accelerating. "Why there?"

Blake clung to the edges of his seat as the car bowled around a corner. "We must stop the liberation before it starts. There's a girl, Francesca. She's my only link with the rebels. They need to know that Tarratona is dead, and that Ortiz is using them to achieve his own ends."

The Plymouth tore along the near empty streets.

The day's siesta was commencing.

"How's he gonna to do it, Blake?"

"The list that Damm and Tarratona drew up named men loyal to the cause as communist infiltrators. Callas and de Vega had them removed, unwittingly leaving the real spies in place. I suspect there are also communist sympathisers camped out on the surrounding islands—the little uninhabited ones around Maliba. It would have been easy for Ortiz, as Paz, to keep them supplied—or, if not him, the submarine. As soon as the fighting is over, they'll move in and declare a new, communist government."

"You think the people will allow that?"

"I do," Blake replied. "Because there's a trusted man right at the top."

Kellaher glanced sideways at the detective, but Blake said no more.

They came to the first barricade, a simple one of portable metal barriers painted yellow, of the type used to hold back a crowd during a procession. To either side of it, a handful of men in police uniforms were lounging on sandbags, smoking and—Blake thought—probably wondering why they had not received orders for a while.

They looked up as the Plymouth Sedan roared towards them, dived for cover as it smashed through the flimsy obstruction, and were still clambering to their feet as it veered around a corner and out of sight.

"My poor headlights!" Kellaher exclaimed. "Reckon you can still buy replacements?"

"You recall that this is a hired car?" Blake asked.

"Sheesh!" The response was comically despondent.

A tougher prospect came into view: a wall of sandbags.

"There!" Blake barked, pointing toward a side street.

Kellaher yanked at the wheel. The car slid sideways, its white-walled tyres smoking and screeching, and shot into what was little more than an alleyway. The vehicle ploughed through a wooden bar table and chairs, sending them tumbling through the air. As it veered back into a main street, it caught the edge of scaffolding, which collapsed noisily into the road behind it.

"Hope that wasn't holding anything up," the CIA man said. "Look out! More police!"

It was a human cordon ahead, easily scattered, but rifles were hastily unslung and shots fired after them as they sped through.

The back window shattered.

"No!" Kellaher hollered. "Gosh darn it! Don't they know this is a classic?"

He sent the sedan careening into the city's main plaza and there hit the brakes hard, screeching to a stop.

The way ahead was blocked by a convoy exiting the presidential palace gates—two large black cars followed by a Cadillac limousine, and another two cars behind, all escorted by eight motorcycle out-riders.

Two small blue and orange flags fluttered at the front corners of the limousine's hood—the first flags Blake had seen on Maliba.

"Doctor Nonales," he said. "Fleeing the scene before the—"

The limousine passed over a manhole and the road erupted. The explosion was tremendous. As heavy as the Cadillac was, it was blown fifteen feet into the air, rising on a ball of flame, spinning over, and crashing back down onto its roof.

The motorcyclists practically disintegrated.

The shockwave slammed into the Plymouth and

cracked its windscreen. Pieces of rubble and twisted metal rained onto it.

"Christ!" Kellaher yelled.

For a moment, Blake was too stunned to speak.

Dense black smoke rolled over the hellish scene.

An unearthly silence gripped the city for what felt to Blake like minutes—mere seconds, in fact—then gunfire broke the spell; first the peppering of single rifle shots, then the furious clatter of machine-guns.

The detective snapped back into focus. He gripped Kellaher's bicep and pointed to a narrow road alongside the police headquarters. "Through there!"

The American put his foot down. The Plymouth jerked forward, rocked over debris, left the plaza, and sped past the tall police building. It emerged onto a wide thoroughfare, raced straight across it, and powered away from the chaos.

"Change of plan," Blake announced. "We need to get to the radio station."

"Which way?"

"Turn left ahead."

Kellaher obeyed. They smashed through another barricade of metal fences, this one unmanned, then had a free run, unhindered along empty roads.

"They assassinated their president!" Kellaher exclaimed.

"No," Blake countered. "Not the islanders. They have never considered him to be anything besides a harmless necessity. He had no power. The notion that he was a brutal despot was disseminated by the press—and the press was controlled by Tarratona."

"Then who—?"

"Ortiz! It was a signal for the liberation to begin. But,

most of all, it was a message to the rest of the world: Behold! Communist forces have overthrown a brutal dictatorship. Hurrah for the Soviet Union!"

Kellaher swore vociferously.

Blake leaned forward and clicked on the car radio. It was already tuned to the city station.

"*...of police violence and suppression, and to throw it off forever! People of Maliba, from this day forth, you will never again be stopped and questioned on the street for no good reason; you will never again have your door broken down in the middle of the night; you will never again have your father or mother or brother or sister or husband or wife dragged away in handcuffs; you will never again be harassed and threatened, beaten and bribed. I plead with you to remain safe in your homes until the People's Liberation Army has secured the police headquarters and arrested the criminal, Carlos Tarratona. I swear to you that once we have forcibly disbanded this nest of traitors—these foolish, deluded men who allowed themselves to be swayed by money and power—we shall see a return to normalcy and the beginning of—*"

The sedan slid to a halt in front of the radio station.

"Get out and keep your hands up," Blake advised.

Six unshaven, bedraggled men—men who looked as if they had been camping in the hills for many days—were standing by the building's entrance steps, rifles in their hands.

Three of them approached the car, levelling their weapons.

Blake and Kellaher emerged slowly, hands raised.

"Francesca sent me," Blake called. "I have vital information for Juan Callas."

One of the men aimed at the detective's head. "You are lying, señor. Francesca cannot have sent you. She is inside."

"Good! Tell her Sexton Blake needs to see her immediately. It is of crucial importance. If you do not do as I have asked, you will become forever infamous on this island."

The man hesitated, then lowered his rifle. "Keep your hands up. If you make a move, my comrades will shoot you. Understood?"

"Understood. Please hurry, there is not much time."

The man turned and ran into the building. One of the others gestured for Kellaher to move around the Plymouth and stand beside Blake.

The American did so, and muttered, "What a goddam awful mess."

"It is," Blake replied, "but we can still get them out of it. Francesca will listen to us."

"Huh," Kellaher responded. "I meant the car."

They did not have to wait for long. The man returned, smiled, and said, "It's all right. This way, please."

They lowered their hands and followed him into the radio station. Blake stumbled slightly on the steps—his vision was impaired, his left eye by now swollen entirely shut.

Francesca met them in a corridor, and her eyes widened when she saw Blake.

"You are hurt!"

He dismissed her concern with a careless gesture.

"Francesca, the signal that ignited the liberation—that detonation? It wasn't a grenade. They set off a bomb beneath Doctor Nonales' car. I witnessed it myself. He's been assassinated."

"Assassinated?" She put a hand to her heart and her dark skin paled. "No, our people would not have done that!"

"They didn't. It was the Soviets. The threat is real. The communists are preparing to take over." He indicated Kellaher. "This is Kellaher from the CIA. He will confirm it."

Her eyes flicked to Blake's companion—who nodded—then back to the detective.

"But—"

He raised a hand to stop her, then spoke rapidly, his tone clipped and urgent. "Maliba has been the subject of an extravagant criminal enterprise. Amelia Tucker was a part of it, and so was Carlos Tarratona. Tucker is now under arrest. Tarratona is dead—"

She gasped.

"—but there is a Soviet agent on the loose and, unless we can stop him, you will lose this island, and it will become everything that Cuba also threatens to be. You need to take me to Juan Callas."

She blinked rapidly, bewilderment written across her beautiful face. Then her eyes flared with determination, she said, "Come!" and wheeled and led the way along the corridor.

They reached the studio just as the red light over the door switched to green. It opened before they got to it. Music wafted out—Jimmy Cliff, Blake thought, the nearest Maliba had to a national anthem—and a young man stepped into view.

Though his name was Spanish, Juan Callas was a Black Caribbean, exceptionally handsome, with hair spiked into short dreadlocks and the most vivid green eyes that Blake had ever seen. He was muscular but slender, attired in a white vest, green combat trousers, and leather sandals. A Luger pistol was holstered at his hip.

He saw Francesca and smiled.

"Mi amor. General de Vega is on his way here. One of his men has just phoned through. You will not believe it! The police headquarters is already ours. There's barely any resistance at all. They say that Tarratona has fled. The police are without leadership and have surrendered! We have won with only a few shots fired!"

She rushed forward and gripped his arms. "No! I don't think so!" She turned and indicated Blake. "This is the detective I told you of: Señor Sexton Blake. And this is an agent from the CIA. Please listen to what they have to say, Juan. It is very important."

The freedom fighter looked inquisitively at them. "All right. I'm listening. What is it?"

Terse and succinct, Blake explained how Violet Damm and Carlos Tarratona had taken advantage of Soviet interest in Maliba in order to steal a fortune; how Tarratona had secretly assisted the Soviet agent Ortiz, to his own advantage and against Damm's interests; how Damm had turned on Tarratona and murdered him; how Ortiz had faked his death, thus fooling Damm that he was out of the picture; and how he was poised to declare a communist government at any moment.

Callas listened, and his face remained utterly impassive.

When Blake finished, there was silence.

Nobody moved.

Then, Callas raised his finger and said, "One moment, please."

He turned and went back through the door.

Over the insistent rhythm of the music, his voice could be heard, rapid and decisive.

He returned to them.

"My men are calling through to the city centre. We are diverting our forces to the harbour and to all parts of the coast that connect by road to Carabanos. If you are correct, and communist sympathisers are coming from the islands, we will intercept them. I also have ordered more men here, to the radio station. It is from here that Ortiz will want to declare his government. We will stop him."

As they made to exit, he turned to the girl. "No, Francesca. You stay inside. It will be safer."

"I can fight," she said.

"You can also be killed or wounded, and I will not have that. You have served Maliba well and need do no more. In the future, my darling, they will sing songs about you."

He kissed her passionately, and she reluctantly stayed behind.

On the steps of the radio station, he surveyed the six guards and murmured to Blake, "Señor, I fear that as a soldier, I have shown myself to be nothing but a garage mechanic."

Blake gave a questioning look.

"The police we found here surrendered as soon as we arrived," Callas explained. "I sent all my men, aside from these six, into the city to join the fight there, where they might be needed. It was, I think, a serious miscalculation." He paused and cocked his head, listening. "Ah, perhaps this is the general. I shall hand over full command to him. He will do a better job than I."

Blake detected the sound of an approaching motorcycle. He, Kellaher and Callas crossed to where the Plymouth Sedan was parked. They watched as the motorcycle roared up the road towards them, braked hard, and slewed to a stop, spraying grit over the side of the car.

"Hey, the paintwork!" Kellaher objected.

The motorcyclist dismounted. He was dressed in dusty khaki, with a holstered revolver at either hip, like a Hollywood cowboy. His hair was short and black, his upper face concealed by dark-tinted goggles.

"Gracias a dios!" Callas exclaimed. "General de Vega! I'm glad to see you, my friend!"

Blake whispered to Kellaher, "Draw your weapon."

Callas went on, "But I'm afraid we cannot celebrate a victory yet. There is more fighting to be done."

Baffled, Kellaher reached into his jacket.

The motorcyclist pulled off his goggles and cast them aside.

His face was bony and sharp, reminiscent of a vulture.

"Juan," he began. "It is time that we—"

"Holy—" Kellaher yelled. "Ortiz!"

The Soviet's hand blurred. A loud report sounded. Kellaher, his gun half out, dropped it, gasped, and went down, clutching his chest, his face contorted with agony.

Blake flung himself forward, his fist coming across in a sweeping right hook. His swollen-closed eye caused him to misjudge. Ortiz ducked back smoothly, then smacked his revolver into the side of the detective's head. Blake went spinning into the motorbike, knocked it over, and sprawled limply on top of it.

Callas shouted, "Wait! What are you—?" and fumbled for his gun.

Ortiz shot him in the bicep. The freedom fighter yelped, and his Luger went bouncing over the ground. Then Ortiz was on him, knocking him to his knees, wrapping an arm around his neck, and pressing a revolver to his head.

"Get back or he dies!" the spy bellowed.

The six guards, only now reacting, stopped in their tracks.

"Drop your weapons," Ortiz commanded, "and put your hands up!"

They all obeyed.

Ortiz dragged Callas backward, only stopping when he felt himself pressing against the Plymouth. Blake was down to his left, semi-conscious. Kellaher was on the ground in front, groaning and bleeding.

"Out onto the road," Ortiz ordered the guards. "Don't come close. Start running. Get away from here as fast as you can. If I see any one of you slow down or turn back, Callas will die. Get going!"

Giving him a wide berth, they did as they were told.

Ortiz bent his head and snarled into Callas' ear, "Juan, this pig of an American here on the ground, what did he tell you?"

Half-throttled, Callas answered hoarsely, "Sufficient! I know who—and what—you really are, Ramon de Vega. I know what you are doing—and my men are prepared. When your pack of jackals comes ashore, we will shoot them down like the rabid animals they are."

Ortiz dug the revolver viciously into the side of Callas' head. "You dumb peasant! If you think your pathetic little mob of—"

A woman screamed.

Ortiz jerked the gun up and aimed at Francesca, who had just emerged from the radio station.

Callas shouted, "No!" and heaved himself to one side. The Soviet, thrown off balance, staggered, and his shot went high. The bullet drilled into the wall six inches above the girl.

Ortiz whirled and, with great force, shoved Callas headfirst into the side of the car, denting the door. He then yanked him back and hurled him away. The Maliban went flailing across twelve feet of ground before hitting the dust and rolling to a stop, unconscious.

The Soviet aimed his revolver at the prone freedom fighter and applied pressure to the trigger.

A shot echoed.

The weapon flew out of Ortiz's fingers. He cried out and clutched at his hand, looked around and saw Francesca's smoking automatic.

"I was aiming for your head, cabrón!" she yelled. "I'll try again!" She squinted down the sights.

Her gun jammed.

Ortiz laughed. With his uninjured hand, he drew his second revolver and pointed it at her.

Sexton Blake came flying over the hood of the car.

He hit Ortiz with his full weight, sending him to the ground, feeling the man crunch beneath him. He kicked the spy's gun out of reach, under the vehicle, then he pushed himself to his feet, hauled Ortiz up, and swung him face-first into the Plymouth's rear door window. The glass exploded into fragments.

The Soviet agent's foot hooked around Blake's ankle and tripped him. The detective stumbled back. A boot lashed out, the heel sinking into his already cracked ribs, and he folded, the pain incandescent, crashing down beside Kellaher, his hand falling onto the CIA man's dropped automatic. He clutched it, whipped it up just as Ortiz twisted to face him, and fired point-blank.

The bullet took half the spy's right ear off and punctured the car's fuel tank. Petrol spouted out and drenched the man.

The Soviet scrabbled forward, rolled, and once again employed his kickboxing skills—and again, a weapon went flying away, Blake's wrist almost broken in the process.

Francesca had by now picked up one of the rifles discarded by the guards. She fired it. The recoil knocked her onto her bottom. A big hole appeared in the Plymouth's front right fender.

Ortiz dropped to his side, rolled back to the car, and groped beneath it for his revolver.

"Blake," Kellaher rasped. "Get back."

The detective heard:

Click-clackety-click.

The CIA man threw his brass lighter.

With a *whumph!* flame engulfed Ortiz. He thrashed and screamed.

Blake pushed himself up, caught Kellaher beneath the shoulders, and hauled him clear.

The Plymouth's tank blew, rocking the big car, turning it into a blazing inferno.

Ortiz twitched and became still.

The guards, forced to run away, came racing back.

Callas sat up. Francesca rushed to him, knelt, and flung her arms round him.

Kellaher chuckled croakily.

"Hey, Blake," he said. "That Plymouth—"

"Hm?" Blake groaned.

"You reckon the rental company will sell it to me cheap, now?"

16

Baker Street idyll

"Violet Damm escaped."

"What?" Edward Carter exclaimed.

"Agent Navarro wasn't very forthcoming about it," Sexton Blake said. "I think he felt rather embarrassed. Probably, she asked him to untie her wrists, so she could go to the lavatory. One way or another, anyway, she got free and proceeded to beat the living daylights out of him." He pointed to his yellowing left eye. "I got one of these. He got two—and a lot more besides. She might have killed him had Curtis and his crew not rushed her."

"Did she recover the bearer bonds?"

"No. They had been taken from the cases and locked in the cabin. She was in danger of being overwhelmed, so sensibly made escape her priority. She fought free of the men, jumped onto the *Calypso*, and sped away, leaving her ill-gotten gains behind. My guess is that she made for Puerto Rico. By now, she could be anywhere."

Sexton Blake and his assistant were sitting in the living room of the detective's modest penthouse flat at the top of the Baker Street house, which they had once occupied in its entirety. The floors below were now converted into offices and rented out. Mrs. Bardell no longer kept rooms in the basement, but lived around the corner and visited daily.

Nowadays, Blake conducted business exclusively from his office in Berkeley Square.

New government regulations had made it a necessity. A private investigator could no longer operate with the freedom that had once been his.

"Accountability" was the new watchword. Five years ago, or thereabouts, he had hired staff—Paula Dane, Marion Lang, and Louise Pringle—to deal with all the bureaucracy, and ever since he had been making the best of the "new order."

In his heart of hearts, he didn't like it at all.

His preferred way of life—his independence and, indeed, his individuality—was being curtailed by politics, which amounted to little more than over-complicated feudalism bound in reams of paperwork and delivered with increasingly hollow and petty rhetoric.

Maliba had been a revelation.

Its lack of anything resembling a central government; the prevalence of voluntary associations—of self-governing communities and extended families; its astonishingly flexible methods of education and apprenticeship, focused on contribution and personal fulfilment; and above all, the manner in which it regarded any crime as a symptom, and so immediately treated the cause; all these things had impressed him immeasurably.

He wanted the island protected, and hoped it would be, now that the Soviet threat to it was exposed.

Protected—but, also, left alone.

As if reading his thoughts, Carter said, "And Maliba? Did Ortiz have people on the surrounding islands?"

Blake filled his pipe and used a tamper to compact the tobacco. He didn't smoke the pipe much nowadays, but he was in a reminiscent mood, and it felt appropriate.

"Yes," he answered. "But his little invasion force was defeated easily, and the communist infiltrators in the People's Liberation Army quickly melted away."

Striking a match, Blake got the tobacco going, pondered for a moment, then continued:

"Ortiz misjudged Maliba. He thought months of police brutality had made the islanders so defiant of the Nonales government that they would willingly embrace a change, even if it came in the form of communism. What he failed to perceive—just as I did at the start—is that there wasn't any Nonales government. There was, in fact, no government of any sort."

"But guv'nor—" Carter began.

The corner of Blake's mouth twitched.

His assistant had taken to calling him "chief" these past few years, but whenever they sat together in the old Baker Street house, he invariably reverted to "guv'nor," which Blake preferred by a considerable measure.

"—surely, when Ortiz joined the resistance in the guise of Ramon de Vega, he learned from the freedom fighters that they were fighting the police, not the president? That his attempt to manufacture the notion of a corrupt and oppressive government had failed?"

The detective blew a plume of smoke at the ceiling.

"There are two factors to consider, Tinker. The first is, why would anyone think he needed telling? And the second is, had anyone said to him 'Doctor Nonales is a powerless figurehead,' I daresay he would have jumped to the conclusion that they were simply demeaning the enemy."

Blake examined the bowl of his pipe.

"Ortiz was—we have all become, I fear—singularly unimaginative where politics is concerned." He smiled. "Nevertheless, I've returned from Maliba feeling considerably more optimistic. There is something very inspiring about the place. I have full confidence that it will quickly recover from the criminal intrigue to which it fell victim."

Carter lifted a glass of pale ale and sipped from it. With a line of froth on his upper lip, he said, "And things really aren't so bad back here in good old Blighty, guv'nor. Don't you feel a fresh breeze blowing across the country? If you ask me, we're more likely to have a revolution than Maliba ever was. I reckon all the old fuddy-duddies are about to get kicked out, and the hepcats are going to take over!"

Blake coughed. "The—what?"

"The hepcats! The beats! The hipsters! The bohemians!"

"Tinker," Blake said.

"Guv'nor?"

"You're fired. You can move your things out of the office in the morning. Go find another job. I never want to see you again."

Carter grinned. "Cool it, daddy-o!"

Blake placed his pipe on the ashtray and glanced around the room. "Where did I leave my gun?"

Laughing and throwing up his hands, Carter cried out, "All right! All right! But my point is: haven't you felt a change in the air since Elvis Presley?"

Sexton Blake blinked. "Elvis Presley? What in blue

blazes are you talking about? What's Elvis Presley got to do with it?"

"Well, not just him," Carter said. He leaned forward in his chair, plainly enthused. "Rock and roll, guv'nor! Music has lit a fire under young people. They're excited. They're engaged. They really feel, perhaps for the first time ever, that they can change the world. Don't you see it?"

"Humph," grunted Blake. He picked up his pipe again. "I very much doubt that music can—"

He stopped.

He remembered Jimmy Cliff—remembered how music had been so omnipresent on Maliba—remembered, and murmured:

"Cuando hay problemas, solo baila!"

"Ha!" Carter exclaimed, triumphantly, and smacked his hand down onto the arm of his chair.

"I wonder," Blake said, in a contemplative tone. "Cuba is red-hot. Kennedy and Khrushchev are aiming atomic bombs at each other. Do you really think we can dance our way out of a situation like that?"

"Of course we can!" Carter declared. "Get with it, guv'nor! It's the nineteen-sixties!"

The End

Sexton Blake

Tuesday 27th April 2023

Mr. Michael Moorcock

Austin, Texas.

My Dear Mike,
By astounding coincidence (I am prone
to them), yours was the first item of
correspondence I opened upon my return
from a short holiday in… Maliba!
That, of course, is not and never
was the island's true name, and, as a
matter of fact, the name it bore during
the time of the "Caribbean Crisis" no
longer applies either, as it adopted a
new one in the summer of 1968.
Aside from that, it remains
surprisingly unaltered. After being
"taken off the map" during the post-
Cuban Missile Crisis negotiations, its
fledgling tourist industry collapsed,
but this turned out to be a blessing
and was more than offset by the bauxite
mines, which continue to be productive
to this day, and which have made the
"Malibans," as I shall call them, the
wealthiest people of the Caribbean.

Yet, they continue to live in an uncomplicated fashion, with little interest in the materialism which has long gripped cultures that would claim themselves "more advanced."

My pleasure at finding the place in good shape was tempered somewhat by the discovery that old Juan Callas is no longer with us. He passed away three years ago, peacefully in his sleep, after a short period of ill-health. His widow, the remarkable Francesca, is a spry and elegant octogenarian, with innumerable grandchildren in whom she finds great solace and delight.

You will recall her claiming that Doctor Nonales was little more than "a telephone receptionist." In 1975, his successor, Martina Eva Gomez, voluntarily stepped down. The duties associated with her role were then stripped to the essentials and assigned to an actual telephone receptionist!

All of which brings me to your request.

It is a timely one, and I am happy to say: yes, I authorise the "restoration and revision" of CARIBBEAN CRISIS. Furthermore, I enclose my case notes sans the redactions that were necessary so long ago. You can, perhaps, now spin a more truthful yarn.

One more item: it occurred to me, while consulting my index for the file,

that none of my previous encounters
with that nefarious villainess, Violet
Damm, have ever been published. I
therefore enclose, in addition, the
notes pertaining to the occasion when
she and I first crossed swords, back in
1935.

Should I find myself in your part of
the world, I shall drop by to reminisce
over the good old, bad old, Fleetway
days.

Until then,

With my (and Tinker's) best regards,

Sexton Blake

VOODOO ISLAND

Michael Moorcock
and Mark Hodder

1

baron pays a call

"BITTE!" LOTHAR LEICHENBERG whimpered. "Ach! Bitte!" He flattened his trembling, wrinkled hands against his ears. On his laboratory bench, test-tubes and retorts jingled and rattled. "How am I expected to work? I cannot endure this endless racket!"

The old man was accustomed to the drums. They thundered nearly every night. On this occasion, however, they were louder, more persistent, and held a special, menacing note. Their rumble had commenced exactly at sunset, their volume and intensity steadily increasing, until now, it felt to him as if the sound emanated from the depths of his skull.

He recognised the looping rhythm and knew exactly what it meant. This was a sacred night for the islanders. A sinister night. The voodoo drummers were battering at that thin partition which separated one world from the next, life from death, the natural from the supernatural. The frenzied tempo hammered on a portal between the material and the daemonic worlds, a portal through which, tonight, some unwilling victim would be hurled.

It had happened at least once in each of the fifteen years he had lived in this half-forgotten part of the Caribbean. This same insistent throbbing intruding into his idealistic dream of making the little island self-sufficient—even rich. There was little he could do to improve a world he had helped to ruin, but to pull this one poor little kingdom out of poverty and superstition—that, at least, might make amends for all his years of arms dealing.

Leichenberg's intentions were good and his influence significant, but the drums told of another power on the island. Every time they sounded this way, the following morning, a corpse would be discovered, eyes wide, mouth fixed in a rictus grin, cause of death: *terror!*

Tonight, however, it felt even more ominous, and a sense of foreboding gripped the old German tycoon.

He was over-tired, of course. Not as young as he used to be. And even a strong, youthful man would find it impossible to experiment in the laboratory under such conditions.

He had been attempting to react carbon tetrachloride with hydrogen fluoride, intent on the creation of a nontoxic and non-flammable refrigerant. With a bark of frustration, he gave it up and stamped out of the chamber, along the corridor, and into his castle's *studiolo*.

He threw himself into a chair and slapped his hands down onto its arms, digging his fingers into the leather.

"Get the damnable noise over with," he moaned. "Let me think. Please... *please*."

He rested his head on the antimacassar and stared up at the stuffed crocodile suspended stomach-side up from the ceiling. Its glass eyes glared back at him, filled with a malevolence he had never previously noticed in them. He shuddered and looked away.

From the walls between the many bookcases, other eyes glittered; those of armadillos, anteaters, bats, owls, wild boars, flamingos, hawks, a plethora of rodents, and—over the door—a baby manatee.

All malicious and vengeful.

On his taxidermy workbench, a box brimmed with glass eyes—well over a thousand of them—and he imagined that, if he went over and peered into it, they would all align to stare back at him.

"You are losing your mind, Lothar," he told himself.

Overwrought and unable to settle, he sprang to his feet, stepped to the mantelpiece, and pressed a small button to summon his manservant, Schiller. He would have him mix a sleeping draught—a strong one.

Leichenberg paced up and down the Persian rug, which covered most of the flagstone floor, passed his desk, upon which he had arranged his paperwork in neat piles, then walked to the door. He threw a nervous glance up at the manatee.

He reached for the handle, then stopped and realised what he was doing. He had been about to call for his secretary, Bölling.

But Bölling had died last week—struck down by a completely unanticipated heart attack.

Leichenberg hesitated, muttered "Verdammt," and opened the door anyway.

"Schiller!" he bellowed into the hallway. "Where are you, man?"

If there was a response, it was lost beneath the booming drums.

"Schiller! Schiller! Herkommen!"

He waited for half a minute then gritted his teeth, wheeled, and strode back into the room, crossing to the carved teak cellarette. He kept a small selection of spirits for guests but was a teetotaller himself. Canada Dry Ginger Ale was his "tipple" of choice. He opened a bottle, filled a tumbler, and moved over to one of the two windows overlooking the great basin of Saint Dorian.

Reaching out his left hand, he placed it against the windowpane, which was vibrating, matching the pulse of the ghastly din. The peculiar topography of the island magnified the sound immensely. The drumming could be on his doorstep but was actually twenty miles distant. Yet, the basin shape of the land did not account for the indefinably different quality of the racket. He supposed that in Yucayeque—the shanty town on the border of the central swamp—the followers of voodoo must be dancing the wildest of deliriums.

He took a gulp of his drink, shuddered, and muttered, "Gott im Himmel."

Movement drew his attention to his refrigeration plant, a line of twelve white blocks, two miles distant down the slope, visible beneath the light of the full moon. One of his "cold trucks" was coming from it, up the road toward the castle, probably on its way into town. He watched as it passed the little runway he had commissioned to create an air route between Saint Dorian and Hayti.

The plant had taken three years to construct, along with the entirety of the fortune he had accrued from arms dealing during the Great War. From the moment it opened, the profit had been greater than he had ever anticipated.

He was now a wealthy man.

Of course, other inventors were experimenting with magnetic refrigeration. He would, in time, face competition. But he had been the first to perfect the technique, and the first to turn it into a commercial venture. He had a head start.

It had amused him to transform this obscure tropical island into the hub of such a business. "The Ice Lord of the Caribbean," they called him on Wall Street.

The truck passed out of sight. He thought he heard its brakes squeal, as if it was stopping at the castle, but that was impossible. It had no reason to halt here. Besides, such a sound could never have penetrated the interminable *boom badda boom badda boom badda boom!* of the drums.

"Why," Leichenberg muttered to himself, "is number nine still closed?"

Twelve weeks ago, the plant manager, a Swede named Max Hellander, had informed him that Unit 9 was faulty. It had been shut down for repairs ever since. Whenever Leichenberg enquired about it, Hellander made excuses. Repair teams had not shown up, parts need to be ordered and delivered, the initial assessment identified the wrong problem, it was fixed but must run for a week before it could be used—then it had failed again. One thing after another.

Bölling, shortly before so inconveniently dropping dead, had told him that his employees referred to it as "the cursed unit." They would not go near it.

Verdammt lächerlich, of course. Bloody ridiculous.

These islanders, the *Aramabuya*, as they called themselves, were a superstitious lot. It was inevitable with a name like that.

Aramabuya meant: *"the Ghost People."*

Leichenberg swallowed the rest of the ginger ale, returned to the cellarette, and left the empty glass on top of it. He walked over to his desk, picked up a folded newspaper, and opened it.

Dated the end of May. European papers normally took about a week to reach him. Its headlines concerned the *Wehrgesetz*, Hitler's new law banning Jews from the armed forces. Now, only "Aryans" were allowed to serve, and from October, such service would be compulsory.

Had anyone been present to witness Lothar Leichenberg's expression as he read through the article for the umpteenth time, they would have perhaps described it as "inscrutable."

He cursed and threw down the paper, pressed his palms against his ears again, and whispered, "For the love of God! Stop! Stop!"

The drums did not stop.

"Wo ist dieser Dummkopf, Schiller?"

Returning to the mantelpiece, he pressed the button over and over.

His manservant's rooms were just along the corridor. Surely, the idiot could not sleep through the voodoo drumming *and* the buzzing of his master's summons?

The Ice Lord stomped to the door, out into the passage, and along to Schiller's quarters. The man deserved a kick, and he was going to get it.

"Schiller!" he roared, hammering at the door. "Aufwachen! Wake up! I cannot work! I cannot sleep!"

He detected the odour of tobacco and was instantly furious.

"Mein Gott! You dare to smoke, you dog? Open up!"

Leichenberg detested tobacco. Pipes, cigarettes, and cigars were strictly prohibited in every part of his castle. Their fumes would damage his stuffed animals and his vast library. He would not have it.

"Ach!" he said, impatiently, and twisted the doorknob. The door was not locked.

Upon entering Schiller's parlour, he noticed first that his man was sitting wide-eyed and motionless in an armchair, and second that the odour was in the passage but not in the room.

"Schiller!" he barked.

There was no response.

"Schiller?"

He bent over the man, a stout Prussian, took him by the shoulder, and gave him a shake.

Schiller was awake—Leichenberg could see the life in his eyes—but appeared unable to move.

Leichenberg shook him more violently. He gently slapped his face. Again, harder.

The man stared fixedly.

There was nothing lying around to suggest that his strange condition was self-induced. His temperature was as it should be. His heartbeat was regular.

Leichenberg stood, fists on hips, looking down at the man and feeling bemused. He saw the button on the wall that operated a bell in the housekeeper's chambers. After pressing it, he decided to pour a glass of brandy into Schiller. The man, like all the staff, was a teetotaller— another of Leichenberg's rules—so perhaps the shock of it would jerk him back into motion.

Leichenberg left the room and hurried back to his *studiolo*.

The corridor stank of woody, pungent cigars. The reek was stronger than before.

Where was it coming from?

And still, the incessant drums growled and muttered.

As he entered the room and strode to the cellarette, the

clock on the mantelpiece creaked, whirred, and began to chime.

He poured the brandy and turned just as the twelfth chime sounded.

It was midnight.

The drums stopped.

As if by the click of a switch, silence fell, immense and appalling.

The Ice Lord froze.

For a second, he thought he was stricken with profound deafness. Then, he became aware of a single drum still thudding loudly, and it took a moment before he realised it was his heart.

"At last," he rasped, but it was a hollow exclamation. He felt terrified.

Why this should be, he could not fathom.

—until someone in the corridor chuckled.

He dropped the tumbler. It hit the carpet, brandy splashing, and rolled under the cellarette.

"Sch-Schiller?" he called.

A mocking voice replied, in a musical tone, "Scha-scha-Schiller?"

"Wer ist da?" he demanded, taking a step backward.

A plume of blue smoke billowed from the right-hand side of the doorframe, from the same direction as Schiller's rooms.

"Hey!" Leichenberg objected, his voice high and tremulous, his knees suddenly weak. "No smoking!"

There came a cackling laugh, and a black-sleeved arm stretched out, the hand gloved in white kidskin, an absurdly fat cigar lodged between the first two fingers. An inch of bare wrist showed, dark in hue and tinged a strange green.

"Ding!" a voice sang. "Dong!"

Compulsively, Leichenberg called, "Komm herein!"

The arm withdrew. Then a foot appeared, clad in a shiny shoe with a white spat, held comically high, the leg bent at a right angle.

In the silence, Leichenberg's breathing sounded like old bellows.

The leg straightened, the foot touched the floor, and a grinning face came sliding into view, its jaw against the doorframe.

"Hallooo!" it said.

The whole figure stepped into view.

Leichenberg said, "Nein," and collapsed onto his bottom, pushing himself back across the rug with the heels of his slippers.

A white painted skull adorned his visitor's dark, greenish face. Cotton plugs stuck out from the nostrils. The left eye was concealed by round sunglasses, the right lens of which was missing. The man—if it *was* a man— was attired in top hat and tails, with a necklace of finger bones swinging across his chest. The stupendous cigar smouldered in his right hand, and there was a large, full, unstoppered bottle of black rum in the left.

Leichenberg recognised the apparition from local legend.

Baron Samedi! The most powerful of the *lwa*—the voodoo spirits. The patron of the dead, of tombs and cemeteries.

"Weee, Lothar Leichenberg, the refrigeration tycoon," the ghoul said, his voice nasal, sardonic, and thickly accented, all singsong "ahh" and "ooh," "daa" and "dee"—the absolute opposite of the Ice Lord's own tightly clipped, precise tones.

Samedi took a big, exaggerated stride forward and held up his cigar. "Did I hear you object to my weed, man?"

Leichenberg panted, struggled to speak but could not. He attempted to get up, but his limbs would not move.

The baron grinned.

"No, no, master of the ice," he said. "You have to live a little before you die. You'll try some of this, now, eh?"

The baron put the cigar to his lips and sucked at it noisily. He took two great steps forward until he was looming over Leichenberg, then blew a noxious cloud into the German's face.

"Breathe deeply. That may be your last breath!"

Leichenberg coughed and managed to say, "Bitte, was—was willst du?"

Baron Samedi cackled. "What do I want?" He gave an exaggerated shrug. "Just for you to die in style, ice man. Do you want a little rum? It will warm you up."

Leichenberg shook his head and held out his hands, palms outward, blocking. He squeezed his eyes shut and whimpered.

Samedi raised the bottle and filled his mouth with the liquor, then leaned over Leichenberg and blew a fine spray all over him.

"Weee, man, that's strong stuff! Do you think it burns some?"

He upended the bottle over Leichenberg, pouring the dark spirit all over him, soaking his hair and clothes and the surrounding rug.

"Hey, now!" he exclaimed, examining the empty bottle. "You have left nothing for me!" He flipped it in the air, caught it by the neck, and swung it viciously into the side of Leichenberg's head.

The bottle did not break. Leichenberg's skull did. He hit the floor in a shower of blood.

Samedi peered at the bottle and exclaimed, "Oh! A sad waste. A sad waste."

He stepped back, placed his cigar between his teeth, held the bottle against his side with his arm, and pulled a box of matches from his pocket. He lit one and flicked it at the prone man.

Leichenberg burst into blue flames.

"The ice is melting now, eh?"

Baron Samedi stalked from the room, laughing, taking the empty bottle with him.

And the Ice Lord burned.

2

broken man

BAJACU CITY IS not a pretty sight. Sprawled across the east-facing slope of the highest of Saint Dorian's low, western mountains, it is a heterogenous pile of colourfully painted but dilapidated board houses, ugly brick residences, decaying colonial edifices, the modest and rather shabby "Royal Palace," shops, bustling bars, small plazas, narrow alleyways, and three ill-attended churches. The front of the short-lived cathedral still stands, the rest having collapsed—two years after completion—during the great earthquake of 1853.

A broad, palm-fringed boulevard cuts through Bajacu from north to south, dividing the higher westernmost districts—which are in a generally good state of repair—from the lower and poorer quarters. The southern end of the thoroughfare continues on out of the city and passes Leichenberg Castle, that one-decade-old, Renaissance-style monument to wealth and eccentricity. It then narrows and curves around the foot of the mountains to where a river, flowing from the central swamp, has eroded a wide valley through to the sea. Here lies the island's principal harbour, Bibibagua—"Mother Sea."

The northern end of the boulevard branches, on the left merging into the road that rings the island, and on the right curving sharply eastward and running on to the shanty town—Yucayeque—twenty miles distant. It then circles the swamp and continues across to the easternmost limits of the island, where a second river flows. At its mouth, a large fishing town hugs the shore.

Small settlements dot the inner slopes of the mountains, all—like the city—overlooking the great malodorous swamp, fifteen miles wide, which bubbles and steams in the dark heart of Saint Dorian.

Most of the cars and trucks on the island belong to the refrigeration plant. The population—approximately a hundred and eighty thousand—gets around by walking, by donkey, or by motorcycle, the latter of which is present in noisy profusion.

Sister Georgina Stark owned a 1929 Royal Enfield that she adored, and on which she sped from her board house just south of the city to her job at the Saint Dorian Royal Sanatorium in the north.

Constructed in 1912, ten years after Denmark sold the island to Germany, the sanatorium was on the bend where the boulevard divides. It was built as a prison—and looked like one, being a blocky and unattractive example of early modernist architecture—but never served that purpose. It stood empty until the island became a British protectorate in 1919, and was then converted for use as a hotel—a misconceived endeavour from the start, the Copenhagen Plaza in the city centre having long since cornered the meagre market.

Ten years ago, in 1925, a syndicate purchased the

building and refashioned it into a sanatorium—a very discreet one—for wealthy clients.

It was run by Doctor Sir Bartholomew Moxton, the eminent physician.

Stark had been in charge of the night shift for the past four weeks. Tomorrow she would have the day off work before then taking up the day shift.

Under the light of the full moon, she parked her motorcycle in the mews at the back of the building and turned off its engine. For a moment, she thought she had somehow fumbled it, the engine was still running, but no, it was those drums grumbling away as they had been since sunset.

"A high old time in Voodoo Town," she muttered to herself as she dismounted.

She crossed to the sanatorium's back entrance, went inside, ascended a staircase, made her way to her office, and there changed out of her overalls and into her uniform. She washed in a basin and tidied herself up in front of a mirror.

After smoothing down her dress, she left the office and commenced her rounds.

What were once prison cells were now, with some walls removed, well-appointed suites. There were twenty-four in total, sixteen of which were currently occupied.

All sixteen residents—referred to that way rather than as "patients"—were awake due to the noise.

"This bloody humidity doesn't help either," the man in Suite Four told her. "'Scuse the language, sister."

"Excused," she said, "because it's justified. But I assure you, the heat is much more oppressive outside than in. These thick walls are a blessing." She smiled. "Aside from the inconveniences, how have you been feeling today?"

"Marvellous," the man said.

He was a rich industrialist from Northern England, shell-shocked during the Great War and still not fully recovered all these years later. There had been occasions when the island's drumming, reminiscent of artillery fire, had sent him into a tailspin, and she had expected to find him a gibbering wreck tonight, the percussive performance being as intense as it was. But, on this occasion, he had somehow withstood the acoustic assault.

"Spa treatment!" he announced.

"Ah," she said. "The miraculous volcanic waters."

"They work wonders!"

The spa was an extension of the sanatorium, built over a hot spring during the misjudged hotel renovation.

"It appears they do," she agreed. "And I'm delighted to hear it. How does your—" she stopped, and exclaimed, "Oh!"

Abruptly, the drums had ceased.

They looked at each other, then he said, "Thank God!"

"On the dot of midnight," she observed after consulting her watch.

He stretched and yawned. "Now, perhaps I'll get some kip."

She left him and continued from suite to suite.

Odd, those drums, she thought. She had heard them many times since arriving at the island, but tonight there was something more ominous than usual about the rhythmic thudding.

She shook her head and continued her rounds.

The residents were fine, relatively speaking. Some were ill, of course—it being the reason they were there—but there had been no deteriorations since she last saw them.

The men in 8 and 15 interested her. Both were extremely well-off, and both were terminal. Trent had cancer, Keegan tuberculosis. "Those two," she muttered to herself as she passed the latter room, "require a miracle."

She made her way to Sir Bartholomew's office and knocked on the door.

"Come!" he called.

She entered.

He was at his desk, a distinguished-looking man, with a full beard, bushy eyebrows, and thick swept back hair, all pure white.

A single desk lamp provided illumination, leaving the room's corners wreathed in shadow, objects on shelves and furniture hardly discernible through a veil of tobacco smoke.

He removed a calabash pipe from his mouth. "Good evening, sister."

She returned the greeting and, at his gestured behest, sat in a chair opposite him.

"It has been a noisy evening," he noted. "How are they?"

He rarely visited the suites in person and, on average, received in his surgery just two or three residents per day, usually in the afternoons.

"They're settling down now," she responded. "None feels unduly disturbed, surprisingly enough."

"Glad to hear it." He put his pipe to his lips, drew smoke into his mouth, expelled it, and said, "Twelve."

She raised an eyebrow. "Doctor?"

"I have been reviewing our records today. In the eighteen months since you've been with us, twelve of our wealthiest guests have discharged themselves unexpectedly. Do you have any explanation?"

Now, both of her eyebrows went up.

"Are you accusing me of something?"

"Absolutely not," he said. "I have never received a single complaint about you. Quite the opposite. The gentlemen we care for appear to consider you the bee's knees. I simply wonder whether you have noticed anything."

"I'm afraid I haven't."

He grunted and puffed at his pipe.

"Perhaps, if another suggests he might want to depart, you could question as to why? Prudently, I mean."

"Certainly, doctor."

"Thank you. Now, to business. Let's make it quick. I'm tired, and I want to go to bed."

He pulled a manila folder from a drawer and, for the next half hour, they went through each patient, discussing matters relating to their condition and their treatment.

This done, the folder returned to its drawer, and his pipe finished but still in his right hand, Sir Bartholomew leaned back in his chair and scrutinised her for two silent minutes.

She sat motionless and endured it.

Finally, he spoke.

"The syndicate is losing patience. There has been precious little to show for your efforts."

She took a deep breath and let it out slowly. "It is a subtle process, doctor. It requires careful handling. Initial momentum must be imperceptible until it becomes unstoppable. Then, and only then, will the results become visible."

"The syndicate does not agree. They require a burning fuse. What they see is a damp squib."

She frowned and crossed her arms.

"With all due respect, doctor, I was hired for my

expertise. If the syndicate wishes to disregard my advice and bypass my methods, that is all well and good, but—"

"There is no but, Sister Georgina," he interjected. "You are in our employ, so you will do as we say. If not—" He paused. "Well, you were made aware when you joined us that leaving prematurely can be—shall we say?—hazardous."

Their eyes locked.

He was the first to look away.

"Lothar Leichenberg," he said.

"The Ice Lord? What of him?"

"During the Great War, he was an arms dealer—an arms dealer for both sides. It is about time he made reparations."

She was quiet for a moment, then: "And how might he do that?"

Sir Bartholomew grinned. "Why, by dying, of course."

She ran her tongue over her top lip and her nostrils flared a little.

"If you—" she began, but he jabbed his pipe's stem in her direction and snapped, "You have your orders. We want quick results, is that understood?"

"Yes," she answered, softly.

"Good. Dismissed. Go about your duties."

Her chair scraped as she stood. She turned and walked to the door. As she was reaching for the knob, he said, "Aren't you forgetting something?"

She stopped, slowly wheeled to face him, and raised her right hand.

"Heil Hitler."

"Heil Hitler," he replied.

* * *

THE NIGHT SHIFT was not difficult. Sister Georgina Stark made the various medicines ready for delivery with breakfast. She patrolled the corridors once every hour to check that all the residents were sleeping soundly, and for the rest of the time sat in her office in case any of them awoke and buzzed for attention.

In her spare minutes, of which there were many, she read *Mein Kampf*, hoping to gain some insight into the Austrian lunatic who was currently subverting history, symbols, fears, and prejudices to create his own warped mythology.

The book was, she thought, a tedious mishmash of thoroughly commonplace clichés, the vapid and vain product of an excruciatingly inadequate clown.

The chaos he was causing, however, might prove useful, and she thought that when she had concluded her business on Saint Dorian, she might make her way to Europe.

At two minutes to four, she rose and left her office.

The dimly lit corridors were as quiet as the grave.

She went down the stairs and passed through the ground floor to the back entrance.

She opened the door.

Hot, clammy air enveloped her.

In the courtyard between the sanatorium and the mews—a slab of silver moonlight bordered by jet black shadows—four figures were waiting, one of them carried by two of the others.

They came forward, and the lead figure, female, whispered, "Sister Georgina?"

"Yes," she responded in a low tone. "Right on time. Follow me, please."

She led them inside, along the main passage, and into a side corridor.

Of the sanatorium's twenty-four suites, eleven were on

the first floor and twelve on the second. Suite 13 was the only accommodation on the ground floor.

There was no logic behind the arrangement but plenty of theories, the dominant being that, back in the prison days, these particular cells were for "death row" inmates. When they were knocked into a single suite, it was numbered 13 to honour the luckless.

A cheery little tale, Stark thought, let down only by the fact that there were no "luckless," the prison never having held a single convict.

She opened the door to the suite, escorted her visitors in, and as the two laid their insensible burden onto the bed, she turned to face the leader.

The woman was spectacular.

Her age was impossible to determine. She might have been anywhere between twenty and forty. Her skin was tawny and unlined; her eyes heavy-lidded and as black as night; her nose straight and wide at the nostrils; her hair—also black—natural, neither plaited nor ironed, yet somehow supremely fashionable in such a way as to make Stark feel a twinge of envy.

There was, in her face, more than mere beauty; it possessed an ethereal force of expression, an occult power radiating from within that made her captivating, yet menacing.

Her figure, draped in yellow, was sinuous and perfectly proportioned, and though she was not as tall as Stark, she dominated her with ease, an experience to which the latter was so unaccustomed as to be rendered completely speechless.

The woman made a slight gesture with her left hand, and the two men, who had carried the other in, left the room, closing the door behind them.

"Look at him, please," the visitor said, her voice deep and exquisite.

Stark blinked, gasped—suddenly aware that she had been holding her breath—and turned to the man on the bed.

Thin rope bound his wrists and ankles. There was a gag over his mouth. His eyes were open, but glazed and unseeing. Mucous caked his nostrils.

He was well-built, burly, with broad shoulders and hard muscles. He sported an imperial beard and moustache, giving him the look of a gentleman. His clothes, however, were torn and soiled, and he reeked to high heaven.

She felt his pulse, looked into his eyes, and placed her palm on his forehead. Then she took hold of his shirt's left sleeve and ripped it from the cuff up to the elbow.

Needle-marks marred the length of his inner forearm.

"Heroin?" she asked.

"Yes," the woman answered.

"How long since his most recent dose?"

"Thirty-six hours, I think."

"And he has been an addict for—?"

"I do not know. Not long, but he went at it hard."

Stark let her gaze rest on the man for half a minute. She shook her head, doubtfully.

Her visitor said, "Already, just to see him, you have been generously paid. If you make him well, I will make you rich."

Stark faced the other. "His name?"

"Andrew Butterfield."

"Who is he?"

"That, you do not need to know. Can you treat him without anyone knowing?"

"Yes, no one uses this suite unless the others are all booked, which they aren't."

"Will you do it?"

After a slight hesitation, Stark answered, "Yes."

"Then take this."

The woman passed over a small bottle of brown liquid.

"A single drop in a tumbler of water every six hours," she said.

Stark nodded and pocketed it.

Then the woman extended her other hand and dropped three small hard objects into Stark's palm.

"There are plenty more where these came from. More than you could ever need. You would be wise to do as I request and keep your lips sealed. I will be in touch. Stay with him. I will see myself out."

She turned, opened the door, and departed.

Stark looked down at her hand.

She was holding three large diamonds.

3

isle of death

"WILL YOU BE a-wantin' your piffle hat?" asked Mrs. Bardell.

"Piffle hat?" queried Sexton Blake, the Baker Street detective.

"What you wears when you go a-gallivantin' in daftest Africky."

Tinker, the detective's young assistant, coughed and snorted.

"Piffle?" Blake repeated, in a bemused tone.

"Yus, them hats what's specially for erotic climbs."

Tinker's ailment spread to his lower ribs. He clutched at his side and collapsed from his chair to the consulting room's hearthrug —much to Pedro the bloodhound's annoyance, the rug being his domain.

Blake buckled shut the suitcase he had been packing and gave his malapropism-prone housekeeper a sidelong look.

"Pith helmet, perhaps?" he inquired.

"That's the one," she responded.

"Darkest Africa?"

"The very place."

"Exotic climes?"

"What I said, sir."

"No, I don't think we'll take them on this occasion."

"Well, you be careful not to get a burnt head," she cautioned. "You know you're a bit retarded around the widder's peak, if you don't mind me a-sayin' so, an' the sun can play the merry devil with a man's audacity to think if he gets too much of it."

"Don't worry, Mrs. B," Tinker interjected, his voice quavering. "I'll make sure he wears a knotted hanky on his head. How about the one with red polka dots that you gave him last Christmas?"

"Yus, it'd be nice if it had grateful employment, fer once," she observed rather haughtily.

The front doorbell sounded.

"Drat!" Blake exclaimed. "If that's a prospective client, direct them to one of the detective inspectors at Scotland Yard—Coutts, Harker or Martin. I can't take on anything new."

Mrs. Bardell nodded and departed.

"Are you going to roll around on the floor all morning or finish packing?" Blake asked his assistant.

"I was finished before you were shaved, guv'nor," Tinker retorted, clambering to his feet.

Pedro stood, too, and gave a prodigious yawn. He looked at Tinker expectantly.

"Go back to sleep, you great lump," Tinker told him. "Me getting up isn't a signal for a walk, you know."

Pedro, hearing the magic word, thumped his tail on the floor.

"Don't worry, our flight isn't until this afternoon, so

we'll have a quick spin around the park before lunch," the lad advised. "And good old Coutts has volunteered to take you out daily while we're away. You be sure to drag him along just as fast as you can, all right? He needs the exercise. The old fellow has been looking positively portly these past few months."

The door opened, and Mrs. Bardell announced, "Mr. Brain Canopy to see you, sir."

"Who?" asked Blake.

"Only me, Blake," said the newcomer, stepping past the old dame.

"Bryant Kennedy!" Blake exclaimed. "My dear chap, how the dickens are you?"

"Just fine." Kennedy smiled. He strode in and gave Blake a hearty handshake, and another for Tinker.

"A pot of coffee, if you please, Mrs. B," Blake requested.

She bobbed her head and exited with a muttered, "These bloomin' stairs'll be the death o' me."

"What are you doing on this side of the pond, Mr. Kennedy?" asked Tinker.

Kennedy was Blake's New York agent; a private detective in his own right, who also from time to time undertook work for the US intelligence agencies. He was a plain-looking fellow, well-spoken, with only a mild New York accent—the kind of individual who, once seen, was instantly forgotten, which in his line of business was distinctly advantageous.

"Following up a lead," he replied. "There's a rumour that Lucky Luciano's National Crime Syndicate is spreading its tentacles—that it wants to go international, starting here in London." He shrugged. "It's probably nothing, but I have to be certain. We don't want another Criminals' Confederation, do we?"

"Most certainly not," Blake agreed. He offered a cigar, which Kennedy accepted, and took one for himself. "How can we help?"

"You don't need to," said Kennedy, lighting up. "It's not why I'm here. I bumped into Detective Inspector Thomas last night at the Venetia Hotel. He told me about Rymer. Is it true?"

"Yes," said Blake. "Yes, I'm afraid it is."

"My God, the poor fellow!"

Kennedy glanced at Blake's desk, then paced over to it. A large and detailed map of the Caribbean had been unrolled on it, the corners weighted with an ashtray, a book, an ink bottle, and a small bust of Blake fashioned by Eric Parker, the renowned artist, back in '26.

"You're going after him?"

"I have to."

"Why?"

That was a difficult question to answer. Sexton Blake and Doctor Huxton Rymer had, for the most part, been bitter rivals ever since their paths first crossed in 1913.

Rymer was brilliant, especially in the field of medicine, and had won decorations from scientific bodies in every quarter. Then, at the very apex of his fame, he had suddenly and inexplicably disappeared.

It had fallen to Blake to discover that some peculiar kink in his mentality compelled this accomplished man to pursue a life of crime.

Before the Great War, Blake and Rymer had fought each other the world over. The doctor was an inveterate adventurer, drawn to exotic locales and committed to extracting from them whatever riches he could lay his hands on.

Blake had vowed to stop him.

That the man was at war with himself, the detective didn't doubt. Frequently, Rymer had resorted to the heavy use of drink and drugs, as if attempting to quell some inner demon, and it was astonishing to Blake that the criminal had somehow managed to avoid complete self-destruction.

The first indication that Rymer was not entirely irredeemable came in 1916, in a small field hospital in Nancy, France, where—in the guise of "Lieutenant Colonel de Loulay"—he had proven again his wonderful medical skills, working tirelessly to mend the hideous damage done to brave young men.

Undoubtedly, the experience affected him and calmed whatever devils drove him, for he was not heard of for five years, and when he eventually returned to England, it was to settle and apply himself single-mindedly to scientific endeavours.

Having negotiated a reprieve from the police, Rymer purchased an estate in Sussex—Abbey Towers—in which he fitted out a large laboratory. There he lived quietly, under the name Professor Andrew Butterfield, researching, inventing, contributing his superb intellect to scientific theory. There, too, he met the girl to whom he gave his heart, Mary Trent.

Like, however, attracts like.

It quickly became apparent that she shared his reckless love of adventure—and was just as lawless. They sailed close to the wind, those two, and over the subsequent years their transgressions were many, though never so serious as to land them in jail. Rymer had become more careful, more humane, and occasionally, he even extricated Blake from tricky situations.

And vice versa.

It could almost be said that an incipient friendship formed.

Blake became convinced, however, that the criminal itch was persistently digging at Rymer and eroding any hope of complete reformation. He feared the worst until, last year, came the wonderful news that Rymer and Mary Trent had married, and that she was carrying his child. This, the detective felt, would be the making of the man.

Fate, cruel and pitiless, had other ideas.

Two months ago, while Rymer was in Edinburgh to negotiate the purchase of an expensive item of scientific equipment, Mary had gone into premature labour.

She haemorrhaged.

In her final moments, she had held her newborn and named him "Huxton," after his father.

Rymer, convinced that, had he been present, he could have prevented her death, blamed himself.

He gave the child into the care of a couple he trusted then fled the country.

"Science, especially medical science, cannot afford to lose an intellect as incredible as his," Blake explained to Kennedy. "And I believe—I have always believed—that he is in essence a decent man. But he carries with him a strange darkness, and if that overwhelms him now, I fear he will be lost forever, as will all the remarkable and beneficial achievements of which he is capable."

"He has attempted to kill you on numerous occasions," Kennedy pointed out.

"And saved my life on others."

"Mine, too," Tinker put in.

With the cigar between his fingers, the American indicated the map. "You think he's in the Caribbean?"

"I do."

"Why?"

"Firstly, because he has frequented that part of the world more than any other, except for England. And secondly—" Blake drew on his cigar. "Because Marie Galante is there."

Kennedy was silent for a moment. Then he murmured, "Before Mary Trent came on the scene, Rymer and Galante—?"

"Yes," Blake confirmed. "She loved—*loves*—him with a passion, with jealous fury. In the past, she has drugged him, mesmerised him, held him prisoner, even shot him—anything to keep him."

"And after Trent?"

"I think Galante bided her time."

Kennedy frowned. "Meaning what?"

Sexton Blake walked around the desk and tapped a finger on the map, on the island of Hayti.

"You might think me a fool, Kennedy, but on this island, Galante is known as the Voodoo Queen. Tinker and I have seen—born witness with our bodies, in fact—that she possesses a power that can alter behaviour, affect health, and even kill from a distance. Call it the occult, if you will, or believe—as I do—that it is a concoction of powerful drugs and skilled hypnotism, but she is capable of things that our science has not yet been able to explain. It would not in the slightest bit surprise me if I were to learn that a voodoo curse was responsible for Mary Trent's tragic death."

Kennedy whistled. "Holy smoke! You reckon Doctor Rymer is out for revenge?"

"Maybe that," Blake said. "Or perhaps, weakened by his grief, he has succumbed to a mesmeric spell cast upon him some years ago—drawn to Hayti by the call of a siren, so to speak."

"Hmm," said Kennedy. "Maybe not Hayti."

They were interrupted by the arrival of Mrs. Bardell bearing a tray with a coffee pot, cups, a jug of milk, and a sugar bowl.

"An excavator!" she declared. "Them moving stairs like what they have in the underground stations. That's what we need."

She exited, taking Pedro with her.

Blake stood looking at his New York agent.

Tinker moved to the tray and quietly got to work.

"Kennedy?" Blake prompted.

The American leaned over the map and pressed his finger on a spot some distance north and a little east of Hayti.

"Here, I think," he said.

Blake bent and peered curiously at the indicated location. "What's there?"

"Strong tidal currents," Kennedy said, "and unfavourable prevailing winds."

"You mean unfavourable to shipping?"

"Yes, before the advent of steam."

"All right, and how is this patch of the Caribbean Sea significant?"

"It's not so much the sea," said Kennedy impassively. "More the island in it."

Sexton Blake blinked at Kennedy, then examined the map.

"It must be a very, very tiny one."

The New Yorker smiled. "About sixty-five miles across."

Tinker, who had re-joined them, said, "Impossible!"

"Because you've never seen it on any map, sonny?"

Tinker threw out his hands. "How could it be missed?"

Kennedy murmured, "Let's have that coffee."

He crossed to the saddleback armchair by the fireplace, the one he knew was reserved for Blake's clients. Blake occupied his chair on the opposite side of the hearth, and Tinker, after placing the steaming coffee cups on side tables, took a seat between the two.

"Let me tell you the history," Kennedy said, "of Death Island."

"I like the place already," Tinker commented.

"It was formed from the caldera of an ancient blown-out volcano. The coastline is forbidding, composed of high cliffs with only two points of access, both from river erosion. There are no beaches. Within the ring of mountains, the island is basin-shaped, its sides providing rich arable land on which the natives grow their various crops. The centre of the basin, however, is slightly below sea level, and is a malodorous swamp, in which plants grow that cannot be found anywhere else in the world. Most of them are extremely poisonous. Moreover, unlike Hayti, which has no venomous snakes, Death Island is teeming with them."

He dragged at his cigar, then sipped his coffee.

"The indigenous population was originally the same as in the rest of the Caribbean—the Taíno people—but this particular tribe, they were isolationists and hostile, killing on sight any visitors. They referred to themselves as the Aramabuya—the Ghost People—and their name for the island was Oubao-Bara: Island of Death."

"Guv'nor," murmured Tinker. "Shall we book a holiday?"

Kennedy gave a curt nod. "I dare say you shall, sonny. But hear me out."

"I wasn't—" Tinker began.

Kennedy talked over him:

"The Aramabuya were expert poisoners and, being constantly exposed to the island's plethora of toxins, they developed a strong resistance to them, which also caused a characteristic green tinge to their skin. The blood of an indigenous islander was itself, according to folklore, poisonous to any outsider."

"You are referring to them in the past tense," Blake noted. "What happened?"

"For a long time, nothing. While the neighbouring islands fell to the slave trade, pirates, and colonialists, the adverse sailing conditions kept Oubao-Bara fairly isolated. The poison darts that invariably showered upon any visitors helped, of course. In fact, the island was so dangerous that it became customary to leave it off maps. Even today, it remains absent from many."

"Including mine," said Blake, ruefully.

"It all changed in 1677," Kennedy went on. "A Danish vessel sent a boat ashore. The men aboard were immediately killed, bar one, who was captured and tortured. This was the first time the Aramabuya had taken a prisoner. What prompted them to do so is unknown, but it was their undoing. The man had smallpox, and the disease ravaged the island. When the Danes visited again, in 1692, the population had dwindled by an estimated seventy percent. Oubao-Bara was claimed by Denmark and renamed. It has since been known as Saint Dorian."

Blake said to Tinker, "Have a look at the index and an encyclopaedia, would you? Let's see if we have anything on it."

Tinker nodded and left the room. The Baker Street Index—that enormous compendium of newspaper cuttings and case notes—had become far too large for the consulting room and now occupied a chamber along the corridor.

"So, it was colonised?" Blake asked.

"Yes," Kennedy answered. "The first wave of settlers arrived and died. The subsequent arrivals fared better and were soon interbreeding with the natives. It has resulted in the oddest-looking people in the region, perhaps in the world. They are dark-skinned, with that green hue I mentioned, especially in their hair and fingernails. Blue eyes are not uncommon. There are even a few blondes among them."

"Does the island still have a Danish administration?" Blake asked.

"No," Kennedy said. "British."

Blake's eyebrows went up. "What?"

"Well, I say that, but it's a little more complicated. The first overseer was a Dane named Dandy Ostergaard. He arrived at Saint Dorian in 1744. Fourteen years later, he declared himself king, and established a rather eccentric monarchy, which still survives. The current monarch is Dandy Ostergaard the Third. He has some measure of administrative power—enough to make a difference—and is revered by the islanders."

He paused to imbibe, then continued:

"In 1902, Germany purchased the island, and a fair few Germans still live there. In 1919, as a part of war reparations, it became a British protectorate. The current administrator is a gentleman named David Woodbine. That brings us up to date."

He leaned back, returning his cigar to his mouth.

"What I'm wondering," Blake said, "is why you happen to know so much about the place."

Before Kennedy could respond, Tinker re-entered and

announced, "Nothing—except that the Saint Dorian flag is blue and yellow with the depiction of a hawk and the moon." He slumped into his chair, disconsolate. It was Tinker's job to maintain the index. He was never happy when it fell short.

"Cheer up," Blake told his assistant, "Kennedy is about to deliver a revelation."

"I'm all ears," said Tinker.

"It's the sea-facing cliffs," Kennedy said. "They are riddled with large, submerged caves, perfect for U-boat bases."

"Ha!" Blake exclaimed. "Germany wants it back."

"According to an unlikely but very credible source, yes. And the directors of US Intelligence are not happy. If U-boats start swarming around the Caribbean, American shipping will be disrupted, and the States could be dragged into a war."

Blake flicked his cigar butt into the fireplace.

"But you can't send agents there to assess the situation because it's British territory, right?"

"Right."

"I'm sorry, Kennedy. You want me to take up the case, that's plain, but I cannot do anything until I find Rymer and get him the help he needs."

"Blake," Kennedy said, "that source I mentioned—"

"Oh," the detective said, as the penny dropped. "It's—"

"Marie Galante."

4

green and blue

AT THE TOP of the low mountain, upon the side of which Bajacu City is untidily arranged, there is a small village. Like every other settlement on the island, it has a Danish name and a German name, but is always called by its Taíno name.

Guaraguao means "red-tailed hawk." It is a bird that breeds in profusion on the island, and the village is, perhaps, named after it because it occupies the highest peak. That does not, by any means, make it inaccessible, for the landward slopes are long and gradual and only in a few places notably steep.

Sister Georgina Stark drove to Guaraguao on her Royal Enfield, racing up the incline at top speed, swerving past the occasional potholes with the wind throwing her hair about and her heart hammering with the thrill of it.

She had only slept for three hours after finishing the night shift, but a small dose of amphetamines had driven away any vestiges of fatigue.

It was, she knew, a dangerous tango she was dancing

on Saint Dorian. At any moment, her Nazi patrons could turn on her and order her execution, or the contents of freezer Unit 9 might come to light, and her involvement be exposed.

The clock was ticking. It was time to wrap matters up and get clear of this godforsaken hole.

When she reached the odd, quiet little village—which resembled a disorganised pile of white blocks—she parked the bike in a corner of its small central square and made her way to a bar named Das Grün und Blau. This was due to the view from its terrace, with green land stretching away on one side and the blue sea scintillating far below on the other. More often than not, however, the sea was a deep emerald hue rather than blue, leading the bar to be nicknamed "Grün Grün."

Whatever the colours, the vista was incredible, and the bar was clean and attractive. The building was low, with a single barroom inside, fronted by big plate glass windows that opened onto the famous terrace. The latter had a waist-high decorative wall running around it, broken by two openings, one giving access to the road, the other, on the opposite side, to a sheer four-hundred-foot drop.

It had a slim stone arch over it, this latter opening, and formed a doorway which, according to the refridgeration plant manager, Max Hellander, was known to the voodooists—but to no one else—as the "Ascension Gate." Images of a vaguely Roman Catholic configuration decorated the stone, but vaguely menacing in appearance, as if taken from a church, and their original symbolism subverted. Talismans, suspended from the top of the arch on varying lengths of cord, formed a curtain.

The gate, according to local legend, was all that

remained of an old *humfo*—a voodoo temple—and was, in the past, used for ritual human sacrifice.

The notion that anyone stepping through it would "ascend" was, in truth, the opposite of what would happen, yet the gate was neither roped off nor in any other way blocked.

Such a lack of attention to public safety was typical of Erik von Bek, the proprietor. He was peculiar and unsociable, not at all the type who might be expected to own a bar or care about the wellbeing of its clientele. He was a man to whom unsavoury rumours clung, whose history no one could ever agree on, and who, in manner, was distant and inexpressive.

Von Bek did good business, but never until sundown. When it was dark, the voodoo crowd drank at Grün Grün. In daylight, no one.

That is why Stark preferred to meet Hellander there. At lunchtime, it was invariably open but empty.

He was waiting at a table on the terrace, a beer in front of him, and he stood stiffly when he saw her approaching. He was a tall, narrow, emaciated man, all elbows, knuckles, and knees, with yellow hair and eyelashes, a bent nose, almost colourless eyes, and skin that could not tolerate the tropics. As always, it was glowing red.

"It is good, no?" he said, as she took a seat, and he folded back into his own.

"You'll have to give me more than that, Max," she responded. "What is good?"

"The air. It is cooler up here." He waved a spidery hand vaguely landward. "I cannot bear it at this time of year. The humidity. The mosquitos. And last night, the drumming, drumming, constant drumming. These voodooists, they disgust me."

"You could always go back to Sweden."

"Ach! But business is business."

Von Bek approached, his face like a mask, his eyes never moving in their sockets, but fixed ahead, dry and lifeless.

"Was willst du?" he intoned slowly, staring at a point between and slightly above Stark's eyes.

"Daiquiri," she replied.

He jerked his head and shuffled away.

"I dislike that fellow," Hellander muttered.

"You don't like anybody."

"I like you."

"Don't start that again."

"But Georgina—"

"*Sister* Georgina—or Miss Stark. Never, ever *Georgina*. We are on first name terms in one direction only."

"If you would just consider for a minute—"

"No," she said firmly. "Not even for a minute."

He frowned and looked out at the distant horizon.

They did not speak again until von Bek had wordlessly and clumsily plonked her cocktail on the table in front of her, arriving and departing as if walking in his sleep.

She took a cigarette from her top pocket. She was attired in jodhpurs, a white blouse, a light jacket, and had pushed her motorcycling goggles up over her hair. She lit up.

Hellander watched her.

Stark inhaled tobacco fumes and blew a plume into the motionless atmosphere. The sky was an intense, unbroken azure. Briefly, she closed her eyes and felt the sun on her face. It was tranquil up here.

She wasn't sure she enjoyed quietness. It made her feel a stillness within, and in that stillness, an emptiness.

"We have a new customer," she said, returning her attention to her companion. "Godfrey James Keegan. English. He has tuberculosis. He also has something in the region of eight million pounds sterling from real estate."

"That is good," Hellander said. "But, under the circumstances, I wonder whether we should—"

"I'm running short of the serum," she interrupted. "Can you get more by tomorrow night?"

"Yes," he said. "I'll go to Yucayeque this evening."

She picked up her daiquiri and sipped, gave an "mmm" of approval, and put down the glass.

"Circumstances?"

"Well," he said, "you know, I can keep the plant running—but, at some point soon, it will either be sold or closed down. Did Herr Leichenberg have any family?"

"I don't know," she said. "What are you talking about?"

"Now that he is dead."

"What?"

Hellander squeezed his hands together. "I thought— that is to say— You don't know?"

She exhaled hard. "Max—"

"It happened last night. He was murdered in his castle."

For the second time in twenty-four hours, just as when the drumming had ceased, she experienced the sensation that time itself had halted—

—then clicked back into motion.

She swore with such intensity that Hellander's mouth fell open.

"How?" she snapped. "By whom?"

"He was burned to death. The killer got away without being seen."

"Do the police have a suspect?"

"Not as far as I know."

"Damnation!"

She struggled to make sense of it. Leichenberg had died the same night that Sir Bartholomew Moxton had instructed her to kill him! Maybe—

Could she claim the credit for it—and a bonus payment?

Would his death placate the syndicate?

For how long might she maintain the deception before being found out?

"Perhaps," Hellander murmured, "you and I could purchase the refrigeration plant ourselves?"

She snorted derisively. "Lose our gains and start all over? Don't be a bloody idiot! Be quiet and let me think."

She smoked and drank and gazed without focus into space, her brow creased, one leg crossed over the other, and the point of her boot tapping compulsively at the air.

Five minutes passed without a word spoken, then Hellander said softly, "I'm sorry, Miss Stark, but if I don't get back to the plant, I will be missed."

"Wait," she replied. "Listen to me. We will proceed as planned with Keegan. Bring me the serum tomorrow, and we'll do it the next day."

"Very well," he agreed.

"But there's something more. A couple of days ago, I received a note along with a thick wad of banknotes. It requested that I admit into the sanatorium a new resident—one who would fall under my care, his presence concealed from everyone else. He was brought to me in the early hours of this morning by a woman. He is an addict. Andrew Butterfield. Have you heard that name before?"

"No, not at all."

"The woman, she was—there was something strange about her. Something—powerful. She gave no name, but she was—"

Stark went on to describe the woman, doing so in detail, and as she talked, she saw that beneath his sun-scorched skin, the blood had drained from Hellander's face.

"God in heaven!" he exclaimed hoarsely. "I think that was Marie Galante!"

"Who is she?"

"The—she is the High Mambo."

Stark glanced past him at the Ascension Gate.

"High Mambo?"

"Voodoo Queen," Hellander clarified. "She is the daughter of a European crook and a Creole devil-woman. All those who practice voodoo follow her, and would die for her."

"Does she live here, on Saint Dorian?" Stark asked.

"No, Hayti is her home, but the swamp—" He gestured toward the island's distant centre. "It supplies the entire Caribbean with the toxins and hallucinogens used in voodoo practices, so she comes here often. I have also heard it whispered that—" He paused and regarded her with a slightly quizzical expression, "—that the source of her great wealth is somewhere on this island."

"How do you know all this?"

"Kaonati of the withered arm—the man who sells me the serum—likes to drink, and when he drinks, he talks. Everything I know about voodoo comes from him."

Stark picked up her glass and drained the last dregs, flicked away her cigarette stub, and reached into her trouser pocket.

She held out her hand.

"She gave me these."

Hellander gasped. "They—they are diamonds!"

"Yes, I know what they are, thank you. And she can afford to give them away. What more do you know about her fortune?"

"Nothing."

"Then find out. When you go for the serum tonight, take Mr. Withered Arm a bottle of rum—two bottles—whatever's required. Get him talking."

Hellander raised his hands in objection, his eyes widening.

"No!" he cried out. "No. To cross Galante—you don't understand what she can do. She won't just kill you—she will torture you for months—for years. Then she will take your soul."

"For goodness' sake, Max, let's not have any of that superstitious nonsense. Besides, when we get our hands on more of these—" She closed her fingers around the stones and shook them, "we can jump into your little monoplane and be in Florida before she knows we're gone. And from there to the other side of the world. How's she going to find us then, hey?"

"She has ways."

"Twaddle!"

"It is not. I have been among these people for a long time. I have seen—I have seen—"

Hellander suddenly jerked to his feet, his chair clattering backwards. His hands were trembling. "I must go. My motorbike is—" He strode rapidly away, not looking back.

"Find out!" she called after him. "Or I'll have your soul myself!"

For a long time after he had gone, she sat alone, deep in thought.

Von Bek came out onto the terrace and asked blankly, "Was willst du?"

"Nothing," she said, paid what was owed, and departed.

As she walked back through the village to her motorcycle, she murmured to herself, "Butterfield might be the key. I wonder what he means to her? I must find out. Who *is* that man in Room Thirteen?"

5

sign of the cat

ENGLAND TO FLORIDA, Florida to Cuba, Cuba to Hayti, Hayti to Saint Dorian—the journey was long and exhausting. By the time Sexton Blake and Tinker stepped into the hot embrace of the island, they were bleary-eyed, muggy-headed, and desperate for their beds.

A motorcycle-rickshaw took them up the hill and into town. They had insufficient energy for sightseeing, and in the fast-fading light of the tropical dusk they received only fragmentary impressions of the environment: palm trees, half-built houses, half-derelict houses, the big and ugly refrigeration plant, makeshift shops, colourfully attired people, music, shouts, barking dogs, braying donkeys, and the odours of coconut oil and grilled fish.

Blake sleepily noticed that the rickshaw motorcyclist had dark skin with a subtle hint of green, and he wondered what the Nazis, with their absurd myth of racial purity, would make of it. The thought amused him, but he was too tired to share it with his assistant.

They were dropped off at the Copenhagen Plaza

Hotel—a grand old colonial pile with balconies that, in Blake's estimation, were in such a condition as to be not worth the risk.

They booked in, dragged their feet up the stairs to their adjoining first floor rooms, and went straight to sleep.

IN THE MORNING, feeling much refreshed, they met in the breakfast room, and were served plantain porridge, poached eggs, herrings, and the strongest coffee either of them had tasted in a long while.

The staff were a heterogeneous lot, the darkest being as black as the coffee, the palest blue-eyed with hair almost as yellow as the egg yolk. Every shade in between was present, with a generous dash of green thrown in for good measure.

"Old Adolf would be blowing froth if he saw this," Tinker observed, echoing Blake's thought of the night before.

"Well," said Blake, in a wry tone, "it doesn't take much."

"What's the programme, guv'nor?"

"We'll pay a visit to Woodbine, the British administrator. He's expecting us. I dare say he will tell us what's what and who's who on the island. Maybe he knows the whereabouts of Marie Galante. It's conjecture, pure and simple, I'll admit, but I suspect that wherever we find her, we shall also find Rymer."

"But does he want to be found? That's the question."

Blake sighed. "I doubt the poor fellow knows what he wants. He has suffered a terrible loss. Depending on Galante's intentions, we may have to rescue him from her, but, more than that, we shall have to save him from himself."

"That may be easier said than done."

"Where Rymer is concerned, Tinker, when has anything ever been easy?"

They finished eating, returned to their rooms, and each slipped an automatic into a shoulder holster.

Both were smartly attired in cream-coloured light cotton suits, white shirts, Panama hats, and spectator shoes. Blake's jacket had a specially made large inner pocket into which he slid a flat case. It contained small, stoppered glass tubes, each an antidote for a particular type of toxin. Bryant Kennedy had recommended that he carry it.

After asking directions from the desk clerk, they left the hotel, and stepped out into ferocious heat.

"Phew!" Tinker exclaimed.

They were on the main boulevard, and made their way along it until they came to a junction, turned the corner, and proceeded up an incline.

It was just past nine in the morning, and the streets were clamorous and dusty, teeming with motorcycles, bicycles, rickshaws, pedestrians, occasional cars, donkeys, and mules.

Women, clad in loose and vividly coloured wraps, swung along with a grace bred into them over generations. Many carried great loads balanced upon their heads. They chattered and laughed together, flashing their eyes and teeth imperiously at the menfolk.

Of the latter, some responded by preening like parrots, others by slouching like whipped dogs, but most were notably gracious, standing aside for the women, greeting them cheerfully, and laughing when they were playfully mocked.

Twice, Blake and Tinker spotted a white-helmeted

police constable, the first a green-hued native, the second Germanic in appearance.

"There it is," Blake said, after they had walked for five minutes, and pointed ahead to a well-maintained, square white building, from the roof of which a Union Jack drooped on its pole like a furled umbrella.

It was the Saint Dorian Administrative Centre, and inside, beneath its cooling ceiling fans, they were greeted by a clerk and conducted to the office of the Right Honourable David Woodbine.

"I'm exceedingly happy to meet you, Mr. Blake," he announced as they stepped in. "You, too, Master Tinker!" He gripped them each by the hand. "Your reputation precedes you."

He was a big, solid man, built like a rugby player, sloppily dressed, and astoundingly ugly in the manner that women seem to find irresistible.

Blake smiled. "Thank you, Mr. Woodbine."

"Oh, please, drop the 'mister,'" Woodbine said, waving them into seats and taking his own behind his desk. "No need for formalities here. Can I offer you anything?"

"No," Blake said. "We're still digesting our breakfast."

"Ah! The ubiquitous plantain porridge, no doubt. Don't worry, you'll get used to it. Well, to business. I understand you have come looking for a gentleman named Huxton Rymer, also known as Andrew Butterfield?"

"Yes. Do you know if he's here?"

"Nope, not a clue. Never heard of the chap." He gave a hefty shrug. "I'm sorry, I know it's not what you wanted to hear. I have asked Tiburon to keep his eyes and ears open—but no, nothing."

"Tiburon?"

"The chief of police."

Woodbine leaned forward and rested his thick forearms on the desk, his fingers entwined.

"You know the history of the island?"

Blake nodded.

"The old Taíno people are long gone," Woodbine said, "but their descendants are plain to see—that bilious green look they have about 'em?"

"Yes," the detective responded, "we've noticed it."

"Those are the people I mean when I refer to natives," Woodbine said. "And Tiburon is a native."

"Does he have poison for blood?" asked Tinker, with a grin.

"Ha! So, you've heard that old folklore, have you? I don't know, youngster, but I'll tell you this: a couple of years ago, a German chap got too fresh with a native girl. She spat in his eye. The next morning, he couldn't see out of it. Permanent blindness."

"Good lord!" Blake exclaimed.

"But don't let that put you off. Whatever he might have in his veins, he's a good, reliable fellow, is Tiburon. The natives can be very fiery if you get on the wrong side of 'em—the hostility of their ancestors, you know?—but he's as steady as a rock."

Woodbine paused, frowned, then went on:

"Which brings me to that other matter—the U-boats and the sea caves. I was informed that a woman named Galante has warned that Hitler's Nasties are nosing around."

"That's so, and we are looking for her, as well," said Blake.

Woodbine nodded. "Her name's familiar enough to me, though I've never set eyes on her. If she's on Saint Dorian, you had best look for her in Yucayeque, the shanty town alongside the swamp. That's where all the voodoo happens, and if gossip can be believed, she is up to her neck in it."

He took a pipe from an ashtray on the desk and fiddled with it absently.

"There's definitely something afoot, Blake. There's a tension on Saint Dorian that I've not experienced in the ten years I've served here."

Blake said, "Expressed how?"

"In the voodoo. We have always had nightly drumming sessions from Yucayeque, while they chop off chicken heads, smear themselves with blood, dance themselves silly, and whatever else it is they do. But these past few weeks, they have been going at it hammer and tongs. And while I'm the last person in the world to give credence to the notion of spells, curses and what-have-you, that drumming has certainly coincided with an otherwise inexplicable eruption of anti-British sentiment. The king—Ostergaard—supports the British and has issued statements urging his people to stay calm, but I'm not convinced that even he can keep things from boiling over."

"Do you think Galante is right—that there are Nazi agitators at work?"

"I do, but I can't offer anything resembling evidence."

"What about the German population? Who among them is the most influential?"

"Was," Woodbine said. "Lothar Leichenberg. He built the magnetic refrigeration plant—that ugly white line of blocks by the airstrip, for which, incidentally, he was also responsible. He attracted a good deal of wealth to the island, raising the living standard here for everyone. A popular man, as you might imagine—known affectionately as the Ice Lord. Personally, I found him insufferable, but that's because he was a non-smoking teetotaller, whereas I am a pipe-chugging whisky guzzler." He grinned mischievously. "Nevertheless, I used to drop by his place now and again. He kept a few bottles for guests, including an excellent Glendronach Finest Highland Malt, which I was determined to polish off. He was an eccentric but sociable fellow, who liked to preach his disapproval of Hitler's mob to an audience. Four nights ago, he was burnt to death. It was not an accident."

"He was murdered?" Tinker exclaimed.

"Yes, lad, and the natives think the British are responsible."

"Why?" asked Blake.

Woodbine grunted. "Hmm, I think Tiburon might be the best person to answer that, what with him being one of 'em—a native, I mean."

He put down his pipe, frowned, and rubbed the side of his neck.

"I say, Blake, how about you take a look at the scene of the crime? I'd like your assessment. Time has passed, and the scent will be stale, so to speak, but I know all the British inhabitants of Saint Dorian, and there's not a single one of 'em I'd consider capable of a ghastly crime like that."

"In that case, yes," said the detective. "I'll certainly cast my eye over it."

"Immediately?"

Blake nodded.

Woodbine reached for his desk telephone. "I'll ring through to Tiburon and have him meet you there. Leichenberg was killed in his home, the hideous castle you'll find on the southern edge of town. You can't miss it, it sticks out like a sore thumb. Also, I have a car you can commandeer while you're with us." He jerked his chin toward the door. "Give me a moment while I make the call, then I'll take you to it."

Blake and Tinker stood, passed out of his office, and waited in the corridor.

"It could be the Nasties, as Woodbine calls 'em," said Tinker. "But that voodoo drumming has me wondering whether Marie Galante mightn't be playing a double game. It wouldn't be the first time she's stirred up trouble of this sort, would it?"

"Certainly not," Blake agreed. "But I'd wager her concern that Hitler might get a foothold in the Caribbean is as genuine as ours. For all the iniquities that Europe has heaped upon this region over the centuries, there are now at least some attempts to improve matters for the population. Imagine how that would change if the Sturmabteilung came marching through, bringing with them their misbegotten notions of racial purity?"

The office door opened, and Woodbine emerged. "All set," he said. "He's on his way there now. The car's out back. Follow me—"

He ushered them through the building to a courtyard at its rear, where he indicated a parked car and asked, "Will this do?"

"My hat!" Tinker exclaimed. "I should say so. A Duesenberg!"

"Model J," Woodbine confirmed, handing Blake the keys. "You know what they say about 'em: 'the only car that can pass a Duesenberg is another Duesenberg, and that's with the first owner's consent.' This beauty can take you from one side of Saint Dorian to the other in less than an hour."

"Are you sure you can spare it?" Blake asked.

"Yours for the duration, old boy. Pop by anytime you need anything. I'm always here. Good luck."

They thanked him, climbed into the vehicle, started the motor, and steered out onto the road.

"Now, let's see if we can squeeze this beast through all the motorbikes and donkeys without getting it dented," murmured Blake, with a despairing sigh.

He turned right, rather than left, going up the hill instead of back down to the boulevard, and the hunch paid off, for they soon came to a junction with a street that ran parallel with the main thoroughfare. It was narrower but much less crowded, and they were able to make steady, albeit slow, progress southward.

Up to their right, the Royal Palace overlooked the city. It was not particularly grand and, as Tinker now mentioned, looked to be in a state of some disrepair.

"Yet the roads are in good condition and the residential buildings along here appear quite new," Blake noted. "It seems that Herr Leichenberg's contributions to the economy have filtered down to the people rather than going to the elite."

"Mr. Woodbine's doing?" Tinker questioned.

"I should say so."

It took them twenty minutes to reach Leichenberg Castle—Bajacu City was bigger than it looked—though it was mainly because, as they drew closer to it, they were forced to navigate roads that were little more than alleyways.

Upon spotting the edifice, they both burst out laughing.

The Ice Lord had built for himself a renaissance-style stronghold so out of keeping with the environment that it looked positively absurd. A square block, with round, cone-topped towers at each corner, it was a squat mélange of columns, pediments, arches, pilasters, and lintels. Apparently assembled with grandiosity in mind, the architecture only served to bring the soundness of that mind into question.

"Obviously," Tinker declared, "he was as mad as a March hare."

Blake drew the Duesenberg to a halt before the castle's main entrance, by which a man in police uniform was waiting, his motorcycle parked beside him.

"Mr. Blake," he said, stepping forward, as the detective and his assistant got out of the car. "I am Police Chief Tiburon."

In appearance, he was extraordinary—tall and muscular, with dark skin, unmistakably green. His eyes were bright blue and set wide, and his long straight hair—down past his shoulders—was very blond. He wore a holstered pistol at his hip, and rather than the peaked cap that was surely a part of his uniform, had on a battered straw hat.

When he smiled, as he did now, he exposed upper and lower canines that were overly long.

"Come in," he said, after introductions. "Herr Leichenberg's manservant and housekeeper are still here. I have not permitted them anywhere near the crime scene, of course. The victim's remains are in the morgue, but aside from their removal, the room is exactly as it was found."

They followed him through the castle's big square entrance hall, along the main passageway, past the manservant's quarters, and to the dead man's *studiolo*.

Stuffed animals were everywhere—mounted on the walls, suspended from the ceilings, on pedestals, and in display cases. Books, too, filled the castle by the thousands, shelf after shelf.

When they reached the murder scene, they stopped outside the open door.

"I responded to the summons at just after nine o'clock in the morning," Tiburon said. "Both servants told the same story. During the late evening, they were in their rooms. They became aware of a sweet scent, then became completely paralysed. They were still conscious but were unable to move a muscle until about half past eight in the morning."

"Drugged?" asked Blake.

"It looks that way. When he was able, Schiller, the manservant, came looking for his master. He discovered the charred corpse there—" Tiburon pointed to a big black patch on the Persian rug. "He immediately put through a call to me. He has a theory."

Blake raised an eyebrow. "Oh yes?"

"There was a lot of drumming from Yucayeque that night. Schiller reckons the voodoo priests caused Leichenberg to spontaneously combust."

"And what do you think?"

"That someone drenched him with strong rum and put a match to him. You can smell the liquor in the rug."

Blake peered briefly at something on the doorframe, then stepped into the room and began to explore.

After a few minutes, he asked, a little distractedly, "Do you have a suspect?"

"Not specifically," Tiburon answered, "but I found this in the corridor just outside this room."

He drew a small cardboard box from his pocket and opened it, holding it out for Blake to see.

"A half-smoked cigarette," the detective observed.

"Yes," said Tiburon. "But Leichenberg didn't allow smoking anywhere in the castle. He was very strict about it; fanatical, even. Yet here we have a cigarette."

"Hmm," Blake said. "It belonged to the killer?"

"Who else? And look, just below the cork tip, there is the tiny image of a black cat."

His eyes met Blake's and held them.

"Black Cat cigarettes are a British brand."

6

to live forever

"Do you understand, Mr. Keegan, what you will have to do every forty years or so?"

Godfrey James Keegan croaked, "Yes," winced, and held a fist to his chest.

"It may be very complicated to alter your identity so completely and so frequently," Sister Georgina said. "But it will be essential."

He signalled his understanding with a gesture.

She leaned over him—he was sitting on his bed—and placed a hand gently on his shoulder. "And don't forget, you will lose loved ones. You will watch them grow old and die. Immortality might turn out to be more a curse than a blessing."

"I can always shoot myself," he said, his voice wheezing.

"That will be an option, of course, but let us hope you never feel the need to resort to it. Better to adapt and prosper." She turned and sat beside him. "You have no reservations?"

"None."

She could practically hear the tuberculosis chewing at his lungs.

"But," he said, "just go through the process one more time."

"It is very straightforward." She reached into her uniform pocket and pulled out a vial of clear liquid. "This serum is filtered from the mixture of plant compounds that the voodoo priests use to turn men and women into zombies. Essentially, it will put you into deep hibernation. Your organs will slow almost to a complete stop. If examined, you will appear to be dead. You will cease to age, and while you are thus suspended, you will gradually heal. I will place you into one of Herr Leichenberg's ice units, set aside for the purpose."

"He knew?"

"He knows."

"But I heard that he had—" A fit of coughing interrupted him. He put a handkerchief to his mouth, and when he lowered it, it was spotted with blood. "One of the other nurses told me he was murdered."

"Herr Leichenberg has received the treatment himself, Mr. Keegan. He is already immortal. It is he who finances this whole wonderful endeavour. We faked his death. He has now taken on a new identity to throw off suspicion."

"Ah."

"If we were to make the process public, everyone would clamour for it, and then where would we be? No, sir, this treatment is—how shall I put it?—*exclusive.*"

He nodded his understanding, and murmured, "You will freeze me?"

"Yes. You will be preserved until restored to full health. The serum will keep you alive. You will not be conscious. It will be like going to sleep. And, I should add, you will wake up very wealthy, for think how your investments will have matured in the interval!"

She noted, with satisfaction, the glint of greed that flickered in his eyes. Then his brow furrowed.

"After I am wakened, I will begin to age again?"

"Yes, of course, but the contract is for repeat treatments, as and when necessary, in perpetuity."

He moistened his cracked lips with his tongue, then gave a slight nod. "All right. I am ready."

"In that case, let us get the paperwork out of the way."

She stood, gave him assistance to do the same, then held his arm as he crossed unsteadily to his desk. After lowering him into the chair, she set three pieces of paper before him.

"You need to sign these, Mr. Keegan. The first is a letter to Sir Bartholomew in which you explain that you have decided to discharge yourself from his care. The second is a cheque for him that covers the period you have been with us. The third is also a cheque, made out to me, which is to pay for your immortality treatment."

"Two million," he said, hoarsely.

"By the time you wake up, I daresay you will have recouped that amount many times over."

He put his signature in the required places.

"Now," she said. "Back to bed with you."

After helping him to lie down, she rolled up his pyjama sleeve, exposing his left forearm. She then took a syringe from her pocket, opened the vial, and injected him with the serum.

"It is very potent, very fast acting. In less than five minutes, you will enter a state of suspension. I'll sit with you, and when you are fully under, I shall call my colleague, and we will transport you to the ice unit." She placed her hand over his. "Night-night, my dear. And goodbye. I should think I will be long dead by the time you awaken."

"Thank you, Sister Georgina," he rasped. "I shall never forget you."

He closed his eyes and waited, and gradually his breathing became slow and shallow—then stopped.

She felt for his pulse, but there was none to feel. She bent and put her ear to his chest. His heart was still.

"Excellent," she said. "You can open your eyes now, Keegan."

He did, and they were dull and empty, like those of a corpse.

"Get up," she instructed. "Put on your slippers and dressing gown."

Slowly and clumsily, he did as he was told, then stood, face slack, arms hanging limply.

She went to his desk, addressing him over her shoulder.

"I must apologise, Keegan. There is an effect of the serum that I neglected to mention. It causes absolute susceptibility to suggestion. You now have no will of your own. For example, you will not show one iota of resistance when I say to you: 'come over here, write another cheque for a million in sterling, make it out to me, date it a month hence, and sign it.'"

He dragged his feet over, slumped into the chair, and did everything she command.

"Hmm. Why not?" she mused. "Since you may be the last. Yes. Another one, please. Same amount, dated two months from now."

He wrote, a line of drool oozing from his lower lip.

When he was done, she pocketed the cheques, and murmured, "Follow me."

She led him out of his suite. He shuffled along, utterly devoid of expression, with no volition of his own.

When they encountered another of the sanatorium's sisters, Stark signalled her to silence, and whispered, "He's in a bad way today, Clarice. The medication, you know."

The other scrutinised him and, under her breath, replied, "Is there anything I can do?"

"No, it's all right. I'm giving him some exercise to get the blood flowing. He doesn't want bedsores, does he? I shall take him back in a minute."

The girl nodded and went on her way.

Stark led Keegan down the stairs and to the same back door where she had met Galante four nights ago. She opened it and squinted into the mid-afternoon sunshine.

She saw one of the refrigeration plant's covered trucks at the side of the road nearby. Hellander was standing beside it. He saw her, moved to the back of the vehicle, and opened the rear door.

Stark lifted a coat from a hook where she had hung it earlier in the day.

"Put this on over your gown," she ordered.

Keegan struggled into it.

"Now, walk to the back of that truck and get inside. The man there will give you further instructions when you reach your destination."

He staggered off.

She gave Hellander a thumbs up, then closed the door and rubbed her hands together. "In broad daylight, too," she muttered, delighted with the audacity of it. "Now for the mysterious Mr. Butterfield."

She made her way to suite 13.

He was as she had last left him, bound to his bed's frame by wrists and ankles.

He rolled his head to stare glassily at her.

"Good afternoon," she said. "How are we feeling today?"

He said, "*Mmmph!*"

"I'll remove the gag, but if you start a ruckus, it will go straight back on again."

"*Mmm-mmph!*"

"You are drenched in sweat," she observed, as she got to work on the knot. "But your colour has improved. Whatever that stuff I'm giving you is, it's certainly doing the trick, and fast. There, that's better. I expect you're thirsty."

"Yes," he said, his eyes coming into focus, his voice a throaty whisper. "Who are you?"

She strode over to a table, on which there stood a carafe of water and a couple of tumblers. She filled one, and took from a drawer the little bottle Galante had given her.

"I'm the same person I was the last time you asked," she said, unscrewing the top. "And the time before that." She carefully tipped it and allowed a single drop to fall. "And, indeed, the time before that." Closing and putting away the bottle, she took a teaspoon from a tray and stirred the water. "I am Sister Georgina Stark. Here, let me help you."

Moving back to him, she slid her right hand under his head, lifted it, and with her left, put the tumbler to his lips. He gulped at it, gasped, then turned his chin away.

She lowered his head back to the damp pillow.

"How many times," he said, his voice stronger, "have I asked where I am?"

"That's the first. You are definitely on the mend! This place is the Saint Dorian Royal Sanatorium, and you are enjoying all the consequences of a short but committed enthusiasm for heroin."

He groaned. "I remember."

"Well, that's good."

"No," he growled. "It isn't. How did I get here?"

She ignored the question, and said, "Here's what we're going to do. I am going to untie your left ankle and left wrist, so you can wriggle about enough for me to get those nasty sheets out from under you and put on some clean ones. I shall also clean you up. If you, at any point, attempt to use your free hand to untie the other, I will jump back to this table, and pick up this carafe. I will then hit you over the head with it so hard you'll be seeing stars until next Tuesday."

He blinked at her, let a few seconds pass, then asked:

"What's today?"

"Wednesday."

"You're a very unusual sort of nurse."

"You don't know the half of it."

She got to work on his bindings.

After a moment, he murmured, "So?"

"A woman brought you."

"What woman?"

"Marie Galante."

He said nothing, and when she glanced from his bound wrist to his face, she saw that it was red and contorted with rage, eyes blazing, the tendons standing out on his neck.

She stepped away.

"Mr. Butterfield?"

"You've got to get me out of here!" he suddenly bellowed. He struggled wildly, kicking out the leg she had loosed. "For god's sake, untie me. I have to get away.

Come on, girl! Now!"

Stepping to the table, she reached for the carafe, and said again, in a warning tone, "Mr. Butterfield."

He strained, thrashed, and gnashed his teeth.

"Damn you!" he roared.

She gave up on the bottle, plunged her hand into her uniform, and yanked out a revolver.

She pointed it at his head.

"This place was once a prison. It has very thick walls and doors. I could put a bullet in you, and no one would hear the shot. So, shut up—or I'll do it."

He glared furiously at her.

"Now then," she said, "you had better explain exactly what is going on between you and this so-called Voodoo Queen. Or, if you prefer, you can lie there in your own filth until she returns to fetch you."

The veins were pulsating on his forehead but, gradually, her gun barrel, aimed unwaveringly at his right eye, lessened his wrath, and he was able to snarl, "She killed my wife, and I'm going to kill her."

Sister Georgina drew her brows together.

"Why did she do that?"

"Because she loves me. The accursed witch loves me. Obsessively. She'll not see me with anyone else. Mary was—" His voice suddenly broke and tears filled his eyes. He turned his face away from her. "Oh, God! Oh, God help me! Galante is a praying mantis, a monster. I'll never escape her. She won't ever leave me alone. She comes to me in my dreams. Nightmares! Drawing me to her, never letting up. I cannot— My poor Mary—my poor—"

He gave way to helpless sobs, and the bed shook under him.

Slowly, she lowered the gun, then left it on the table and went to sit beside him.

"Who are you?" she asked softly.

"Rymer," he whispered. "My name is Huxton Rymer. I am a doctor."

"I'm pleased to meet you, Doctor Rymer," she said. "And now, I will tell you my real name, and let that be a bond of trust between us. I believe we can be very useful to each other, so let's begin at once."

She gave him a broad smile, displaying the wide gap between her top front incisors.

"My name is Violet Damm."

7

toxin for tinker

AFTER EXAMINING THE scene of Lothar Leichenberg's murder, Sexton Blake and Tinker said goodbye to Police Chief Tiburon and drove out of the city, intending to spend the afternoon touring the island to get the lay of the land.

"Black Cat cigarettes," said Tinker, as they left the southernmost buildings behind them, "are manufactured in Britain, but they are smoked all over Europe."

"They are," agreed Blake, manoeuvring the Duesenberg past a flatbed truck loaded with building materials. "Including Germany."

"It seems to me, then, that Tiburon has put all his eggs into one rather dubious basket. And I wouldn't be at all surprised if that cigarette was planted."

"To cast suspicion on the British?"

"Exactly so, guv'nor. But no Englishman would commit a murder like that. It's too horrible."

Blake pursed his lips. "Are you suggesting that some murders are better than others?"

"Well," Tinker said, "maybe not better, but certainly cleaner."

Blake grunted in agreement. "I take your point, though I consider it dubious at best. You and I have seen plenty of foul deeds committed by fellow countrymen, have we not?" He was quiet for a moment, then added, "Did you happen to notice that, despite the stench of the fire, the corridor reeked not of Black Cat cigarettes, but of particularly pungent cigar tobacco?"

"I did," said Tinker. "Furthermore, I found a shred of it on the floor farther along the corridor, near Leichenberg's laboratory. To judge by the curve of it, the cigar in question was preposterously fat."

"You kept it, of course."

"In an envelope in my pocket."

"Good lad. I'll have a look at it later."

Bajacu faded into the heat haze behind them. They were now driving through open land, which rose to the peaks on their right, and formed a long and increasingly shallow slope to their left. Farms were much in evidence—coffee, corn, banana, and plantain—and livestock could be seen in pens or roaming free, mostly goats and pigs.

"It is rather curious," Blake said, "that in a household which strictly prohibits smoking and limits drinking to guests—of which there were none—there should be so much evidence of both activities."

"I'm not convinced anyone drank the rum, guv'nor."

"No, but someone dropped a tumbler of brandy. I found it under the cellarette."

"My hat! It sounds like Leichenberg was having a regular shindig."

"Perhaps a costume party."

Tinker looked at him. "Why do you say that?"

"The most peculiar item of evidence of them all, young 'un! There was white greasepaint on the doorjamb. A clear imprint of someone's jawline. The housekeeper swore it wasn't there before her master's death."

Tinker furrowed his brow, thought hard, but could form no theory.

They turned their attention to the island.

The harbour, they found to be noisy and industrious, with busy docks on its western side and a marina to the east. It was considerably more Caribbean in character than Bajacu, with a greater prevalence of people of African ancestry, and much shouting in English, Danish, German, French, and Spanish.

It felt like exactly what it was: the point that tethered obscure little Saint Dorian to the rest of the world.

By contrast, the swamp—which they visited next, and which Tinker dubbed "the Devil's Stinkpot"—was the island's primordial heart. When they drove alongside it, they found that it discharged such a fusion of pungent, flowery odours that their senses began to reel, and Blake lost confidence in his ability to steer.

He took—a little clumsily—the first outward-bound turning they came to and accelerated up into the fresher air of the mountains.

"No wonder they practice voodoo in the shanty town," he murmured. "They must exist in a permanent scent-induced hallucination, thinking themselves in a world where mad gods and amulets dictate the course of their lives."

Tinker shuddered.

They sped on to the fishing town on the east coast—large, tranquil, but inhabited by a sullen, unwelcoming, and exceptionally green-skinned populace, all adorned with facial tattoos. They then circled the northern parts of the island anticlockwise, passing towns and villages, some of the smallest consisting only of *caney*—the old Taíno roundhouses. From these, people emerged to gape in bewilderment at the Duesenberg, the like of which they had apparently never seen.

It was late afternoon when Bajacu came back into view, and though the sun was still above the mountain peaks, the city—being on the east-facing slopes—was already falling into shadow.

They swept into its northern outskirts, and Blake eased pressure on the accelerator as traffic closed around the car.

Their road joined the boulevard, and they passed the prison-like building signposted "Saint Dorian Royal Sanatorium."

As they did so, a big Royal Enfield came roaring out of its driveway, swerved, and accelerated past them. Tinker, an ardent motorcycle enthusiast, turned his head, and saw that it was being driven by a tall, athletic young woman, her features concealed behind goggles. A man, riding pillion, looked back at him, and their eyes locked.

"Rymer!" Tinker yelled, as the machine shot into the traffic ahead. "Guv'nor! Rymer's on the back of that bike!"

Blake instantly put his foot down, but where the bike could—and did—weave between the traffic, the big Duesenberg was blocked from the outset, almost colliding with a donkey-drawn wagon piled high with watermelons.

"He's getting away," Tinker cried out, frustrated.

"Let him," said Blake. "There's nothing we can do. Except—" He jerked the car into a spot suitable for parking and drew to a stop. "We saw where that motorcycle came from—and that's where we're going."

Locking the car, they walked back along the road.

"Phew!" Tinker exclaimed. "Fancy spotting him on our very first day here."

"Did he see you, young 'un?"

"We looked each other full in the face! He recognised me, no doubt about it."

They came to the sanatorium.

"A rather unprepossessing place," Blake observed, but when they passed through the front door, they found themselves in a smart and plush lobby.

A receptionist—a young British woman—greeted them, and Blake nodded at the portrait of a white-haired, bearded gentleman hanging on the wall behind her.

"Sir Bartholomew Moxton," he read aloud from the brass plaque beneath the painting. And, ignoring the long line of qualifications following the name, added, "Director. Is he available, perchance?"

"I am afraid not, sir," she answered. "He conducts his surgeries during the afternoons."

"Maybe you could help me, then." He gave his most charming smile. "I'm searching for a man named Andrew Butterfield."

"I'm sure there is no one of that name here, sir. Neither on the staff nor as a resident."

"What about Huxton Rymer—or perhaps a good-looking fellow with an imperial beard?"

She shook her head.

"All right—one more try," he said, with a grin. "A young lady who rides a big motorcycle."

"Ah," she responded. "That will be Sister Georgina."

"Where might I find her?"

"I am not permitted to give out home addresses, sir—you understand—but she will be here tomorrow, from nine o'clock."

"Sir Bartholomew, too?"

"Yes, he's always here by then. Would you like an appointment?"

"I would."

"Nine, tomorrow, then. Your name?"

"I'm Sexton Blake."

On the way back to the car, Tinker said, "Rymer will probably do a flit now he knows we're snooping around."

"Possibly," Blake responded. "It depends on why he is here and what condition he is in."

They got into the car.

"Let's get back to the hotel to freshen up and have dinner," said Blake. "Then we shall see what Woodbine can tell us about this Moxton fellow and his sanatorium."

They resumed their drive back to the Copenhagen Plaza. The sky was purpling by the time they reached it. They left the Duesenberg in the parking space at the rear of the hotel and made their way to the first floor.

"Come sit with me for a few minutes," Blake said, indicating his door. "We should sketch out a map of the island while our tour is still fresh in our memory. I want to examine that strand of tobacco, as well. You know how often the brand of a—"

He had unlocked the door and now pushed it open. A small click sounded and at the same moment Tinker barged sideways into him.

"What the—!" Blake cried out, almost knocked off his feet.

"Booby-trap!" Tinker gasped.

Blake recovered his balance and looked into the room.

He saw a thin wire stretching from the inner door handle across to a chair, upon which was affixed a crossbow-like device.

"What did it shoot?"

"A dart."

The detective moved past his assistant, stepped into the room, and ran his eyes over the doorframe and the surrounding wall.

"Where?"

"Here," said Tinker, and pointed at his own chest.

Blake's jaw clenched. He crossed to a table and dragged a chair from it, placing it beside the door. "Sit down and stay absolutely still. Keep your breathing slow and shallow."

Tinker, moving carefully, lowered himself onto the seat.

Three inches of a needle-like dart with feathered flights was sticking out of his jacket's lapel, over the right side of his chest.

Blake peered at it. "Has it gone through to the skin?"

"Oh, yes, definitely," said Tinker. "And I can feel my chest muscles tightening up already."

"You confounded young idiot! Pushing me aside like that!"

Gingerly, Blake took hold of the end of the dart and pulled it out. It was four inches long and smeared with a sticky-looking red paste. He sniffed at it, clicked his tongue, and murmured, "Organic, but I can say nothing more than that."

"Look, guv'nor." Tinker jerked his head slightly to the right.

Blake turned in the direction indicated and saw, painted upon the wall, a large black swastika.

He reached into his jacket and pulled out the flat case he had been carrying since their arrival on the island, opened it, and ran his forefinger over the glass test tubes within.

"Maybe this," he muttered, and extracted one that was filled with a white liquid. He pulled out the stopper and held the tube to Tinker's mouth. "Drink it down, young 'un."

Tinker did so.

"Yuck."

"I hope it'll slow the effects," the detective said. "But your pupils are dilating already. I can see no option. We are going to have to find her—and find her fast!"

"Find who?"

"Marie Galante."

"Surely, a doctor—"

"*I'm* a qualified doctor! Have you forgotten? But, no— on this island, with its surfeit of toxins, there is only one person who—"

He stopped talking. There was no time to spare.

Taking an envelope from a bureau, he dropped the dart into it and slipped it into his jacket pocket. He strode back to Tinker.

"You're not to move a muscle, young 'un. So—"

He bent and hoisted his assistant up in a fireman's lift. Then he left the room, pulling the door shut behind him, ran along the corridor, and descended the stairs. Guests and staff gaped in open amazement as he raced through the hotel and out to the car.

The drive through Bajacu was so agonisingly slow—the streets teeming with people—that, at one point, Blake slapped his hand against the steering wheel in frustration, something that Tinker, in all their years together, had never seen him do.

Then they got out onto the Yucayeque road, and the detective slammed his foot right down. The Duesenberg roared and surged forward.

"Symptoms?"

"Chest feels constricted. Breathing is a bit laboured. I have a ringing in my ears. Why should she help, guv'nor? She has a long list of grudges against us."

"True, but we appear to be working for a common purpose. Let us hope she can suspend her antipathy at least until Saint Dorian is safe from the Nazi threat."

"Don't count on it."

"We have no other choice."

Night had fallen, and the sky was bright with stars.

The car tore along, dust billowing behind it.

Tinker's respiration slowed and began to creak and wheeze. His head drooped forward.

Blake forced every last ounce of speed out of the car, careless of the irregularities in the road's surface, allowing the chassis to take the punishment. He would replace the vehicle ten times over if it would only get him to the shanty town in time to save his loyal and capable assistant.

If Marie Galante was there.

If she was willing.

If she had an antidote.

"Tinker?" he said.

There was no reply. The lad was unconscious.

At last, far ahead, he saw the lights of the town.

The main voodoo temple—the *humfo*—would most likely be located in a central district, and, if it followed the Haytian model, would consist of a roofed-over dancing court with a carved centre-post rising out of a stone altar. There would be buildings circling the area, with rooms opening onto it.

The drums led him straight to it.

They commenced at exactly the moment he sped past the town's outermost shacks.

The streets were empty, and nothing slowed his progress. It was as if they knew he was coming.

He slowed, allowing his ears to guide him.

The streets were of hard-packed dried mud. No building exceeded two storeys in height, and even in the moonlight he could see they were all painted in bright primary and secondary colours. He glimpsed talismans dangling from veranda roofs, and symbols painted on walls and doors.

Then, the roads became too narrow for the car. He stopped, heaved Tinker onto his shoulder, and continued at a run, through tightening alleyways, the deep, throbbing rhythms drawing him on, his assistant as still and heavy as a corpse.

"Galante!" he yelled. "Marie Galante!"

He heard someone laugh.

A trumpet sounded nearby—one discordant note.

"Marie Galante!"

Seemingly out of nowhere, a crowd materialised, swarming from doorways, windows, and side streets, surrounding him, buffeting him this way and that.

"Wait!" he cried out. "Listen to me—"

Someone shoved a handful of leaves into his face. Earthy, overpowering odours flooded into his nostrils, made his eyes water, and instantly dried the back of his throat. His senses swam and his knees buckled.

Tinker was hauled from his grasp.

Blake was grabbed, borne aloft, and sent careening from hand to hand, the drums in his ears, the stars in his eyes, his head spinning. The perfumes of the swamp coursed into his bloodstream and rendered him helpless. Drugged, he had no control over his body, and could barely maintain a grip on consciousness.

Men and women chanted and shouted and jeered beneath him.

His gun was snatched from its holster.

"Stop!"

But he went flying along, and became increasingly disorientated, feeling reality warp and shimmer around him.

"Please," he whispered.

His awareness of time and place folded into an oblivion.

Abruptly, he emerged from it, shockingly lucid, a different scent filling his lungs, a vegetation-filled hand coming away from his face, someone stepping back.

He was upright, bound to a post, and intensely aware of the beautiful and powerfully alluring woman standing before him.

Marie Galante smiled seductively and swayed forward until her face was just inches from his own.

"Now, Sexton Blake," she whispered huskily, "we shall have our reckoning."

8

compromising position

"I RECOGNISE A crook when I see one," said Rymer, "even when they come packaged as nicely as you, my girl. Whatever scheme you have got going, you need to cut your losses, bring it to an end, and get off this island while you can. Sexton Blake is impossible to beat. Believe me, I have been endeavouring to get the better of him for nigh on quarter of a century."

"But why is he here?" Violet Damm asked.

"I have no idea. You should hope it has nothing to do with you."

They were in her kitchen, in the house to the south of the city. Rymer, at the table, had just finished picking at a light meal. Damm mixed a drop of Galante's medicine into a glass of water and passed it to him.

"No," he said. "I'll not take any more of her damned potion."

"Are you craving heroin?" she asked.

"No."

"You certainly will be if you don't drink that. Whatever

267

it is, it works wonders. Here, put the bottle in your pocket. One drop, every six hours. You can take responsibility for your own recovery now—if you *want* to recover."

He glowered at her, hesitated, then drank the water and took the bottle.

"Blake saw us leave the sanatorium," he said. "He will go there. He will get your name and address, and he will come looking for us."

She shook her head. "This house is not the address I registered when I joined the staff. You're safe." She pressed her hands together and put them to her lips, thinking. "Nevertheless," she said, presently, "perhaps it would be wise to get out of the city. I already have rooms rented at a tavern in Bibibagua. The Carl Magnus. It overlooks the harbour."

"Your bolthole," Rymer stated.

"I was always going to need one at some juncture," she said. "And it's useful to have it ready and close to my boat."

Rymer gave an appreciative nod. "I see. Your getaway is all planned. Good. I like a crook that thinks ahead. Now tell me, what on earth have you been up to?"

She considered him for a moment. He had once been a powerful man—physically, intellectually, and in character—that much was obvious, but it was also plain that he was broken. She could see it in his pain-filled eyes, in the way his hands trembled, and in the slump of his shoulders. He was no threat to her, but he could easily become a complication. She felt inclined to direct him to the nearest opium den and leave him to his squalid fate.

There were, however, those diamonds.

To get at them, she required him, and to get him, she must establish trust.

So, while she tidied the table, she told him all about her and Hellander's immortality scheme.

Rymer slapped down his hand, threw back his head, and laughed uproariously. There was a hint of hysteria about it that unnerved her.

"Wonderful!" he declared. "By god, girl, you're a villain through and through!"

He put his fingers to his beard, a crease appearing between his brows. "Do you mean to tell me that these zombies you've created are just sitting doing nothing in a disabled refrigeration unit? Won't they starve to death?"

"To all intents and purposes, they are dead already," she said. "They don't require nutrition. I suppose, if left unattended, they would eventually cross fully into the afterlife, if there is such a thing—but they will probably be discovered before then."

"I can see why you went into nursing," Rymer said, in a sarcastic tone. "You are simply bursting with compassion. Is there an antidote for the serum?"

"Not that I am aware of."

He looked down at himself, at his filthy, stinking clothes, and his torn shirt sleeve. The puncture marks on his forearm.

"So, you have made yourself rich. You should already be on your boat, far away from here. Instead, you have purposely made an enemy of Marie Galante by pulling me out of her clutches. That was not a wise move. I must presume, then, that you have your sights set on a fortune so large as to be worth the risk—and that you need me to help you get it. Since the only thing I have to offer is my association with that sorceress, I must also presume that the fortune is hers."

"Correct."

"You are a fool. You haven't the faintest conception of what you are up against."

Damm smiled.

"You've made my case for me, doctor. I *don't* know what I'm up against. You do. Therefore, I need you."

"And why should I be inclined to assist you?"

She went to a cupboard, took from it two glasses and a bottle of dark rum, and brought them to the table. Pulling out the chair opposite, she sat facing him.

"Imagine how it would feel to look Marie Galante in the eye and inform her that you had deprived her of her fortune, and with it, her power. Then, perhaps, you would kill her—or, maybe, you would prefer to leave her in abject poverty. Either way, you would have half her riches—the other half, of course, belonging to me. Recompense for what she has done to you, perhaps?"

"There can be no recompense," he snarled. Damm had piqued his interest, though, and he asked, "What is this fortune?"

She poured two generous measures and pushed one over to him. Then she took a packet of "Luckies" from her pocket and offered him one.

"When she delivered you into my care," she said, striking a match, and putting it to their cigarettes, "she paid me with three diamonds and told me she had plenty more. I asked Hellander to find out where she got them. He did. He was told by a drunk voodooist in the shanty town."

"A nice, reliable source," Rymer mocked.

She ignored the comment, and went on:

"During the sixteenth century, there was a pirate named William Angell, whose ship, the *Santa Dorrito*, was wrecked here. Survivors managed to get three chests ashore, all filled with gemstones, and hid them in a cave in the cliffs. Those men, however, did not live for long. This is Death Island! The chests are still here, supposedly protected by a voodoo curse—which, of course, is nonsense."

"Don't be so sure. The voodoo religion is ages old. Those who follow it possess knowledge the so-called civilised world has barely touched upon. Dismiss it at your peril." He drew on his cigarette. "So Galante scoops out a handful of diamonds every time she's in need of funds?"

Damm put her glass to her lips, swallowed the contents in a single swig, and said, "Yup."

Rymer contemplated.

"All right," he said, eventually. "What do you propose?"

"I'm going to buy you some fresh clothes," she answered, "because you look and smell like a tramp. I shan't be long. You, meanwhile, will have a bath. After I return, you'll sleep the night through. You need to gain whatever strength you can. Then, in the morning, we shall move to the Carl Magnus. Do you have money?"

"No."

She took a ceramic jar from a shelf, placed it in front of him, and removed the lid, revealing rolls of banknotes.

"Take what you need from there. Fill your pockets, if you must. From the Carl Magnus, you'll ride my spare motorcycle to Yucayeque—the shanty town—to contact Galante." She gave a gappy smile. "Into the lion's den for you, sir."

"I'm to seduce her, am I?" he said, curling his lip in disgust.

"Don't look so glum about it. She's a ravishing beauty."

"She killed my wife," he roared, slamming his fist onto the table so hard that his glass toppled and spilled rum, while hers rolled to the floor and broke.

Damm, jumping up and back, drew her gun. She aimed it at him, her hand shaking.

But his sudden fury had already abated.

"Put that away," he said. "I will do as you ask. I'll get the location of those chests out of her, then return to you, and we'll go claim 'em for ourselves. All right?"

She holstered her weapon.

"All right," she agreed.

She cleared away the broken glass, then left him and went into town.

Damm was convinced that Rymer's forthcoming encounter with the Voodoo Queen was going to shatter whatever remained of his sanity. He was already close to being a full-blown maniac.

She would have to dispose of him quickly and cleanly.

Certainly, she had no intention of sharing the diamonds with him.

First, though—

The shops in Bajacu usually opened late in the morning and did not close until about ten in the evening. It was now around half eight, giving her plenty of time to purchase for her guest a razor and shaving soap, and a complete outfit.

She also paid for a jerrycan of petrol, which, when she returned to the house, she emptied into the tank of her spare motorcycle. It was a rickety old machine, but would serve its purpose.

She had been away for an hour and a half, and found Rymer sitting at the table, clean and wrapped in a towel. He was reading her copy of *Mein Kampf*.

Despite his recent addiction, he was, she noted, in good physical shape.

"The man who wrote this book," he said, "is a pitiful idiot, and a bad writer, to boot."

She suddenly became very still.

Then she checked her pistol, and murmured, "I'm going out again."

He raised an eyebrow.

"You just made me realise something," she said. "I think I know why Sexton Blake is here. There is a Nazi agent on the island. I will lay you ten to one that the detective is after him."

"So?" he asked.

"So, the Nazi is the one person who could set Blake on my trail. I am, therefore, now going to shoot him in the head."

Rymer stretched and said, through a yawn, "That's good. Dead Nazis are my favourite sort." Then he added, "If you're not back by morning, I'll assume he was quicker on the draw. What's the name of your boat? I might need it."

"Best not to take me for a fool, doctor," she replied, and departed.

Damm rode her Royal Enfield across town to the sanatorium and parked it in the courtyard.

Entering through the back door, she made her way up to her office. She checked it with painstaking thoroughness, ensuring that it was free of any clue which, should he come poking around, might cause Blake to become suspicious of her.

The scrum and syringes went into her pocket.

When she was satisfied that all was well, she left the room and passed along to Sir Bartholomew Moxton's office.

It was now ten o'clock.

She caught a whiff of a pungent, smoky odour, and simultaneously, the voodoo drums began to thunder.

Though she did not know it, Blake had just driven into Yucayeque with Tinker, unconscious, in the seat beside him.

She hesitated for a second, then knocked on Moxton's door.

"Come!" he called, and as she entered, closing the door behind her, he went on, "Ah, Sister Georgina, I wasn't expecting to see you tonight. Sit down, please."

She took a seat, facing him across his desk.

"They are off again," he said, gesturing into the air to indicate the drumming. "I'll tell you what, when we have secured this island, there will be no more of that mumbo-jumbo."

He reached into a drawer and withdrew from it a bulging envelope.

"Matters are proceeding as planned. I have been in contact with the syndicate, and you will be pleased to know that your prompt dispatching of Leichenberg has met with much approval. Your bonus—"

He pushed the envelope across the desk.

She took it, and slipped it into her pocket with a murmured thank you.

Moxton continued, "They intend to send one of our people to occupy the castle and take over the refrigeration plant. What of this Hellander fellow, the manager? Do you know anything about him?"

"I've never met him," she said.

"Swedish or Swiss, I think. Should be easy to convert to the cause, if he isn't already one of us. Now then—"

He opened a pouch of tobacco and took up his pipe.

"—the Britisher, Woodbine, is next. Do you think you could do away with him by, say, Sunday?"

She frowned. "Sir Bartholomew—"

He looked at her curiously.

"Yes?"

"Have you changed your smoking mixture?"

"No. Why do you ask?"

"It smells diff—"

But even as she said it, the odour changed, and sweetness filled into her sinuses. A disquieting sensation overcame her, as if she were floating.

It was time, she decided, to do what needed to be done, then get out quickly.

She stood, drew her pistol, and aimed it at his forehead.

"Good lord!" he exclaimed, and as if unable to think of anything more appropriate, added, "Why aren't you wearing your uniform?"

Damm squeezed the trigger.

Nothing happened.

Moxton looked past her, at the door.

She heard it creak open, and that pungent stench of cigar smoke came again, intense, supplanting the cloying sweetness.

Moxton froze, his eyes fixed wide, not moving.

She tried the trigger again, and realised that the problem was not a jammed gun, but a stuck finger. She was unable to move—not a single muscle. Utterly paralysed.

"Weee!" came a deep, strongly accented voice from behind her. "Look at this. What am I interrupting? Is it a party?"

Tobacco smoke billowed past her.

There was a long pause. Then, still from behind:

"I have been thinking to myself that it is time to kill an Englishman. It looks to me like this girl, she has the same idea!"

Baron Samedi stalked into view, to her right, hat on head, plugs in nostrils, a string of finger bones around his neck.

She willed herself to twist and shoot him, but her weapon remained as it was, aimed at Moxton.

Violet Damm was breathing, her heart was beating, her senses were functioning, but she simply could not move. Moxton, evidently, was experiencing precisely the same immobilisation.

The baron raised his gloved right hand to his mouth and drew on a ludicrously huge cigar. He puffed out a curling plume, then raised his other hand and gulped from a big bottle of rum.

Turning his white-painted face to Damm, he said, "You are a killy killy girl, hey? Well, you go right ahead and do it."

He placed the bottle on the desk, held the cigar between his teeth, and took hold of Damm's extended wrist with his left hand. He put his right thumb on her trigger finger and pressed it.

There was a loud report and a hole appeared in Moxton's forehead. Blood spurted out and down over his face, vivid on his white beard. His eyes remained wide. He did not even twitch.

"Weee! That was a good shot," Samedi exclaimed, smiling happily. "I could not have done it better myself."

He flung out his arms and spun around laughing, then he leaned forward and planted a kiss on Damm's cheek.

"Bee-ootiful woman," he said into her ear. "You have pleased me so much tonight, that I'm going to give you another job. You are going to tell whoever finds you that foreigners are not welcome on Oubao-Bara. You get me? This island is not for the English or the Germans or the

Danish or nobody else. Aramabuya only! The Ghost People! The rest can get off. You tell them! You tell them when they come for you."

He took up his bottle, gave her a comical wink, and moved to the door and out of her sight.

Sir Bartholomew Moxton stared past her.

Violet Damm stared at Moxton.

A wisp of smoke curled from the barrel of her gun.

The voodoo drums kept beating.

9

unlikely alliance

SEXTON BLAKE WAS at the centre of a frenetic, primal storm of dancing, singing, and drumming—voodoo devotees whirling and jumping around him, limbs flailing, eyes turned up in their sockets, perspiration flying off them.

The air was thick with fetid odours, of bodies, of smoke, of incense, and of the swamp.

Desperately, he strained at his bonds, but they would not give in the slightest.

"Galante!" he hollered, but she had vanished into the surging throng.

Tinker! Where was Tinker?

A man, swinging a headless chicken by its legs, pushed out of the crowd and jerked the still pulsating carcass at Blake. Blood spattered over the detective, then the man whirled away, and another emerged, with a burning brand in his hand. He shouted and gibbered frenziedly, raised the brand and blew on it—a "fire-eater"—causing its flame to crackle into Blake's face. Then he, too, was reabsorbed into the mob, to be replaced by a short, bulky figure dressed in top hat and tails, with a white-painted face, a cigar in one hand, and a bottle of rum in the other.

Ever since his first encounter with Galante, nearly twenty years ago, Blake had studied voodoo. He knew enough to recognise the costume as representative of Baron Samedi, the debauched, disruptive and unpredictable spirit of chaos, and as that figure came stalking toward him, the clues spotted at the Leichenberg murder scene clicked into place.

Someone, made up as Samedi, had killed the Ice Lord.

Leichenberg had suffered a voodoo execution.

Blake leaned his head back, and as the man splashed rum over him, puffed smoke into his eyes, and babbled incomprehensibly, the detective bellowed, "Marie Galante! Why did you kill Leichenberg? Why did you kill Leichenberg? Why did you do it, Galante?"

The drums stopped.

The crowd melted away, and it was so fast—and Blake's senses had been so assaulted—that it struck him as magical, this sudden silence, and incredible vanishing of the multitude.

They were there, then they were not.

The *humfo* was empty but for Blake and one other.

She paced forward, with all the threatening grace of a tiger, and stopped in front of him.

"Do you accuse me, Sexton Blake?"

"Mademoiselle," he said, his voice terribly hoarse, "I know what you did. I want to know why. It makes no sense to me. I thought you were working with the Americans to protect this island. Why would you murder a man who brought so much wealth to it? Was he a Nazi agent?"

"I do what is best for Saint Dorian," she said. "And so, too, did Lothar Leichenberg. He was not an agent—and I am not responsible for his death."

"Do you give me your word?"

"I swear it before Bondyé, my god."

"In that case," said Blake, "I believe we have a common enemy."

She gazed at him for a moment, then murmured in a softened tone, "Your assistant is close to death."

He lowered his chin to the left. "In my pocket. An envelope."

Galante moved closer and searched his pockets until she found it. She opened the envelope, withdrew the dart, and put it to her nose. She turned and called out.

A man emerged from a doorway and approached.

She spoke to him, her patois too rapid for Blake to understand, handed him the dart, and sent him on his way.

"He will apply the antidote," she said, turning back to Blake.

The relief was so intense that the detective wilted, and only his bindings kept him upright.

She drew a knife from a fold of her dress, moved behind him, and sawed through the ropes confining his ankles, then those around his wrists.

He fell to his knees.

"A reprieve only, Sexton Blake," she warned. "Why did you think it was I who had Leichenberg killed?"

"Cigar," he rasped, "rum, white face paint. All the evidence at the scene is suggestive of someone in Baron Samedi costume."

She blinked, and the muscles of her jaw tightened.

Blake struggled to his feet.

"Not the man you saw just now," she said. "His named is Loquillo, and he was with me on the night of the murder."

"In that case, I suspect that someone is using your religion to further their own ends. It is forbidden for a non-believer to dress that way, is it not?"

"To do so is to disrespect Baron Samedi. The sentence is death."

She stared at him, her face unreadable, then, motioning for him to follow, led him to one of the open-fronted buildings facing the *humfo*.

Inside, they sat on the floor either side of a low cane table.

Galante snapped her fingers and a man entered. While she issued instructions in a low tone, Blake examined the spacious room.

Brightly painted poles held up its thatched roof. Against each of the three walls, stood stone altars. On one, there was a basin of water; on another, a black wooden cross; and on the third, a brazier from which projected an iron bar.

An internal doorway—from which the man had emerged and through which he now exited—was framed by animal skulls, with that of a goat on the lintel, and those of birds down the sides.

The walls were almost entirely hidden behind strips of colourful material, pinned onto them, and a great many small hessian sacks, tied shut and hanging from hooks, their contents a mystery.

"For what you did to me two years ago," Galante said, "I should have you tortured to death. Instead, I am going to feed you."

"Two years ago, you were intent on sacrificing an Englishman to your god. I prevented it."

"And because that sacrifice was not delivered, as I had promised, I lost much of my influence," she said. "It has taken me all this time to rebuild it."

"I never doubted that you would succeed in doing so."

Blake sighed and used the back of his hand to wipe spots of chicken blood from his face.

"Marie—will you permit the familiarity?"

She gave a slight nod.

"Marie, I want you to understand something once and for all. I have never stood against your ambition to make of the Caribbean a black empire. As a matter of fact, I support the notion. It is the way you go about it that troubles me. I have opposed your actions but never your intentions."

Her dark, wonderful eyes met his and held them. Then she, too, sighed, and looked over to the altar with the black cross.

"The world changes," she said. "We must change with it, or we become irrelevant and useless. I have been... rethinking my strategics."

The man returned with two others. They put a large basin of water, in which a sponge floated, onto the floor, and on a chair placed a towel, a clean pair of trousers, a shirt, a jacket, and, to Blake's surprise, his automatic. Then, they put a bottle of red wine and two glasses onto the table, together with a carafe of water, a big bowl of rice, another of chicken stew, two plates, and cutlery.

They departed.

"Clean yourself," Galante murmured, and set about pouring wine and dishing out the food.

Blake stripped to his underwear, sponged himself down, towelled himself dry, and dressed in the fresh clothing, which proved rather too tight. He put on his shoulder holster and slipped his gun into it.

Then he settled back at the table, sipped the wine, and said, "Tinker?"

"He will recover," she answered. "But it will take a little time. He will remain here for now." She forked rice and stew into her mouth, chewed and swallowed, and added, "Only we voodooists know of that poison, Sexton Blake. It suggests that one of my own has betrayed our secrets. When I discover who it is, I will force into them a drug that keeps them conscious while their skin is peeled off strip by strip."

"I am eating," Blake commented.

She smiled.

He said, "You informed American intelligence of a Nazi agent on Saint Dorian. How did you find out?"

"My people intercepted radio communications."

"Do you think the agent and the murderer of Lothar Leichenberg are one and the same?"

"No, it is not possible. Not even one who has betrayed me would work with the Nazis. If Hitler gained this island, it would mean the end of voodoo in the Caribbean—and voodoo is our life."

"Yet," said Blake, "whoever is responsible for the booby-trap that shot Tinker also painted a swastika on the wall beside it." He frowned, thoughtfully, a vague suspicion forming. "And also dropped a British cigarette at the castle."

"There is a faction on this island," Galante said, "that would like all foreigners removed from it. Its members would restore it as the Oubao-Bara of old, isolated and hostile to all."

"And if this murderous Baron Samedi impersonator represents that faction," Blake suggested, "then he is committing these crimes and planting evidence to set foreigners at each other's throats?"

"Yes."

"Which means we have not just one common enemy, but two: the faction and the Nazis."

They continued their meal in silence, both wrapped in thought.

Blake's mental processes did not run along the usual logical and insightful channels. His mind was working in a disjointed manner, vivid images arising, tastes and sounds intruding, deductive reasoning drifting into flights of fancy wherein he imagined himself fulfilling a predestined role that repeated over and over.

Wrenching himself into focus, he wondered whether the food or wine was drugged, and whether Galante, through a lifetime of exposure, was immune to whatever was affecting him.

But no, it was the swamp. He was, he realised, succumbing to the pervasive fumes from that giant cauldron of bubbling toxins.

As if reading his thoughts, Galante murmured, "My apologies," stood, and crossed to the wall. Pushing aside dangling strips of cloth, she took something from a hidden niche and returned to the table with it, passing it to Blake.

It was a small tin, like those that hold shoe polish.

He opened it to reveal a clear, soft, waxy substance.

"Smear some beneath your nose," Galante advised. "It will clear your head."

He did so, and it worked immediately.

He said, "Give some to Tinker."

She nodded, but indicated that he should keep that particular tin.

He slipped it into his pocket.

The offering, though but a small gesture, convinced him of her good faith. He decided to trust the Voodoo Queen.

"It is essential that we work together," he said. "Will you, for once, have faith in me?"

"I will," she replied, "if you reciprocate. Under the circumstances, it would be a good idea, I think, to put the past behind us."

"Good! Now, this faction you speak of, you must get to the heart of it. Find out as much as you can and tell me whatever you learn. I, meanwhile, will set out to unearth the Nazi."

He paused, then added:

"But there is a third factor we must consider—"

She looked at him inquiringly.

"Doctor Huxton Rymer is on Saint Dorian."

"Oh."

"Tell me truly," he said, "were you already aware of it?"

"No," she answered impassively, "I was not."

He lifted his wineglass to his lips and scrutinised her over its brim.

She returned the gaze, steadily, and asked, "What is he doing here?"

"I do not know. Maybe looking for you."

"For what reason?"

"Perhaps you can tell me."

"I cannot."

Blake put down his glass and scraped the last forkful of chicken and rice from his plate before pushing it aside.

"How do matters stand between you two?" he asked.

A flicker of fury flared in her eyes.

"I have not seen him for five years," she said. "You will recall the affair of the oyster beds around Santa Margarita?"

"When you both slipped through my fingers and sailed off in your schooner? Yes, how could I forget it?"

"Another of your many failures, Sexton Blake," she observed in a sardonic tone.

"I spoiled your crooked scheme, if I remember rightly." He smiled. "Shall we not bicker?"

She pushed her plate away, took up the wine bottle, and topped up their glasses.

"Five years," she repeated. "It is a long time. He means nothing to me. But, if you see him, you can tell him I said hello—and goodbye." She chuckled, throatily. "And tell him to get off my island."

"I will personally remove him. He needs a friend, Marie, and despite everything, I have taken it upon myself to be that person."

She shrugged.

"It is your business. I do not care."

He took a big gulp from his wineglass, stood, and brushed down his too-small clothes. "I shall leave my assistant in your care. Should anything happen to him—"

"He will sleep," she interrupted, "and when he awakes, I will have him brought to you."

"I'm at the Copenhagen Plaza."

She got to her feet as he made to depart. "There is a condition."

"Condition?" he asked. "To what?"

"To my cooperating with you."

He waited for her to elucidate.

"When this is over," she said, "and we have exposed the killer and the Nazi agent—"

"Yes?"

"You will represent me to your government with a view to opening a discussion concerning the future of this island."

He nodded.

"Very well."

Galante summoned her servant and instructed him to guide Blake back to the Duesenberg. The dangerous gleam again showed in her eyes as she nodded farewell to the detective, reminding him that his new ally was a powerful and unpredictable woman.

By the time he drove into Bajacu, the sun had risen. He had not slept at all, but there was no time for rest now. He had a nine o'clock appointment at the sanatorium, which would, he hoped, lead him to Huxton Rymer.

At the Copenhagen, he was accosted by the manager, who complained vociferously about the swastika daubed on the wall in his room. Blake explained that he was not responsible for it and agreed that the police should be informed. Apparently, he noted, someone in the hotel did not much like the British.

He then changed into a clean set of clothes, returned to his car, and drove to meet with Sir Bartholomew Moxton.

As he arrived at the sanatorium and turned into the driveway from which Tinker had seen Rymer emerge on the back of a motorcycle, he reflected upon Marie Galante's words.

She claimed no knowledge of Rymer's presence.

Blake was certain she had lied.

10
zombie!

VIOLET DAMM HAD been standing all night with her arm outstretched and her pistol aimed at a dead man.

Dawn came glimmering through the window, and with it, agonisingly, her muscles gradually unlocked.

Her arm, with that weight at the end of it, had dropped until the wildly trembling pistol was now pointing at Sir Bartholomew's stomach.

The pain was unendurable.

Through clenched teeth, she had been screaming for almost an hour.

Tears were pouring down her cheeks.

Thirst tormented her.

And somebody knocked at the door.

She was terrified they would enter and catch her in this compromising position—but, also, she was desperate for them to come and give assistance; to at least remove the appalling burden from her hand. The conflicting emotions, adding further anguish, caused her to pant rapidly, her heart hammering.

There came a click and the rasp of hinges. A male voice started, "Excuse me, Sir Bar—" and stopped.

Involuntarily, she emitted a quavering, animalistic wail of despair.

The door clicked shut, footfalls sounded, and a man stepped into view. He was tall, broad of shoulder and narrow of hip, with a lean, handsome face, steely blue-grey eyes, and dark hair brushed back with a deep widow's peak.

He took the weapon from her fingers and placed it on the desk.

"Gaah!" she cried out. "God!"

Deprived of the weight, her arm rose back to its former position.

The man watched it, his eyebrows going up.

He peered into her eyes, And murmured, "You have white face paint on your cheek. Was there a sweet odour?"

"Yaah," she sobbed.

"The servants at Leichenberg Castle smelled it, too, before they were stricken by paralysis. I gather Baron Samedi has been here?"

"Yaas."

Suddenly, she felt hope—and with it, her legs abruptly folded, and she crashed to the floor.

The man crouched, slipped one arm under her shoulders, the other under her knees, and—tall and athletic as she was—lifted her as if she were a child.

He carried her to Sir Bartholomew's reading chair—a big old eyesore of cracked leather—and lowered her into it.

"I am Sexton Blake," he said. "Are you Georgina Stark?"

"Ya—yes," she gasped.

He crossed to a bureau upon which stood a decanter of brandy, poured a glass, and brought it back to her. It went down her throat like fire.

She cried out as cramps assaulted her, contorting her limbs.

"It will pass," he reassured her.

Silently, she employed every expletive she knew—which was very many.

Blake left her and moved back to the desk. He briefly examined the corpse, which was still gazing in bewilderment at the door, then used his thumbs to press the eyelids shut.

Moving around the office, he scrutinised every part of it, until he was close to her again.

"Ah!" he exclaimed.

With great effort, she turned her head to see what he was doing.

He had, apparently, found something of interest on a bookcase.

He put his finger against a book and pressed. There came a soft clunk, and a whole row of book spines levered down.

"There you are," he murmured.

"Wha— what—is it?" she croaked.

"There is a concealed radio receiver and transmitter. Your employer, I'm afraid, was a Nazi agent."

"Wha—what?" she said, in feigned shock. "But—but he was so—so *nice*."

Damm thought fast. Blake would surmise, she felt sure, that if Moxton was an agent, then he must also have an operative. Since she was that operative, she needed to deflect the detective's attention onto someone else. Her first thought was Hellander, but she quickly dismissed the idea. He could incriminate her, and to save his own skin most assuredly would.

To play for time, she said thickly, "Can I… have water, please?"

Blake immediately moved back to the bureau, and as he poured from a carafe, he gave her the solution she needed:

"Beneath the make-up, was Baron Samedi, in fact, Doctor Huxton Rymer, Miss Stark—maybe you know him as Paul Butterfield?"

He handed her a glass and held her arm steady while she gulped the water down.

She was shaking uncontrollably as the effect of the gas wore off, which made play-acting all the easier.

She moaned and allowed the tears to flow. "Oh! That aw—awful man, Mr. Blake! I—I don't know. I—yes, I suppose it could have been Butter—Doc—Doctor Rymer. But—I couldn't move my eyes, and he was only ever at the periphery, if you know what I mean. I never got a clear look at him."

"What about his voice?"

"He spoke strangely, putting on a heavy Caribbean accent."

Blake looked puzzled.

"You are not certain that it was Rymer, yet you say Rymer is awful? Why?"

"He—he held a knife to me. He made me take him on my motorcycle to the—to the refrigeration plant. There were—he needed me to— Oh god, the bodies, Mr. Blake! The living dead!"

She hid her face in her palms and sobbed, hiding her eyes, in case they gave anything away. She was thinking fast, throwing it all at Rymer. The apparition, whoever or whatever it was, had unnerved her. Bad enough that Sexton Blake was poking about. Now a costumed lunatic! That, and night-long paralysis, had sharpened her sense of urgency almost to the point of panic. Time to snatch those diamonds and get off this damned island!

Blake placed a hand on her shoulder.

"Living dead, sister? Do you mean zombies?"

"He has been... removing residents from here—the rich ones—and..."

She stopped and clutched her hands to her chest, as if to protect her heart.

"And?" he prompted.

A means to deal with this nosy detective had suddenly occurred to her. She quelled the impulse to smile and said, "I don't know how to explain. I don't even understand it. Will you—will you come to the plant with me—allow me to show you?"

Blake cast his eyes around the office, then looked back at her.

He appeared to reach a decision.

"Are you able to stand?"

"I think—" She reached out, and he gave assistance.

She heaved herself up, staggering a little as they moved to the door. After the first three or four steps, it became easier to walk, and by the time they were out in the corridor, she no longer required his help—but pretended otherwise.

He closed the office door behind them.

When they reached the lobby, the receptionist—the British girl—asked, "He was there, Mr. Blake?" then she noticed Damm. "Oh! Georgina!"

"He was—" Damm said, then pretended to be incapable of any further word.

"Sister Georgina has had a bad shock," Blake told the girl. "You need to ensure that no one enters Sir Bartholomew's office. I am afraid he's been killed."

The receptionist cried out and half rose from her chair.

"Call the police," Blake said firmly. "Ask for Chief Tiburon. Tell him I have examined the scene, I am pursuing the case, and I will contact him presently."

"Y-yes, Mr. Blake," she said, and began to cry.

"Hey!" he snapped. "Time for that later!"

She nodded and reached for her telephone.

As the detective guided her out of the sanatorium, Damm regretted that her pistol was still on Moxton's desk. She had more weapons in her house, and others at her rooms in the Carl Magus inn, but right now, she was unarmed, and did not appreciate the feel of it at all.

They rounded the building to where the Duesenberg was parked, got in, and he started it up and steered out onto the road.

"Tell me what you can," he said.

"We need to go to Mr. Hellander's office," she responded.

"Who is he?"

"The manager of the plant. He will open Unit Nine for us. That is where the doctor—"

She stopped as if overcome by emotion.

That will be the tricky part of it, she thought. *If Max reacts badly—if he shows fear or hesitancy—*

Hellander tended to be calm under most circumstances, but he had lost his icy Scandinavian equilibrium when she revealed her intention to steal Marie Galante's fortune. That same unbridled emotion in front of Blake could—

"Miss Stark," Blake said. "Are you suggesting that Rymer is turning people into zombies and freezing them?"

"Not freezing," she said. "The unit is broken. He just—just stores them inside it."

"Why?"

"For experiments, I think."

Blake navigated the car onto the road, which sloped down to the plant and the airfield.

"And for what did he need you?"

"Not me specifically. He just required a nurse, and I happened to be the one he chose. He took me to the unit, and—"

Her mind raced. *And what? Come on! Think!*

"And," she said, recalling what she had learned about Rymer from conversations with him, "he performed surgery. On two of them." She cleared her throat. "Surgery. I was forced to assist."

She looked sideways at him. He was frowning.

"What sort of surgery?" he asked.

"A heart transplant."

She could have kicked herself. Of all the options, she had to blurt out something idiotic—incredible—impossible!

Idiot! Calm Down!

To her surprise, however, the detective, after making a noise of astonishment, said, "Experimental operations of the sort have occurred, with dogs as the subjects. There was one just two years ago, though the animal survived for only eight days. Certainly, it is proposed that such procedures might one day be possible with people."

He shook his head slightly and gave a low whistle of amazement.

"I cannot think of anyone more likely to succeed in transplanting a living heart than Rymer. As a surgeon, he is a genius of the highest order. Unfortunately, there is something twisted in his mentality, and recently, Miss Stark, he suffered a personal tragedy so profound that I fear his sanity is at risk. To practice the operation on men turned zombie, in his warped view, must make total sense. To such as you and me, though, the immorality of it—the rejection of any notion of ethics—is absolutely monstrous."

"Yes," Violet Damm agreed, quietly.

They rounded a bend and came alongside the airstrip.

"Stop!" she cried out. "There's Hellander."

Blake pulled over. Before he could say anything, she opened the door, got out, and leaned back in.

"I'll fetch him over, Mr. Blake. He knows me—as a matter of fact, he's a little sweet on me. It will be a big shock for him to discover that a unit he has thought disused is employed for such a purpose. Best the news comes from me—"

She closed the door on the detective's objection and moved rapidly away, passing between a couple of palm trees and striding across a wide patch of grass towards the strip's parking bays.

Blake called after her, but she pretended not to hear him.

When she reached a sufficiently safe distance, she glanced over her shoulder. He was standing beside the car, watching her.

Max Hellander was checking the wheels of his little Gee Bee Sportster monoplane. He straightened as she approached, looking surprised.

"What are you doing here?"

"Max," she said, in a low and urgent tone. "Do you have the keys to Unit Nine?"

"I carry all the keys, all the time."

"I am with a British detective named Sexton Blake. He wants to look inside it. You must stay calm, come with us, and open it up."

He stepped back, shocked. "No! I can't do that! You know what will happen to us if—"

"Lower your voice, you fool!"

"But Georgina—I mean, Miss Stark—we cannot allow him to see—"

"Shut up and listen!"

She spoke rapidly, and the fear in his eyes gradually turned to doubt, and from doubt to resignation.

He accompanied her back toward the car.

"But this," he muttered, "it means we must forget those diamonds and fly away from here with what we already have. My aeroplane is ready. I have the key for it in my pocket. We can go today, this morning, within the hour."

"No," she said. "I'm going to buy us a little more time."

"You cannot possibly think that—"

"Shhh!"

Then, approaching the car:

"Mr. Blake, this is Max Hellander. I have explained everything to him, as far as I can understand it."

"But it is not true, surely," Hellander said, shaking Blake's hand. "If the unit was used for anything—anything at all—I would have noticed, I think."

"Let us see, Mr. Hellander," Blake replied.

They got into the Duesenberg. Hellander pointed ahead to the line of big white blocks.

"It is only a little way. We will find unit nine empty, I am positive."

Blake drove the short distance and stopped when the Swede said, "Here."

They disembarked and approached the unit. Damm looked around and saw that, while there were plant employees at work around all the other units, there were none near this one.

Massive double doors of steel fronted the block, but it was to a normal-sized one, set into the left-side wall, that Hellander led them. He drew a big bunch of keys from a loop on his belt, selected one, and put it to use.

They entered a long passage with fat pipes running along its length, turned right into a room of gauges and control consoles, crossed to another door, which Hellander unlocked, then entered a large chamber.

Though the refrigeration machinery was dormant, it felt cold, and while this came as a marvellous respite from the island's all-pervasive heat, it quickly needled into Damm's bones, and she began to shiver.

Blake turned to her and asked, "Where?"

She made herself appear hesitant and a little afraid, but then said, "This way," and led the two men across the floor to where a series of big rooms, like cells, lined the main wall.

She entered one and murmured, "This is it."

Inset into the walls to either side, there were alcoves, thirteen of which were occupied, each by a prone figure.

"Herregud!" Hellander cried out, his voice echoing. "Vad är det som händer här?"

Blake crossed to one of them—it happened to be Godfrey James Keegan—and felt for a pulse. He shook his head. Then he held the glass of his wristwatch beneath the man's nose. It did not mist over. Finally, he pushed up an eyelid and stared at the exposed glassy orb.

"Dead?" Hellander asked.

"Yes," Blake replied, then he straightened, jabbed his forefinger into Keegan's shoulder, and snapped, "Sit up."

Keegan sat up.

Damm let out a convincing scream.

Steady, she told herself. *Don't overdo it. He knows you know what they are, remember?*

"Interesting," Blake murmured. He turned to her. "On which two did Rymer operate?"

She cast her eyes around, then pointed to the man lying closest to her.

"This is one of them, Mr. Blake. The other—I am not sure."

He stepped to her side, bent over the dormant zombie, and set about unbuttoning its shirt.

Damm took something from her pocket.

Hellander positioned himself on the other side of the detective and asked, "What are you looking for?"

"Evidence of surgery," Blake said. "But I think this must be the wrong man. There is no sign of—"

Violet Damm leaned over him and thrust the needle of a syringe into his neck, simultaneously pressing the plunger.

She and Hellander both jumped back as Blake cried out and jerked upright.

He groped for the syringe, pulled it out, and regarded it with a confused expression. It dropped out of his hand.

"What—?"

"You have the last of my serum, Mr. Blake," said Damm. "But I suppose it has not been wasted. No more of your interference, thank you very much."

Blake's arms dropped limply to his sides. His mouth moved, but no words came, and after a minute it simply hung open.

His eyes went dull.

"Hand me your pistol," Damm instructed.

Slowly, as if in a dream, he drew his weapon and held it out to her.

She took it, examined it, and murmured, "I've half a mind to make you put a bullet through your own head."

Raising the weapon, she pointed it at him.

"But I shall shoot you myself," she said, then added, "Max."

She swung the pistol to the right and shot Hellander in the chest.

He staggered back and gaped at her.

"Sorry," she said, as he crumpled to the floor. "Partnership dissolved."

11
the fly

IT WAS SLIGHTLY before dawn when Huxton Rymer awoke, and upon entering Violet Damm's kitchen, found nothing disturbed since the night before.

He knocked on her bedroom door, at first softly, and when there was no response, more loudly, then opened it and looked in. The bed was neatly made.

"Perhaps," he mused, "her Nazi was too quick on the draw."

He went back to the kitchen and prepared a light breakfast of melon, cured ham, and coffee. With appetite satisfied, he took his medicine, lit one of the "Luckies" from the packet that Damm had left for him, and sat pondering his next move.

It did not take long to come to a decision.

He was going to deprive Galante of her diamonds.

From that fortune, he would invest however much was necessary to systematically destroy her. Killing would not do. His vengeance required her to suffer. She must be humiliated, rejected by her people, outcast, and condemned to a miserable life of abject poverty.

As for Violet Damm, he did not care—she did not matter. He had never intended to share the fortune with her, anyway.

He found motorcycle goggles hanging from a hook, and a military-style cloth cap, which he donned, pulling the peak down low. Then, he went outside, mounted her spare motorcycle, and drove out of the city.

She had told him the route, which was straightforward, and he was soon able to open up the throttle and speed ahead, passing through and around the light traffic with reckless impatience, kicking up great swirls of dust.

The sun was just sending its vivid rays over the mountaintops, the sky deepening into the day's azure.

As the city fell away behind him, the road became less busy. He put his head down and pushed the bike to its limits.

UPON ARRIVAL AT Bibibagua, which Rymer immediately found more to his liking than Bajacu, it having the familiar ambience of the Caribbean that the city in some indefinable manner lacked, he made his way to the busy waterfront.

The Carl Magnus was not difficult to locate, a rambling and ramshackle, two-storey, harbour-facing tavern. It was a place of villainous aspect, not at all suitable for a young woman as outwardly beautiful as Violet Damm— but perfectly in keeping, Rymer thought, with her cold, wicked heart.

He entered it without hesitation. As was usual with establishments of the sort, it was even at this early hour crowded with seafaring riff-raff, some just beginning their day's drinking, others still going strong, loudly and unsteadily, from the night before.

At first, he could see nothing, his eyes struggling to adjust to the exceedingly dim interior. Then, he discerned a tall Carib standing behind a long bar, and, shouldering his way through the crowd, ordered a beer and asked to see the proprietor. This worthy proved to be an obese, red-faced old British woman with a plethora of moles and an incipient moustache. She was introduced to him as "Mama C."

She eyed Rymer up and down and leered at him. "Wot can I do yer for?"

"Have you a room?" he asked.

"Yus, but I won't be in it until late tonight."

She winked at him.

"To rent. I'll need it for a day or two," he clarified.

She sighed, clicked her tongue, and said, "Foller me. Mind the stairs, they ain't safe."

The room, halfway along a corridor, was small and seedy but adequate. When she demanded more than double its worth—payment up front and in full—he pulled a roll of bills from his pocket and handed over the requested amount.

Fingering another couple of notes, he said, "I'm supposed to meet my colleague, Sister Georgina, here. Has she arrived?"

"That gap-toothed young—?" Mama C stopped, cleared her throat, scratched her belly through her stained apron, and went on, "I ain't seen her in weeks. Room's still all paid up, though."

"I'll knock on her door later, then," said Rymer. "Which one is it?"

She sniffed.

He handed over a banknote.

"Right hopposite your 'n."

"Thank you."

"You want some grub sent up later?"

"No."

"Suit yerself."

She waddled off, and a few moments later, he heard the "ain't safe" stairs creaking, cracking, and squealing beneath her vast weight.

Quietly, he crossed the passage to Violet Damm's room and tested the door. It was, as he had anticipated, locked. To a man like Rymer, this was no impediment at all. In less than thirty seconds, with a sharp click, he had breached the portal and was closing it behind him.

Damm's room was bigger than his own, and in a much better state of cleanliness and repair. It contained many personal items—clothes, shoes, books, jewellery, and various knickknacks. This suggested some special arrangement with Mama C—payment considerably over the odds, no doubt—to keep the chamber secure.

But not from him.

It took only five minutes to find what he was looking for. It was in a dressing table drawer, concealed beneath the paper liner—a key, on a ring, to which was also attached a little brass disc embossed with the words *The Promise*.

"Careless, my girl," he muttered. "Very careless. If you intend crime as your career, you had better learn to be a lot less sloppy."

He left the room, relocked the door, and ensured that his own was also locked. Then, he went downstairs, through the bar, and out into the blinding sunshine.

The harbour front was all hustle and bustle, giving—

like all small harbours in the West Indies—an impression of complete chaos. The loading and unloading of cargoes, sailors milling about, and dockhands gesticulating and yelling or, where opportunity allowed, loafing and smoking—bedlam!

Rymer sauntered through it all and along to the marina, where he passed from mooring to mooring until he found *The Promise*. It was a six-foot, raised-deck cruiser, a little shabby but perfectly capable, in his assessment, of island-hopping all the way to Florida.

He clambered aboard and hid the keys beneath the pilot's seat.

Twenty minutes later, Huxton Rymer roared out of Bibibagua on his motorcycle, satisfied that he had his means of escape arranged.

That was the easy part.

But now—

A fly into the spider's web!

He powered along the road to Yucayeque, drawing ever closer to the sorceress who had prowled remorselessly through his dreams for more than a decade.

"I can do it," he told himself. "I can do it. I have faced down far greater challenges than that poisonous hellcat."

The image of Mary Trent, his deceased wife, rose to occupy his mind's eye.

"Oh, no Mary," he cried out. "No, no, my dear, it is not a betrayal. I would never do that to you. I will be acting, that is all. Acting. Surely you understand?"

Her large eyes seemed to drill into him.

"I promise! I hate Galante! You cannot imagine how much I hate her. I despise her to the depths of my soul!"

It was by no means a long journey from the harbour to the dark core of the island, but he spoke to himself—

believing he was addressing his wife—the whole way there.

By the time he swept into the outlying districts of the shanty town, though he felt as calm and as impenetrable as a rock, Rymer had done irreparable damage to himself.

He approached Galante with a fractured mind.

The streets were swarming with people. He stopped twice to ask directions—where is the *humfo?*—and was pointed on his way.

Navigating, without knowing it, the very same roads traversed by Sexton Blake only hours before, he came to the town's centre and was all of a sudden alone.

These streets were empty—aside from a few chickens scratching at the hard-baked ground—and preternaturally silent. There were no drums to greet him, just a pervasive air of expectancy, and the echoes of his motorcycle's grumbling engine.

He steered slowly into the covered open space of the voodoo temple, came to a stop, and switched off his motor. Pulling the cap and goggles from his head, he threw them down into the dust.

Then he sat against the bike and waited.

Nothing happened.

Time passed, stretched, slow and distorted.

Somewhere nearby, a goat bleated into the stillness.

He unwittingly breathed the perfumes of the swamp—the pollens, gases, and spores. Gradually, they infiltrated his blood, altered his consciousness, and made him susceptible to suggestion. By the time Galante emerged from a doorway, at the exact minute of noon, he had fallen into a light trance.

She crossed to him, radiant, an elemental force, wearing a blue and orange knee-length summer dress, hair pulled into a topknot, bangles on her arms, and beads strung around her neck.

Her beauty, profound; her manner, alluring; her welcome, simple: "Rymer."

He smiled and extended his hands.

"I came."

Galante took them. "I knew that you would, once you were sufficiently recovered."

"Why did you put me in that place, Marie?"

"The sanatorium?" She gave a small shrug. "There were many matters requiring my attention. I could not afford to sit with you until you were better, much as I wanted to. And our history—yours and mine—is a complicated one. I was concerned that there might be some among my followers who would think it well to remove you, had I left you with them."

"And—" He broke eye contact and looked at the ground, "—and where did you find me in the first place, before you brought me to this island?"

"In an opium den in Port-au-Prince."

"I don't remember."

"That is probably for the best."

She pulled him from the bike and led him to the same structure in which Blake had sat, into the open-fronted room, through the skull-framed door, across another room—illuminated via slots high in the wall—and down a passageway. They passed openings to the right and left, then entered a square chamber, in the middle of which stood a long altar—in voodoo, called a *pè*—with Roman Catholic saints depicted in bright colours around its sides.

Tables stood against the walls. They were all crowded with flickering lamps, bottles of strange herbs and mysterious solutions, vials of powders, baskets of dried leaves and bleached bones, decanters of rum, bowls of pebbles and oils, crucifixes, platters of roots and berries, skulls, and little figures fashioned from sticks and string.

Galante pushed Rymer onto the *pè*, and finding himself strangely incapable of resistance, he allowed her to stretch him out, full length on his back.

"I need to know—" he started, but she placed a hand on his chest.

"You need to know nothing but this," she said, her voice low and mellifluous. "Your treatment must be completed, else in your grief, you will seek heroin again. At present, my love, you are *chwal*—a horse, ridden by a *lwa*—a malign spirit. I must force you into the *crise de lwa*—a purification ritual, to drive away that which possesses you."

"My addiction?" he said. "No, it is not necessary to—"

"It is!" she declared, firmly. "The road divides before you, Rymer, right here, right now. The spirits have made it so. One way to glory. The other to destruction. Which shall you take?"

He hesitated, then nodded, wanting only to get it over with, and murmured, "Do what you must."

She took his shirt in her hands and jerked it open, buttons popping, exposing his broad chest. Then she went to a table and returned with a small silver bowl. From it, she took a long, narrow thorn, and pushed it into the skin of his left pectoral. Then another, and another.

At first, he felt only a little discomfort, then—

Something more.

12
in absentia

DURING THE AFTERNOON, the din of someone's sustained and terrified screaming periodically brought Tinker to consciousness.

It was appalling—the shrieking of a man confronted by a fear he could not possibly conquer; a man taken beyond the limits of endurance, past any last shred of sanity.

Horror had rendered the voice so grotesque that Tinker—in his lucid moments—could not identify the source. He knew only that it was an Englishman, for though no clear words were discernible, there were many half-strangulated utterances that had about them the form and accent of his own language, sans Caribbean inflection.

Then the screams died away, and Tinker drifted back into a healing sleep that lasted all the following night.

When he next awoke, the quality of the light and the level of heat and humidity suggested early morning.

He vaguely recalled those awful ululations, and a dreadful idea occurred to him.

They might have issued from Sexton Blake.

Tinker believed that, under even the most despicable of tortures, his "guv'nor" would have maintained a stubborn, implacable silence. It was, however, conceivable that, if dosed with strong drugs, the detective's staunch character might be broken, and this possibility gave the youngster a desperate strength.

He sat up and saw he was in a small room, with light beaming through high slots. It had linen-covered walls, but no furniture aside from the cane bed beneath him and a small table crowded with odd bric-a-brac.

There was also a chair, by an open doorway, upon which sat a tall, cadaverous, bald-headed black man, in white cotton shorts and a washed-out blue and yellow striped shirt.

"Where am I?" Tinker asked.

The man got to his feet, all bones and joints and incredibly long legs, like a deckchair unfolding, and smiled, revealing enormous teeth.

"You stay there," he said. "You still got the bad stuff in your blood. More sleep, hey? But this—"

He stilted across to the bed.

"—you have more of this now, boy."

He took a small tin from his pocket, opened it, twisted a finger into the substance within, then—before it was apparent what he was going to do—reached out and smeared the stuff over Tinker's upper lip.

"That will stop the swamp a-getting into you," he said. "Here, now that you are awake, you take the tin and keep it, okay? Whenever you feel your head puffing up like a balloon, you put a bit of the cream under your nose."

Tinker accepted the tin, and put it into his pocket.

"This is Yucayeque?" he asked, clutching at dim memories.

"Yes. Mademoiselle Galante, you are under her wing now." The man gestured. "So, you sleep until she says otherwise, you understand?"

Tinker remained seated at the edge of the bed.

"I heard someone screaming."

"That was yesterday afternoon. No business of yours."

"Who was it?"

"Never you mind. Lie down."

The man placed his hands on his protruding hips and stared hard, as if by doing so, he could force Tinker to obey.

To no avail.

"I feel fine. I think I'll go now, if you don't mind."

"Me minding or not minding makes no difference any which way," said the man. "I was told what to do, and that's what I'm a-doing. You sleep, boy, all right?"

Tinker nodded, said, "All right."

He lay back and closed his eyes, and, after a few minutes, slowed and deepened his breathing. He feigned sleep so well that he drifted back into it.

A snore jerked him to consciousness.

Stupid! he thought. *I'll not be able to jump the fellow if I carry on like that. Sleeping on the job! The dear old guv'nor would give me a right ear-bashing!*

He wondered how much time had passed.

Another snore sounded.

Tinker opened his eyes in surprise. He looked across the room and discovered that he had not been woken by his own slumberous snorts but by those of his guardian. He grinned, very carefully sat up, gained his feet, and crept silently out through the door.

He stepped into a corridor, proceeded along to the right, came to a room in which a woman was sewing, with her back to him, and successfully tiptoed past her. Then, through to another passage, slipping by more rooms, some occupied, and into a chamber with a doorway in each wall.

He knew how shanty towns such as this were constructed, the buildings interconnected, all jumbled up. The people lived like rabbits in a warren, where they could move from premises to premises without exposure to the relentless sun.

He was also aware, by the curve of the passages, that he was passing through structures that circled something— probably, a *humfo*.

This was sufficient to give him a vague sense of his bearings, enough that he knew which doorway would take him in the direction from where, now that he thought about it, the screams had most likely come.

He explored a little until, quite unexpectedly, he heard the deep, musical tones of Marie Galante.

Her voice, muffled, was coming from the other side of a storeroom wall.

Tinker moved silently past shelves crammed with tinned and bottled food, past sacks of flour and dried beans, until he found a corner where her voice sounded loudest. He hunkered down behind a pile of coconuts and put his ear to the wall.

"—with no need to ever return to England. And you have always loved the tropics, have you not? Now they are your home."

A man answered, and Tinker instantly recognised the voice as Huxton Rymer's, though it sounded weak, and very hoarse.

"How can you expect me to stay with you when I have absolutely nothing?"

"I don't require anything from you."

"It is not what you do or don't require, Marie. It is what I demand of myself. Do you seriously think I can live like a savage? I have work to do. Great work. By God, my radium treatment of cancer is in its infancy—who is there to take up that baton, should I let it drop?"

Tinker frowned. There was something odd about Rymer's tone. He was speaking passionately, but in a manner that sounded—to Tinker's ears—strangely hollow.

"Everything you need is already here."

"On this pathetic little backwater island? I find that hard to believe!"

"It is true. At one o'clock today, the British administrator, Woodbine, and I, are to meet with the king to discuss the future of the refrigeration plant. The king has it in mind to nationalise it. But I am going to persuade him to sell it to me. There are big mechanical workshops that come with it. You will have free access to them."

"You don't underst—" Rymer began, but she cut him off.

"Furthermore, I have already purchased the Leichenberg castle. It will be your new home. It is fitted out with a very advanced chemical laboratory. I have already had delivered to it samples of the herbs and flowers that grow in the swamp. Unique organic compounds, doctor, that are found only here—nowhere else in the world. Imagine the discoveries that await you, the miraculous medicines that you'll create. You can begin work as soon as you are recovered from your ordeal."

"How have you done that?" Rymer demanded. "How could you have got possession of it so quickly? How can you possibly afford to purchase the refrigeration plant? Two years ago, Sexton Blake left you almost destitute."

She uttered a low, throaty laugh.

"He thought so! But I have always had a considerable fortune in diamonds hidden here on Saint Dorian."

"Nonsense," Rymer said, derisively. "This confounded place is too small to conceal anything so valuable."

"You underestimate the power of voodoo. A powerful curse protects the diamonds. To reach them, a thief would require the courage—and foolishness—to pass through the Ascension Gate. But no one, without the proper charms to protect them, would survive such an act. They would be stricken by lunacy and condemned to death by fire!"

"And where exactly is this accursed gate?"

"That, my love, you do not need to know. All that matters is that whatever you need for your scientific experiments, I can provide."

"It seems too good to be true," he protested. "I can really start over? Build a new life? Here, with you?"

"Together," she confirmed. Then, after a pause, she went on, "I must go to the city now, and I will not return until late, by which time all that was Lothar Leichenberg's will be ours. Until then, stay here and rest. The purification ritual has exhausted you. You need a few days to recover."

"But Sexton Blake is on Saint Dorian!" Rymer protested. "I have seen him! What is he doing here?"

"I am aware of his presence, and it need not concern us. He is pursuing a Nazi agent and will not interfere with our plans. Besides, we are not involved in anything illegal, are we?"

"I suppose not. But I cannot feel secure with him nosing around."

"I have insurance should he become a problem," Galante said. "His young assistant is in my power. I will hold him until the hour of Blake's departure."

Tinker silently mouthed, "Oh, you will, will you? Not if I have anything to do with it!" and quietly left the corner. As he made his way across the room, he heard Galante say:

"You must rest. Here, drink this mixture, it will give you—"

Her voice faded as Tinker slipped out of the storeroom and along the passage. He was now searching for any door that would open onto a street leading away from the *humfo*. It was not long before he found one.

So far, luck had been with him, and he had been able to creep past the few people encountered. Outside, it became apparent that caution was no longer necessary. He was seen, but no one took any notice of him.

Moving rapidly, he flitted from alleyway to alleyway until he happened upon a parked motorcycle. With a muttered apology to its absent owner, he commandeered it.

Minutes later, he was speeding along the Bajacu road.

IT WAS TEN o'clock in the morning when he arrived at the Copenhagen Plaza.

He knocked on Blake's door, but there was no response. After washing and changing into clean clothes in his own room, he returned to the other and picked the lock. Inside, he found a shirt and pair of trousers thrown over a chair. He did not recognise them, and they looked a little too small for Blake.

A mystery!

Another was waiting in the hotel's car park. The Duesenberg was there—Blake had evidently returned from Yucayeque—and when he opened it and got inside, he found a big bunch of keys on the passenger seat. He had no idea where they had come from or what doors they fitted. They were too bulky for his pocket, so he strung them onto his belt.

Tinker then took a long, slow breath. It confirmed that a woman had been in the car. Her perfume was subtle but, once detected, unmissable.

"Who goes there?" he muttered to himself.

He returned to the hotel and ate a late breakfast—he was absolutely famished—then headed to the police station, fifteen minutes' walk away.

When he entered the low, white building, he said to the man at the front desk, "The chief here?"

Before an answer could be given, a door to Tinker's right opened and Tiburon, with a cigarette in his mouth, gestured for him to come into the office.

"I've been waiting for you," the police chief said. "Have you tracked her down?"

"Who?" asked Tinker, taking a seat.

"Sister Georgina Stark."

"The motorcycle girl? No. How did you know about her?"

"She didn't turn up for work. No one has seen her since the murder."

"I have!" Tinker countered. "The guv'nor and I caught a glimpse of her coming out of the sanatorium."

"When was this?"

"A couple of days ago."

"But that was before Moxton was killed."

"Moxton!" Tinker exclaimed. "I thought you were talking about Leichenberg! You mean, someone murdered Sir Bartholomew?"

"He was shot dead late last night." Tiburon frowned and drew on his cigarette. "Mr. Blake was first on the scene. He had the sanatorium's receptionist call me—said he was following up a lead. You weren't with him?"

"I walked into a booby-trap," said Tinker. "I've been out of commission."

He described the incident.

"Where's Blake now?" Tiburon enquired.

"That's what I came here to ask you."

The police chief blew a plume of smoke, gave a puzzled shrug, and crushed his cigarette into an ashtray on his desk.

Tinker took the big bunch of keys from his belt.

"Do you know where these are from? I found them in our car."

Tiburon took them, examined them, and nodded.

"As a part of my duties, I have to occasionally inspect the island's facilities. I've seen these before. They belong to Mr. Hellander, the manager of the refrigeration plant."

"Perhaps I should have a word with him," Tinker suggested.

Tiburon nodded, handed the keys back, and reached for his uniform cap, which was hanging from the corner of a chair, his straw hat on the other corner.

"You probably should," he said, "and I'd like to accompany you—but there's a meeting at the palace, and I have to be there. As a matter of fact, it's to discuss the future of the plant. I think the king wants to nationalise it." He pushed the cap over his long hair and raised his eyebrows at Tinker. "When you find your master, will you both come to see me? I would like to know what sent him away from the crime scene."

Tinker, glancing at the ashtray, murmured, "Yes, of course."

They left the office and, outside, went their separate ways.

Tinker was deep in thought.

The cigarette Tiburon had been smoking was a Black Cat.

13
the gate

In Unit 9—the day before Tinker's return to Bajacu, while he was still unconscious and fighting the toxin, and Rymer was waiting in the *humfo* for Marie Galante— Violet Damm searched Max Hellander's corpse and retrieved from it the key for his monoplane. She also took his big bunch of refrigeration plant keys.

"Blake," she said. "Where are you staying?"

"At the Copenhagen," the detective slurred, in a slow, dull voice.

"Give me your car keys."

He complied, moving mechanically, and when she took them from his hand, it dropped limply back to his side.

She pointed at an empty niche. "Lie down there."

Not bothering to stay and watch—knowing he had no option but to obey—she strode from the room, crossed the big chamber, and retraced the route by which they had entered.

Once outside, she selected the key with "9" engraved into it and locked the door.

She walked to Blake's car, got in, and threw the plant keys onto the passenger seat.

It was midday by the time she parked the Duesenberg at the back of the hotel.

Her Royal Enfield was still at the sanatorium, and she did not dare to go anywhere near the crime scene. Unhappily, she abandoned it, and walked to the city's motorcycle dealership—a thriving business on this island of two-wheeled vehicles—where she purchased a cheap, low-powered machine, knowing it would soon be discarded.

She drove it home, and there discovered that Rymer was gone.

There was every possibility that she would not see this house again, so she set about gathering those few possessions she was reluctant to leave behind—her make-up box, a couple of summer dresses, three blouses, a selection of jewellery, her favourite jodhpurs, three pairs of shoes; and from a compartment hidden beneath the floorboards, a 1922 Browning service pistol, a Walther PP semi-automatic, a Smith & Wesson revolver, a Webley, knuckle-dusters, and a trench knife. All this, she crammed into a big rucksack. Then, she set off for the harbour town.

Violet Damm arrived at the Carl Magnus inn late in the afternoon.

"Hallo stranger!" Mama C exclaimed. "There was a feller askin' arfter yer this mornin'."

"Pointed beard?"

"That's the one. Took the room hopposite your 'n."

"Still here?"

"Nope, came an' went, an' I ain't seen 'im since."

"All right. Would you send me up something to eat and

a couple of bottles of beer? I'm going to settle down and wait for him."

The old woman gave a salacious grin. "Sweet on 'im, are yer?"

"No, Mama C, I don't like him at all—but, for the moment, he is useful."

"Ah! Good gal!"

Damm went up to her room, swung the rucksack into a corner, sat on the bed, and removed her boots.

All she could do now, was wait.

RYMER ARRIVED AT ten thirty the next morning.

Unknown to him, Tinker had departed Yucayeque just over an hour before him and headed off along the Bajacu road. Galante had travelled the same road in a car, just thirty minutes behind the youngster.

Damm opened her room's door and found him on the threshold.

He looked shocking, his face devoid of colour, his hair pure white at the roots, eyes like craters, mouth in a fixed, rictus grin.

She let him in and stared at him, aghast. "My god! What did she do to you?"

"She took away my addiction, Mary" he rasped. "And my memories."

Mary?

"But I got what we need. I know where the witch keeps her diamonds."

"Where?" Damm asked.

"Somewhere guarded by a curse. A place called Ascension Gate."

She leaned against the doorjamb and laughed. How

many times had she and Max Hellander met at the Grün Grün? And all the time the diamonds had been right under their noses!

"Oh!" she exclaimed. "This will be easy!"

"You know where it is?"

"Yes, and it's unguarded. We can go there immediately and fill our pockets."

Rymer's breath caught in his throat, and he clutched his fists to the middle of his chest. With a sob, he cried out, "Then we can go home, Mary?"

She took a step back.

"Yes," she said, cautiously. "Straight home."

He grinned, face like a skull, and she put her hand to her pocket, feeling the outline of her pistol.

"Wait here," she instructed. "I have to take some things to the boat. It won't take long."

Like a child, he nodded and sat on her bed with his hands pressed together between his knees.

She considered him, and wondered whether it might be better to shoot him now. Mama C would be all right about it. She would help dispose of the body.

However, Rymer, though he had plainly lost his mind, still had his muscles, and they could prove useful.

Damm left him, took her rucksack to *The Promise*, then returned and packed the rest of her belongings.

She looked under the lining of a dressing table drawer, then turned and glared at him. "Did you take the key? For the boat?"

"Yes," he said. "I hid it under the pilot's seat."

"I see."

When she delivered the second load of personal items, she checked the hiding place and, indeed, the key was there.

She left it, and returned to him.

"Are you ready?"

"Yes."

"You have my motorcycle?"

"Your spare, yes."

"So, you follow me, all right?"

"Yes, Mary."

They went down the complaining, unsafe stairs.

Outside, Damm and Rymer mounted their motorcycles and set off along the road to Bajacu, intending to pass through the city, and up to the peak above it.

DAS GRÜN UND BLAU was, as always in daylight hours, empty.

Violet Damm and Huxton Rymer selected the table closest to the Ascension Gate and sat down.

Erik von Bek shuffled over.

"Was willst du?"

"Daiquiri," said Damm.

"Whisky," said Rymer.

The proprietor lurched back inside to fetch the drinks.

"That," said Damm, using her chin to indicate the stone arch, "is the gate."

Rymer peered at it. "On the other side?"

"A sheer drop."

"Stay here, while I have a look."

He pushed back his chair and got to his feet, crossed to the arch, swept aside the curtain of dangling talismans, and leaned carefully out, looking down at the vertical rock face and distant sea.

In doing so, he unwittingly broke a taboo. The consequence was immediate.

Von Bek charged from the bar like an enraged bull.

"Verboten!" he bellowed. "Weg von dort!"

"No!" Damm cried out, jumping up.

The doctor turned just as von Bek's extended hands slammed into him. He flung out his arms and grabbed the stone arch.

Von Bek gave an inarticulate screech and shoved.

The arch cracked, folded, and crumbled backwards out into the void.

With a wild yell and flailing limbs, Rymer fell with it, gone in an instant.

Damm drew her gun and shot von Bek. He swivelled and threw himself at her. She caught a glimpse of his face, holes in both cheeks where her bullet had gone through, then he was on her.

He caught her wrist in a vice-like grip, jerked her forward, and used her momentum to fling her into the air.

She cartwheeled into the terrace-facing plate glass window and crashed through it, fragments exploding around her, thudded into the bar inside, and hit the floor.

She swore, shook her head to clear it, took a breath, and hoisted herself up.

There were lacerations on both arms, her left shoulder, and her left calf, the blood flowing but not spurting, no arteries sliced.

She was still holding her gun.

She raised it as von Bek came at her. He smacked it aside and slammed his forehead into the bridge of her nose.

Incandescent whiteness flared, followed immediately by absolutely nothing.

She was unconscious for only a few seconds. When her

senses returned, she found herself being dragged by the ankle through shattered glass towards the gap where the gate had stood.

Her pistol had clattered away over the floor.

Snatching up a long triangular sliver, Damm employed all her strength to bend her leg—the one being held—and slid forward on her shoulder blades until she was within reach of von Bek. She lashed out with the glass and sliced through the back of his left knee.

He staggered and fell, but his fingers remained tight around her right ankle.

Rolling and twisting, she thudded her left heel into the side of his face, once, twice, three times, hearing the bones of his cheek crack.

It did not seem to bother him at all.

"By God! What the hell *are* you?" she panted.

He released her leg, clambered over her, and put his fingers around her throat, squeezing, tightening them like bands of steel.

Immediately, her vision reduced to a narrow tunnel, then to a receding pinprick of light.

She was still holding the glass shard.

With her last vestiges of strength, she swung it up and buried it deep in von Bek's ear.

He crumpled onto her and lay motionless.

Her pinprick awareness expanded, her eyes filled with the azure sky, and suddenly, she was gulping air, filling her lungs.

"Ik haat dit verdomde eiland!" she muttered hoarsely, speaking her native Dutch for the first time in many, many years.

I hate this damn island!

She heaved von Bek aside and rolled to all fours, her

head hanging down, blood dripping from her nose and dribbling from her arms and legs. From the corner of her eye, she watched the dead man, half expecting him to sit up. Had she really killed him? She shuddered, suddenly aware, with a thrill of fear, that voodoo was much more than the primitive religion she had considered it. She had employed its drugs to con rich patients out of a fortune, but drugs are drugs … science explains them. Could it also explain why von Bek had not shed a single drop of blood?

She quietly whimpered.

A voice called, "Mary?"

Damm coughed, gasped, and regained control of herself.

"Mary?" it repeated.

"Wait," she groaned.

She crawled on hands and knees toward the gap in the low wall, reached it, and looked over the edge.

A vertical cliff of black rock dropped four hundred feet down to where the blue-green sea swelled against it. From the broken stanchion that had been the right-hand base of the gate's frame, a rope dangled, with knots every couple of feet along its length. As her eyes followed it to its end, a head suddenly emerged from the cliff, twisted, and Rymer's face looked up at her.

"You didn't fall," she observed, her voice made husky by her exertions.

"Caught the rope!" he exclaimed. "There's a narrow cave. It goes in for a short distance, then turns sharply to the left. A table at the end. Three small chests on it, all brimming with gemstones. We are rich, Mary!"

She sighed.

"All right, how are you going to get them up?"

"Go and find me a curtain or something that I can fashion into a sling."

She nodded, shoved back from the edge, then got clumsily to her feet and stumbled into the bar. There was nothing useful in the saloon, nor in the kitchen or back sitting room. However, she then passed through into a bedroom—which looked as if it had never been used—and there found sheets.

She quickly ripped one into strips and used them to bandage her limbs and to wipe the blood from her face.

Then she took two more, knotted a corner of one to a corner of the other, and took them outside.

On the way, she found her pistol lying amid broken glass, and reclaimed it.

"Rymer," she called, lowering the rope of sheets down. It was not long enough.

"Drop it," he said. "I'll catch it."

This was done, and he disappeared back into the cave.

Damm returned to the bar and mixed herself the daiquiri that von Bek had never delivered. She took it outside, sat at a table, sipped, checked her gun, and waited.

As the shock of the sudden, unanticipated violence diminished, she started to feel her injuries, and when she lifted her drink to her lips, her hand was shaking.

She surveyed the damage and von Bek's motionless form. She wondered why her gunshot had failed to bring anyone running from the village.

An odd place, the Grün Grün. Shielded by voodoo spells, perhaps.

"Where next?" she muttered.

She lit a cigarette and smoked.

Again, she considered Europe. It was in upheaval. War

seemed inevitable. Opportunities would abound for a woman of her calibre. Besides, as much as she enjoyed the tropics, she needed to give her skin a rest. She did not burn as easily as Hellander, but her complexion was by no means dark, and if she—

A hand came over the edge and Huxton Rymer heaved himself up. He had knotted the sheets around his shoulders and neck, wound them around three box-like shapes, which bulged on his back, stacked one atop the other. They were each about eighteen inches in length by eight in width and height.

"Phew!" he gasped. "I was afraid the sheets would rip, and the whole lot would plunge into the sea."

She threw away her cigarette, joined him at a table, and helped him out of the makeshift pack.

They put the chests—of hard, dark wood banded with silver—onto the table and Rymer clicked one open, raising the lid.

Damm's mouth dropped open.

She could hardly credit that so many diamonds were in one place—riches beyond her wildest dreams.

"We can go to my castle now, Mary," Rymer declared, happily. "Think of all the laboratory equipment I'll be able to buy. The materials. We are set for life!"

"Well," she said, drawing her pistol. "One of us is."

She pointed it at him.

He said, "Oh!" and swift as lightning, snatched it out of her hand, lifted it, and clunked it down onto her forehead.

For the second time that day, Violet Damm's lights went out.

When she came to, she was sitting behind him on her spare motorcycle. The sheets, cleverly fashioned into a pannier, secured a chest to either side of the vehicle and the third on the seat between her and Rymer.

Damm's hands were bound tightly—cruelly so— behind her back.

The old bike, straining under the weight of its two passengers, clattered down the mountain road towards Bajacu.

And she thought:

"What did he mean, 'castle'?"

14

a horse, mounted

WHILE RYMER AND Damm were at Das Grün und Blau, tyre tracks guided Tinker to Sexton Blake.

The youngster had driven the Duesenberg down to the refrigeration plant and parked it beside the last in the row of twelve units.

There were, in addition to the big white blocks, administrative buildings, mechanical workshops, and sundry other structures, and he had no idea where to start until he glanced at the dusty ground.

Blake had trained him well. Tinker's observational skills, refined by daily practice, operated very proficiently without effort. Often, he would know who or what had passed over a stretch of ground—and even when—without having consciously to analyse the evidence. Other times—such as now—something would suddenly leap into his awareness, as clear as a written signpost.

The road was well-marked by the passage of trucks. Over the top of those impressions, however, there was a set of imprints made by the narrower wheels of a car.

He stood, scrutinised them, glanced at the Duesenberg, and saw that they matched. It had been here before—and fairly recently.

He followed the tracks to Unit 9, next to which the vehicle had apparently parked, before then turning and going back the way it had come.

Unlike the other units, there was no activity around this one.

Tinker looked through the keys, selected "9," and used it to enter the structure.

It did not take him long to find the room of corpses.

There were fifteen, one on the floor with a bullet in its heart and blood pooled around it, the rest in alcoves— Sexton Blake among them.

"Guv'nor!" Tinker cried out, rushing to the prone man's side.

The detective's skin was cold and clammy, there was no pulse, no heartbeat, no respiration, and no life in the milky eyes.

"Guv'nor!" The despair in Tinker's voice echoed around the chamber.

He collapsed to his knees, clutching at a lifeless, unresponsive hand.

For years, Blake had been his surrogate father, a mentor, an example, a friend. The bond between them was forged through years of adventuring, time and again saving each other's lives, until Tinker—though he never would have said it—had thought them indestructible.

But now—

Minutes passed, the grief too cruel to process, until it abruptly turned to fury.

"Who did this?" Tinker yelled, jumping to his feet. "Who killed you, guv'nor?"

He would find out. Whatever it took, he would find out. He would hunt the murderer down remorselessly, across the world if necessary, even if it consumed the rest of his life, and he would—

"Georgina Stark," said Sexton Blake.

"Gaah!" cried Tinker, falling backwards onto his bottom. "What? You're—you're—?"

Blake said nothing else. He remained dead.

"Guv'nor?"

No response.

Tinker scrambled to the detective's side and again felt for a pulse or heartbeat.

There was nothing!

"Are you alive, guv'nor?" he asked.

"Yes," Blake answered, in a monotone.

"Can you sit up?"

"Yes."

Blake did not move.

Tinker blinked, and raised a hand to his own head, clutching at his hair.

"Um," he said. "What is wrong with you?"

"I was injected with the serum the voodooists employ to create zombies. I have no volition of my own."

After considering this for a moment, Tinker said, "Sit up."

Blake sat up.

"Is there an antidote, guv'nor?"

"I do not know."

Tinker stepped forward, grabbed the zombie by the shoulders, and looked intently into its blank eyes. "But there must be! There must! Someone has to be able to—"

He stopped, then exclaimed, "Marie Galante!"

Positions reversed. Blake had needed Galante to save Tinker, now Tinker needed Galante to save Blake!

And he knew exactly where to find her.

"Stay here!" he instructed, only later realising that it was a rather ridiculous utterance.

He raced back to the external door, went out, locked it behind him, and sprinted to the Duesenberg.

It was no great distance to the palace, but people and traffic clogged the route through the city. There was even a farmer herding goats along the boulevard, blocking the way just as Tinker was attempting to cross the thoroughfare.

He got through eventually, and steered up the sloping streets to the palace, parking outside its gates.

Two police guards eyed him curiously.

"I need to see Chief Tiburon," Tinker urged. "It's important! Is he here?"

"He is," one of the men responded. "But he's meeting with His Majesty. You'll have to wait."

The other added, "Go to the police station if you have a problem."

Tinker gritted his teeth in frustration, then returned to the car, drove it around the corner, and parked again. He left it and ran alongside the palace's perimeter wall to the quiet rear of the premises. The king, it appeared, required little pomp and circumstance, or even protection—for when Tinker jumped, grabbed the spikes atop the eight-foot-high wall, and heaved himself up, he peeked into the grounds, he found them to be empty.

"No guards?" he muttered. "That's convenient ... but dashed peculiar."

With an acrobatic avoidance of the spikes, he vaulted over, dropped behind a bush, and landed square on a recumbent form.

"Oof!" he said. "Sorry!"

It was a guard, flat on his back, breathing deeply, his pupils so expanded they near filled the irises. Tinker felt the nonresponsive man's pulse. "Drugged. My hat! What's the blessed game now, and who is playing?"

He peered between the leaves at the palace gardens, and spotted another prone guard half concealed in an overgrown flowerbed. No one else.

"Here goes, then."

He jumped up and dashed across to the main building, expecting at any moment a shouted challenge or the bark of a dog. None came.

The palace, a decaying colonial edifice, was fairly modest in size. He saw three wide open ground-floor windows, and even the back door was standing ajar.

He entered without being seen, moved quietly and cautiously from room to room, and discovered two maids and a manservant, all slumped in chairs, minds flown elsewhere.

With a low whistle of amazement, he moved on.

Voices approached. Tinker ducked behind an open door.

"—upstairs?"

"Clear."

"And the men?"

"All out. We are the last. We should get going. He will do the rest. I wouldn't want to be here when the fumes are—"

They passed beyond range of hearing.

Tinker allowed two minutes to pass then continued to explore.

Finally, he found what he was seeking. He opened a door, and there she was, the High Mambo, the Voodoo Queen.

Galante was seated at a long table in a high-ceilinged, well-furnished dining chamber. The Honourable David Woodbine was opposite, and between them, seated at the head of the table, was King Dandy Ostergaard III.

The monarch appeared every inch a Viking. He was a stocky, meaty-limbed man of about sixty, with long greying blond hair and an enormous beard wound into two thick plaits. His face was wide and his eyes pale blue.

Unmistakably, he was descended from the Danes, but, too, the island blood flowed in his veins, for his skin showed the characteristic tinge of green.

It so happened that he had been looking directly at the door when Tinker silently pushed it open a little and peeked in.

Their eyes met.

"Ho!" Ostergaard boomed, his voice deep and immense. "Dost thou dare invade the king's chamber, stripling? Enter thou, and kneel before thy monarch, else thou shalt lose thy head!"

Tinker moved into the room, clutching his hands together, and said, "Forgive the intrusion, I do not mean to—to—Mademoiselle Galante—Mr. Woodbine—I need—"

Ostergaard grinned and his eyes twinkled. "I'm joking. Come in, young man. Take a seat. You know my guests? Who are you? Is there something you need?"

Moving forward to the end of the table, opposite the king, Tinker said, "Your Highness, please, I have to speak with Mademoiselle Galante. It is a matter of life or death."

"Then speak with her, by all means," said Ostergaard, gesturing.

"But also," Tinker continued, "I fear an attack of some sort is in progress."

"Attack?" The king's eyes widened. "Where?"

"Here, Your Majesty. Your guards and staff have been drugged. They are unconscious."

Ostergaard frowned, muttered, "We'll see about that," then tipped back his head and roared, "Van der Meer!"

To Tinker, he then continued, "More likely they are all sleeping on the job, as usual. My private secretary was here but a minute ago. I shall have him look into the matter. In the meantime—" He again indicated Galante.

"It's Mr. Blake," Tinker said, turning to her. She was regarding him with an expression of surprise, no doubt having thought him still in Yucayeque, half-patient, half-captive. "He has been dosed with serum and turned into a zombie."

"No," said Galante. "That is not possible. The serum of which you speak is used only by my people, and there is not a single one of them who would have administered it to Blake without my express order. And I have given no such order."

"It wasn't one of your people," Tinker responded. "It was a sister from the sanatorium. Georgina Stark."

"If what you say is true, then—" Galante hesitated, and her eyes hardened. "I have become aware of a separatist faction on this island. If Miss Stark is a part of it, and they have used the serum, which is reserved for the most secret of our rituals, then she and all those who count themselves a part of it have forfeited their lives."

"Please," said Tinker. "I need an antidote. An antiserum."

"I am sorry. There is none. A zombie cannot be made to live again."

"There *has* to be a cure!" Tinker cried out, desperation cracking his voice. "It is not as if the guv'nor is really dead. He is just—just—*suspended!*

"Wait," Woodbine put in. "Start at the beginning. Where is Blake now?"

"In one of the units at the refrigeration plant. There are others with him. Maybe properly dead, maybe zombies, I didn't check."

King Ostergaard rumbled, "Where the devil is van der Meer?" Then, "The refrigeration plant, lad? But surely Mr. Hellander would have—"

He was interrupted by Galante, who abruptly jumped up and held out a silencing hand.

"Hold!" she cried out. She sniffed the air.

Woodbine grunted and nodded. "Yes, I smell it. A bad cigar. Strong!"

"No," she said. "For your life, hold your breath! I recognise the odour. It is used in certain ceremonies. It is paralytic gas!"

Tinker immediately became aware of a cloying odour. In a flash, before he even knew what he was doing, he snatched a small tin from his pocket, twisted it open, screwed a finger into the waxy substance it contained, and smeared the stuff across his upper lip.

He passed the tin to Galante, who, with a nod of approval, quickly did the same.

She slid it across the table to Woodbine. He reached for it, then froze.

The king's face set in an expression of comical surprise.

"Don't move," Galante urged Tinker. "Keep your breathing slow and shallow."

Tinker recalled that, when he had received a poisoned dart in the chest, Sexton Blake had issued the identical command.

He decided that Saint Dorian was his least favourite of the Caribbean islands.

A minute passed, then another.

Galante was positioned to Tinker's left, Woodbine to his right, and the king opposite, with the table between them. Beyond the monarch, there was a door.

Tinker saw it ease open a few inches.

A cloud of blue smoke plumed in through the gap, followed by a white-gloved hand with an enormous cigar between its fingers.

"All hail the king!"

The voice was nasally, sardonic, with an extremely strong Caribbean accent.

Baron Samedi stalked in and bowed melodramatically, his right arm extended to the side, a big bottle of dark rum in the hand.

"Weee!" he said, straightening, and stalking slowly to the king's side. "What a party this is! Everyone here!"

He sucked at his cigar and blew a thick cloud into Ostergaard's face.

"The king of the island, who has filled it with people who don't belong here."

Moving to Woodbine, he gulped from his bottle then sprayed rum from his mouth, showering it over the British administrator.

"The man who thinks Oubao-Bara belongs to his country."

Tinker remained absolutely still as the macabre figure stepped around the table and stood at his back. He felt the baron lean in close, and as he was enveloped in tobacco fumes, the whiny voice sounded close to his right ear.

"The youth-man who comes to poke his nose where it don't belong."

Samedi paced around to Galante, also motionless, and planted a kiss on her cheek.

"And the Voodoo Queen that is not of the Ghost People—not of the Aramabuya—but thinks she has power over them."

He prowled back to the king and stood at his side.

"This day, it ends."

Tinker contemplated drawing and shooting, but then recalled that he was unarmed. When had he last seen his pistol? Was it taken from him while he was unconscious in the shanty town?

"This day," Baron Samedi continued, "we Aramabuya, we take back Oubao-Bara."

He gestured with his bottle toward Woodbine and Tinker.

"You two—along with all the Danes and the Germans and the English—will be thrown from the cliffs into the sea. That will show the whole world that none but the Aramabuya are welcome here. And you—" He pointed his cigar at Galante. "You will be sacrificed to Bondyé. We will show our god we are his faithful people with this tremendous offering."

He turned to Ostergaard, whose face was still frozen in absurd surprise.

"As for you, Majesty—you die now!"

He flipped the bottle of rum into the air, caught it by its neck, and swung it full force at the king's skull.

Before the blow landed, Tinker slapped his hands to the edge of the table and shoved it with all his strength and weight.

Ostergaard and Samedi were both knocked backward, the king's chair toppling, his legs going up, while the baron staggered back, the bottle flying from his hand and breaking on the stone floor.

Tinker scrambled around the table and, as Samedi recovered his balance, planted a terrific right-hander on the apparition's chin. The baron reeled backward into the wall, but immediately braced himself against it and sprang back, launching shoulder-first into his assailant. Tinker went sprawling.

Snatching up the broken bottle, Samedi held it like a dagger, raised it, and pounced.

"Stop!"

Marie Galante's voice rang out like a striking bell.

The baron hesitated, then turned, his eyes locking with hers.

She grinned.

Tinker, looking up at her from the floor, saw her expression and shuddered, realising immediately that, by meeting her eyes, Samedi was already lost; knowing the man's death was now inevitable—and would be hideous.

He realised, too, that if he interfered, he would suffer the same fate.

"And now, Baron, just like that, you are mine," Galante said, her voice a sibilant, venomous hiss.

Mesmeric power radiated from her.

Perhaps, Tinker thought, for Galante to achieve such a hold over anyone who was not a practitioner of voodoo, they would need to be drugged. For Baron Samedi, however, steeped to the marrow in the old secret religion, the woman's eyes alone were utterly overwhelming.

He stood transfixed.

"You think," she said, "to supplant me?"

"Yes," he whispered.

"You lead a faction against me?"

"Yes."

"Sister Georgina Stark is one of your followers?"

"No, though she was useful when it came to killing the Nazi."

"Who?"

"Sir Bartholomew Moxton."

"Ah, I see. Many wheels, it appears, have been turning." She paused, then continued, "You think to supplant me?"

"Oubao-Bara is for the Aramabuya. No one else. Not even you, you Haytian witch."

"So, you think to lead the voodoo here? You have the strength to command the *lwa*—the spirits and elementals?"

"Yes."

"You think you have the wherewithal to be *chwal*—a horse, to be ridden by the *lwa*—without losing your sanity?"

"Yes."

"Even an *Iwa* as formidable as the *true* Baron Samedi?"

"Yes," he repeated, his voice a croak.

"Then let us see. And, if your confidence is justified, I shall willingly hand over to you this island."

Galante extended her left arm toward the baron, fingers spread wide, and began to murmur in a bizarre singsong tone.

Tinker would swear ever after that what he then witnessed actually occurred, though he knew it was impossible.

The air around Galante appeared to darken, and the temperature of the room, on that hot, humid afternoon, plummeted.

David Woodbine, still paralysed in his chair, suddenly slumped as if boneless and slid to the floor. The king's legs flopped down to one side.

Only Galante and Samedi remained upright.

A peculiar buzzing filled Tinker's ears.

The Voodoo Queen appeared to grow taller. Her

beauty coarsened, the bones of her face becoming heavier, her body broadening, the essence of her taking on a masculine cast.

Tinker blinked rapidly to force away the crazy notion that she was wreathed in blue cigar smoke, and attired in top hat and tails, her face painted white.

"Weee!" she said, in a nasal tone. "Do I see me a-standin' there?" She cocked her head to one side, clicked her tongue, and decided, "No, I don't think so."

She moved—loping strides—around the table, and to Baron Samedi's side, looking him up and down, sneering as if he were carrion. "Going to mount the horse now. You ready for me, mister?"

"Yes," rasped Samedi, his weak utterance filled with abject terror.

She chuckled and placed her left hand on his right shoulder.

"Here it comes," she said. "The *real* thing!"

Samedi screamed.

The cries Tinker had heard in Yucayeque had been appalling, but this—it was like nothing he had ever experienced before. A ululating wail of absolute despair, it was the sound of a soul plummeting into the deepest levels of hell. He knew, the moment it was wrenched forth, that there were nights to come when it would invade his dreams, and cause him to jerk awake, bathed in perspiration, his heart hammering wildly.

That scream echoed and echoed, fading slowly into an eternity of torment, then finally, mercifully, terminated with a dry rattle.

Tinker felt a sensation like the snapping of an internal elastic band.

He moaned with relief.

Galante looked down at him, and was herself.

Woodbine stirred, emitted a groan, and tried—but failed—to rise.

Dandy Ostergaard III shifted on the floor and muttered, "By the gods!"

Tinker pushed himself to his feet. He swayed, and was steadied by Galante, who took him by his arm.

"It is over," she said. "Quick and easy." She was radiant and beautiful again, all traces of her transfiguration gone. "That was a clever reaction, Tinker, with the lotion. You saved us from paralysis and death."

"I—" Tinker began. But he did not know what to say.

He looked at Baron Samedi.

The man was on his knees, his eyes wide and fixed, gazing into space, the whites showing all around. His mouth was hanging slackly open with the tongue protruding, drool oozing from it.

Tinker saw the long canine teeth, and muttered, "Ah."

He stepped to the baron's side and lifted the top hat. Long blond hair flopped to the shoulders.

Throwing the hat aside, Tinker took out his handkerchief and wiped the greasepaint from Police Chief Tiburon's face.

He sighed.

"Why?" he asked.

"A fanatic," Galante said. "The madness and hostility of his ancestors was strong in his blood. He wanted Saint Dorian to return to its past. Some people cannot adapt to change, despite that change is the one and only constant in this, our material existence."

"What will happen to him now, mademoiselle?"

She shrugged. "I will have him taken to Yucayeque. Maybe someone there will choose to feed and bathe him when necessary. Maybe one day he will wander into the swamp and not return."

Woodbine at last managed to sit up. "Ugh! I'm soaked through with rum and have pins and needles from head to toe."

"You'll be all right," Galante told him. "Give the king assistance, would you? Tinker and I have to go."

"We do?" asked Tinker. "Where?"

"I owe you a debt of gratitude, young man. And I have an idea."

She paused, considered for a second, then nodded to herself, as if reaching a decision.

"Tinker," she said, "I am going to summon the one spirit I know that might—perhaps—save Sexton Blake."

15

Rymer redux

Violet Damm, her hands bound behind her back, dismounted the motorcycle.

Doctor Huxton Rymer had found no difficulty in locating his new home, it being the only castle in Bajacu. He slung the sheets holding the three diamond-filled chests over his shoulder, took her by the arm, and dragged her to the front door, upon which he then hammered insistently.

When he withdrew his fist, the pounding continued by itself.

It took a second before Damm realised that the thudding was, in fact, drumming, which had just commenced from somewhere in the city. From those initial beats, it suddenly thundered out in a throbbing, complex rhythm, like a primordial Morse code.

"That's unusual," she murmured. "It usually comes from the swamp. A message for the voodooists there, perhaps."

To undermine Rymer's confidence, she added:

"I daresay it's relaying news of von Bek's murder to the Voodoo Queen. She is being informed that her diamonds are stolen. She will be sending a horde of zombies after you, doctor."

"She doesn't know it's me who's got 'em," he responded.

The door opened, and Rymer demanded of the stout man who stood at the threshold: "Who are you?"

"Schiller, sir."

"Your function?"

"General factotum, sir. May I ask—"

"I am the new owner, Schiller. Doctor Huxton Rymer. This is my wife."

"I am not—" Damm objected, but he squeezed her arm with vicious force, causing her to snap her mouth shut and clench her teeth.

"Ah, yes, sir. I was told you would come, though I didn't expect you so soon. Won't you enter?"

Rymer pulled Damm with him into the parquet-floored entrance hall, keeping her positioned in such a way as to conceal her bindings.

She cast her eyes over the stuffed animals arrayed upon the walls and grunted in mild disgust. Rymer made a noise of agreement.

"Are you content to stay on, Schiller, under the same terms as with your previous master?"

"Oh, quite so, sir!"

"Excellent! But my wife and I would like the place to ourselves for a little while, just to get the feel of it, settle in, and make decisions about how it will be redecorated and furnished, you understand? We can fend for ourselves for the night. No doubt there is food in the kitchen. Anyone else here?"

"The housekeeper, sir. There is a maid who comes in every couple of days—but not today, sir."

"Do you and the housekeeper have lodgings in town?"

"Yes, sir."

"And the castle, has it vehicles?"

"Two cars, sir, in the garage."

"Very good. Bring them both around to the front, then take one for your own use. Drive the housekeeper into town. I am giving you both a night off. No need to come back until, let's say, tomorrow evening. Here—" Rymer fished a roll of banknotes from his pocket—one of the many he had taken from the ceramic jar in Violet Damm's kitchen—and handed it to the German. "Share this between you. Call it a bonus to help you through the change of circumstances."

"Thank you very much, sir. Is there anything we can do before we go?"

"No. Thank you, Schiller. We'll see you tomorrow."

Schiller nodded and went off to find the housekeeper, looking slightly bemused.

"Let us tour our new home," Rymer said to Damm.

"I'll not be staying," she commented.

He pulled her across to the main passage, along it, past what appeared to be Schiller's quarters, and into the *studiolo*.

This, it was plain, was the room in which Lothar Leichenberg had burnt to death. If there had been a carpet, it was gone, but scorch marks showed on the flagstone floor and the chamber reeked, despite the open windows.

Damm peered with disdain up at the stuffed crocodile, and back at the baby manatee over the door, and muttered, "What a pity he died that way. He should have been filled with sawdust and put on display."

Rymer let go of her arm and placed the cloth-wrapped diamond-filled chests onto the floor by the cellarette.

"Remember," he murmured, as he selected a bottle of Highland Malt from the furniture, "I'm armed, and I'm quick. Don't try anything."

She sighed, muttered, "This really isn't the sort of marriage I ever envisioned," and stepped over to Leichenberg's taxidermy workbench. She gave the appearance of idle curiosity, but was searching for any sort of bladed tool with which she could surreptitiously slice through her bonds.

She looked into a box, and thousands of little glass eyes looked back at her.

"Ugh!"

There was a drawer, liable to contain what she was looking for, but it was locked.

She gave up and joined Rymer at the window.

"You could at least pour me a glass," she observed reproachfully, upon finding that he was sipping from a half-filled tumbler. "I judge von Bek a better bartender than you, and he beat the living daylights out of me!"

"My sincere apologies, I'm forgetting myself." Rymer said, and returned to the cellarette.

"Yes," she muttered, "I've noticed."

She looked out of the window and took in the vista, the refrigeration plant and airstrip, the land sloping into the hazy distance beyond them.

The drumming suddenly ceased, seeming to echo from the city, away across the island.

"This room," she said, turning to him, "has the stench of death."

He lifted a glass to her lips and she emptied it in two gulps.

"We'll not stay in here," he said. "Come, let's find the laboratory."

He returned to the passage, and she, with no better option, followed him along it.

The laboratory turned out to be the next room, on the opposite side.

Rymer stepped into it and gave a whistle of appreciation.

"Why, this is splendid! I couldn't have asked for better!"

Leaving her in the doorway, he set about examining the equipment.

On a table, he found bundles of dried herbs stacked beside a great variety of small bottles.

"From Galante!" he exclaimed. "There are undoubtedly organic compounds here no other scientist has ever seen. In even this small selection there could be the means to develop a cure for cancer, for the common cold, even a remedy for ageing! With Galante supplying further materials from that unique swamp, I could—"

"You appear to have forgotten," she interjected sharply, her tone stern, "that you despise Marie Galante and that, when she discovers you have stolen her fortune, she will return that emotion a thousandfold. Listen to me, Rymer. When love turns to hate, it gains an obsessive vindictiveness that will only be satisfied by cold, hard vengeance. If we don't get off this island immediately, we are doomed. Maybe you are too insane to care—God knows what that woman has removed from your mind—but personally, I would rather abandon the diamonds than be sacrificed in some hideous voodoo ritual, so—" she raised her voice, "*let—me—go!*"

She wrenched at her bonds, but to no avail.

Rymer threw up his hands impatiently. "You and Galante have never seen eye to eye, Mary. It has to stop.

We must find a way to—"

"I am not Mary!" Damm yelled.

Someone rapped loudly at the castle's front door.

Rymer turned and snapped, "Who the blazes is that?"

"A zombie horde," Damm suggested. "Come on, you fool. Let's get out of here. My boat is waiting."

"I'll not abandon Abbey Towers. This is our home."

"Abbey Towers? Now you've *named* this crackpot castle?"

The knocking at the door repeated, more persistently.

Damm backed away as Rymer strode over to her. He grabbed her arm and propelled her from the laboratory and along the corridor.

"You're surely not going to answer it?"

"Only to send whoever it is away," he countered.

He hauled her into the entrance hall.

"What if it's Galante?" Damm protested.

"Don't be stupid. Galante thinks I'm still in Yucayeque."

Before they reached the door, a key clicked in its lock, it swung open, and the Voodoo Queen stepped in.

"Wonderful!" Damm murmured in a tone of resignation.

Tinker was at Galante's side, and behind them, Sexton Blake.

"Oh," said Rymer, stumbling to a halt.

Galante gazed at him, her dark eyes inscrutable, and said, "How do you come to be here? The drums have only just instructed that you be brought to the city."

Rymer shrugged. "I came of my own accord. I was eager to see the place. The laboratory is marvellous. The herbs and—"

"Mademoiselle!" Tinker cried out, his voice filled with dismay. "*He* is the spirit you referred to? Rymer, of all people? Why, he is less likely to help my guv—"

Galante cut him off with a curt gesture.

She turned her attention to Violet Damm.

As the woman's gaze skewered her, Damm felt the roots of her hair stiffen. There was a quality about those eyes that reminded her of the unfathomable ocean, devoid of illumination, with leviathans stirring in the impenetrable depths.

"Who are you?" Galante asked quietly. "Do *not* say Sister Georgina Stark."

Damm determined that she would not answer, and would not be made to answer, but against her will, and before she knew it, she spoke.

"Violet Damm."

After a moment's silence, Galante said, "I paid you to look after this man." She indicated Rymer. "I gave you a tincture to administer."

Damm shrugged. "I did as you ordered, and here he is, as fit as a fiddle."

"I did not give you permission to use *another* potion, on *other* people. From whom did you get it?"

"I don't know what you are talking about."

Galante's gaze hardened. "In his current state, Miss Damm, Sexton Blake is able to respond to questions. I have had all the details out of him."

Damm's mouth went very dry. She cleared her throat, and muttered, "From Max Hellander."

"Who now lies dead in a refrigeration unit. You shot him?"

"In the chest."

She cursed herself. Why was she responding? Why was she standing here, hands tied, unable to move, like a pinned butterfly?

"And From whom did Hellander obtain the potion?"

Tinker said, "Mademoiselle—" but again, Galante silenced him with a cutting motion of her hand.

Once more, Damm felt a compulsion to answer.

"A man named Kaonati of the withered arm."

"I am much obliged," said Galante. "You have just issued a death sentence."

She wheeled, stepped to the front door, and closed it. Then she returned to the group and stood facing Huxton Rymer.

"This woman. What is she to you?"

Rymer squeezed his eyes shut, as if forcing himself out of a dream, then opened them, crossed his arms over his chest, and stood tall and defiant.

"She," he said, "is Mary, my wife. You thought you had removed memory of her with your toxins and rituals, but I am stronger than you, Marie Galante, and here she stands, at my side, where she has always belonged."

Galante snarled and slapped his face, viciously and without any restraint.

The crack echoed around the entrance hall.

Before he could recover from the shock, she grabbed his bearded chin and twisted his head, making him face Damm.

"Look at her!" she commanded, in a voice hissing and sulphurous. "*Look!* Is that Mary Trent? Does she resemble in any way the accursed Mary Trent? Look at the gap in her teeth! Look at her height, her build, her hair!"

Damm, having retreated a couple of steps, saw Rymer's face contort in agony. She felt she was witnessing the shifting of internal tectonic plates, a mental upheaval that would either reconfigure him or result in utter annihilation.

How much more, she wondered, *can this man take?*

The doctor was much bigger than Galante, but her force of personality was so intense that, to Damm, Rymer appeared to shrink in her grasp, seeming little more than a child.

"*Is—*"

Galante's teeth showed in an animalistic grimace.

"*That—*"

She shoved his head forward.

"*Mary—*"

Rymer whined—

"*Trent?*"

—and he wailed out a single word.

"No!"

He folded down to his knees. Tears welled and spilled over his cheeks. A sob wracked his body. He wept, and for three minutes, Galante allowed it, warning Tinker to silence with a glance. Then, she raised the doctor's face, met his eyes, and said, "Stop. You are done."

He gulped, sniffed, and became quiet.

She stepped away and turned to Tinker. "All right, you can ask him."

Tinker took a deep breath and hissed it out through his teeth. He moved closer to Rymer.

"Doctor," he said, his voice hoarse. "Sexton Blake has been injected with the potion of which Miss Galante has just spoken. It has turned him into a zombie. He shows no signs of life, but if you tell him to move, he will move, and if you ask him a question, he will answer it. Only responses. No volition."

He moved aside, so Rymer could look past him at Blake.

The doctor did so, and something new filled his wet eyes.

It was wonder.

"A zombie?" he whispered.

"There is no cure," Tinker said. "Unless you can find it."

Rymer suddenly jerked out a hard, pitiless laugh. He slowly shook his head. "After all these years, all I have to do is tell him to go away—and he will? To put a bullet through his own head—and he will?"

"Doctor!" Tinker barked. He pointed at his guv'nor. "This man might be your only friend in the whole world. When he learned of the tragedy that had befallen you, he dropped everything, and came all the way to the Caribbean, intending to spend whatever time and money it took to locate you. Not to hunt you—but to *help*. And he did so without a second thought. He did so out of *compassion*, doctor, and if you do not help him now, knowing that truth, then you are no man at all, but a confounded beast!"

Rymer swayed on his knees.

"Why would he do that?" he asked. "We have been at each other's throats for years."

Tinker threw up his hands. "Why? Because he knows that you are brilliant. He believes that you have it in you to rein in that criminal streak, which has so tainted your reputation, and to make amends for it. He has told me time and time again that, of all the extraordinary men and women he has ever met, it is you who has most to contribute to the world; that if you would only conquer whatever demon drives you, you could be regarded as a scientific saviour."

Rymer hung his head.

"I cannot," he whispered throatily. He jerked his head toward Galante. "This enchantress attempted to drive that demon out of me with her hocus-pocus—and failed!"

Galante murmured, "I have yet to see any evidence of failure."

Rymer bent, punched the floor, and uttered a great guffaw of laughter.

"No evidence, woman? No evidence? Why, not even a day passed before I stole all your diamonds!"

Galante's dusky face paled. She staggered back from him.

"You—?"

"Go check for yourself. The cave beneath the Ascension Gate is empty. I have gutted you. You are ruined!"

She stood, unmoving, mouth open, and Violet Damm, watching her, carefully backed away, all the time pulling and twisting at her bonds, in which, finally, she sensed a little give.

Galante suddenly lunged, snatching a dagger from the folds of her dress, and raising it high over Rymer. Her eyes were ablaze, her teeth bared like a carnivore's.

"No!" Tinker yelled, jumping forward and catching her arm as the knife came sweeping down. "Mademoiselle! You promised!"

"I'll kill him!" she screeched.

"No!"

They struggled, her fury so extreme that Tinker, whose strength was considerably above average, found himself retreating before her onslaught.

Then he shouted, "Sexton Blake! Restrain this woman until I—and only I—say otherwise!"

Blake lurched across the floor and threw his arms about Galante, pinning her own to her sides. He lifted her, then froze, his grip implacable, and though she twisted and kicked and hollered, she was unable to break free.

She went limp.

Then, she laughed.

"You are dead, anyway, Rymer," she proclaimed. "If you went through the gate, the curse is upon you. That great mind of yours—already half gone—will fast rot to nothing. And you will burn. Death by fire, for you!"

Rymer flinched from her.

"Half gone?" he said, hoarsely. "No. Damn it! Despite everything you have done to me, I am still what I've always been—a surgeon, a scientist, a pioneer. I shall prove it, you hellcat! I shall prove it!"

He addressed Tinker.

"Bring Sexton Blake to my laboratory."

16

not so perfect escapes

SEXTON BLAKE STRETCHED and groaned.

His eyes found focus.

He saw Marie Galante regarding him with an expression of surprise; Doctor Huxton Rymer, intent on a retort he was holding with tongs over a Bunsen burner; Sister Georgina Stark, sitting smoking a cigarette with sullen disinterest; and Tinker, standing with his pistol aimed at her head.

Stark was covered from head to toe in cuts, bruises, and abrasions. She had a split lip, a swelling eye, and blood caked around her nose. There were makeshift—and bloodstained—bandages on her arms. Her clothes were in tatters.

Tinker was also sporting evidence of conflict, his right eye half closed, and his crooked stance suggestive of a badly battered ribcage.

Blake felt a yawning absence, a sense of time having passed with nothing in it.

"Guv'nor!" the youngster exclaimed. "Are you back? Are you with us?"

"Water," Blake creaked out.

Galante obliged, moving to a table, where she filled a glass from a carafe, before approaching and handing it over.

"I had hoped," she murmured, "but in truth, I did not think it possible. A zombie revived. Never, in the long history of my religion——"

The detective downed the water, rasped, "More, please," and took a measure of the situation.

He was seated on a chair in a laboratory, which he recognised as belonging to Leichenberg Castle. His head was aching, his mind felt sluggish, and his stomach was painfully empty. The last thing he recalled occurred in the refrigeration unit, when he handed his pistol to Georgina Stark. The memory ended with the shooting of Max Hellander.

He peered curiously at the woman. She and Tinker were surrounded by debris: overturned workbenches, smashed chairs, and shattered chemistry equipment.

What had happened?

His assistant answered the unspoken question.

"She broke her bonds and attempted to escape, guv'nor. Put up quite the fight!"

Blake cleared his throat and, in a voice that was slurred and hoarse, said, "Sister Georgina. You will be given over into the custody of Police Chief Tiburon for the murder of Mr. Hellander."

She smiled crookedly, drew on her cigarette, tipped back her head, and blew a perfect smoke ring into the air.

"My name," she said, "is Violet Damm. As for what you just said, I very much doubt it."

"Tiburon is no longer with us," put in Tinker. "He is as good as dead."

Blake took the refilled glass from Galante and quenched his thirst. He was confused, sensing that much had occurred, but unable to assess what time had passed since Hellander's demise.

"Explain," he said. "What has happened?"

"It was the police chief all along, guv'nor. He murdered Leichenberg and Moxton—and was, I'm next to certain, responsible for the booby-trap that nearly did me in. Then, he set out to kill the king, but Mademoiselle Galante stopped him."

Blake turned his questioning gaze to the Voodoo Queen.

She said, "I think, Mr. Blake, that Tiburon had only just started his campaign of murder. He wanted to make it appear that the Danes, English, and Germans were killing each other. The resultant political strife would provide justification for a coup. He intended to wrest control from the British administration and restore Saint Dorian as Oubao-Bara, the Island of Death, forbidden to all outsiders."

Violet Damm murmured, "I like his style. I might try the political angle myself sometime. I'll be sure to make a better job of it, though."

"He also," Galante added, "meant to depose me, becoming High Houngan, the Voodoo King."

"He led the faction we spoke of?" Blake asked.

"Yes," she responded. "But thanks to Tinker's fast reflexes, he is defeated, and without him, it will quickly fall apart."

Blake glanced at Rymer. The doctor was wholly preoccupied, mixing chemicals, heating liquids, oblivious to all else.

Standing, his limbs terribly stiff, the detective limped across to Damm, and scrutinised her.

Tinker backed away but did not, for even a second, relax his aim. The automatic—not one of his own, Blake noted, so gained elsewhere—remained resolutely directed at her.

"You murdered Hellander, Miss Damm. What of those thirteen other corpses in the refrigeration unit?"

"Not corpses, zombies," she responded, in an airy, carefree tone. She dropped her cigarette and crushed it with her heel. "They can be restored now that Doctor Rymer has developed an antiserum. He made plenty."

"But how do they fit into the picture?" he asked.

She gave him a wide, guileless grin, showing the gap between her upper front incisors, and causing her split bottom lip to start bleeding again.

"They don't, Blake. It was an entirely separate matter, a rather splendid con job dreamed up by yours truly. Hellander got hold of the zombie serum, I convinced rich residents at the sanatorium that it would extend their lives, possibly forever, and once they were pliable zombies, I had them sign over considerable sums of money. Hellander then put them into Unit Nine to keep them out of the way. It was all going swimmingly, and I was about to depart with a considerable sum when Madam Galante turned up with Doctor Rymer, and tempted me with diamonds. Then, Chief Tiburon chose to kill Moxton while I was in his office. After that, schemes have tripped over each other, and here we are."

"I see," said Blake. "Were you also Sir Bartholomew's Nazi operative?"

"Why do you pin that on me?"

"It feels in keeping with your character."

"You surely don't think me a Nazi?"

"Not at all. I think you an opportunist."

Again, she grinned, and blood tricked down her chin.

"It's marvellous, isn't it?" she said. "This demon that has possessed the soul of Europe. How wonderful for such as me when fascism preaches that the common man knows nothing—that only an uncommon man can save us. It is miserable nonsense, of course, but with the economic depression, people are afraid, and they look for leadership to charismatic, confident men. Men who, I feel certain, I shall twist around my little finger."

"I don't doubt that, given the chance, you could do just that," Blake observed. "Men with confidence enough to seek power are frequently also stupid men, intent only on an illusion of glory."

"My point exactly," Damm agreed, triumphantly. "They must rail against the truth as if it were an enemy because, for them, it is! And when lies become the common currency—"

"The crooked prosper."

"And I shall. I was no agent, Blake. I possess no allegiance to Hitler or to anyone else. I was simply cheating Moxton's Nazi syndicate by accepting payment for jobs not done. Easy pickings gained from vain, oafish thugs. As a matter of fact, I took credit for the murder of Leichenberg, and was generously rewarded for it."

"A very dangerous game, Miss Damm."

"I think," she mused, "I shall play it in Germany next. The bigger the lies, the bigger the prospects—what do you think?"

"That your confidence is misplaced. You presume a future freedom that is unlikely to—"

Then it happened again, just as it had in refrigeration unit 9, only much more abruptly:

A gunshot sounded, and Sexton Blake's lights snapped out.

* * *

HE RECOVERED HIS senses in the midst of chaos, enveloped in thick, black, acrid smoke that scalded his lungs and prickled his eyes. Hands under his shoulders were dragging him along the floor. A female voice screamed, "He's got the diamonds!"

Coughing, Blake rolled sideways and to his feet.

Fingers gripped his arm.

"This way, guv'nor!"

The detective, stumbling, followed Tinker's lead, and suddenly the smoke thinned, and he saw that they had emerged from a corridor into the castle's entrance hall. The front door was wide open.

He plunged out into the open air, falling to all fours, gasping, Tinker to his right, and Galante dropping to his left.

"My diamonds—" she panted.

"Don't—" Tinker began, but gave way to hacking and wheezing.

Blake heard a car accelerating away. A motorcycle engine barked then roared into life.

The detective's instincts took over. He shoved himself up. "After them!"

Tinker pointed. "The Duesenberg."

They assisted Galante and reeled over to where Tinker had parked the big car. The youngster took the wheel. Blake threw himself into the passenger seat. Galante got into the back.

"There!" The detective cried out, pointing to where a motorcycle was speeding down the hill.

Tinker jerked the car into motion and put his foot down.

"What hit me?" Blake asked, massaging his jaw, which felt as if a horse had kicked it.

"Violet Damm, guv'nor," Tinker said. "Phew! What a haymaker! It came out of nowhere, straight to the point of your chin. One second, she was sitting there all relaxed; the next, *bang!* Knocked you silly. I've seen you fight championship boxers who couldn't do that. She must be strong as an ox, fast as a panther. My hat! You're not having a good time of it, are you?"

"I am not," Blake agreed, ruefully. "But I'm still in the game. Look out!"

Tinker yanked the steering wheel, swerving the car past one of the plant's refrigeration trucks, which was just steering out from a junction. The Duesenberg's wheels shrieked, but he regained control.

"I think she made off in the car parked outside the castle," Tinker added. "That's Rymer ahead. Broader shoulders."

They could still see the motorbike, a good distance in front.

"Tinker," the detective said, "was the castle on fire? There was smoke."

"I don't know," Tinker said. "I jumped at Damm, she kicked me in the unmentionables, and while I was curled up on the floor, the room filled with smoke—"

"It was the doctor," Marie Galante put in, leaning forward from the rear seat. "He threw that flask of chemicals he had been working on to the floor. Immediately, an enormous black cloud billowed out."

Tinker said, "And under cover of it, he escaped. That white cloth on the back of the bike, mademoiselle—it is wrapped around three small chests."

"My diamonds."

She explained—and it was the first time since their initial encounter, eighteen years ago, that she claimed a fortune which Blake could agree was justifiably her own. It was, in effect, salvage.

"If you've had those diamonds all along," he asked, "why have we run against each other so many times? Why the crimes, Miss Galante?"

She uttered a low laugh.

"Your empire robbed my people for its own benefit. When I sought to create a black empire, I simply followed the example you set."

They grabbed for a hold as Tinker was again forced to steer dangerously, this time to get past a donkey-drawn wagon.

"We're gaining a little," the youngster observed. "He's making for the harbour town."

They continued on in silence for a few minutes, then Blake, noting by the sun that it was early afternoon, asked, "For how long was I in that zombie state?"

"I was still recovering from the poison when you were injected," Tinker answered. "Two days passed before I found you. The mademoiselle and I then got you to the castle, and Rymer worked for almost forty-eight hours with barely a break. He must be utterly exhausted."

Blake whistled.

"He created an antiserum in just two days? Incredible! We have to save him. A mind like that cannot be lost!"

Galante murmured, "It is too late. That demonstration of brilliance was his last. Now, he goes to meet his destiny, and his destiny is—death by fire."

The car flew along, kicking up a great wake of dust, and less than a mile distant, Rymer leaned low over his machine and forced every little he could out of the rattling old machine. The town was ahead, and moored in its marina, *The Promise*.

Ten minutes passed.

An open road now lay before them, but the outer buildings of Bibibagua were visible in the distance. There, the narrow and populated streets would force Tinker to check their speed, allowing the more manoeuvrable motorcycle to outpace them. But—

"We'll catch him!" Tinker cried out. "He can't match our horsepower. Look at the fumes pouring out of his exhaust. We're going to—"

With a thunderous roar, a monoplane swept down from the right, flying so low over the car that one of its wheels came perilously close to hitting the Duesenberg's windscreen.

Tinker cried out in alarm and lost control of the vehicle. It slewed sideways, tyres shredding, dust surging up around it, and slammed into a palm tree with a tremendous crash of crumpling metal and smashing glass.

The engine howled, stuttered, and stopped.

Shock brought time to a halt and muted every sound.

Then the world snapped back into motion.

"Marie?" said Blake.

"I—I'm all right."

"Tinker?"

"A poached egg and grilled kippers, please, Mrs. Bardell."

"What?"

"Sorry, guv'nor, misplaced humour. It's what happens when I have had a bellyful. Let's vacate this heap."

They clambered out and stood unsteadily. It was immediately apparent that Galante's right arm was broken. She cradled it, her dark skin an unhealthy pallor, her lips drawn back, perspiration beading her brow.

Blake took a step toward her, but she looked past him and gasped.

The detective wheeled and saw the monoplane, a Gee Bee Sportster, flying low in a wide arc. It was coming back for another run at the road, though far ahead of them.

"I'll wager that's Damm," Tinker yelled. "Must have made her way to the airfield. She'll land, pick him up, and we'll lose 'em both, worst luck!"

"*Run!*" Galante barked the order. "If that's what she means to do, they both have to stop their vehicles. You'll catch up with them. I can walk from here to the harbour."

Without hesitation, they both set off.

The aeroplane's wings straightened. It was coming at the road from their left, straight toward Rymer, who was forcing the last dregs out of his straining vehicle.

Blake and Tinker quickly discovered that running was easier in theory than in practise. The detective had not eaten in four days, and while it was true that for most of that time his body had not required sustenance—its functions suspended—he was painfully aware of the lack.

Tinker, on the other hand, having been assaulted by Damm, was in considerable pain.

They ploughed on.

The monoplane dropped in altitude, swooping close to the ground.

It did not land. Instead, it streaked across the road and knocked Rymer from his motorbike.

Whether it actually hit him, Blake did not see, the distance was too great. However, if it missed, it was so close as to produce the same result. Rymer hit the dust, rolled over and over, and the bike went somersaulting away from him, crashed to a stop, and burst into flames.

He lay motionless.

The plane rose, its right wing dipped, and it turned tightly on its side before straightening and flying parallel to the road, coming in their direction.

As it buzzed past, they clearly saw Violet Damm waving at them from its cockpit.

Then, she was gone, flying into the blue, making a successful escape—though without the diamonds.

Blake got his second wind and drew ahead of Tinker, who was by now limping and struggling for breath.

As the detective drew closer to Rymer, he saw the doctor push himself to his feet, and walk unsteadily to the white sheet in which the pirate treasure chests were wrapped. He picked it up, slung it over his shoulder, and spotted Blake.

Rymer gave a yell of dismay, turned, and set off at a run toward the town.

It was a strange chase, that one! Two men so battered and exhausted that, in any other circumstance, even walking would have been a challenge. Their clothes were tattered rags, they were covered in blood and dust, and both were half starved.

A child could have outpaced them.

Yet on they pushed, into Bibibagua, past the outermost board houses, past astonished men and women, who stopped and stared, and in some cases pointed and laughed. Then, through the central district and onto the slope that eased down to the harbour.

Rather than making it easier, the incline challenged their rubbery legs, and both fell repeatedly, at one point crawling the length of a block on their hands and knees.

Blake slowly but surely closed the gap between them, until they were within shouting distance.

"Stop, Rymer, I want to help you!" The words came out as a barely audible squawk.

The sea was just ahead, a dazzling deep turquoise.

The detective laughed, feeling delirious, thinking it best to simply lie in the street and go to sleep.

He kept going.

They were about sixty feet apart now. To the right and left of them, a small crowd gathered, and walked alongside, following their progress, by turns encouraging and mocking, with no idea of what the two men were doing, but finding the bizarre spectacle thoroughly entertaining.

No one interfered.

Weaving this way and that, stumbling, dropping the chests, heaving them up again, Rymer forced himself along the quayside to the marina.

Blake, on his tail, resembled a drunkard after a particularly dedicated days-long session.

Fifty feet.

Forty feet.

Inch by inch, he lurched closer.

Rymer came to *The Promise*. He reached into his pocket, withdrew a roll of Damm's money, and pushed it into the hands of the nearest bystander.

"Cast off the ropes," he mumbled. "Do it before he catches up, then stop him, and I'll throw you more cash."

He fell into the boat with a thump.

The man, glancing first at his unexpected windfall, then back at the approaching Blake, responded with alacrity.

Rymer divested himself of the treasure chests and, with their weight gone, gained sufficient strength to scramble to the raised deck and the pilot's seat. He retrieved the key, inserted it into the ignition, and on the fifth fumbling try, started her up. He propped himself upright against the helm. Without even checking that the ropes were off, he slammed the throttle forward and twisted the wheel.

True to his word, as the boat jerked away from the quay, he fished out another bankroll and, without glancing back, tossed it carelessly over his shoulder.

The money reached the intended recipient's hands—but served to distract him. Sexton Blake evaded the man, summoned a final reserve of strength, and flung himself from the quay.

He arced over the water and crashed down onto the deck.

"Doctor," he gasped. "Stop!"

Rymer turned and glared at him.

"Never!"

Blake sat up. With immense difficulty, his legs shaking wildly, he stood and clambered to the upper deck.

"You are a scientist," he said. "Not a villain."

Rymer's eyes resembled those of a wild animal.

"I made the cure," he said. "Tell Galante that it proves my mind is sound, and cannot be affected by her pathetic curse, by her drugs and arrant superstition. Tell her, I spurn her, and I reject everything she believes in and represents."

He got up, stepped back along the deck, and faced Blake.

"As for you, whatever obligation brought us together, it is paid in full. I neither need nor want your help, and if I ever see you again, I will kill you."

"I believe your genius must always come to the fore, doctor," persisted Blake. "I cannot abandon hope that you will—"

"Go away."

Rymer stepped forward and shoved hard.

Blake hit the rail, overbalanced, and went overboard.

He splashed into the water, surfaced, and watched *The Promise* speed away.

Exhausted, the detective swam slowly back to the quay. He found a ladder and hauled himself up.

Tinker and Marie Galante helped him onto dry land. He sat, panted, and dripped.

"How did you get here so soon?" he finally managed.

"A truck came by and gave us a lift," said Tinker.

Blake turned to Galante. "If we are to retrieve your diamonds, we need to commandeer a very fast boat."

She smiled, though the pain of her injury made her wince at the same time.

"Let him go. Whatever his destination, eyes will follow."

"Voodoo magic?"

She uttered a low laugh. "No. *Tinker* magic!"

Blake looked interrogatively at his assistant. "What's going on?"

Tinker grinned.

"Nothing much, guv'nor. Except, a while back, while Rymer was obsessively brewing his potion, and Mademoiselle was guarding Violet Damm, I wondered into old Leichenberg's study, and found the chests filled with diamonds."

Blake frowned. "So?"

"I also found a box filled to the brim with little glass eyes."

"And—*you didn't!*"

"I did. I remembered all the times in the past when he slipped through our fingers, and—just in case he should do so again—I swapped the contents. Rymer has just made off with shiny baubles of immense value—to a taxidermist!"

17
epilogue

Two DAYS LATER, after the drums had throbbed all night, a corpse was discovered beside the road to Yucayeque, its face frozen in an expression of abject terror.

It was eventually identified as Kaonati of the withered arm.

In the evening of the same day, Sexton Blake, Tinker, and Marie Galante enjoyed dinner with the Honourable David Woodbine.

All three were due to depart the island on the following morning.

"I am not convinced this is the appropriate venue," Woodbine said, gesturing around at the Administrative Centre's dining room. "Perhaps the hospital would have been better. Look at the state of you. What horrors!" He smiled at Galante. "I should clarify that I am referring to your battered companions, mademoiselle, not to you. Your arm sling, while unfortunate, is perfectly inoffensive, whereas these two—"

"Our faces will heal, Mr. Woodbine," Tinker said.

"Yours, by contrast, will stay just as it is."

"Ha!" Woodbine barked. "Cheeky young beggar! How do you put up with him, Mr. Blake?"

"It's not easy," Blake replied, "but he occasionally makes himself useful."

"Yes," Woodbine agreed. "That stunt with the glass eyes!" He laughed. "Just wonderful! Simply wonderful! What I wouldn't give to be a fly on the wall when Doctor Rymer opens those chests."

"I have my moments," Tinker observed, modestly.

Woodbine jabbed his fork into a pork chop and, while he was slicing, asked, "Do you think you've lost him for long?"

"Whether we see him again or not," Blake said, "I think we have lost him forever."

Galante nodded. "You are right. His mind is destroyed. If you encounter him again, he will not be the man you knew before." She paused, then added, "And his time is short. Fire will get him."

Blake exhaled through his teeth.

"I mean no disrespect, mademoiselle, but it is my opinion that, if Rymer dies by fire, it will be because drugs and mesmerism have manipulated him into believing it to be his inevitable fate. His own actions and reactions will precipitate that manner of demise—if it happens at all. The Ascension Gate curse can have no effect in and of itself."

Marie Galante sipped at her wine and shook her head.

"You dismiss my people's rituals and symbols as something primitive, but has it never occurred to you that the gods and elemental spirits that we petition, and to which we give offerings, are merely aspects of our own minds made external? That when we summon them and honour them and pray to them, we are, in fact, operating in precisely the same field of endeavour as Europe and America's psychologists and psychiatrists?"

Blake's eyebrows went up.

"That's an intriguing proposition. You imply that both our perspectives are valid? That we are, in fact, in agreement, but perhaps speaking in different languages?"

"Perhaps so," she agreed. "But please resist the notion that translation might be possible. The language of voodoo has a far greater and deeper vocabulary than the language of science. You must not overlook the fact, Mr. Blake, that we blacks created it because you whites made it necessary. Thus, to your inability to truly comprehend voodoo, I have only one response."

"Which is?"

"I am delighted."

Woodbine let loose a great guffaw, pounded his hand on the table, and bellowed, "Bravo! Bravo!"

Blake's eyes twinkled with appreciation.

"You were a good enemy, Marie Galante," he said, "but I have it in mind that you will be a better friend."

She turned her beautiful face to him, and her impenetrable eyes were hard.

"No," she said. "I shall be a willing ally, I can promise you that. And if you and Mr. Woodbine can convince your government to keep this island off all maps, and to give its people control over their destiny, then I will strive to achieve what I know you want."

"You will press for an end to the practise of human sacrifice in voodoo?"

"I will, but—" She paused, and her expression grew bleak. "But such as you and I, Sexton Blake, cannot be friends. Not until my people can look back on a long history of yours proving themselves such. In that respect, you, and many future generations to come, have a great deal of work to do."

Blake held her eyes for a moment, then nodded and turned his attention back to his meal.

For eighteen years, he had considered Marie Galante, the Voodoo Queen, an irremediable criminal.

That evening, he changed his mind.

The End

CARIBBEAN CRISIS, RESTORED, REVISED, EXPANDED—AND "PREQUELLED"

Caribbean Crisis was not Michael Moorcock's first novel. That honour belongs to a manuscript which was, unfortunately (Mike might say fortunately), eaten by rats before it saw the light of day. Nor was it his second, that being *The Golden Barge*, written when he was eighteen. *Caribbean Crisis* was, however, the first of his novels to be published. He wrote it in 1959, while working as Editorial Assistant at THE SEXTON BLAKE LIBRARY, but had resigned from that post by the time it was released, three years later, in June 1962.

As Mike has explained in his foreword, the outline for the "murder in a bathysphere" storyline came from his friend, Jim Cawthorn. The politics of the tale, however, were Mike's own... until W. Howard Baker, Chief Editor of the SBL, interceded. Mike's sympathies were pro-Castro, a common sentiment among left-leaning observers at the time, before Castro's dictatorial proclivities were in evidence. Baker, however, slanted at an acute angle in the opposite direction. He therefore subjected the manuscript to an extensive overhaul to bring it in line with his own views... and rewarded himself for the work with half of Mike's fee.

The result was, according to Mike, "a dog's breakfast." Baker's crude anti-communism had entirely reversed the message.

As might be imagined, this was a disappointing outcome for a young, up-and-coming author, tempered only by the relief of having the novel published under the house pseudonym of "Desmond Reid."

Mike has, ever since, more or less disowned *Caribbean Crisis*, and with the original manuscript long lost and presumably destroyed, there is no likelihood that the pre-Baker version will ever see the light of day. And why should it? Curiosity might be satisfied, but that does not equate with relevancy. The world has changed. Mike's politics have matured. What would be the point?

That is how matters stood for nigh on sixty years... until I jabbed a figurative finger into Mike's metaphorical ribs and yelled, "The point is: SEXTON BLAKE—BY MICHAEL MOORCOCK!"

Such impudence was permissible due to Mike and I having become friends through our mutual enthusiasm for Blake. Had our relationship been otherwise, he might have counter-attacked by pretending to throw my imaginary typewriter out of a non-existent fourth-floor window. He is dangerously rock 'n' roll like that.

As it is, our regard for the most-written-about-ever British detective is such that, when I bellow, "Blake!" at Michael Moorcock, Michael Moorcock responds.

Providing I chance upon *exactly* the right moment, of course.

Which I did.

So, Mike agreed to take another swing at *Caribbean Crisis*.

There were conditions. It would be a collaborative effort... but I would be the one hammering at the keyboard (fair, considering he had already written the novel). The "restoration" part of the project would involve adding a flavour of Mike's politics as they are now, as opposed to what they were then. The story must contain more action. And there should be improved female characters.

Mike's role was to advise, approve (or not), edit, and to telepathically torment my sleeping hours with visions of what might occur should I make a mess of it.

We got to work.

The "Bill Baker version" was basically a Cold War thriller of the "corrupt fascist dictator versus Soviet-style communism" variety. We decided to retain that but undermine the premise by turning it into a big red herring. In our update, Blake discovers about two-thirds in that, in fact, he is investigating an audacious crime rather than a Soviet plot. This felony, committed against the people of tropical Maliba, enabled us to give the islanders a political system (or, rather, the opposite of one) of their own. By the end of the yarn, the people of the island are revealed as being entirely independent of the two political extremes. They live in a self-sustaining condition of "compassionate anarchism," with none of the trappings of traditional Left-Right politics.

Until Chapter 12, the story proceeds scene by scene almost exactly as originally published, albeit with nearly every paragraph rewritten to varying degrees. These alterations include, among much else, the addition of more detailed "local colour"—descriptive passages based on my own experiences in Cuba. I had visited the island in the mid-1990s, the year it first tentatively opened to foreign visitors. The place, at that point, had barely altered since the late 1950s, so I hope these expanded descriptions give "Maliba" a more authentic feel than did the original.

After Chapter 12, pretty much everything is new, though with bits and pieces from the original final chapters integrated. The plot becomes considerably more complex, with plenty of twists and turns introduced. This new material expands the novel by nearly ten thousand words.

The transformation of Amelia Tucker into the newly created Violet Damm proved to be the most significant change. While writing her scenes, Mike and I fell in love with Damm, and it was then that the notion of a second story took form.

"More work!" I warned, while smashing my bleeding, blistered fingers against the keys.

"We'll manage," Mike bravely declared, settling back into his satin pillows, and bracing himself with a sip of aged malt whiskey.

Thus, we powered into the prequel.

Many of the old Sexton Blake stories are remarkable for featuring strong female characters. This is especially true of the tales published during Blake's "Golden Age" (the 1920s and early '30s), but less so of the "New Order" era, from which had come *Caribbean Crisis*.

We therefore felt it would be fun to write about a younger Violet Damm in a 1930s setting, which would enable us to team her up with one of the original "Blake women." It then occurred to us that, if we continued the

Caribbean theme, this old character could be one of our favourites, Marie Galante, the "Voodoo Queen." That, in turn, led us to Galante's sparring partner, another of the classic villains, Doctor Huxton Rymer.

Both these were created by George Hamilton Teed (1886-1938), widely regarded as the best of the 200+ Blake writers.

Having settled on this approach, we required a plot. I dipped into some of Teed's many Huxton Rymer stories (there are around 80), hoping for inspiration, and quickly noticed a peculiarity. In the last handful of yarns, the doctor's character is, without explanation, radically altered. Rather than the brilliant and innately honourable scientist he had been since his debut in 1913, he was, in the mid-1930s, depicted as a barely recognisable thuggish brute. This was never explained by G. H. Teed, but I also noted that Rymer's partner and love interest, Mary Trent, was absent from those later stories. This got me thinking, and when I read the final story, circa 1938, in which Rymer is killed when his home, Abbey Towers, burns to the ground, it all clicked into place. In *Voodoo Island*, Mike and I would tell the story of what had happened to poor old Rymer.

This being an entirely new project, I was now subjected to the full force of Mike's creativity. It worked like this:

Me: "Mike, I've got the story to this point, but I'm uncertain what should happen next."

Mike: (Levels his double-barrelled, sawn-off, Shotgun of Creativity). BOOM!

Me: "Aaargh! My head!"

The thing about Mike is, he knows exactly *what* needs to go where in a story, but when you request a *what*, he'll shoot a hundred at you, all suitable and all brilliant.

He presented the options. I made the choices. That said, and in my own defence, there were occasions when, having had the nature of the required *what* demonstrated, I shelved his multiple offerings and came up with a *what* of my own. It means I now possess a library of unused Moorcock *whats*, which, one day, when all this is long forgotten, I shall dust off and present as my very own. (Don't tell him).

Our collaboration was a blast. We both thoroughly enjoyed it. There were a few weeks when his computer was on the fritz, and I received emails along the lines of G0t idea b@T mYYy KeY,BBoRd iS foKdED U-$p! but aside from that, it all went astonishingly smoothly. In addition to these two tales, we also wrote a non-Blake novel, which also features Violet Damm, and which we hope to see published soon. Another is currently in the planning stage. We want to do more—and, if we can squeeze it into our heavy workloads, we shall.

In helping Mike to "restore, revise, and expand" *Caribbean Crisis*, I feel I've righted a wrong dating from the dawn of his remarkable career (1962, as it happens, was also the year I was born). And, with *Voodoo Island*, I shared the full creative process with the man who, when I was 11 years old, instilled in me the ambition to become an author.

Two, possibly three, full circles there!

— **Mark Hodder, Valencia, Spain. June 2023**

ACKNOWLEDGEMENTS

With acknowledgements to George Hamilton Teed (1886-1938), from whom we have borrowed Doctor Huston Rymer and Marie Galante. Teed was an adventurer, a traveller, and is widely considered the greatest of all the Sexton Blake authors.

ABOUT THE AUTHORS

Michael Moorcock

Michael Moorcock is one of the most important and influential figures in speculative fiction and fantasy literature. Listed recently by *The Times* (London) as among the fifty greatest British writers since 1945, he is the author of 100 books and more than 150 shorter stories in practically every genre. He has been the recipient of several lifetime achievement awards, including the Prix Utopiales, the SFWA Grand Master, the Stoker, and the World Fantasy, and has been inducted into the Science Fiction Hall of Fame. He has been awarded the Nebula Award, the World Fantasy Award, the John W. Campbell Award, the British Fantasy Award, the Guardian Fiction Prize, and has been shortlisted for the Whitbread Award.

Mark Hodder

Mark Hodder's debut novel, *The Strange Affair of Spring Heeled Jack*, won the Philip K. Dick Award in 2010. He has since written five sequels and a number of other novels, including *The Silent Thunder Caper* (2014), which was the first officially sanctioned Sexton Blake story since 1978. Mark created and manages the BLAKIANA website, and is widely acknowledged as the foremost authority in all things Blake. He lives in Valencia, Spain.